D0969201

UNTRACEABLE

The Nature of Grace – Book 1

by S.R. Johannes

Coleman & Stott

Untraceable: The Nature of Grace series, Book 1
Copyright © S.R. Johannes, 2011
www.srjohannes.com

All rights reserved

This book is a work of fiction. Names, characters, places, and incidents are products of the author's imagination or are used fictiously.

Cover photograph by Vania Stoyanova at VLC Photo.
Photograph copyright © 2011 Vania Stoyanova at VLC Photo
Internal design and typography by GraphicCat.com

All right reserved. No part of this publication can be reproduced, stored in a retrieval system, or transmitted in any form or by any means—electronic, photocopying, mechanical, or otherwise—without prior permission of the publisher and author.

ISBN: 978-0-9847991-2-1

Dedication

To my parents who always instilled courage,
persistence, and a love of reading

"Courage is just grace under pressure."

- Ernest Hemingway

Preface

Nature will talk to you if you listen.
Every sound tells you something.

I know the exact moment I went wrong.

Three weeks, two days, twenty-two hours, and thirty-three minutes ago.

I had no clue a few small decisions could puncture the perfect bubble of my existence.

I zigzag through the forest's brown pillars like I'm barrel riding in a local rodeo. The internal rhythm keeps me running at a steady speed along the broken path. *Left, right, left, right.* My muffled breath echoes in my ears, making me feel as if I'm underwater. Sinking. Drowning.

Don't stop, Grace, or you will die.

I veer off the main path and into the arms of the darkening woods. Gnarled branches, shaped like broken fingers, comb my hair and scratch my skin. I fight against a clump of twisted vines grabbing at my ankles. Jerking. Pulling. Ripping. The rhythm of my running becomes choppy and uneven as I sludge my way through the curled tangles of vegetation. My lungs sear from the lack of oxygen. Burning.

As soon as I round a corner, I slip behind a mammoth oak to catch my breath. A brown rabbit scurries by me and disappears into the safety of a prickly bush, giving me hope that maybe I can escape too.

My eyes dart across the monotonous woods, searching for a way out. I need to calm down. Can't lose it now.

My chest rises and falls as my lungs finally pull in enough oxygen to settle my nerves. Pure air sweeps through my body like the dry wind over a starlit desert. Blowing away the doubt, and erasing aside the fear. Everything Dad's ever taught me about wilderness survival comes flooding in.

Suddenly, I know exactly what to do.

Examining my GPS watch, I pinpoint my coordinates and map a way out. After assessing the area, I tiptoe out of my hiding place and backtrack down the trail, careful not to disturb anything along the path that will give away my position.

I disguise my tracks all the way back to Dead Man's Cliff. After securing my backpack, I clutch onto the cragged rocks and scale the steep wall, careful to place every toe and finger just right. My palm hits a sharp edge and begins to bleed as both my arms spasm from the strain. My toes cramp underneath my weight as they press against the tiny ledges. I slowly creep up the steep rock like a lizard, careful not to send showers of rocks or crumbling dirt onto the path that now lies several feet below me. My arms quiver, threatening to numb.

When I finally reach the top, I fight against the pain and summon all my strength to pull myself over the ledge. Instantly, I roll onto my stomach and flatten against the cool dirt, scanning the horizon. Tiny pieces of sun punch through the thick canopy, dotting little amoebas of light along the forest floor. I listen for the slightest sound, search for the tiniest movement.

Nothing.

As a wildlife enforcement officer, Dad believed the woods would talk to me if I could be still enough to listen. Closing my eyes, I concentrate on the space around me.

Listening. Waiting. Afraid to breathe.

A light breeze slithers through the ghostly forest. The leaves rustle and the trees hiss as if whispering secrets to each other. The forest appears to exhale then hold its breath. Everything goes as quiet as a graveyard at midnight. Nothing scurries, burrows, or twitters. The trees stop swaying and freeze, as if they're hiding too. And then I hear it: the distant snap of a random twig. The hair on my neck bristles.

They're still after me.

Survival Skill #1

A good tracker learns to follow every print and every lead—one at a time.

Dad used to always say, *nothing is untraceable.*

Everything that touches this earth leaves a special imprint, a unique mark that proves we existed in some way—no matter how invisible we may feel.

I follow the thin trail, staying a few feet to one side, and search for any sign of humans. Every time there's the slightest blemish in the dirt, I drop down and study it, to see if it's something important—something my dad left behind. Even if it's nothing, I draw a circle around it with a stick and mark the spot with orange surveyor tape. Just like Dad showed me. Then I document it by snapping a few photos with my digital camera and logging some notes. A tracker never knows how two separate things might be related. Connected in some way.

At the next bend in the path, I squat and scour through a mound of dead leaves. The Arnold Schwarzenegger of ants pops out from under a stick, lugging a dead beetle ten times his size. No matter how much he struggles, he never gives up. Another lesson to me from Mother Nature herself.

A few feet away, a squirrel rifles through a pile of twigs, searching for acorns. He freezes and stares at me as I inspect a nearby shrub. An earth snake, or *Virginia valeriae* as Dad calls it, slithers over my hiking boot. I pinch the tip of the snake's tail and dangle him in front of my face. "You seen anything out here?"

His forked tongue darts out and kisses the tip of my nose.

"Great, now I'm talking to animals." I sigh and place him down gently then watch him slither away.

Dr. Head thinks I'm in denial, Captain thinks I'm distrusting of his police investigation of my dad's disappearance, and my mom just thinks I'm nuts. What if they're right?

I pick up a stone and chuck it at a nearby tree. The rock bounces back and hits my kneecap. "Owwww!" My voice echoes a little before being swallowed by the thick humidity. My body relaxes after I drop down onto a boulder. Leaning forward, I rest my forehead in my hands and inhale deep breaths, trying to let the woods calm me.

Three months, and not one solid lead.

Finding evidence should be easier than this. Especially for me.

Technically, I've been a wildlife officer's assistant since I could trace my own hand in the dirt with a stick. My first friend was a bear. My first potty, an oak tree. My first swing, a forest vine. I've lived in the North Carolina Smokies my whole life. Tagging along behind Dad when he patrolled, I've soaked up everything he taught me about wildlife, tracking, and wilderness survival. Over the years, I've created a mental map of every side trail, memorized plant species, and studied the scientific name of forest animals.

One time, when I was smaller than a river otter, Dad hid from me in the woods. Took me less than sixty minutes to track him down. I remember him being shocked. But it didn't surprise me. After all, I've been his shadow all my life. I know his gait, how his right foot drags slightly when he walks because of an old motorcycle injury. I memorized the tread of his size 11 hiking boot—ranger standard issue. Mostly, I know how his mind works.

Yet none of this seems to help me now.

Even though it's pretty unlikely that a sixteen-year-old tomboy—who can build a fire from scratch, yet can't seem to cut her own bangs straight—could dig up something when more than a hundred searchers couldn't, I know deep down that if anyone can find Dad, it's me.

After looking a few more hours with no finds, I reluctantly stop my search for the day. I flatten my trail map against a boulder and smooth out the tiny creases.

I wish it were that simple.

To wipe my hand across a crumpled page in my life and erase any unwanted wrinkles.

After studying the map of the Smoky Mountain National Park, I highlight my search coordinates.

Marking another failed day.

I dig my notebook out of the backpack to jot down my findings before heading home: *absolutely nothing.*

I stroke the pink camo cover. Dad used to tease me about how the bright color stood out against the all-real green backdrop. Strange how random things pop into your head at strange times. The little, insignificant things you never think about until they're triggered by something totally unexpected, without any warning.

A tightness fills my chest when I picture his smiling face, so I quickly put away the notebook. Beads of sweat race along my spine as the humidity presses down on me. The heat seems much worse this year. I dampen my bandana with water from my canteen and drape it across the back of my neck. I steal a drink, letting little droplets of water trickle down my chin. Pulling the sticky strands off my neck, I roll my long, black hair into a bun. The warm air is a small relief to my suffocating neck.

After gathering my things, I begin the long five-mile hike back to my bike. Along the way, I get lost in the simple sounds of the woods. The crunching of my boots through the dry leaves. The bickering birds and crickets in the trees. All the random sounds that don't seem like much on their own but, when put together, create a special song.

Just as I reach the main trail, I spot an azalea bush with a few broken limbs on one side. A scar on the hand of nature, marking an unnatural break. My heart stumbles as I stop abruptly. To the average person, this is nothing. To me, it could be everything.

As I inspect the jagged branches, the bugs beneath me stop buzzing. I peer into the thick foliage and spot a splash of orange. Even though the limbs scratch my face and arms, I reach into the brambles until my fingers skim something stiff and crinkly. I pinch the edge and retract the object slowly before laying it on the ground.

It's an old Cheetos bag.

Dad's favorite snack.

At first, I freeze, not sure what to do. Then I remember how to recover items properly. My hand trembles as I slip a Ziploc and tweezers out of my pocket. It takes me a few minutes to get the evidence into the bag and seal it. Once it's safe, I stare through the dirty barrier. Who would have thought a cheesy snack could mean so much? That a simple piece of trash could crack Dad's case wide open. I shove the plastic baggie into my backpack.

I need to get it back to town. Now. After three months, time is definitely not on my side.

Before I can stand, the bushes ahead of me shiver.

My body tenses as I spot a dark shape crashing through the dense underbrush. I wait quietly, not sure what it is.

Then a deep groan pierces the silence.

Survival Skill #2

To avoid wild animals when hiking, make lots of noise and stay alert.

About one hundred feet in front of me, a huge black bear lumbers onto the path, blocking my exit.

His dark fur glistens in the broken streams of light, and his nose twitches. Bears have a wicked sense of smell—seven times that of a bloodhound. They've even been known to detect a human's scent hours after the person has left a trail. I'm not worried. If I stay upwind, I can probably go unnoticed long enough to sneak away.

As if on cue, a slight breeze strokes the back of my neck. My body stiffens.

I'm downwind.

Whether this guy has seen me or not, he'll get a good whiff in about two seconds. The bear rears up on his hind legs and wiggles his snout, sniffing the air. His beady brown eyes shift around until he locates me. He huffs a warning and stares me down.

I remain still and size up my opponent. Black bear. Adult male. About four hundred pounds. Six-feet tall. Definitely the largest one I've ever faced out here without Dad. This is the first time I'm totally on my own.

I keep my eyes on the bear, remaining stiff. Even though black bears are generally passive, Dad once told me they cause more injuries to hikers than any other bear species. Partly because people don't seem to be afraid of them like they are grizzlies. Unfortunately, thanks to Yogi Bear, people wander too close to them. I assume they think the bears are cuddly, tame animals just out looking for a picnic basket.

7

I scroll through all the facts Dad has drilled into my brain over the years.

Can't run. Bears can bolt about thirty miles an hour.

Forget climbing. They can scale a tree trunk faster than you can yell "bear."

My best chance is to retreat slowly and try to widen the space between us. I suck in a breath and inch backwards. The bear immediately senses my small movements and drops down on all fours. A series of huffs and growls pour from his throat. I keep my feet grounded, but my heart takes flight.

Time for Plan B: when a 140-pound girl scares off a 400-pound *Ursus americanus*.

Waving my hands over my head, I speak in a loud voice. "Go on! Get outta here!" I stomp my feet on the path a few times for show.

The bear is not amused. He swings his massive head from side to side and snaps his jaws, displaying long, sharp fangs. And I'm almost positive he's not smiling. The bears roars an awful sound.

My chest heaves, my mouth turns dry, and my stomach cramps. I force my eyes to stay open and prepare for his next move, "The Bear Two-Step," as Dad calls it.

Just as I predict, the bear lunges forward, invading the small space between us. His feet hammer the path as he charges. My legs threaten to move, but fear has kidnapped my entire body and shackled my feet to the earth.

Lucky for me, I'm right about the bluff. When the bear's only a few yards away, he suddenly jerks to a stop and stares me down.

I drop my head and look away, breaking any eye contact, so he doesn't consider me a threat. However, my brain remains on high alert. If this thing charges again, I need to be ready or I'm dinner. I peer out of the corner of my eye. It's only then that I notice a white necktie marking on his massive chest and a single scar running over his left eye.

Simon.

I'm amazed at how much he's grown since I last saw him.

Years ago, Dad found Simon when he was just a cub. His mother had been killed, and Simon had been shot right above his eye. Against his own rules, Dad brought Simon home, hoping to nurse him back to health. During the months of rehabilitation, the little cub and I were inseparable. He was a silly animal. Forty percent human, forty percent dog, only twenty percent bear. The day Dad returned Simon to the wild was one of the worst days I can remember. For a year after that, every day after school, I'd hike deep into the national park, hoping to catch a glimpse of Simon.

But I never saw him again.

Until now.

Part of me wants to run up and hug him, but I force the feelings aside. Even though we have a history, Simon is wild at heart, and that's how it should be.

Simon notices me watching him out of the corner of my eye. His amber eyes seem to soften and his eyebrows twitch, giving him a strange human-like quality. He moves his lips around in a circle as if he's trying to tell me something. I wonder if he recognizes me.

A few minutes later, he finally gets bored and lumbers off, uttering grunts under his breath, getting in the last word.

As soon as he disappears behind the green curtain of leaves, my legs crumble underneath me and I slump to the ground. Even though my body has already surrendered to my nerves, I keep an eye out, just in case Simon decides to give a surprise encore.

Once I'm positive he's gone, I muster the courage to leave. During the long trek back to Luci, every rustling noise and crackling stick sends my heart skipping. I'm relieved when I finally reach my bike safely. I hop onto my motorcycle, throw on the helmet, and stomp down the pedal with one foot.

The bike sputters a couple times before dying a slow death. I holler out, "Geez, Luci! Do you *ever* start on the first try?" Luci, short for Lucifer, has been temperamental since the day I got her. My boss, Tommy, restored the vintage motorcycle for my sixteenth birthday. Except for the testy starter, the bike works fine.

I attempt to wake Luci again. This time, more gently. She forgives my outburst and springs to life. I pat her engine like she's a horse and steer her out of the woods. As soon as I hit the main drag, a breeze welcomes me.

On my way into town, I try not to think about the Cheetos bag stashed in my backpack. About what it could mean. I can't help but allow a drop of hope to sneak in. I rev the engine and increase my speed, eager to get to the police station and show Captain what I've found.

Somewhere along the winding road, I think about Simon. Even though I was almost bear breakfast, seeing him brings back good memories. Feeding him milk from a bottle. Playing chase in the woods. Catching fish in the river. (Actually, I hooked the fish; Simon just scared them away.)

Through my rearview mirror, I watch the forest fade into the background and smile.

I love these woods, and so does Dad.

Protecting bears like Simon is what got us here in the first place.

Survival Skill #3

*Understanding all aspects of the terrain
is critical to successful hiking.*

"**C**ome on, Grace. We keep having the same conversation over and over." Captain Carl Stevens readjusts his police baseball cap and pops two huge pieces of bubble gum into his mouth. As his tongue wrestles the sticky wad, he eyes me warily.

"But you *can't* close Dad's case. Not yet." I clear my throat, hoping to shake loose the words that have gotten stuck. "He's still alive. I can feel it." I shift in the wooden seat, not from nerves, but because my butt's numb from sitting too long.

Obviously, Carl didn't hear me ask, *do you have a minute?* because he's been lecturing me for exactly fifty-three.

Carl sighs. We've been at this a while. "Look, I know you're upset, but it's not up to me. Your daddy was a wildlife officer, so it's the U.S. Fish & Wildlife Service's call. They're always by the book. To them, it's been over three months, and they want this thing wrapped up."

Wrapped up or thrown away? My hands tremble as I display the plastic bag housing my newly found evidence. "I found something today. Something big."

He frowns and grips the corners of the plastic Ziploc. "Dang it, Grace. I told you not to touch anything out there." He wrinkles his nose and peers into the bag as if it's a dirty fish bowl.

I cross my fingers behind my back and watch him inspect the snack bag, half expecting one of his unlimited professional opinions.

I can't help but wonder how many he has left to go.

Carl scoffs. "In my professional opinion, this doesn't mean a thing."

I point to it. "It's a Cheetos bag."

"I see that." He rolls his thin shoulders, triggering the familiar cracking sound of a wrecked collarbone. "But we don't know how long it's been out there. Let alone who it belonged to."

My shoulders sag forward as an invisible force pushes down on my back. My hope drains a little, and I try to mask the frustration scratching at my vocal chords. "But Dad loves Cheetos."

Carl shakes his head and smacks a bubble. "So does Chester Cheetah. Along with half of America, I might add."

I ignore his bad joke. "Yeah, but he *always* carried them when he patrolled. Bags of them. This is his. I'm sure of it."

Carl removes his hat again and brushes one hand over his spiky blonde hair. "Listen, Grace, I saw the bark with sap—that you thought was blood—and the empty toilet paper roll you found a few weeks before that. Nothing came of those items either. This is what we like to call *litter.*"

I twist the ring on my middle finger. "That far out? Who goes out there to snack and leaves no other tracks? I spent ten hours looking in that area and didn't see anyone or even a sign someone else was out there."

Carl reaches over to pat my hand. "Grace, do you hear yourself? You spent almost half a day in the remote woods, by yourself, and this is all you have to show for it." He holds up the crumpled bag. "Only thing this proves it that the person eating it is pretty cheesy." He smirks at his joke.

My frown doesn't crack. Though in any other circumstance, I might have laughed. "I covered twenty acres. No other signs of anyone but this. Doesn't that seem odd to you?"

He sighs. "Twenty acres? If I'm not mistaken, the Great Smoky Mountain National Park is over 500,000 acres. At this rate—"

Carl whips out his ancient desk calculator and punches on the keys. He turns it to face me, displaying large block numbers that I could probably see from 1.2 miles away.

"—it'll take you 25,000 days to search all of that land. And that's if you search every day for 65 years. Forget sick days and vacation time. You'll be 79 years old. Think how much trash you could clean up in that amount of time. Might even be able to save the earth."

I drop my head and try to breathe, even though panic is cinching my insides. My fingers graze over the black leather bracelet Dad gave me last year. I stare at the flyfishing symbol engraved on the little silver circle. Two words are embedded into the flat surface. *Fly High.* My eyes sting, but I pinch back the tears. "Please."

Carl comes out from behind the desk. I can't decide what he resembles more, a Q-Tip or a teaspoon. When he passes by a statue of a man holding the North Carolina flag, it plays "Dixie." Carl stops in his tracks until it finishes, as if he's respecting the national anthem. I almost expect him to salute.

When it's done, he pulls me to my feet and positions my body in front of the smudged mirror hanging on his wall. "Grace, honey, look at yourself."

I stare at my scruffy reflection. My hair is knotted and jutting out in all directions like I'm Einstein. Lines of dirt are smudged down my pointy nose and a deep scratch marks my jawbone, covering my cheek in dried blood. I flip over my hands and notice the grime caked under my nails. My spirit sags, weighing me down.

Maybe he's right. I'm going nuts.

Carl cups both of my shoulders with his hands and stands behind me, looking over my shoulder in the mirror. "I'm getting worried about you. Don't you think this might be going a bit too far?"

Without saying anything, I study his eyes. They're similar in color to mine, except mine resemble algae; his are more of a muted pine green, which reminds me of the deep forest. Which reminds me of my dad. My throat swells, making it hard to swallow. I drop my head and focus on my muddy boots to avoid Carl's stare. A frayed thread on the toe teases me. I fight the urge to bend over and tug on it.

No sense in making anything else in my life unravel.

Carl steers me back to my seat and sits in a chair next to me. "Sweetheart, maybe it's time you drop this for a while and focus more on your future." He catches my eye and smiles a little. "Maybe get your head out of the woods."

Carl's on a roll for the dumb jokes today, 0 for 3. A quote from Dad's wilderness survival course pops into my head. *Never let an animal see your fear.* Problem is, Carl can smell the stuff a mile away.

I raise my chin a fraction of an inch and decide to use my first secret weapon. "Please, Carl?"

He snorts, "It's *Captain* to you."

I flash my second tactic. My ex-boyfriend, Wyn, says my puppy eyes get him every time. "Sorry … *Captain.*" Ever since I've known Carl, he's insisted everyone call him Captain. Including his family. I bet he secretly wishes everyone would salute too.

Instead of falling into my pity trap, Carl returns to his chair in silence.

Time to pull out a new tactic of persuasion: The Art of Brown Nosing. Though I must say, I've never been very good at it. I clear my throat. "Captain, with your position and reputation, I know you can do something. Maybe convince the USFWS to keep my dad's case open. For just a little longer. Maybe test for fingerprints or something?"

"First of all, don't blow smoke up my ass, Grace. It's not you." Then he waves the air, as if I'm an annoying fly. "Secondly, this is not a *CSI* marathon. No matter how much you want there to be something out there, doesn't mean there's anything to find, especially if we haven't found it already."

My brain takes a second to process his attempt at being profound. I stare up at the flourescent light buzzing above me and focus on the popcorn ceiling. I will not cry, no matter how frustrated I become. "Captain, I can't give up what happened."

"We may never know. All of our evidence points to an accident. Grace, there's no proof he's even alive."

The A-word stabs me in the heart, but I try not to physically jerk from the pain of it. My voice shows no sign of the turmoil going on inside. "Even if it was an accident, he could still be out there. Last year, a lost camper survived sixty days before anyone found him. Dad could survive for months longer than that on his own."

Carl sighs and closes his eyes, appearing to be meditating. "Joe knows those woods better than his own backside. You and I both know he isn't *lost*. Don't we?"

I shrug off the doubt. "Maybe someone kidnapped him?"

"Why would anyone do that? Besides, there's no evidence of any foul play."

I grasp at straws. Anything. "Maybe he's so hurt, he can't call for help."

Carl scratches the top of his head. "He'd signal, use smoke or something. Joe would find a way, but there's been nothing. His trail's as dead as a dinosaur."

I hold up the Ziploc bag. "Maybe *this* is his signal? Maybe he dropped this for us to find. Please. Just dust it. To be sure. For me. I swear I won't ask you for anything else."

Before he can answer, a knock on the office door interrupts us. Carl's secretary enters the room and smiles, revealing teeth stained with cherry-red lipstick. Bernice kinda reminds me of an eggplant. Not only in shape, but because she pins up her purplish hair with an enormous green leaf clip.

Carl stands and stuffs both hands into his pockets. "What is it, B?"

Bernice teeters in the hall like a weeble-wooble and winks at me before speaking. "Captain, Wyn called. He wants you to meet him over at Bob's place for lunch."

Carl looks a bit surprised. "Really? That's odd. Okay, tell him I'll be right there." As Bernice waddles back to her desk, Carl snatches his police belt off the brass hook and cinches the leather strap around his wafer-thin waist. "Grace, I've known you your whole life. Grew up with Joe who was always a dang good friend. I want to find your daddy as much as you do."

I wheel around in the chair to face him. "Captain, all I need is for you to believe me. Trust that I'm not being crazy or emotional."

He pats my shoulder. "I don't think those things, kiddo. Just wondering if you're havin' a hard time lettin' go."

It's only then I notice I'm still shaking my head "no" as if trying to convince myself. "Not until I see a body."

Carl stands in the doorway with his hands on his guns, trying to look intimidating like he's in some kind of western standoff. He exhales slowly. "For the record, I don't think this Cheetos bag is relevant at all. And I certainly don't have to remind you that I, as an officer of the law, don't have to discuss the details of any investigation with you, a *teenager*. But because I like you, I'll dust the bag. But this is the last time I'm playing cops and robbers with you."

Without hesitating, I jump up and bear hug him. He remains stiff, his hands still gripping the butt of both weapons. "Thanks, Captain!"

He blushes at the unexpected human contact and grunts under his breath. "Uh, you're welcome."

I step back a few inches to let him recover. "And if you find something? You'll talk to the USFWS so they don't close the case?"

"If I find something, yes, I will. But if I come up empty, I want you to drop this and try to move on."

I can tell by his tone, he's not asking, so I tell Carl exactly what he wants to hear. "Sure, Captain, whatever you say."

He doesn't fold that easily and narrows his eyes. "You promise?"

I hold up three fingers. "Scout's honor."

He appears to mull over my response. "I don't remember you ever being a scout."

I wave him off. "Well, I was." Lucky for me, he's obviously forgotten I got kicked out of my troop for punching his daughter, Skyler, in the boob. I quickly recite the promise. After all, no one ever doubts a Girl Scout. "On my honor, I will try to serve God and my country, to help people at all times, and to live by the Girl Scout Law."

Carl studies me for a minute as if I'm on display at some museum for the strange. "So we have a deal then?"

I nod and shake his hand quickly. "Yeah, and you won't regret this, Carl. I mean, *Captain.*"

He sighs and pops another bubble with his gum. A few pieces of it cling to his bottom lip as he shakes his head. "I already do." Carl pets my head like I'm a mangy street mutt he doesn't really want to touch yet can't ignore. "Take it easy. I'll let you know if anything shows up."

Before I can say a word, he leaves me sitting there. In his office.

Alone.

I suppose since I've known him my whole life, Carl assumes he can trust me.

Unfortunately, he's wrong.

Peeking through the office blinds, I watch Bernice picking off her Press on Nails and wait for my diversion to arrive. A few minutes later, the bells on the door clang, and she squeals in delight at her unexpected guest.

Wyn has finally arrived.

I was starting to wonder if he'd even show. Better late than never. I was lucky to get him here at all, considering we haven't spoken in a couple of months.

My on-the-fly plan to get Carl out of his office worked.

Survival Skill #4

In survival situations, don't be afraid to utilize any and all resources you may find.

With a quick glance through the plexiglass window, I check Bernice, who's pointing at Wyn with her nail file. I don't have long but already know exactly what I'm looking for.

I beeline to the cabinet and pull out the drawer labeled "Closed Cases." My fingers walk past the Walkers and the Watkins until I reach "Joseph Wells." As I slide out the crisp manila folder, the fact that criminals have been convicted and possibly jailed for doing what I'm doing is not lost on me. My hands quiver a little until I remember what Dad said once: *If you want to get something done, sometimes you have to do it yourself.*

Wonder if that'll hold up in court.

In the next room, Wyn bursts into a coughing fit.

The warning signal forces me to hide under Carl's desk just as the door swings open. I peer through a crack in the wood, wondering if this is what a roach feels like. Bernice reaches in and flicks off the light. Even after she closes the door, I remain hidden for a few minutes just to be sure. After stuffing the folder in my backpack, I sneak out the door and down the hallway. As soon as I'm clear, I race into the alley where Luci's waiting.

I jump on my bike and tear out of town.

When I pull down my dirt driveway, Mom's truck is already gone. Nothing new. She always works. These days, the only time I see her is in a photo. For once, I'm relieved she's not here.

I charge up the porch steps and yank open the screen door. The frame flies off the hinges and crashes onto the floorboards.

Great. My whole world is deteriorating right before my eyes, and there's nothing I can do about it.

Skipping every other step, I bound up to my room and lock the door behind me. After ripping off my shoes, I fall back into my duct-taped beanbag. A few tiny white balls escape and hide under the dresser next to a crowd of dust bunnies.

I sit there and fumble with the file for God knows how long, flipping it over and over like a hot pancake. Maybe this is it. Maybe I'll crack this case wide open. Maybe I'll find something everyone else missed.

Maybe. Maybe. Maybe.

I take in a deep breath and open the folder.

The first thing I see is a photo paperclipped to the inside. Dad's sitting in a chair with a trophy with a few men flanking him. I remember the moment perfectly. The picture was taken last year after he won the *Wildlife Management Excellence Award.* Staring at his face, it suddenly dawns on me how much I look like him. Same black hair, bright green eyes, and athletic build. When I was little, I always wanted to look more like Mom—curvier yet petite—but I got over that wish years ago.

My jaw clenches as I take note of Dad's crooked smile. Whenever I was in trouble or scared, if that grin appeared, I instantly knew everything was okay with the world.

Panic takes over. I toss the file on the carpet like it's a scalding pan and push it away with my foot.

My lungs feel like they've been sawed in half. I scramble to my feet and hang my head out the open window. As I gulp in air, the tide of panic recedes. I have to pull myself together. Freaking out isn't going to help anyone.

Breathe, Grace. Just breathe.

My eyes water as I realize all the tiny details of Dad are dimming like a used lightbulb. His smell is gone. The sound of his voice, muted. And his hands? Why can't I remember his hands?

Sitting back down, I take a deep breath before opening the folder again. This time, I avoid the picture and dive straight into

19

the stack of papers. On top is a form filled out in Carl's handwriting.

Case File: 763452NC
Date: 5/07/11
Name:　　Joseph Wells**DOB:**　07-26-56　　　**Age:** 54
Race: Caucasian**Sex:** Male　　**Height:** 6'0"
Weight: 190 lbs.　**Hair:** Black　**Eyes:** Blue

NOTES:

Last seen wearing a Wildlife Officer/Game Warden uniform – green pants, grey button-up shirt, green baseball hat, and black hiking boots. Size 11.

I flip the pages and read all the details of the case.

CASE ACTIVITIES:

4/9 – Joseph Wells left home on patrol at 0600 hours
4/10 - Wife Mary reported Joe missing at 0100 hours
4/11 – Point last scene, Oconaluftee River. Located radio in river. Hiking boot print (confirmed to belong to Joe), size 11, standard issue
4/12 – Search Party.
4/18 – Dogs. Search Party.
4/20 – Cross-referenced anon tip on 4/8 before incident. Refer to Call Transcript.
4/21 – USFWS enters investigation, Reviews case file
5/1 – Evidence: a partial boot track (make unknown)
5/11 – No blood DNA or other forensics evidence.
5/31 – Another search party sweep
6/1 - Presumed dead. Cause: drowning Oconaluftee
7/15 – CASE CLOSED
ADDITIONAL INFORMATION:
Evidence catalogue/photos: JW125543.doc

My eyes focus on one entry. *A partial boot track (make unknown).* I sift through the file. No picture? Wonder if it's the same as the tracks I found in the woods. At the bottom of the case is an evidence file name, JW125543.doc, probably stored on Carl's computer. Good luck hacking in there. There's no way Wyn will help me again once he finds out I actually stole the file from his personal hero.

After jotting down the clue, I page through some interview notes until I find the referenced call transcript.

Hiker reported suspicious campsite about a mile from Sidehill.

From the date, the anonymous call came in a few days before my dad disappeared. Worth noting.

With hands trembling, I wipe my finger over Dad's reddened face, remembering how embarrassed he was about the attention he got the day of the awards. There's something so boyish about his face in this picture. Something I'd forgotten. Something I miss. I unclip the photo, replacing it with a different one from my drawer, and hide the new picture in my fly-carrying tin. No one will notice.

As my chest starts to tighten again, I shove the case file back in my sack and zip it closed, as if the Gor-Tex bag can prevent the picture from hurting me. Chewing on my bottom lip, I think about the facts in the case. Aside from the anonymous call and the random prints, Carl's right. There's not much to go on. I massage my forehead and think about all the places in the National Park.

Sidehill doesn't ring a bell.

Maybe Google knows. I sit down at my clunky computer and conduct eighty-seven keyword searches on "Sidehill" over the next couple of hours. Not much turns up, except for a few unreliable sites suggesting it's some kind of historical trail. I scour through all my trail maps to see if I can spot anything. Nothing.

Eventually I go to bed, hoping everything will make sense later. For now, I know what I need to do.

Find Sidehill.

Survival Skill #5

When meeting a stranger, take note of every detail to create a composite in your mind.

The next morning, I hide in bed until my mom leaves for work. Then I ride Luci deep into the Smokies to start another search. The morning air is warm yet crisp, hinting at the beginning of fall. After passing the bent "bear crossing" sign, I skid my motorcycle into a turn and roll down an overgrown path. Hunching over Luci's handlebars, I dodge the low-hanging branches and go as far as I can before trekking in the rest of the way.

Using the trees as handrails, I slide down the sloped forest, taking in the details of my lush surroundings. How the bark scratches my palms and how the crisp grass crunches under every step. The sweet smell of pine teases my nose, reminding me of the dreaded holidays only a few months away. I can't imagine them without Dad's light display, secret stuffing recipe, and our annual Christmas morning fishing.

To avoid the scent, I breathe through my mouth and refocus my attention on how the blooming bushes splatter the green forest with blotches of pale pink. I take in their sweet perfume, letting it replace the holiday scent.

After hiking a couple more miles, the murmur of gurgling water beckons me. I gallop to the tree line and stop to watch the river. Mossy boulders crowd Bear Creek as it glistens in the sunlight. I close my eyes, inviting the sun to stroke my cheeks and warm my soul. I'd give anything to go back to last summer when Dad and I spent every morning fishing and every afternoon patrolling the forest. Everything seemed so easy then. I can actually remember wishing for more adventure in my life. More excitement.

Be careful what you wish for.

Staring out at the river rushing by, I suddenly want so much to fish first, but it's more important to get in another search before dusk. Eating a MoonPie with one hand and chewing a hangnail on the other, I spread out my gear and highlight a search path on my map. The plan is to fan out in a one-mile radius from the point where I found the Cheetos bag. My breath speeds up with excitement and anticipation. I don't know if it's the rush of hope I'll find something more or the fear I'll find nothing else.

Pulling on my backpack, I blaze the trail and sweep in an arch, searching for another sign. For hours, I move slowly and deliberately. Careful not to step on anything that could be evidence. A small something off to one side sends off an alert in my head. I bend down and inspect the compressed area filled with tiny crushed plants, a random pebble, and a broken stick. To the average person, these are just part of your everyday woods. To me, they're prints. Signs, like this heel strike, that prove someone is out here. I lightly run my hand over the area and can tell the mud is dry. It hasn't rained for a couple weeks so it's at least that old. I quickly note the find and move on to find a scuff marking on an old dead log. After inspecting it further, it appears someone climbed over it, damaging the surface with a boot. On the other side, I spot a partial track. Up ahead, I can make out a faint trail someone left behind where the leaves bend at funny angles or are flipped over, showing their light underbellies.

After finishing the planned grid, I sit down to note everything. Chewing on the pencil eraser, I scan the forest. My spirits lift a little.

I was right. Someone is out here.

The question is who and if it's related?

Even though it's only four o'clock, the woods are already growing dark as if nature is slowly drawing its shades. The silver on my bracelet gleams in the dimming light. It's too dark to keep searching. Maybe I have enough time to fish. Reward myself for a search well done. Relax and clear my head before the sun sinks behind the treetops.

After unpacking my stuff, I slip into my waders and a waterproof vest before slithering into the river. The current tugs at my boots, urging me to play. The soft sloshing sounds of the water stroke the embankment, and the crickets hum along to the forest's natural buzz.

I start casting. Once I get a good rhythm going, my body relaxes and my chest fills, allowing me to breathe again. There used to be a time when Dad and I would fish for hours. Without talking. Without any worries.

Whipping the line back and forth, I focus on the meter of my technique. Two o'clock, ten o'clock. Two o'clock, ten o'clock. The moist air wets my face. I lick the droplets from my lips, tasting the pure mountain water. Being in the river makes me think about the fishing trip Dad was planning for us. A lump grows in my throat, blocking my airway. My chest hardens at the thought of possibly never fishing with him again.

Suddenly, I have a huge urge to get out of here, before my heart explodes.

I spin around and slosh out of the water. So much for relaxing. I pull on my backpack and stand at the tree line, watching the river slide by like a conveyor belt. Here, nothing has changed. Somehow, life keeps moving at the same speed it did before.

But for me, everything is different.

Before I can invite anyone else to my pity party, a few twigs snap behind me.

Instinctively, I squat behind a boulder and scan the horizon, wondering if Simon's making another star appearance. It takes a few minutes for my eyes to notice a human silhouette snaking through the trees. By the gait, size, and shape, it appears to be a male. My heart rate skyrockets along with my curiosity. During all my searches, I've never come across anyone out here. This place is always deserted. It's why Dad loves it here.

As the person moves further away, I decide to follow. Maybe this is the guy who owns the prints I've been tracking all day. I silently move through the leafy cover by using an old Apache stalking method, Fox Walking. Or as Dad called it, the Ostrich Shuffle. It comes in handy when tracking bears, so I assume it can fool humans too. Maintaining my balance, I lift each leg high in the air and lightly touch the ball of my foot to the ground. No matter how effective the technique, I always feel like a complete idiot doing this. Pretty sure I look like one too. Unfortunately, the silly walk only works if I'm patient, so I take my time and find a rhythm.

Lift. Bend. Step. Lift. Bend. Step.

The figure darts through a clump of trees in the distance. No matter how fast the shadow moves, my body remains on cruise control. For a second, I lose him, but then a slight movement notifies my peripheral vision. I work hard to continue the method, but it soon becomes clear I'm falling behind.

Without hesitation, I shoot off toward the intruder, only to anger a dry stick.

Crack!

The figure stops.

I slip behind a mountain laurel, letting the fat bush conceal me, and wait a few seconds. Then, in a stealth move, I inch around the side and survey the wooded landscape, listening for any sound.

Nothing.

A deep voice cuts through the silence. "Oi! What are you doing?"

I spin around to face a guy standing only a few yards away. My wilderness survival class comes back to me. *Always size up your opponent. Note every detail.* I conduct a quick once-over and etch a physical profile into my brain. Never know when you might have to do a composite sketch. The subject is about 6'2", 200 pounds, with longish dark hair. Probably my age. Looks older due to the thin scruff covering his face. He's sporting khaki cargo pants, hiking boots, and an army-green t-shirt. A leather pouch hangs across his chest, and he's carrying a small blue cooler. I look up into MoonPie-brown eyes.

He frowns. "Why are you following me?"

This time, I detect a slight accent that straddles the fine line between English and Australian. I can't tell for sure because, to be honest, they both sound the same to me.

Never show your fear. I assume that's the case any time you come across something threatening, whether it's a big animal or a hot guy. After straightening my posture, I make sure to project my voice, hoping to mask any nerves as well as my thick Southern accent. "Saw you in the woods. I was curious. No one comes out here."

"You do."

I center my weight over my feet, just in case this dude comes at me. "That's different."

He shrugs. "Not to me."

This chitchat is not productive, so I change the subject to something more interesting to me. "You lost?"

"You a tour guide?"

"Obviously not."

"Right. First off, I wouldn't be lost. Second, if I was," he holds up his wristwatch, "I have this handy little gadget called a … compass."

I cross my arms and bite back at his sarcastic remark. "Then I guess you know where you can go."

One side of his mouth curves. Somewhat crooked but stark white teeth sneak-a-peek through his fullish lips. "You're a bit cheeky."

Whatever that means. "Thanks. Now why did you say you were here?"

"I didn't." He gives me an indignant look then crosses his arms in defiance.

"You seen anyone else out here?"

His eyes dart around as if he's watching a mosquito. "No."

"So you're out here alone?"

"If you must know, I was fishing."

26

I narrow my eyes to slits and look him over. "You fish?"

"Abso-bloody-lutely." He points to a short, stubby rod leaning against a nearby oak.

I frown. A bait fisherman. Flyfishing is about more than just fishing, not to mention it takes way more skill. Bait chunkers splash through the water, ruining peaceful runs with loud yelps and incessant booze breaks. How can slapping a fat, sedated worm on a hook be called *fishing*? I stare at his fishing rod, which is actually too short for his height. This guy is invading my turf, stealing my fish. "Haven't you ever heard that *size matters*?"

The guy's eyes darken slightly, but I swear I see a sparkle. "No need to be rude. I'll leave you to your business. This time, don't follow me."

I notice how his words go up at the end of every sentence like every statement is a question. "I'm rude, but *that's* polite?"

He rubs the scruff on his chin with his thumb and forefinger. "Hmmm. Let me try again. *Please* don't follow me. Much better I hope." Before I can claim the last word, he pivots on one foot and trudges off into the trees.

I spy on the mystery guy until he fades into the green abyss, wondering what he's really doing out here. I make a conscious decision to trek back to my bike off the main trail. That way, if this dude tries to track me, I'll hear him first. Not that I'm worried. Then again, Dad and I have come across some whacky characters out here so one can never be too careful.

As I hike toward Luci, I can't help but think more about the stranger.

Questions cloud my head like the early morning mist over Bear Creek. *Who is this guy? Where is he from? And, out of all the places to fish, why is he hanging around my fishing spot?*

In fact, why is he out here at all?

Survival Skill #6

Never let an opponent see any sign of weakness or fear.

As soon as I wake up the next morning, I spread out my notes, hoping to spot something I haven't seen before. Detect something I've missed.

"Grace!" my mother shrieks from downstairs.

I ignore her and scramble to gather the papers sprawled across my bed. After shoving everything into my bag, I jump over to my desk and quickly begin tying flies to replenish my fishing stock. Mom'll freak out if she sees me obsessing over Dad's case.

What she doesn't know won't hurt me.

A few seconds later, she bursts into my room. The door slams against the wall, enlarging the long-standing hole caused by a missing doorstop. Mom is frowning and breathing heavy from skipping up the stairs in a hurry. "Grace! Did you hear me calling you?"

"Mm-hmm." I study the diagram on my computer screen. Following the instructions, I position a size-twelve hook in the vice and load black thread into the bobbin. Holding a small duck feather in place, I loop the delicate string around it several times and add a few hackles. To top it off, I tie a perfect whip finish. It's critical to make the fly just perfect down to the gnat's eyebrow or the fish will know it's a total fake.

She stomps over and flips off my screen. "You're being rude."

Without looking up, I mumble under my breath. "Ditto."

Her face pops up over my shoulder. I catch a whiff of her flowery perfume and unwillingly soften at the familiar scent. Until she speaks. "Why do you keep tying flies? Don't you have enough?"

Without looking up, I pin a fly onto my rack. *Why do you care?*

Her breath tickles the nape of my neck. "Not talking? Why are you so crabby today?"

I hang up another one of my masterpieces. "Why is it that you come in yelling at me, and I'm the one who's crabby?" Blowing my self-inflicted "bangs" away from my face, I lean in and admire my handiwork.

Mom grows strangely quiet behind me.

I twirl around on the wobbly stool, nervous she's found my case notes. Instead, she's strolling around the room, hands clasped behind her back as if she's visiting a museum. I cross my arms in front of me. "Mary, can I help you with something? Or are you just browsing?"

She scowls back. "What's this *Mary* thing lately? I don't like it."

"Sorry ... *Mary.*" Fighting with her seems unavoidable. We can't—or maybe won't—stop tromping on each other's hot buttons. The days of swinging on the porch together, sipping lemonade, are a distant memory.

Mom ignores me and continues perusing my room like it's a cheap souvenir shop. She picks up a horse statue and flips it over, possibly checking for a price. "Heard you went to see Captain yesterday."

I rub my temples and curse my oversight. Two of the hundred and eleven things that suck about living in a small town? One, dumb news travels fast; and two, it always visits the wrong people first. In this town, if I blow my nose wrong, it's sure to be breaking news in the "Medical Section" of *The Smoky Review.*

Before I can reply, she sneaks in a dig of her own. "I called Jim."

"I figured."

"He's expecting you at noon."

Great. I rub my forehead. "I'll be sure to count the minutes." It's embarrassing enough that I'm forced to see a shrink, but one named Dr. Head? And I still don't understand why I'm the one sentenced to whacko sessions when she's the one who really needs it. "By the way, how come you get to call him *Jim*, but I have to call him Dr. Head? Or, should I say, Dr. Head-ache?"

She exhales a long sigh, at least twenty seconds. "Because I've known him since high school."

Seated on the stool, I twirl in a circle so my world becomes one big blur. "Sounds like a conflict of interest to me."

She snaps back. "You know you're my only interest."

I mumble. "I'm not crazy, Mom."

"Never said you were. But you concern me."

"Why, because I ask questions that you don't want to know the answers to?"

Mom sighs again. "I can't get into this again right now. I'm late."

I finally notice she's wearing her Daisy's Diner apron. "Thought you weren'tgoing in until later?" Since Dad went missing, I never see Mom anymore. She's either taking on extra shifts at Daisy's or locking herself in her room until she leaves again. Some nights, she cries. Sometimes she just watches TV. Other times, I don't hear anything at all.

As far as I'm concerned, both my parents disappeared on the same day.

She gazes into the chrome lamp and adjusts her apron. "I have a few things to do first."

I try to hide the frustration in my voice. "Like what?"

"Like none of your business. You just worry about getting to Jim's on time."

After a few awkward minutes, I try to be nice. "We having dinner tonight?" A faded memory sizzles in my mind. Mom, Dad, and me sitting around the dining table, eating Sloppy Joes. I miss those days. Mom was different then. A tide of sickness churns through my belly.

She avoids my eyes and rolls on her lipstick. "Can't. Already promised Susan I'd eat with her. How about lunch?"

"Sure, whatever."

She gazes at me, and for a split second, I think I see her eyes moisten. A hint of regret for pushing me away? Maybe an apology for all the times she's blown me off? As the staring contest ticks on, I suddenly notice how much older she looks than a few short months ago. Her once professionally highlighted hair has surrendered to a mousy gray-brown. Instead of her hair down, it's slicked back into a bun. New worry lines crease her once-smooth porcelain skin. Tiny crow's-feet frame her brownish-yellow eyes. Under them, black smudges that would make a raccoon jealous, peek through her concealer.

Mom looks tired. Worn down. Similar to those women with no smile, hiding in dusty, faded photos from the past. Of course, the puce diner uniform and black nursing shoes don't add much cheer either. A rush of sadness trickles through me. She used to be so full of life. Now she's hollow. Her energy sucked out. A zombie waitress ambling through life, decaying without even noticing.

For a brief moment, I want nothing more than to hug her. I wish she'd let me comfort her. Then she could stroke my hair while singing *Blackbird* in my ear. When I was little, her singing could fix anything.

Now a song just isn't enough.

Mom turns away. "I better go."

"Yeah, see ya." I spin around on my stool and pretend to start tying another fly.

She sighs as she leaves the room. Once the front door slams shut, I spy on her from behind the old curtains splattered with large flowers. My dad called them "antique." He had a way of making cheap things sound beautiful.

Mom hops into my dad's "antique" faded-red truck. My throat tightens as I watch her, wishing I'd been a little nicer. Still, I can't help but want to give up on Mom the way she's given up on Dad.

The same way she's given up on me.

I press my forehead against the cool window and watch as she inches down the pebbled driveway like an old lady, braking every few feet. As soon as the truck rounds the corner, I hear the familiar crunching sound of a tired clutch as she shifts into

31

second gear. After the countless hours Dad spent teaching her, Mom still sucks at driving a stick.

I smirk. In a backward kind of way, the scraping sound comforts me. It's one of the only things I can still depend on with her. That god-awful noise gives me hope that maybe one day, things will be normal again.

The alarm on my watch sounds off, pulling me from my thoughts. Great. Now I'm going to be late for Dr. Head.

I can hear him now. *Being tardy makes you look like an "avoider lost in denial."* After stripping off my PJs and squeezing into my getting-too-small-but-I-don't-care jeans, I yank on a vintage green t-shirt of Oscar the Grouch that says, "Scram!", tie back my hair, and race out the door.

Survival Skill #7

Utilize stress management techniques to help you remain calm and focused in the wild.

Sitting in Dr. Head's office, I zone out, staring at the smiley-face clock above him. The eyes look left and right with every tick and tock, like a crazy person. Only thirty-seven minutes and twenty-nine seconds to go.

I silently celebrate. This is the longest I've gone in a session without talking. I sit Indian-style in the fabric chair. Dr. Head sits across from me in a raggedy, brown leather recliner, and packs his pipe. He lights it and settles back into his favorite La-Z-Boy, making him look about thirty years older than he really is.

Seriously, who smokes a pipe these days besides authors or grandfathers?

Not to mention, what kind of therapist sets up a business in a small town? A bad one, maybe? One who doesn't know what he's talking about? Plus, I happen to know Dr. Head moonlights as a janitor at my school to get extra cash. What real therapist does that?

Dr. Head's eyes are hidden behind ebony horn-rimmed glasses, and his wavy black hair skims his shoulders. He's kinda handsome in a hippie-professor sort of way. Then I stare down at his feet, wondering why Vans shoes were ever made in the first place, let alone, remade.

When I glance up again, he smiles and waves at me with his fingers. A smoke ring curls out of his pipe. I turn my head away and fake cough at the sweet fumes as they coil in the air. My legs bounce up and down, pumping out nervous energy fueled with a growing urge to speak. I recount the number of crooked pictures hanging on the walls and reread the battered sign above the door for the umpteenth time.

It's better to be mad and know it then to be sane and have one's doubts. Probably true.

I shift in my chair, trying to contain myself. Boredom taunts me, begging me to speak. The only sound in the room is the psycho-clock clicking in the background. Eleven minutes and sixteen seconds. Nine minutes, fifty-seven seconds. At eight minutes and ten seconds, I surprise myself by blurting out, "I suppose you want me to talk about my dad." Where did that come from?

I sigh at the defeat. I hate to lose. Probably from years of Dad always winning when he played board games with Wyn and me. Though I'd give anything to lose to him right now.

Dr. Head answers in a monotone voice. "Is that what you want to talk about? Your dad?"

I huff and throw my head back against the puffy headrest. "Geez, this is so stupid. I told you before, there's nothing left to say."

Dr. Head cocks his head to one side resembling a bird. "Well, then why don't you tell me about your visit with Captain?"

Great, here it comes. "Doc, it wasn't a big deal. I asked him a few questions, that's all." Rocking back and forth, my chair repeatedly slams into the wall. I laugh on the inside.

Dr. Head seems completely unaffected by the thumping. He's either really, really balanced or just plain dead inside. "Did you ask him questions about your dad?"

"Maybe."

Dr. Head takes a drag off his pipe. When he speaks, smoke trails out of the corner of his mouth and spirals to the ceiling. "I thought we were coming to terms with your situation."

My volume turns up a notch. "You mean *me*. Not *we*. *You* don't have to work through anything."

"So then, are *you* letting your investigation go?"

I blow out lightly. "Not until I prove he's not dead." As soon as I say it, I slap my hand over my mouth. Busted! I've barely spoken a word in all my sessions and now, within a matter of seconds, I throw open the door to my brain and invite Dr. Head in. And like a vampire, he will now suck me dry.

Dr. Head's eyebrows shoot up into perfect arches. He leans in and fixates on my pupils, seemingly excited. "Good, at least you're finally being honest. Maybe we're getting somewhere. Let's go over what we know. I can talk you through it."

I mumble, "Lucky me." The walls slowly start to close in around me, forming a tight box. My head pounds and my mouth turns dry. I circle my fingertips on my temples, attempting to push the emerging pain back into my brain. There's only one small window in the incredibly shrinking room. My only escape.

Outside, a branch scratches a rhythm on the glass pane. I will the tree to break through and set me free.

I need air.

Breathe.

In through the nose. Out through the mouth.

Dr. Head continues poking his mental probe into my psyche. "After your dad went missing, the police said they found his radio in the Oconaluftee River."

I fixate on the small square of freedom and suck in enough air to respond, the whole time spinning my bracelet on my wrist. "Doesn't mean he drowned."

Dr. Head perches his glasses on the bridge of his nose and reviews his notes. "Lester Martin's been a park ranger out there for years. He said your dad told him he was going to the river."

I tug at the collar of my shirt that's suddenly choking me. Squeezing tighter and tighter. "Doesn't mean my dad *died* there."

"The dog didn't pick up your dad's scent anywhere else. Only at the river's edge."

I wring my hands together and remember something my dad once said. *Don't lose your cool, it's harder to get it together than keep it together.* I work hard to steady my voice. "Bear's not a hound. He's an old dog. He probably got confused."

"Your dad wasn't the best swimmer. Even he admitted that."

I avoid hyperventilating before I can answer. "He saved people from that river. He wouldn't *drown* there. Besides ..." My voice trails off as the words stick to my larynx like a dead moth to light. I bite the inside of my cheek, careful not to reveal any information from the stolen file. Information I shouldn't know.

Dr. Head urges me on. "Besides what?"

I swallow hard and keep my eyes on the glass portal, leading to safety. "Never mind."

"Do you think you're getting a little obsessed with this?"

I glare at him. "Don't you mean, we?"

His face doesn't move as if it's frozen in place. No expression. "Grace, I'm trying to help you. I want to know where you think we can go from here."

My voice comes out sharper than I intended. "I'm sure you're going to tell me."

He isn't bothered by my tone. Totally different than Mom. Dr. Head is more robotic.

"I think maybe you should consider letting go a bit. Focus on letting yourself move on. Let yourself try to be happy."

I choke out one word. "Happy?"

He nods.

My chest feels as if someone is sitting on top of me and bouncing. I squeeze my eyes shut as emotions start to bubble beneath my hardened shell. *How can I be happy?*

I don't want to cry, but my body doesn't seem to care what I want anymore. I'm on the verge of crumbling just as the alarm clangs.

Saved by the wacko clock.

I leap out of the chair like a lemur in a tree and clamber for the door. Knowing freedom is waiting for me on the other side. "Time's up!"

Dr. Head tails me. "So I'll see you next week?"

Without looking back, I wave over my shoulder and sing out, "Saaaame time. Saaaame place." I hurl myself down the steps, barely avoiding injury, and sprint around the corner until I'm out of sight. I lean against the wall and fight to regain my mental strength.

That was close. Almost bought a one-way ticket to Meltdown City.

I regain my composure and drag my heavy body down the cracked sidewalk toward work. Immediately, people recognize me. Dad's case has turned us into local celebrities. Only without the red carpets and expensive dresses. A few young girls from the local middle school stare with gaping mouths, while others eye me, searching for an excuse to say something. One couple avoids my gaze all together.

I walk faster down the sidewalk toward work. The dilapidated buildings make the town look as old and poor as it is. The store banners are faded and even missing a few letters. A "for sale" sign hangs on the door of an empty storefront. One shop down, only twenty-three to go. When I pass by the general store, Mr. Fields is standing outside with a short bald man.

He sees me and waves. "Well, hello Grace. How's … everything?"

I pretend not to notice his awkward pause. "Fine, thanks." I speed walk past him with my head down to avoid any more questions. What am I supposed to say? People only want to hear the good stuff so they can go on with their day without feeling guilty. Mr. Fields doesn't ask anything else. He stares up at his sign and continues his conversation with the man I've never seen before.

As I turn the corner, Ms. Green, the town's hairstylist and gossip expert, sets her sights on me like a nuclear missile to its target. Before she reaches me, I veer off the town's main drag and duck down a side street, taking a shortcut to work. These people don't get it. Just because they've read about my family and the missing case in *The Smoky Review*, doesn't mean they know me.

At least not the *real* me.

I'm so deep in thought, I almost don't notice the footsteps echoing behind me.

In perfect rhythm with mine.

I speed up. They speed up.
I slow down. They slow down.
No doubt about it. Someone's following me.

Survival Skill #8

Pay attention to your surroundings and be prepared for attack.

𝕼 stop dead in my tracks. "I can hear you, you know."

"Man. You're good. I'll give you that."

"It's not hard to hear an elephant coming." I spin around and my heart slips a little when I see Wyn.

He looks better than usual. I cock my head and try to figure out what it is. Is it the new dark jeans, the navy Coldplay t-shirt, or the Converse shoes.

My voice cracks as I shake off the all-too-familiar feeling of attraction and confusion. "What do you expect? I'm trained in self defense and wilderness survival."

Wyn rolls his eyes. "Yeah, yeah. I know. You're a badass."

I nod once. "And don't you forget it!"

He smiles and tilts his head to one side like a little puppy. I've seen that look so many times before. Wyn and I have been friends since we were babies. Pooped and played together. Last year, we even started dating and everything seemed okay until Dad disappeared. Wyn tried to comfort me, but it was just too weird, so we broke up at the worst possible time. I guess he was tired of me pushing him away, and I felt smothered.

Now I've heard Skyler Stevens has been draping herself all over him, trying to get noticed. I wonder if he just hangs out with her because Carl's her father or because he really likes her. After all, Skyler's petite, pretty, and perky. The total opposite of me.

Never got what GI Joe saw in that blond doll anyway.

"Dating Barbie yet?"

Wyn raises one eyebrow. "Why? Is Skipper jealous?"

"You wish." I poke the chicken-pock scar in the middle of his forehead. "You're certainly no Ken."

He puffs out his chest ever so slightly. Assuming I don't notice. "Thank goodness. Because I hear he has no banana in his hammock. If you know what I mean."

I try not to laugh because it's true. "That's because *Barbie's* got them."

He smirks and flexes his skinny arms. "Ken's got nothing on this."

Even though he's kidding, I know Wyn's always been a little sensitive about being on the skinny side, so I squeeze his bicep. "You definitely have much better hair. Anyway, you're changing the subject." I glance around, all spy-like. "So where is she? Your shadow."

"If this isn't an official inquiry on who I really want to be dating, then I plead the fifth. Besides, it would be rude of me to talk about another girl in front of a lady." He flashes me a bright-toothed smile.

I give him a look. "Oh brother, you're such a shyster."

"Are you from the '50s? Who says shyster anyway? Kinda dorky."

"Like *dorky* is any cooler."

Wyn shoves his hands in his pockets and strolls next to me. "You know, you almost gave me a heart attack the other day." His strides are longer than mine, so he does a lot of starting and stopping. Reminds me of how my mom drives, first accelerating then braking every few feet. He pushes my shoulder. "You're lucky I lured Carl out of the office and distracted Bernice for that long."

I wink at him. "I knew you could handle it. Bernice loves to flirt with you."

"Ha, ha." Wyn grabs for me.

Without warning, I clutch onto his wrist and fold his arm behind his back. He didn't even know what happened. "Gotcha! Magic phrase, please."

"This game was funny when we were five."

I pull on his arm a little but not enough to hurt him.

He mumbles. "Amazing Grace." He jerks on his arm. "Now let go. I have a rep to protect."

I release my grip and smile. "So you've said."

Wyn steps back a few inches to safety. However, the scent of his cologne lingers in the air, making me think back to all the times I could smell him on my jacket hours after he dropped me off. He rubs his shoulder and gives me a strange look. "Man, you are strong. You sure you're not a guy trapped in a girl's body?"

"Are you sure *you're* not a guy trapped in a girl's body?" I cover my mouth and smirk.

He puts his palm against my forehead like a church healer and pushes me backwards. "Very funny." He keeps a straight face, but I can tell he wants to laugh. He waits a few seconds. "Weeeeell? Did you find the file?"

"I did better than that." I stare at him with a look that says, *Come on, think about it.*

His silly grin fades, and he throws his head back and looks at the sun. "Ah man! Come on, G." He leans in closer and lowers his voice. "Seriously, did you steal it?"

"Does a one-legged duck swim in circles?"

Wyn ignores my joke and smacks his forehead. "You said you were going to look at it, not steal it. Captain's gonna kill me if he finds out I helped you break into his office. Probably dock my pay too. I need that job."

I feel bad for a second. Not only does Wyn work for Carl doing odd jobs, but ever since Wyn's dad left when he was five, Carl's been a stand-in father to him. I definitely don't want to jeopardize the only male connection he has ever had. He needs it. "Chill out. I didn't break in, he *left* me there. There's a difference."

"Shoot. Tell that to Judge Huey. If you get caught, you're on your own."

I pluck a piece of fuzz off his shirt. "You mean, if *you* get caught."

The corners of his mouth turn down. "I don't follow."

41

"I got what I needed. Now, I want to see if you can put it back," I whisper. Adding some drama, I survey the area before sliding the file out of my bag and hold it against his chest.

"Ohhhh, no!" He backs away with his hands up, as if touching it will contaminate it. Then again, knowing Carl, he's probably already got Wyn's fingerprints on file, since Skyler is his daughter. "You're whacked if you think I'm going in there with that. Besides, I already did you a favor."

"*Psst.* You didn't do me a favor, you *owed* me a favor."

He leans in and pokes my shoulder with one finger. "Hey! You can't keep holding that against me. You only changed one grade and that was over a year ago. I've paid you back, in more ways than one." He winks.

I wrinkle my reddening face and lightly smack the back of his head. "Whatever. Anyway, I didn't just change your grade; I illegally hacked into the school's computer. So I say, eye for an eye, know what I mean?"

Wyn glares at me for a second before snatching the file out of my hand and stuffing it into his leather messenger bag. "Fine. But we're even now. I'm puttin' my foot down. I'm tired of doing all your dirty work."

"If it makes you feel better, we can call it even." I shrug and watch an older couple walk by holding hands. "At least, for now."

"Ha! You're dreaming. So was the B&E worth anything? What'd you find out?"

"Not much new. Just notes on a partial boot print and an anonymous call about a place called Sidehill. Ever heard of it?"

Wyn thinks for a second. "No, but have you asked Tommy yet? He's lived here his whole life. He knows every trail out there."

"I'm heading to work now, so I'll ask him."

"What kind of boot was it?"

I shake my head. "Didn't say. 'Make unknown.'"

His eyes light up. "You might be able to track that down. There was a case Carl was on last year. You know how they

42

caught the guy? They tracked his tread to some custom boot maker and found the purchase order. I think Mama Sue still owns that boot place on the reservation."

"She's still alive? I totally forgot about her." I glance at Wyn out of the corner of my eye. "You know? You're not as dumb as you look."

He can't help but laugh out loud. "Gee, thanks."

I hook my arm through his and walk along with him. For a second, it feels like six months ago when he used to escort me to work. Before everything bad happened. "Seriously, the boot lady is a good idea, but there was no picture. Must be on his computer."

He keeps his eyes straight ahead. "Don't look at me."

I study his face as he continues walking. "Wyn? Thanks for helping me. I know Carl would be pissed if he found out."

"Why? Because I'm aiding a felon? No harm in that."

"That, and because the case is pretty much closed at this point." I stare up at the white puffs spotting the perfect blue sky. "Unless I find something concrete he can use."

Wyn swaggers next to me and pats my hand, still hooked through his arm. "G, you know he'd help you if he could. It's out of his hands."

"Geez, you're hanging out with him so much, you're starting to sound like him." We stop in front of my work, and he looks down at me. I notice the familiar freckle under his right eye. I used to love that little sun spot.

I immediately break away, putting some space between us. I don't want to want Wyn back. I lean back against the wall with one foot up, standing like a plastic flamingo, and try to go on with the conversation as if the thoughts about him aren't going on inside my head. "Carl could fight to keep the case open."

"Why do you say that?"

I tell him about the Cheetos bag. "I'm betting it belongs to my dad."

Wyn mimics my stance, and his eyes grow wide. "Man, I'm getting a little worried about you. Seems like you're getting obsessed with this whole thing. I mean, you're hanging your hat on Cheetos."

I push off with my foot and cross my arms. "Obsessed? That bag could be evidence. It shouldn't be out that far, and my dad's missing, and he just happens to love them. Maybe it's a clue. And if you don't want to help me, I'll do it on my own." I turn away, but Wyn circles around me and blocks my exit.

He cups my face with hands. "Easy, tiger. It's me, and last time I checked, I *am* helping you. I mean, come on, Grace. You don't talk to me for three months. Three. And the minute you call, I drop everything to help, so that's not fair."

"I know."

He moves my bangs away from my eyes with his finger. "I'm just worried, that's all. Doesn't mean I'm against you. Neither is Captain. But you gotta chill out a little."

The tension in my body drains. "You're right, but I'm serious, Wyn ... I won't stop until I figure out what happened out there." I stare at the distant mountains cloaked in mist. "I need to know."

"Fair enough. But don't push me away again. Deal?"

"Deal." I nod and squeeze his hand. "Hey. I'm sorry I snapped at you."

He holds my hand longer than the average shake. He smiles at me. "No, you're not. And don't you go all soft on me now."

I tug on his hand, hoping he'll set mine free yet hold on to it at the same time. "Don't worry. I won't."

He squints his eyes as if trying to read my mind. "Look, I'll put your stupid file back today, but you better make sure Captain doesn't find out you're still snooping around." He mimics Carl's signature phrase. "Or he'll have to shut you down."

His impression of Carl is spot on, and I can't help but crack up. Then I spot Mr. Fields carrying out another box from his store. "What's going on with Fields' place?"

Wyn tries on his serious look for a minute. "I don't know. He came by to see Captain yesterday. Evidently, the bank didn't give him enough money. So he's closing up shop. After thirty years. Can you believe it?"

My heart sinks as I watch Mr. Fields hug his wife. "That sucks. He loves that place. This is the second shop that's closed in the last few months. If this keeps happening, there won't be a town left."

Just then, Skyler appears from around the corner. Compared to my standard black and tan look, she is overly colorful in turquoise jeans and a bright yellow top. Skyler tosses her over-processed hair and waves like an excited three-year-old. "Hey, Wyn! I've been looking for you! Want to join some of us for lunch?"

"Hold on a second." As soon as he faces me again, Skyler shoots me a dirty look. Typical. To this day, she hasn't forgotten the Girl Scouts incident. Personally, I still don't see the big deal. At least she has boobs.

I can't help but rearrange my hair a little. I look like a mess compared to her. The before and after shot at an Oprah makeover show. I point over his shoulder. "Looks like love's a-calling."

He smirks and his cheeks flush a little, as if someone pinched them. "Maybe it's a wrong number." He brushes his hand across my shoulder, pushing my hair to the back. Something he used to always do. "You wanna come with?"

I laugh. "Me? Somehow, I'm guessing I'm not on Skyler's Evite. But you go, I gotta get to work anyway."

He looks at Skyler then at me. "You sure you're okay?"

"Go. I'm fine."

He bites his lip. "You know what FINE means, right?"

Dr. Head's definition of FINE scribbles across my brain. "Feelings Inside Not Expressed?"

"No. Freaked out, insecure, neurotic and—."

"Emotional." I roll my eyes and play along. "Gee, I'll try real hard to keep my tears in check." Behind him, Skyler crosses her arms and taps her foot to a silent beat. "Um, I think Barbie's about to kick Ken's ass."

He winks. "I'm not worried. Kinda hoping Skipper will save me." He presses his finger into the dimple on my chin. "See ya later, Little Miss Independent."

When he joins Skyler, she makes a point of touching his arm and laughing a little too hard for my taste. I bird-dog them until they disappear around the corner, half wishing he'd stayed.

I had forgotten how good of a distraction Wyn can be. I shake off the thought and turn away. How is it, after three months, Wyn can just jump back in and mush up all my feelings again. I thought I was over him. Because, to be honest, my heart can't take any more drama.

I have more than enough as it is.

Survival Skill #9

A good knife is an essential tool that can be used as a weapon or help construct other survival items.

The wooden sign swings above me—Tommy's Fishing Shack: Where Anyone Can Fly—squeaking in the breeze. As I push through the door, ready for my morning shift, the slight smell of leather finds my nose. The store is quiet and empty. Tan clothes, fishing vests, and waders hang on racks, and rows of fishing rods line the back wall. Soothing Native American music floats through the comfy space. No matter how much time I spend here, entering the shop always feels like I'm wrapping up in an old sweater on a chilly night.

Comfy and warm.

I call out to my boss. "Tommy?"

A bass-toned voice answers me from the back room. "Elu! Be out in a second." I grin at the Cherokee nickname he gave me when I was just a kid, or an *usdi. Elu* means "full of grace."

I'm full of something, but it definitely isn't grace.

I stroll toward the front counter, staring at the old pictures hanging along the wall. Some are of Tommy posing with famous fishermen who have frequented his well-respected shop. Others showcase him with large fish he's caught in tournaments. I always tease him about not displaying the smaller catches. Each time, he explains it away.

Only show your best side. No one wants to see the ugly one.

A picture hanging on the wall catches my attention. The second my eyes settle on it, I jerk my head away as if I've been slapped. Chewing on a fingernail, I glance back at the photo of Dad and Tommy, both wearing disarming smiles. I gnaw on the next nail as I lean in closer. Dad's wearing his favorite t-shirt with a flyfisherman on the front that says, *Fly Me to the Moon*.

How could I not have noticed this before?

It's the same shirt he was wearing the last time I saw him.

Tommy appears from out of the storage room with a large box in his hands. I smile at his outfit. Even when he's on land, Tommy dresses as if he's going fishing or just coming off the river. Shoulder-length, white hair peeks out from under a fishing hat, decorated with tons of lures.

He glides up to me. "You're late again."

I give him a hug. "How do you know? That old watch hasn't worked in years. Can't believe you haven't fixed it yet." I've never seen him without it since his wife died. Ama gave him the gift for their 50th anniversary.

Tommy bends over and sets the box on the floor. "Time is nothing but an illusion."

"Good. I'll remember that next time you dock me for being late."

He chuckles. "Smart girl. Too smart, if you ask me." For the first time, he takes notice of me. His face crinkles, revealing the map of his long life. "Good lord, you look tired."

"Gee, thanks." I brush my bangs away from my face. "Is that how you make a *ge ya* feel good?"

His eyes flicker in the artificial light. "Elu! You've been practicing your Cherokee."

"Not really. I think I got lucky on that one."

He stares for a minute then frowns. "All right. What's wrong?"

I try to pretend I have no idea what he's talking about. "Nothing. It's just been a long week."

He sits down on the stack of boxes. "I'm all ears."

I cave instantly. "I found a Cheetos bag in the woods. Gave it to Carl."

Tommy's eyes widen. "I don't get it."

"Don't you remember? Dad always carried those with him. Carl promised to dust the bag for fingerprints if I let the case go."

Tommy snaps out his pocketknife and zips it across the box. "No matter what you think, Captain's a good cop."

As he pulls out a bundle of waterproof socks, I launch into the next topic, not wanting to debate Carl's effectiveness. "Oh yeah, and yesterday, I came across some guy while I was out fishing. By Bear Creek."

"Who was he?"

"That's what I wanted to know. Said he was fishing." Tommy returns to his inventory as I review the store checklist. Then a question pops into my head. "I almost forgot. Do you know anything about a place called Sidehill?"

Tommy pauses for a second as if searching his memory bank. "Hmm, don't think so. Why?"

"In the file, there was a reference to a place called Sidehill. I thought you might have heard of it since you were born in these mountains."

He fumbles with a stack of price tags and answers quickly. "Doesn't ring a bell, but let me think about it."

I huff and puff. Another dead end. "That sucks."

Tommy eyes narrow. "By the way, what *file*?"

"Huh?"

"You said *in the file*. What file?"

No use lying to him. I suck in a deep breath. "Okay. I'll tell you, but promise me you won't get mad."

He squints and folds his arms across his chest, resembling a real chief. "Uh oh. What'd you do this time?"

"I borrowed my dad's case file from Carl's office."

He frowns. "Borrowed? You mean *stole*? Are you *nuda*?"

"Crazy with a capital K. There wasn't much in the file. Anyway, Wyn's putting it back for me. Carl never even missed it."

Tommy covers his ears with his hands. "I'm going to pretend I didn't hear this. I can't get involved in your shenanigans. Got too much on my plate. Forget *Elu*. I should call you *du-la-di-nu-li-ni-gv-gv*."

"Nah. Doesn't sounds as cool. Plus, it's a mouthful."

Tommy doesn't smile. "Well, Ama used to be 'strong-willed' too, when she was younger. But she always knew where to draw the line. You and Wyn are both lucky you haven't been busted for any of your crazy antics. If you aren't careful, you're both going to get into real trouble one of these days. And to be honest, I can't afford any trouble around here. Got enough of my own."

I stop what I'm doing. "What do you mean?"

He waves me off. "Things are tight. Got Ama's medical bills I'm still paying off."

"Man, seems like everyone's having problems in this town."

Tommy goes back to what he was doing. "Never mind all that. You don't need to worry about me. You got enough on your mind."

"You can say that again." I stack some papers on the counter and count the cash in the old cash register.

He walks around the counter and hugs me tight. "You know I support you in what you are doing to find your dad. However, I don't want you doing things that'll get you into trouble. Promise me one thing."

"What?"

He cups my shoulders with his large hands. "If you find out anything new, you'll talk to Les or the Captain first. Promise me you won't do anything dangerous, especially on your own."

"I promise." I cross my fingers behind my back and jump into a new subject. "You'll never believe what else happened."

Tommy grins as he stacks fishing tins in a perfect column. "You gonna make me guess?"

My eyes widen for emphasis. "I ran into Simon. Face to face. From here to there." I point to the back room.

Tommy stops working and gives me his undivided attention. "Go on." After I tell him the play-by-play of my encounter, he whistles. "How did he look?"

"Big and bad."

He chuckles. "Good for him. What do you think it means?"

I think about the animal totems I studied on the reservation. "Well, bears are sure of their power, so sometimes they forget to show caution. If a bear symbol shows up, it means you have to pay more attention to how you think and act."

"Interesting." Tommy straightens some shirts on a rack. "Either that or he was just hungry."

I can feel my face redden. "Very funny. Hey, speaking of bears. Did you talk to Chief Reed about closing the Cherokee Bear Pit yet?"

Tommy sighs and removes his hat. "Elu, there's nothing I can do."

I turn away from him and straighten a t-shirt display. "I don't see how we can let this happen. Those bear pits are a disgrace to the reservation. It's animal abuse. Offensive. Disgusting."

"I don't disagree. But Chief Reed says it brings in a lot of income. Nothing I say will change his mind."

I face him and keep from yelling. "Tommy, as you *know*, those bears live their lives in a cement pit, sitting in their own crap. Grizzlies. Sun bears. Last time I went there to see Chief Reed, the poor things walked in endless circles, begging tourists to feed them Lucky Charms or old cat food. One bear was so depressed, he had sores from lying in the same spot for so long."

"I know all this."

"Then why can't you do more to stop it? You live there. Chief Reed is your *nephew*. He should set them free."

Tommy places his hat back on his head and frowns, shaking his head. "Those bears wouldn't stand a chance in the wild anyway." My mouth hangs open, and he puts up his hands in defense. "I'm not saying it's right. I'm just saying, it's bigger than me. There's nothing I can do. Reed isn't going to impact the whole reservation for an old man like me."

I flop down in a chair. "I know. It's just so hard to watch something so awful and be so helpless to change it."

Tommy pats my shoulder. "I know, I'm sorry. It'll work itself out. You'll see." He squints at me. "Maybe this will make you feel better." He reaches behind the counter and pulls out a long wooden box.

I trace my finger over the three intricate carvings decorating the lid—a bear, a wolf, and an eagle. I look up at him in surprise. "You made this?"

He nods and smiles proudly. "With my own two hands and a load of love. I know you're into animal totems, so I did some research." He points to the pictures. "The bear, or *yona*, tells you to be aware of your limits. The *wa-ya*, or wolf, will help you develop strength in your decisions. And the eagle, *we-ha-li*, says that you can soar to great heights."

I gawk at him. "This is awesome, but I thought you didn't believe in that stuff."

He shrugs. "This gift isn't about me. It's about you. Are you going to open it?"

I slide back the lid to reveal a knife set resting atop soft, purple-velvet padding. Tiny turquoise and red beads line up in perfect rows, decorating the deerskin sheath. I ease the knife out of its pouch and hold it up to the light, admiring the craftwork. Tommy even carved "Elu" into the shiny blade. "It's beautiful."

He lightly runs his finger along the ridge. "Hand cut from steel. Strong, like you."

I throw my arms around his neck. "I love it … and you."

Tommy half bows. "*Gv-ge-yu-hi* too, Elu." Then he eyes me. "Well? What are you waiting for? Get back to work. I'm not paying you to stand around and chitchat."

I salute. "Right away, Chief."

Tommy shuffles off to the back office as I tuck the present into the side pocket of my backpack and assume my position behind the counter. As I wait for customers, the soft music, a blend of beating drums and sorrowful chants, sways around me. The end of summer is so slow in this town. My eyelids grow heavy from a lack of sleep. I flip through my notebook, reread my notes, and doodle little flowers in the corners. My tummy protests. Only one more hour until my break: sugar, caffeine, and a catnap.

Someone whistling a song breaks my trance.

At first, I think it's the music. Until a big burly man with a pockmarked face steps in front of me. I recognize him from Mr. Fields' store. He's decked out in a Cabela shooting shirt with suede patches on both shoulders and expensive-looking pants. Dude screams hunter from a mile away. Rich one, too.

He speaks with a thick country drawl that even I find hard to understand. "Yew work here?" Before I can answer, the man frowns and, for some reason, speaks slower and louder. "I ... SAID ... DO YEW ... WORK ... HERE?"

Obviously, he's confused because I'm not deaf or stupid.

I suppress a deep sarcastic urge to answer, *Noooo, I'm hanging out behind the counter wearing a store apron and a name badge.* Instead, I simply reply, "May I help you?"

He places both hands on the counter and leans in a little too close for my comfort. "You got any guns?"

Survival Skill #10

If lost, do not be impulsive. Patience can be the difference between life and death.

𝕼 smother my sarcasm and motion toward the back wall where rods are obviously on display. "Sorry, sir, this is a *fishing* shop."

He removes his hat and glances around the store until his muddy-brown eyes fixate on a glass case. "Let me see them knives." Without waiting, he moves around the counter and eyes the locked display. "How about that one?"

"Sir, that's a limited edition. What kind of knife are you looking for?"

He leans in and reads the sales tag of the weapon he's admiring. "A Browning Russ Kommer Custom Limited Edition Knife."

He chuckles as I unlock the case and take out the box. "This is custom made. Hand carved with a black ash burl handle."

"Yeah, I can read." The man gives me a nod without even looking at the knife. "I'll take it."

I hesitate at the thought of someone dropping this much money on a knife. Must be nice to just walk in and buy something off the rack without caring about the price tag. "Sir, it's a thousand dollars."

He waves me off and browses through the display of GPS watches. "Okay, go ahead and ring her up."

"Sir, are you sure? We have other ones that are cheaper. But just as good." I have no clue why I'm talking this guy out of buying, and my piggy bank out of a large commission.

He frowns. "I said, I'd take it."

"Okay." I feel a bit guilty for protesting in the first place. Tommy really needs a big sale. My hands shake as I punch in numbers on the register. This transaction is as much as the store makes in a week. Maybe even a month. I can feel the man staring at me. Without looking up, I recite his total. "That'll be $1,007.37. Do you want a bag?"

He pulls a wad of cash from his back pocket and counts out ten one-hundred-dollar bills plus a twenty. "Nah, I'll just take it with me." The man chuckles as he takes the box. When the receipt pops out the top, he rips off the little piece of paper and turns away from the counter. The whole time whistling the same song that I still can't name.

I call after him. "Sir, your change?"

He doesn't even bother to look back. "Keep it. This place needs it more than I do."

Before I can protest any more, the wooden wind chimes on the front door clap together, announcing his exit. I sit on the stool, staring at the money before dropping it in the donation jar on the counter for Save the Bears.

A few seconds later, Wyn struts up and leans on the counter. "Hey you."

I can't help but grin. "What are you doing here?" I look at my watch. There's no way he could have eaten lunch in thirty minutes. Poor Skyler, she probably had to have her Cobb salad and water all alone. The thought lifts my spirits.

Wyn winks. "I thought I'd stop by to bug you before I head out."

"Oh, lucky me." I glance through the window to see if the redneck is still in the street. "Hey, did you see the big dude that walked outta here?"

Wyn thumbs over his shoulder. "The jolly *red* giant? Yeah, why? Was he bothering you? 'Cause if he was, I can take care of him."

I scoff because he isn't nearly as tough as he talks. I happen to know he's been afraid of spiders since the first grade. Freaked out every time we watched *Charlotte's Web* in class. I snicker. "Oh? And what will you do? *Talk* him to death?"

"A real man never gives away his fighting strategy."

I rub my eyes and give a fake yawn. "Of course you don't. Anyway, the dude just came in here and slapped down a thousand big ones for a really expensive knife. Barely blinked."

"Must be nice." Wyn plays with the fishing lure display. It topples over, spreading hooks and flies all over the ground.

I groan. "Smooth move, Slick." We both bend over to pick up the pointy hazards and almost knock heads.

He doesn't move back. Instead, he hovers an inch from my face. "Did you ask Tommy about that hill?"

"Sidehill? He's never heard of it."

"Want me to ask my connections?"

I put my hand over his face. "If you mean Carl, no. He probably knows it's in the file, and he'll wonder why you're asking."

"Speaking of file, I put it back already."

I prick my finger on a hook and suck on the bead of blood. "That was quick."

"Yeah, well, I didn't want to carry it around town. Captain was out for lunch, so I went for it. Almost got nabbed too. And if I had, don't think for a second I wouldn't have taken you down with me."

I plant a fake punch on his chin. "I know you better than that."

"I hate it when you're right."

"I love it." I flash him a big smile and return the display to its upright position.

"Well, I'm going to go meet … I mean, I gotta go." He's obviously about to meet Skyler and just didn't want to say the S word.

"Okay."

He turns around to walk away then glances over his shoulder. "Hey, you up for a game night tonight? Haven't hung out in a while. I need to get my revenge for the last time we played Scrabble."

I pretend to fiddle with the little boxes of impulse buys on the counter. "You seem pretty confident for someone who lost."

"Persistence is a state of mind."

"So is *crazy*."

"You would know." He widens his eyes. "Anyway, it's not about winning. It's how you play the game that really matters."

I roll my eyes. "Yeah, right. You don't believe that anymore than I do."

He flashes me a wide Cheshire-cat grin and shrugs. "Yeah. I know, but it sounded real sportsmanlike. So are we on?"

I check my watch. Break time. "Can't. All I can think about when I get home is food and bed."

His gaze turns soft for a brief moment. A few uncomfortable seconds pass between us until he breaks through the awkward silence. "Okay, maybe next time then?"

I straighten a stack of invoices, trying to hide my disappointment that he's leaving again. "Uh, yeah … sure. I'll call you."

His face flushes a bit as if he's hot, and he abruptly heads for the door. "If you're lucky, I'll answer." He waves over his shoulder without looking back. As he walks out, he rubs the back of his head, which tells me he's smiling. Somehow, even when I can't see his face, I know exactly what's going on just by his gestures. I know him that well.

After Wyn leaves, a mixture of emotions stirs around inside me. Why is it guys always seem cuter after you break up? In Wyn's case, he's never been *hot* cute, just *adorable* cute. But mostly, I've always digged his sense of humor. He makes me laugh even when I don't want to. On paper, we're probably the perfect pair. A comfortable blend. So different, not alike in most ways, yet still go together somehow. Like peanut butter and jelly or cookies and milk.

I rubberneck out the window, watching him kid around with shop owners as he passes them on the street. It's funny how people act when Wyn's around. The men slap him on the back as if they've always been great friends. And the women smile and giggle. Wyn makes everyone happy. And when he's around me, my world is brighter even if it is upside down.

Just then, a little dark cloud rolls through, and her name is Skyler. She sneaks up behind Wyn and covers his eyes with her hands like a bad game of *guess who*. Doesn't she have a life? When he spins around, she gives him her best fake smile. I swear, she even sticks out her boobs.

Maybe I should have punched them harder.

☙

I sit at my usual booth in the diner and wait for Mom to bring my double order of caffeine and Cinn-O-Bun. Chrome booths with cracked yellow seats fill the large space. A long counter is off to one side of the room, ending at the kitchen, while a buffet borders the far wall, filled with potato salad, mac and cheese, and jellos and puddings. Even though the diner is old, it's usually packed this time of day. After all, it's the only place in town with decent food. And that's not saying much.

Mom finally strolls up with a pencil over one ear and a tray on her hand. Instead of taking my order, she slides a plate full of real food in front of me and annoyingly pinches both my cheeks. "Eat up! You're getting too skinny."

I scoff at the ridiculous comment. "You're not eating with me?"

She stares at the top of my head, unable to lock in eye contact. "Can't, too busy."

I duck around, trying to capture her gaze. "You want to hear about my session?"

Mom smiles at someone as they walk in the door. "Be right with you!" Then she addresses me. "Can it wait until later? I'm slammed today. We're a person short."

I mumble, "Sure."

I try not to look too dejected, but before I even answer, she scoots off to take care of her patrons.

Only instead of waiting on tables, she walks back into the kitchen and starts chatting with Kenny, the short order cook. I stare down at my stale turkey sandwich with mayo, a wilted salad, and a milkshake. Somehow, Mom's forgotten her daughter is vegetable-resistant and lactose-intolerant.

She's lost it.

Finally, we have something in common.

I slide the drink away and nibble on the bread like a chipmunk. Scanning the room, I observe all the people stuffing themselves. Up at the buffet, people scoop all-they-can-eat onto a plate, determined to get their $6.99 worth. Dad loved the buffet here. Then again, he loved anything on sale.

I soak in my surroundings and listen to the buzz around me. I study each person, noting peculiar things about them most people wouldn't catch. The way they walk. The way they laugh. One lady slips on a smudge, and a man drops food on the floor then pretend he didn't. It's amazing what you see when everyone assumes no one is watching.

At the end of the line, a large man scans the dessert selections and sticks his finger in the pudding to test it. Gross! He spins around and faces my direction. That when I notice him. The redneck from Tommy's store. He lumbers toward me, balancing two overfilled plates. I slouch down in my seat, hoping he doesn't notice me. Luckily, he slides into the booth in front of me. I sigh in relief but continue to spy on his reflection in the window.

He chews his cud and talks at the same time. A drizzle of ketchup cakes both corners of his mouth as he stuffs in a double cheeseburger and a spoon full of mashed potatoes at the same time.

A twiggy dude with a thin mustache, already eating in the booth, leans in and speaks with a lisp. "Think we gonna get close this time?"

The redneck jams a few fries into his pie hole before he's even swallowed the previous bite. He struggles to speak clearly. "Billy, I told yah already. All we gotta do is get us some donuts and corn. Maybe rub some honey on us. They'll come beggin'."

Billy scoffs. "Aw, geez, Al. I just want to catch 'em, not *date* 'em."

Corn? Honey? Either these guys want to hunt bears, or they're trying to be the next big hit on YouTube. Some people do whackadoo stuff just to get a kill. One guy even tried baiting a bear by holding marshmallows in his teeth. That didn't go over so well with the bear or the guy's face. Dad's told me some crazy stories. A few sick ones too.

Al whistles the song I still can't place. He wipes his mouth on his t-shirt. "You ready?"

Billy nods. "*Bear*-ly."

Al cackles. "Ha! Good one." I roll my eyes at how many times I've heard that joke up here.

Billy stuffs some of the free bread and packets of crackers into his pockets. "Let's get goin' then. Catch us some you know what."

Al lowers his voice and smacks Billy upside the head. "Sshhhh."

Both of these guys are a donut short of a dozen. For one, this is not bear season. Two, unnaturally baiting bears in North Carolina is illegal. Any way you look at it, these guys are breaking the law. Big time.

Whether they know it or not is the question.

Al snorts. "No need to waste your last brain cell worryin'. We won't get caught this time."

My ears perk up like a dog tuning into a high pitch. *This time?* I hold my breath for fear I'll miss something important. My hands tremble under the table. There are only two people here who would bust these guys for illegal hunting.

Les.

Or Dad.

Billy whispers with a slight lisp. "You sure?"

Al hisses like a deflating tire. "Positive."

I slink down even further, praying they don't see me as they stand to leave. After the two men pay and walk outside, I peek through the mini-blinds. They walk down Main Street and disappear into the back alley. As soon as they're out of sight, I sprint out of the diner and bolt to the corner. Peering around the side, I watch them climb into a shiny green Dodge Ram with temporary tags.

I hesitate for a second. Should I tell Les, or should I follow them and see where they go first? What if they're totally innocent? That'd be the last thing I need. Carl and Les would never believe me again. On the other hand, if these guys are hunting around up in these mountains, maybe they know something about my dad?

Out in the woods, these are the tiny decisions that contribute to someone losing their way. To act or not to act. To move or not to move. Those basic questions can make a huge difference.

Between life and death. Lost or found.

I bolt toward Luci.

If these idiots know something about Dad, there's only one way to find out.

Survival Skill #11

By moving slowly, you decrease the chance of detection and conserve energy you may need later.

Dark, billowy clouds roll across the sky like tumbleweeds as I snake up the mountain, leaving a safe distance behind the truck. Once the men turn down a dirt lane, I wait a little before inching my bike around the bend. Their truck is parked off to one side, partially concealed by the trees. What Dad called a 4-5-9 or suspicious vehicle.

As Luci rolls closer, the reality of my decision to follow these guys finally clicks. This plan would definitely be a "don't" in the *Dumb Girl's Guide to Wilderness Survival* handbook. However, if I don't chase after these idiots now, they may be gone by the time I get help.

I park Luci behind some bushes and sneak along the tree line. When I peer inside the shiny truck, a new cowboy hat rests on the shiny leather seat. I scan the area and notice a few shoe prints leading away from the truck. Dad called this a confirmed sign or spoor.

After taking pictures, I pause at the mouth of the trail leading into the darkening woods. It's late, and the woods will only allow a couple more hours of light. I hesitate only a fraction of a second before allowing the trees to swallow me whole.

My plan? Sneak in, get coordinates of their camp, and sneak out. Then I'll go get Les or tell Carl so they can haul these guys in and arrest them.

What could go wrong?

I trek along the overgrown green alleyway, weaving in and out of trees while inspecting the path for prints. Shafts of sunlight break through the lush foliage, creating orange stripes along the forest's green floor, reminding me of the setting sun. Oaks, pines, and spruces border the trail. I move noiselessly. As if my feet aren't touching the ground. These guys could be anywhere, so I need to find them way before they notice me.

After barely escaping a fence of poison ivy and almost stepping on a sleeping timber rattlesnake, I stop to regroup. Fear and anxiety is a tracker's Achilles' heel. Dad used to track poachers all the time. So I know I need to pay attention to the whole world around me, not just the trail. Any place where these guys have disturbed the natural grain of the forest. Broken twigs. Crushed weeds. Pebbles pressed into dirt. A good tracker anticipates movement and searches for forced lines that blemish the natural flow of the forest.

Every nerve switches on and tingles, probing to find something out of place. I trek for a couple miles. Suddenly, a soft whistling and the smell of smoke hitch a ride on the wind. Cupping my hand behind my ear, I zero in on their location. With each step, I breathe and release.

Step, roll foot, weight transfer, and breathe.

I inch my way to the border of their campsite and hide. To conceal the whiteness of my eyes and teeth, I squint and close my mouth. It's surprising how those two things can give you away in an all-green environment. Then, like Dad taught me, I poke my head around the side—not over the top—of a fat shrub to get a better view.

Al sits next to a blazing fire, methodically scraping his new collector's knife back and forth along a sharpening stone as he whistles. The campsite seems scant, except for a couple of small iceboxes, a few large duffle bags, and some scattered trash.

Off to one side, Billy stuffs a few things into a large satchel. "Why do we need all this crap anyways? We got guns." His lisp is magnified in the still evening air.

Al stops whistling but keeps a steady rhythm with his knife. "You never know when we might need 'em. Them creatures is unpredictable."

"Yeah, but bear spray? Seems like that's for a buncha sissies."

I roll my eyes. It's hard to take these idiots seriously. Some men drink from the fountain of knowledge.

Obviously, these guys only gargle.

Or maybe they're just plain parched.

Al chuckles. "Got it off one of those bear-huggin' sites. Wanted to be sure we were prepared to dance."

Billy reads the label aloud. "Bear Smart. Repels bears in a non-toxic, non-lethal manner. This pepper spray will not permanently injure the bear or the outdoorsman. Holster is also available."

I smile thinking of how many times people end up hurting themselves by spraying into the wind.

Al opens one side of his hunting vest, revealing a gun. "I got me a holster right here."

I only get a glimpse, but from the shape of the handle and length of the barrel, it appears to be some kind of .44 Magnum. All those hours of watching Dad polish his antique gun collection might finally come in handy.

Billy loads another bag. "Where we huntin' this time? Some place new, I hope."

"Doesn't matter. Everything's under control. We don't need to be afraid of none of those forest cops this time."

Forest cops? Wildlife officers, game wardens, and park rangers are often referred to as forest cops around here. Hard to tell the difference unless you know the uniform or what each person actually does.

My brain shuts down, and my ears buzz as if a swarm of bees is trapped inside my head. Their voices sound all nasally and distorted, like a McDonald's drive-in operator. I jerk out of my daze and quickly note the coordinates on my GPS watch. When I spin around to leave, my head is so jumbled, I forget about staying quiet and step into a pile of dead leaves and twigs. A horde of birds explodes from the bushes around me. I stop and look back to see if the two men heard me.

"What was that?" Billy grabs his rifle. From the size and color, I'd guess it's probably a Winchester or a Colt.

Al glances in my direction and slips a hand into his vest. "I dunno. Let's check it out."

Billy's voice quivers as he stares off into the trees, his gun cocked. "Maybe it's that friggin' bear again. Feels like he's huntin' *us* sometimes."

Al slides out his pistol and storms in my direction. "I got me a weird feeling about this."

Without too quick of a movement, I slowly slink to the ground and press my body against the earth. Keeping my eyes down, I spy on the men, hoping they don't investigate my location too closely. I bury my face in the leaves. As footsteps pound toward me, I suck in my breath and breathe shallow so they can't hear the oxygen filling my lungs. The loud crunching of Al's shoes gets closer and closer. He stops on the other side of the bush and rattles the branches directly above me.

Billy whispers from further away. "See anything?"

Al kicks his foot into the roots, stirring up some dirt and leaves. A gritty cloud of dust particles billows around me. My nose twitches as I fight against the urge to sneeze.

Unfortunately for me, I lose.

Al's voice hisses above me as he leans over the line of bushes. "Well, well, well. What we got here?"

Survival Skill #12

To fend off a predator, always target the most sensitive spot.

𝔔 lift my eyes and stare at the dirty pair of boots in front of me. My eyes trace up two tan pant legs until they settle in on Al's pitted face.

He motions with his gun as if it's a pointer. "Get up."

My mind circles through different reasons on how to explain why I'm lying on the floor several few yards away from their camp. "Sorry, guys. I was just hiking through."

Al must sense I'm lying, because his eyes narrow and a smile slithers across this face. "Funny way of hiking. Sure you weren't spying?"

My head shakes vigorously. "No, no. Not at all. Just didn't want to bother you. I'll just leave you guys alone." I stand up slowly with my arms out, like a tightrope walker.

After I turn and take a step in the opposite direction, Al grabs my ponytail. "Wait a minute, missy. You ain't going nowhere 'til I say so. Move into the light where I can see you. What's your name?"

I stall. "Actually, I'd rather not say. I'm not supposed to talk to strangers."

Al frowns. "Smartass."

"Actually, it's standard danger stranger stuff."

He pushes me towards his camp. "Shut up and walk."

I stumble forward, planning what to do next. Should I play it cool until I can bolt out of here or run for it, hoping they don't shoot? Self Defense 101 says, *Never let an attacker take you to another location.*

I lift my foot to take a step forward but instead kick my heel back into Al's shin. He collapses onto his knees, and the gun pops out of his hand. My legs start moving before my brain signals to them. Unfortunately, the thick trees slow me down, and I only make it a few yards when a shotgun clicks behind me.

I stop in mid-stride.

Billy sings out. "Leaving so soon? But you just got here."

I turn to face him with both my hands in the air. "Okay. Okay. Seriously guys, take it easy."

Al limps toward me and clutches onto my bicep, squeezing tight. He jerks me beside him. "Not very polite for a guest, are you? This time, I'm not going to be so hospitable." He half-drags me to their campsite, and Billy flanks me, jamming the gun into my spine.

Once we reach the fire, Al hammers down on my shoulders with both hands, forcing me to sit on a log. "Take a load off." He grabs a cola from an ice cooler and holds it out to me. "Soda?"

I keep my eyes down. "No, thanks. I'm trying to quit."

Squinting, he pops open the can and chugs down the liquid.

Billy pipes up. "Well? What are we gonna do with her?"

Al rubs his temples. "Shut up for a second."

"We can't keep her here."

Al growls. "I said, shut up!" He wings the empty can at Billy's head, clipping him in the forehead.

Billy whines and rubs his head. "Man! What'd you do that for?"

Al glares. "I told ya to be quiet. I'm thinking."

I take a shot at him. "Looks like it hurts."

Al lifts my chin with his hand, forcing my face up, and checks me out. His face is strained. Veins pop out on his forehead as his brain straddles the line between recognition and confusion. "Don't I know you from somewhere?"

My heartbeat thumps like the sound of spinning helicopter propellers. "I doubt it."

Al scratches his head. "Why are you here?"

I do a quick scan of their camp. Beer cans and trash are scattered throughout the site. "Don't you know it's against the law to litter?"

Al laughs but squints at me, obviously agitated. "Billy! We got us a smarty ass."

Billy parrots him, which seems to make his lisp worse. "Yeah, a smarty ass."

I straighten up and pull my shoulders back. Confidence is everything out here. "By the way, you can't hunt here, or I'll have to cite you."

"Cite me?" Al chuckles for a second then acts innocent by placing his hands on his inflated chest.

"Either that or I could make a citizen's arrest for poaching."

"Is that what you think we doin'? Naw, naw, sweetie, we ain't huntin'. We're camping."

Billy echoes him again. "Yeah, we's *camping*."

I roll my eyes. "Yeah, right, and I'm Mother Nature." I immediately wish I hadn't said it. Maybe if I was a little more passive, these guys would back off. In these situations, you never know what is better, to be tough or meek.

Al snatches my bag and rifles through it until he finds my wallet. He stares at my license. A smile starts in one corner and cuts cross his face. He moves around me like a shark circles chum. Then he snaps his fingers. "Heeeyyyyy, wait a minute. I know who you are. You're that chick from the fishing store." Al cackles. "Billy, this is the girl that sold me my new knife. Gave me attitude. Thought I couldn't afford it or something."

Billy and Al break out into laughter.

Al dumps out my stuff out onto the ground and picks up my fishing tin. He opens the case and stops. I hold my breath as his eyes widen. Al holds up the photo of my dad. "Well, well. You know that ranger guy who's been missing?"

How would he know that? These guys don't seem to be the newspaper-reading types.

I study my shoes, admitting nothing. Terror slithers through my body as the severity of my situation becomes clear. What was I thinking? After everything Dad's taught me, I should've known better than to come out here alone. He would be so disappointed.

I soften my voice. "Guys, listen. I'm sorry I stumbled on your site. Seriously, it was an accident. Just let me go, and I'll leave you alone."

Al shakes his head and flicks the photo at me. "We can't let you go now, sweetie."

"Come on. Do you really think I'd be out here alone without telling anyone where I was?"

Billy and Al glance at each other then back at me. Al shrugs. "So what if you did? They ain't here now."

Amazingly, my voice doesn't waver. "Because if I don't show up, they'll come up here looking for me."

Al snorts. "How would they know where to find you?"

My stomach lurches at his words, but I clench my teeth, not giving him the satisfaction of a quiver. Instead, I improvise and hold up my wrist, displaying my GPS watch, praying they haven't a clue how it works. "With this. Gives off my location. So if you do anything then they find me, don't you think I'll tell them about you?"

Al leans in until his face is close to mine. I wince at the smell of stale alcohol on his breath. "Maybe they won't find you *alive*."

At that exact moment, I bolt off into the woods, crashing through the brush. It feels as if my legs are trapped in a vat of goopy molasses. Behind me, footsteps hammer the ground until someone plows into me and slams me on the hard ground. My temple clips a rock, and stars twitter on the edge of my vision.

Before I can get up, Billy pounces on me, twists both arms behind my back, and yanks me to my feet by my wrists. I yelp at the pain and start begging them to let me go. Repeatedly. All my survival training seeps out the window as fear engulfs me.

Billy shoves me against a tree. I scream and kick, desperate to escape, but he's strong and confident especially for a small guy with a speech impediment.

"Remember this?" Al draws the large knife from its sheath and twirls it in the dimming light, his eyes crazy and wild. "Billy, put a sock in it, or she's gonna yap all night."

Billy tugs on a dirty green rag out of his pocket and secures it over my mouth.

I gag on the musty cloth, tasting a mixture of sweat and dirt.

Al sighs dramatically. "Ahhhh. Peace and quiet." I struggle to breathe through the non-permeable material. Tears cling to the corners of my eyelashes. He gets right in my face. "Awww, you gonna cry now?"

Billy mimics a baby by rubbing his eyes with his fists. "Boo hoo."

My eyes dart between the men and the woods, searching for a way out.

Al nods once. Billy clutches my hair and yanks my head back, forcing me to stare up at the stars spying on us from the grayish sky above. I scream, but instead of piercing the eerie silence, my voice tumbles out in a muffled wail.

Al teases my throat with his knife. The razor-sharp blade burns my skin. "Now you'll see what happens when you stick your cute little nose into our business." Licking his lips, he snuggles up close to me. "We gonna have us a par-TAY!"

I take that exact moment to force my knee up and into his groin.

Al hollers and clutches his crotch. He bends over with his mouth hanging open, yet no sound escapes.

Billy retracts his lips, showing his teeth like a rabid dog. "You gonna get it now!"

Before he can make his move, I side-kick him in the chest. Billy stumbles backwards as he gasps for air.

Somehow in those few seconds, Al's recovered and snatches my wrists. My arms pulse in pain, threatening to dislocate. He spins me around to face him and backhands me across the face. My head snaps to one side, my cheek stinging as if a million killer bees have attacked all at once. I stumble to the ground.

As I lie in the dirt below him, Al speaks through grinding teeth. "Bitch, you fight me again, and you'll die ... slowly."

For some strange reason, I suddenly wish I had more friends. At this point, I'm pretty sure there are only a few people who care whether I live or die. And even those aren't a hundred percent guaranteed. My emotions boil over, and I start to cry.

"Not so tough anymore, huh?" Al snickers at my defeat and waves the knife in front my face. He grabs my hair with one hand and chafes the edge of his blade along my mouth, slicing my bottom lip. I scream through the cotton, eyes wide. The muffled sound of my voice only jazzes him up even more. "Billy, I don't think she should see this."

On cue, Billy ties a cloth over my eyes, forcing me into total darkness.

Even though I can't see, I pinch my eyelids together to block out the pending scene, preparing for the worst. My other senses are heightened. I swear, I can hear every little bug skittering through the leaves while Al and Billy whisper behind me.

Then everything goes quiet.

The silence is shattered by shuffling and grunting noises followed by a primal wail.

This time, it's not mine.

Billy's hands slide off my arms as his body crumples at my feet. Someone from behind yanks off the cloth covering my face. The sun blinds me for a second, and I'm afraid to move. Paralyzed by the ribbon of fear weaving through my gut. I'm not sure what happened.

All I know is my days just got renumbered.

Survival Skill #13

Proper preparation means having the right survival items and knowing how to use them.

Something whimpers.

I look down and see Billy writhing at my feet in pain. Blood seeps through a wound in his thigh. An acidic taste sloshes around in my mouth, and my gut performs somersaults. I'm not sure if my stomach's upset because I taste my own blood or because I smell Billy's.

Al stands frozen directly in front of me. With bulging eyes, he fixates on something over my shoulder. His voice cracks. "Take it easy, man. We just foolin' around."

Behind me, someone grapples with the bind on my wrists. As soon as I'm free, I yank the sopping cloth out of my mouth and bend over. Fresh mountain air revives my lungs, and the smell of the sweet woods drowns out the stench of the cloth. As my breath returns, I spin around and spot a familiar face.

The cute guy I saw by the river stands only a few feet away, pointing a gun at my attackers. He does a once-over and frowns. "Bloody hell, are you all right?"

I nod but can't help staring at the gun in his hand.

My rescuer walks over to Billy and yanks a knife out of his leg. Billy screams in pain as the guy wipes both sides of the dirty blade on Billy's pant leg. "Sorry, mate, but I'm going to need this back. You understand, right?" Still holding the gun, he motions to me. "Hold this while I tie them up?"

He sounds amazingly polite and calm considering the situation. My voice quivers. "Me?"

The guy nods. "Unless you see any other damsels in distress around?"

Damsel? I take the gun and hold it in my hand. The barrel is shaking as Al practically kills me with his eyes. The guy ties Al's and Billy's hands together. "There. That should do it long enough for us to get out of here."

Billy whimpers as Al growls. "You know we're gonna get you back, don't yah?"

The guy ignores them and takes back the gun. He picks up my bag and shoves all the contents back in before offering his hand to me. "I believe we've worn out our welcome here."

"Hold on, I lost something!" I drop to my knees and scower the ground, frantically searching for my bracelet. I can't lose the only thing I have left of Dad. Thankfully, I find it tucked under some brambles and slip it on my wrist, sighing a breath of relief.

Cute guy is standing there staring at me. "Any time you're ready?" I move close to him and clutch his hand. He bows toward Al. "Thank you, sir, for a lovely evening." Then he takes off into the trees, towing me close behind.

I stumble every few steps because my legs keeping curling underneath me like limp, wet noodles, but the guy keeps me on my feet. About a mile or so down the trail, a few drops of water sprinkle my face. Within moments, the sky cracks open and dumps a wetload.

The guy races ahead of me, slopping through the soggy underbrush and yells over his shoulder. "Come on. This way!"

I scramble after him, trying to track his fuzzy figure through the downpour. Squinting through wet bangs and waterlogged contacts, I catch sight of him way ahead, slithering along a rock wall. I race after him to try and catch up.

What if Al and Billy get loose? What if they're already following us? What if they were right behind me? By the time I reach the wall, the guy's gone.

Once again, I'm alone.

I scan the ground to find some sign of where he went but the water was coming down so hard and fast, it was hard to see. A few yards away, something crashes through the thick foliage. I frantically hunt for a place to hide. Hysteria gurgles below the surface and my nerves begin to fray. It takes me a second to realize I'm mumbling to myself. "Oh God, please."

Just as I surrender to the sheer panic, someone clamps a hand over my mouth and drags me backwards into a dark cave. A mixture of fear and adrenaline pump through me. Instinctively, I fight back against the hold, determined to get free. Scratching. Punching.

My arms are pinned to my sides, and the cute guy from earlier whispers in my ear. "It's me. Calm down." My body sags into him. He catches me and lowers me to the ground.

I stare blankly and struggle to find words. "I ... I ... I'm sorry. I ... didn't know it was you."

He plucks a string of soggy hair off my cheek. "Don't worry. Those blokes aren't getting out of those binds any time soon. Knot tying is one of my specialties. Trust me, you're safe."

"Says the mysterious stranger who fishes with a gun."

He pats my shoulder. "Sit tight. We'll stay here until the storm passes."

My hero shuffles around the small, dry cave, collecting sticks and clumps of dry moss. In a few seconds, a cozy fire lights up the cramped space. The flames offer warmth, but I continue to shiver from the mixture of cold and fear. Every now and then, droplets of sap pop in the fire, mimicking gunfire, causing me to jerk back with each bang. I hoped the rain would hide the smell of smoke from the fire.

"Cold?" The guy slings his thin jacket over me like a cape. When his hands brush against my neck, I flinch. He gives me some space and speaks in a calm tone as if he's merely ordering food. "Guess I should introduce myself. My name's Mo."

I answer in a hoarse, raspy voice that I don't even recognize as my own. "Grace."

Mo flashes me a look of concern. "You all right?"

"Never better," I mumble, watching the raindrops drip off his dark, wavy hair. His cheeks are flushed from running. I force my mind to focus on something else for fear I'm staring.

He tugs on his longish, unkempt hair. "How'd a pretty girl like you get mixed up with those blokes?"

He called me pretty. I choke on the compliment. "Long story."

Mo gestures outside with his thumb in a hitchhiking motion. Only then do I notice the sheets of rain blanketing the entrance. He smirks. "I think we have some time."

I lie back against the stone wall, my body stiff like a corpse, and fixate on the ashes as they glow a reddish orange. Eventually, I muster up the energy to talk. "I overheard those two guys talking about hunting bears and wanted to check it out."

His eyebrow arches. "Are you a secret agent or something?"

I shake my head. "No. Just curious."

"Right. I seem to remember that about you." His dark eyes swirl in the firelight. "Little Nosey Parker."

I frown. "Excuse me?"

"Sorry, English expression." His face flips serious again. "You almost got in a load of trouble back there."

"Thanks. I think I got that part." I sweep the damp hair away from my eyes and think for a second. "How did you find me, anyway?"

He shrugs and rakes his hands through his black hair. "Lucky, I guess." He smiles, and I can't help but notice how one tooth sits forward a little. I find his slightly misaligned front teeth kind of cute. Matches the gap between mine.

Outside the storm intensifies with loud cracks and booms. I focus away from the explosions. "What's up with the weapons? Are *you* a secret agent?"

"Protection. The Appalachians attract a bunch of nutters. Can't be too careful."

I nod in understanding. Dad always carried a gun, like an executive does a pen. It's the way of the woods. "Fair enough."

Mo eyes my swelling cheek and lightly touches a sore spot on my neck. I jerk away when his flesh skims mine. "What are you doing?"

He holds up his finger, smeared with blood. "You're cut." He pours water out of his canteen and soaks a cloth before holding it a few inches from my face. "May I?" I cover my wound with one hand as he speaks softly, trying to reassure me. "I'm not going to hurt you, Grace."

At first, I stiffen. Wyn said that to me after my dad went missing. For some reason, I couldn't take a chance then, but for some reason this guy relaxes me. My body sags and my hand drops, allowing Mo to dab my neck with the cloth. His face is only a breath away. The whole time he tends to me, I'm pretending to study the stalactites on the ceiling.

When Mo's done, he wraps my hand around the cloth and holds it to my lips. "Keep this here." Little pulses of electricity tickle the place where our skin briefly made contact. I've just been attacked and now lusting after my hero? What's wrong with me?

I clutch the cloth and nurse my wound as Mo lines more sticks across the fire. Flames spark a few times before dancing to life again. The longer I stare, the more the burning embers resemble little red worms wiggling through charred mounds of ashes. The scene with Al and Billy replays in my mind. A chill travels through me, and I hug my knees to my chest, determined not to shed any tears in front of this guy.

"You want to tell me what happened?" He doesn't look at me when he asks, but his voice is low and serious.

Licking the cut on my lip, I force my voice past the huge lump forming in my throat. A quick image of Al flashing his knife in my face. "Not with a stranger."

"Thought I already introduced myself." He raises one eyebrow. "Weren't you paying attention?"

I can't help but smirk a bit. "That doesn't matter. I don't know anything about you."

"Fine. Ask me a question."

Survival Skill #14

During long periods of sheltering, you will need to manage your supplies, including food and water.

I turn to face him. "Will you answer them this time?" Maybe it can't hurt to give this guy a chance. Drilling him is much better than being grilled about my encounter. My body tenses as I wait for him to speak.

He plays with his hair in the back. "Abso-bloody-lutely. What do you want to know?"

Immediately, I fire off questions at rocket speed, probably from the nerves and adrenaline raging inside. "How old are you?"

He licks his dry lips. "Seventeen."

I jerk back, shocked by his answer. "Really? I thought you were like twenty-two or something."

"Should I take that as a compliment?"

I shrug it off. "You just seem older, that's all."

He thinks for a second as a nervous laugh brushes over his lips. "Must be my posh accent."

I smile a little. "Maybe." Before he can say anything else, I jump back into my interrogation. "Where are you from?"

Mo seems mesmerized by the firelight. "England, but lived in Australia and France for a stint. Moved to Tennessee a few years ago." His lips move steadily as he speaks.

I let his sexy voice drown out any recurring visions of Al and Billy threatening to resurface. "How'd you end up here?"

He rests his forearms on his knees and pinches his bottom lip. The t-shirt tightens around his biceps, proving he's in pretty good shape. "Quite a long story. But to keep it short and sweet, I graduated early and just started a semester in the Geology program at Appalachian State University."

"So ... you study rocks?"

He straightens into a defensive posture. "Not just *rocks*. I'm working on a study that examines ultramafic bodies in the Southern Appalachian Mountains. Supposedly, these mountains have gneiss rock exposures that date back 480 million years ago. You probably know all this since you live here."

I almost laugh right in his face. "Me? No way. I can tell you anything you want to know about plants and animals. But I'm not the rocker type."

Mo tugs on the top of his hair again. I wonder if he's nervous or if it's just a habit. "Am I boring you?"

"Not at all." Nevertheless, I'm exhausted and fight hard to suppress a yawn so I don't appear bored. The day's events are taking their toll on me as the adrenaline drains from my blood. "So you live out here? In the woods? All the time?"

He nods. "I fancy the outdoors."

I think about my dad who would rather sleep on a bed of leaves than a mattress. "I get that." And I do. Nothing is better than being surrounded by nature. I can definitely relate to this guy. But now, as I settle into the warmth, I'm all out of questions.

Mo pulls a brown paper bag out of his rucksack. "Biscuit?"

"Sure." Careful not to touch his hand, I take one and inspect the treat.

I must look confused, because he explains, "It's a cookie."

"Yeah, I guessed that." When he tends to the fire, I check him out again.

At first glance, his deep-set eyes appear jet black. But if I zoom in, the dark color resembles Dad's famous chocolate mousse with little swirls of caramel inside.

Pulling myself back, I take a bite of the cookie and cover my mouth with my hand, praying no loose crumbs spray his way. Not attractive.

Mo rests his chin on his fist and looks at me sideways. "Well? What about you?"

"What about me?"

"What's your story?"

Shifting in my seat, I shrug and nibble at the snack. "I don't really have one. Not a page-turner anyway." He laughs but doesn't press me. For the next few hours, we trade small talk. I don't reveal anything too personal, and he doesn't say much more.

Eventually, Mo peeks out the cave entrance. "The rain's let up. You ready to go?" He holds out his hand to me.

"Sure." I ignore any trepidation and use him to pull up.

He places his hand on my lower back and returns me to the gray world. "Ladies first. But stay close to me."

I thought you'd never ask.

Mo remains on high alert as we slosh through the wet leaves. Drops of water jump from the trees and splat on the ground. Each ping sends tremors through my body. Now that I'm out in the open again, Al's face hovers in my mind. My eyes dart around, searching for any sign the guy might be watching.

Mo must sense my tension, because he leans over and whispers, "It's safe, Grace. I promise."

It's impossible to relax because all my senses seem heightened. Every strand of hair tickles my face. The smell of wet leaves fills my nose, and I can hear bickering squirrels as they reemerge from their dry hideouts. All the fear from earlier pumps through my veins at a quickened pace.

Mo brushes up against my arm. When he touches me, I can almost hear the sizzle between us. A look of concern skims across his face. "You sure you're all right?"

I roll my shoulder. "I'm fine, really."

Mo drops his hand, taking my hint. "Don't worry, I'll stay with you. Where do you need to go?"

I check my watch for a location and point north. "My bike's only about a mile away."

We hike all the way back to Luci in total silence, pointing and signaling. Every now and then, we signal which way to go with our hands. As if we both know it's not the best time to talk. Or maybe because there's a certain comfort level between us. Who knows.

As soon as I spot my bike, I signal to him while keeping silent. He scans the dirt road to be sure we're alone.

Al's truck is still there.

Mo steps out of the trees and stands in the open. "Told you they wouldn't get out of those ropes."

"You sure they aren't just hiding and waiting for us?"

"Positive." He grabs my hand and leads me to Luci. His skin feels rough yet his grasp is soft. I follow him, relishing in the heat of his grasp until he stops in front of my bike and faces me. "Do you plan on telling anyone what happened?"

When I shake my head, my thoughts clink around like ice cubes in a glass. "I don't know, why?"

Mo shoves his hands into his pockets as if searching for money and studies his boots. "Well, if you don't mind, I'd like to be left out of it. I knifed that bloke back there and don't want any trouble."

I ponder his request. "Sure. No problem."

"I appreciate it." Mo flashes his crooked smile. I watch his irises pulse in the changing light. He steps to the side, allowing me to pass. "Do you need any help?"

"Thanks, but I got it." I swing my leg over Luci's seat. Risking total humiliation, I wrestle with asking him one last question. "I'll probably go fishing tomorrow if you wanna join me. To thank you and all. I mean, you don't have to if you're busy. But you're welcome to … if you want to. But you don't have to." My words trail off when I realize I'm rambling.

Mo's reaction isn't what I expect. He wrinkles his face. "Fishing? Bit daft, considering what you just went through. Maybe you should stay clear of this place for a while."

My body stiffens at the thought of seeing Al again in the woods. But I won't let Mo know I'm afraid. "I can't hide out in my house just because of a couple of jerks. Besides, Bear Creek is miles from here."

He gawks at me for a second before looking away and off into the woods. "Well, suit yourself. Thanks for the invite, but I'm not sure it's a good idea."

"Okay. Whatever. I understand. No big deal really. I was just asking. Trying to be polite and all…" I lock my jaws to stop from droning on any longer and making a fool of myself. Hoping to conceal any changing colors revealing my total embarrassment, I slip on my helmet and attempt to start Luci.

No such luck.

This guy must think I'm a total loser.

He points to the bike. "You sure this is yours?"

My cheeks heat up. "Positive. She's just stubborn."

"I know how she feels." He winks.

"Very funny." On the fourth try, Luci growls to life. I mumble through the thick, plastic shield, wanting a quick exit from my visit to Awkwardville. "I better go. Thanks for everything. You saved my life back there."

Mo pauses for a moment as if he's going to say something spectacular. "No worries. Stay safe, Grace."

&

All the way home, I can't shake the feeling I'm being followed and constantly glance over my shoulder to be sure. Luckily, when I pull into the driveway, Mom's still not home. Good, I can only imagine how I look.

After locking myself in the house, I get ready for bed, wishing I wasn't alone but there's no one to call. Looking in the mirror, I study the cut on my neck and poke the bruise on my cheek.

Man, I'm lucky Mo showed up when he did. Can't believe how close I was to something awful. I guess I never expected them to turn on me like that.

What caused such a viseral reaction? Was it me, or was he just nuts?

Then I remember what happened right before he went all Christian Bale on me.

Al found my fishing tin and recognized my dad's picture.

That means he's seen Dad somewhere before.

Survival Skill #15

If alone, stay aware of your surroundings,
even if they appear to be safe.

$\mathcal{T}$he next day, I head into town for work. After parking Luci in the back alley, I slink down the alleyway to the store's rear entrance, just in case Al and Billy are hanging around again. I hurry inside, letting the door slam shut behind me.

Tommy snaps his head up, and his fishing hat falls off on the floor. "Good heavens, you scared me, Elu."

"Sorry. I didn't know you'd be back here."

He picks up his cap and puts it back on his head. "Hey, what happened to you yesterday? In case you're confused, your break is only thirty *minutes*, not twenty-four *hours*."

I slump against the wall for fear my legs will buckle underneath me. "Sorry, Chief."

He leans back in his desk chair and crosses his arms. "Sorry? You left me high and dry without any notice. I don't appreciate it, Elu. Not one bit."

Dr. Head always says that you can tell a lot by someone's body language. According to his rules, Tommy is shutting himself off to me. I drop my eyes to avoid his disappointing gaze. "Something came up. I promise it won't happen again."

Tommy glances at the clock and frowns. "Wait a minute. Why are you on time, and why are you sneaking in the back door?"

Wringing my hands together, I shuffle over to him. "I'm not *always* late. Besides, I come in the back sometimes."

His scowl intensifies. "Since when? What's going on with you?" He approaches me and holds my chin, looking at my face into the light. "What the hell happened to your cheek?"

I step to the side and push a stack of unmarked shirts off the tweed chair before plopping down. "Okay, listen, I need to tell you something, but you have to promise to keep it a secret."

Deep-set wrinkles burrow into his tan forehead. "You've got one red cheek, a gash on the other, and a cut on your lip. This can't be good." I stare at him until he unfolds his arms. "Fine. Who am I to say anything anyway? It's none of my business."

That's good enough for me, so I explain everything. Well, *almost* everything. About overhearing the two men at the diner, following them to the campsite, and getting busted. I skim over the really, really bad parts, like being tied up, threatened, and almost sliced to death by a limited edition knife I sold him. No use worrying Tommy any more than I have to. When it comes time to explain Mo's part in the situation, I skip it all together. One of the few promises I've kept lately.

Tommy rubs his face. "What were you thinking?"

I massage my head. "I know, it was stupid, but they were talking about bear hunting. And I think they know something about my dad. When Al found his picture in my stuff, he went ballistic."

Tommy widens his eyes. "And they let you leave? Just like that?"

I shrug and avoid his dissecting gaze. "Yup. That was it."

Tommy rubs his hands together, as if he's washing them. "Jesus, Elu. You need to talk to Captain."

"What? No way! He'll kill me for following them."

"Maybe he should." Tommy stands and paces around the room with his hand cupped behind his neck. "I know you're going through a lot, but this is getting out of control."

"You said you wouldn't get mad."

"I'm not *mad*, I'm worried. These guys sound dangerous. We can't keep this to ourselves."

"You promised you wouldn't tell anyone."

He balls up his hands on his hips. "I won't *if* you promise me you will."

I surrender. "Okay, fine, but I can't talk to Carl. He'll totally freak. He's already warned me."

Tommy stops and raises his eyebrows. "How about Les? If you tell him what these guys might be doing on his turf, as a park ranger, he has to do something. Right?"

I get what Tommy's suggesting. "If Les can find them, he'll at least bring them in. Then Carl will have to question them about Dad."

The wrinkles on Tommy's forehead fade in relief. "When does Les get back from his ranger meeting in Colorado?"

My knees bounce up and down. "Today or tomorrow, I think."

He nods emphatically. "Great, then it's settled. You'll talk to Les?"

My body slumps further down into the chair. "Yes. But I can handle this on my own. Trust me."

Tommy straddles a chair in front of me and cups my pale hands with his tan ones. His voice softens. "You don't have to sacrifice yourself like this."

My chin quivers, but I bite my lip. "I'm not trying to. Why do you say that?"

"Because you can't help your dad if you get hurt. And you don't have to get hurt in order to help him." Tommy grabs a picture frame off his desk and hands it to me. "Look at this."

Gripping the picture, I rub my thumbs across the dusty glass and study the man's strong face. I can tell just by looking he's someone important because he's got that air about him. "Who is this?"

"My great-great grandfather, Tsali. He was a simple farmer. Until the Trail of Tears."

It's easy to tell the man in the photo is related to Tommy. They have the same eyes, the same wise look. As if they've both witnessed a lot in their lives, more than most. "Why, what happened?"

Tommy sucks in air before jumping into his story, telling me it is probably a long one. "During that time, Tsali and his family were taken from their home. When Tsali's wife stumbled along a mountain trail, probably out of sheer exhaustion, one of the guards prodded her with a bayonet. Tsali got so angry that he and some others made a plan to overtake the soldiers. During the attack, they accidentally killed a guard. Tsali and his family fled here to the Smoky Mountains."

I stare at the man's eyes in the photo and can almost sense his zest for life. "What happened to him?"

Tommy walks around the room, motioning with his hands as he talks. "Since a soldier was killed during the escape, Tsali became a hunted man."

I lean forward on the edge of my seat. "Did they ever find him?"

His eyes take on a distant look. Then he shakes his head. "Not at first. They searched these mountains and killed many Cherokees looking for him. Eventually, General Scott in the U.S. Army offered the Cherokee Indians a deal. If Tsali turned himself in, Scott would give the Cherokee people some mountain land to rebuild their lives."

"Did Tsali go in?"

Tommy pauses before answering. I watch his Adam's apple bob, as he swallows his emotion. But I can't tell what he's feeling. Or hiding. "He turned himself in and was sentenced to death. Only as a last wish, Tsali requested to be shot by his own people."

I cover my mouth. "Surely, they said no. I mean, how could they kill him after everything he'd done for them?"

"Because he wanted to die for them. To help them live on in peace. A hero dies for something, a fool dies for nothing."

I twirl the end of my ponytail. "Did the general give them the land he promised?"

He leans forward, and his voice drops lower. "Yes. The remaining Cherokees, the Eastern Band, still live in these mountains."

I recall my history class lesson on the region. "I remember, the Qualla Boundary."

Tommy nods. "That's right."

"So what happened to Tsali?"

"Legend has it that Tsali was buried under the blue waters of Fontana Lake." A sad look scrolls across Tommy's weathered face as he sits in silence.

I study the photo, curious to know more about the man behind the soft eyes. What does a Cherokee hero have to do with a small-town nobody like me? "Why are you telling me all this?"

Tommy takes the photo back and props it on his desk. "Elu, Tsali meant to help his wife that day. He didn't *mean* to kill a soldier. He didn't mean for any of it to happen. But sometimes innocent mistakes kick off a chain of serious events with dangerous consequences that you can't know until it's too late. I want you to remember that." He squats down and cups my chin. "What I'm saying is this. Decide the best way to *help* your dad. Don't be careless and let mistakes force you down a different path. A path that might take you farther away from him. A path you might regret."

I hug him. "Thank you."

He pats me on the back. "I didn't do anything. Now go home and rest. I'll take care of the store and keep an eye out for those guys."

As I sit outside on my bike, I mull over what Tommy said and realize he's right. I'm being careless. Taking too many chances. Maybe I need to chill out and not let all of this consume me so much. Maybe I can give myself a break and just enjoy a moment now and then. Try and relax, so I don't make another mistake that could hurt someone I love or ruin my chances of finding Dad.

My phone sings in my pocket. My heart skips. It's been a long time since I heard Wyn's ringtone. Thought I'd deleted it. I almost answer but press DECLINE instead. My phone might as well have said REJECT. I feel awful but don't want to lie and hide anything from him. He'll know.

I jump on my bike and take off. As my bike snakes along the narrow road through mountainous terrain, I revel in my surroundings. I pass split-rail fences and old farmsteads, enjoying the wind rushing through my hair. The hot air burns my cheeks as I take in the spectacular views of the distant mountains and neighboring valleys.

Other than Luci, the river is the only place in the world where I feel a kind of lightness. As soon as I think about fishing, I recall Mo's rejection. His response was so direct, I feel stupid for even saying anything. It's obvious he's about as interested in me as a dog is to fruit.

I shake it off. Doesn't matter. Mo's a complication. A distraction. The last thing I need right now.

Then again, maybe he's just what I need to live a little.

I'm so busy daydreaming about Mo, it takes a minute for my brain to register the grumbling noise growing louder behind me.

I glance in my rear view mirror but the sun is so bright, it takes me a second to make out the outline of a truck tailing me way too close for comfort.

My heart drums against my breastbone.

Al's back.

Survival Skill #16

When facing a desperate situation, don't panic. Stay calm to avoid fatal mistakes.

$\mathcal{I}$ punch down on the pedal with the toe of my shoe and lurch forward.

The truck speeds up and inches closer, like a wild dog nipping at my heels. I climb to a hundred miles per hour, knowing this speed is dangerous but hoping my knowledge of these winding roads will help me lose the truck. Squinting in the bright sun, I glance back again. The vehicle is so close I can practically count the bugs splattered on the grill.

The vehicle swerves into the opposite lane and moves next to me. A semi whizzes around the mountain bend and forces the truck back in line behind me. I focus on the swervy road and accelerate, adding more distance between us.

My hands tremble, making it hard to keep the handlebars steady. The dry air blows through my mouth and nose. One move can send me to my death. Cars whiz toward me, forcing the truck to stay in our lane. The engine seems to growl and nip at my bike's heels. One time, I react quickly and jerk the handlebars too hard. Luci panics and fishtails, but I manage to steady her without crashing.

As soon as the opposite lane clears, the pick-up truck changes lanes, almost clipping my back tire, and speeds up next to me.

My breath rushes out in rapid, shallow bursts. My knuckles are white from grasping the handlebars so hard. I can't tell which is worse, crashing at this speed or seeing Al's face again.

The rumbling beast hovers only a few inches away. So close, I can hear the music's bass pounding from inside the cab.

For fear of losing control, I avoid looking and zero in on the pavement rolling under me.

Then the horn blares and someone yells out the window. "Hey, Graceless. Get that piece of shit off the road!" A thunder of laughter follows. As the truck speeds by me, a zit-faced kid from my class shoots me the bird.

I scream from underneath the helmet, "Asshole!" As tears fill my eyes, I slam on the brakes. Luci fishtails again and skids along the shoulder of the road.

Once we stop, I clamber off my bike and bend over the guardrail. My stomach burns, and my muscles clench. A burp sends a swirl of acid up my throat. I take deep breaths, willing my gut to relax. Even though I know I'm safe, my body still reacts as if I'm not. Clenching and shaking.

When I'm finally stable enough to drive, I mount Luci and sit for a second. Glancing down, I spot the faded picture of Dad and me duct-taped to Luci's black and red gas tank. I exhale slowly, wishing more than anything he was here right now to hold me. Tell me everything's going to be okay. Eventually, I roll out onto the highway and putter home going twenty-five an hour, my slowest speed in history.

As soon as Luci rolls to a stop in my driveway, I race up the porch steps and bolt inside, locking the doors behind me. I flip off all the lights and draw the curtains before crawling to the top of the stairs.

There, I sit. In the dark. Alone.

My body quivers like one of my grandma's little chihuahuas. I pull out my ponytail elastic and rake my fingers through my hair before twisting it up into a tight bun. My fear shifts into anger. Stupid boys. Maybe I'll get Wyn to kick that kid's skinny ass for me. Serves him right for almost mowing me down.

Then again, maybe I'll just do it myself.

Thank God it wasn't Al. His sneering face flashes across my mind, causing me to rub my neck. Can't help but still feel that knife pressing against my throat, a centimeter from slicing my jugular. The blade burning my skin. Most of all, I can't stop thinking about how his eyes bore into mine. How cold they were. How empty. I bury my head in my knees, trying to block out his face. Tommy's right, I need serious help.

After what seem to be hours, I force myself off the stairs and into my room so I can change into PJs. Lying on my bed, I watch the ceiling fan spin above me. Now I know how the fan feels, spinning in circles, going nowhere. Eventually, I get dizzy and shut my eyes. But just as I'm about to fall asleep, a clattering noise barrels up the driveway. I jolt upright as if my heart's been electrocuted back to life. I roll off the bed and crawl on all fours to the window. It takes me a second to muster up enough courage to peek over the windowsill, half expecting to see Al's truck.

Instead, Les's heap rolls down the driveway.

Relieved, I pull on my favorite bear slippers and race downstairs, skipping every other step. Just as I step onto the porch, Les climbs out of the cab and ambles toward me dressed in a green park ranger uniform. His belly slumps over a tight belt working to contain a suffocating waist. Les is bald except for a thin ring of coarse red hair that stubbornly clings to his freckled head. He sports a red and grey speckled goatee and constantly chews tobacco, reminding me of the poor fat goats stuck in petting zoos. He never looked like a real ranger to me. But according to Dad, Les knows this national park better than anyone.

"Mornin', Grace," Les grunts as he trudges up the porch stairs in his familiar cruddy boots, the same nasty ones he's been wearing since I was about four. Les calls them his lucky boots; I designate them as a health hazard. There's no telling what's on or in those smelly things.

As Les teeters up the steps, each wooden plank screeches, threatening to cave beneath his weight. Panting, he throws out his chubby hand. "How yah doing?"

"Hey, Les." I stare at his pudgy hand. Shaking it totally grosses me out. His palms are always clammy, and his grip never quite firm enough, like clutching onto a limp fish. I give his hand a speedy shake and discretely wipe my palm on my PJs. "What're you doing here?"

He gurgles out some slobbery words. "Your mama said you had a broken door."

Since Dad went missing, Les has made an effort to come by the house and help Mom with her "honey-do" list. As he breathes, a whiff of tobacco punishes my nostrils. I press one finger under my nose and nod to the screen door lying on the porch. "Over there."

Les waddles over and inspects the rusted hardware. "This'll be no problem." He drags the frame across the porch. "Wanna help?"

I scrunch up my nose and motion to my pajamas decorated with little bears and trees. "Thanks, but I'm not really dressed for hard labor."

"Suit yourself." He jiggles the door hinges. One falls off and clangs against the wooden floor. He huffs, "Dang thing is completely stripped." He reaches over and grabs a screwdriver, offering me another sneak peak at his smiling buttocks.

I avert my eyes. "Les? Can I ask you something?"

He keeps his eyes on the project at hand and spits over the side of the porch before answering. "Sure thing."

I try to sound casual. "Have you seen anything unusual on patrol lately?"

Les stops and squints at me. "Can't say I have. Why?"

I shrug and try to appear all relaxed, even though every muscle in my body is stiffening. "I ran into a couple guys in the woods and they sort of ... threatened me."

Les dribbles black goo into a white Styrofoam cup. "What do you mean, sort of?" I recap the event, using the Cliffs Notes version, but leave out all the gory details to avoid getting into trouble. Les is like Carl. He doesn't favor people snooping around his domain.

When I finish, Les whistles. "You're lucky. Never know what hunters can do. Bad thing about them is that you can guarantee they will always be armed with something. Where are they now, do you know?"

I shift in my bear slippers and think about what to say before answering. "No, but I know the coordinates of their campsite and a license number."

He takes out a tiny notepad from his back pocket. "Well, good for you. What'd those fools look like?"

My body relaxes as I let the large burden roll off my shoulders. "One was big, the other skinny."

He writes as he nods. "You get their names?"

I swallow and force out the words. "Al and Billy."

He chuckles as he jots more notes down in his little book. "You're a regular Nancy Drews."

I sigh at the incorrect reference. "It's Nancy *Drew*. Anyway, they were sitting behind me at the diner, and I overheard them talking about bears. I followed them so I could tell you about it."

Les chuckles. "Well, good fer you. You shore got some balls, Grace. Just like your daddy."

The comment totally grosses me out, and I'm not sure how to respond. "Uh, thanks? I think."

"You tell Captain?"

I pick at the loose button on my jammie shirt. "Not yet. I knew you'd want to handle it and check them out first. I mean, since it's your territory and all."

Les sniffs and straightens up. "Yeah. You're right about that."

"There's more. I think these guys knew my dad. Recognized a photo." I look down at the floor, afraid to see his reaction. "Maybe they had something to do with him going missing."

Les leans over and snatches a nail between his fat fingers, getting back to work. "Hm. I must say this is all mighty ... interestin'. Can definitely bring them in for questioning. If I can find them. Usually these kind of guys run off once they're seen."

Part of me wonders if he is saying that to get me off his back. Like Carl does. Then again, Dad trusted Les, so I know I can too. "Will you ask them about Dad?"

"Of course, I will." He trudges back toward the truck and calls out over his shoulder. "Don't you go out in them woods 'til I call you. Those guys sound like they could be trouble."

I nod. That's an understatement.

Cℨ

Early the next morning, I stand at the window, waiting for Les's call. The distant sky seems darker than usual. Clouds shaped like massive clumps of cauliflower hang on the horizon. I press my face against the cold window, letting my breath create patches of fog so I can draw little hearts. Through the glass, I squint at the dense woods enveloping my house. What once was my best friend, my retreat, seems to be turning on me a little. But I can't let those guys scare me away from everything I know. Or I'll lose everything that's keeping me safe.

Chewing my fingernails, I pace in a square along the room like a caged lion. No matter how much I want to head out, I promised Les I'd wait.

An hour later, Les still hasn't called. Forget this. I'm going fishing whether those guys are busted or not. No way I'm holing up in this place any longer. Probably not something my dad would approve of.

Then again, he's not here.

I check my backpack for all my supplies and jump on my bike. The whole ride, I feel fine. Until I start walking deeper into the woods. Every rustle and every creek rattles my nerves. My body stiffens and tension balloons in my chest, crowding my lungs. I force the fear aside, telling my nerves there's nothing to worry about; Al and Billy are probably miles from here. It's just for a couple hours of fishing then back home. I need this.

Most people don't get why I love flyfishing so much. They seem to think the sport is about having the perfect looped cast like in *A River Runs Through It*. Or about snagging the largest fish. To those of us who spend hours and days on the river, it's about so much more.

Thoreau's quote trails through my mind. *Many men go fishing all of their lives without ever knowing that it is not fish they are really after.* So true. After suiting up, I wade into Bear Creek's quickening tide. As I strain to find a rhythm, the angry water slams against my ankles, pushing me off the slimy rocks. It takes me a few tries, but I finally manage to dig my heels into the silt and cast smoothly. However, instead of finding peace, my brain jumps around from Dad to Al to the case and back again. There's got to be a missing piece to this whole puzzle, one I can't wrap my brain around.

Seconds later, something snags my line. I rejoin reality, only to find my tippet trapped in a low-hanging tree. Great. I wrestle with the line, hoping the branch will release my fly. No such luck. Instead, the line snaps in two and coils around me. Resting on a boulder, I pick at the jumbled knot, reminding me of when Mom used to untangle my hair, a tiny clump at a time. Somehow, this mangled mess becomes a metaphor for my life.

No matter how much I try to straighten everything out, it remains muddled.

Eventually, I tuck the twisted mess into my pocket and tie on a new leader and fly. Just a few more minutes of fishing before I hunt for more clues. Scanning the river's brown canvas, I spot a few fish splashing downstream and stalk my quarry, teasing the surface with my line. One of Dad's fishing tips scrolls across my brain.

Take it easy, Gracie. You're better off letting it happen than making it happen.

Instead of recasting, I let the line float along the glassy surface. Just as I'm about to give up, something nibbles my fly. Breathing evenly, I do a quick jerk before reeling in the line. Seconds later, a shiny fish flaps along the surface, trying to escape. I counter his reaction by anticipating his next move. My body tingles with excitement. I feel more alive than I have in a long time.

For one brief moment, I forget all my problems.

I grab my net and scoop up my catch before he flops on the sand. The fish's brown-spotted body gleams with water and a reddish-pink band decorates his side. A rainbow trout. I hold him up to my face and stare into his big, bulging eyes. The fish opens and closes his mouth, as if telling me his life story.

The current tugs at my ankles, begging me to release him back to nature. I ease up on shore and carefully remove the hook from his mouth. It's important to respect every catch or it isn't flyfishing. Since I'm not going to eat him, I need to let him go. Nature shouldn't be wasted.

I whisper, "Thank you," just like Dad always did and open my hand. The slimy fish slides down my fingers and plops into the gurgling water. As he squirms away to freedom, I envy him. Wishing it was that easy for me to swim downstream and start over as if nothing bad had happened.

As I take off the waders and gather everything, my sixth sense kicks into overdrive. The hair on my neck rises.

I'm not alone.

I freeze and tune into every noise around me, waiting for the one that's out of place. A cricket. A bird. A fish jumping. Then I hear it.

Two pebbles clap together.

Then another crunch. This time, much closer.

I wait and let my intruder approach, knowing I'm not prepared to face Al alone.

Survival Skill #17

Nature can be unforgiving; therefore, you must be prepared to defend yourself in a variety of situations to survive.

As soon as my ear detects a sound behind me, I pivot, sweeping my leg along the ground. My foot clips two black boots, catching my attacker off guard. He trips and as soon as he falls, I pounce on top and jab my knee into his chest, pinning him to the ground.

I do all this in a flash, without thinking or even realizing who it is.

Mo stares up at me with wide eyes. "Bloody hell!"

It takes a second to register his face. "Jesus. Don't you know it's rude to sneak up on someone?" I roll off him and jump to my feet, still tense and on guard. Darting my eyes, I search the woods to be sure someone else isn't with him.

Mo lies on his back with his mouth hanging open. "I wasn't sneaking. I was *walking.*" He sits up and smacks dirt off his pants. "Anyway, I believe it's much ruder to *attack* someone who's only armed with a fishing pole and a smile."

I take my hand off the handle of my knife before he notices I almost drew a weapon on him. "Well, if we're getting literal, I wasn't *attacking.* I was defending."

He holds up two hands. "Is it safe for me to get up?"

I shrug and hide a smirk. "If you can."

Mo stands and massages the back of his neck. "Crumbs, I can't figure you out, Grace."

My tummy flip-flops when he says my name. "Are you trying to?"

He teases me with his eyes. "Maybe."

I recoil, surprised at his bluntness. "So then, what's the big mystery?" After all, Dad says I wear my emotions on my sleeve so I can't be that difficult to read.

He picks his bag up off the ground. "Do you always react like this?"

"Do you always *stalk* girls? In the woods? When they're alone? Anyway, after the other day, do you really blame me?"

Mo frowns and shakes his head. "No, I guess I don't. You're right. It was daft of me not to say anything. I apologize. Then again, I told you not to come out here alone. So in a way, maybe it was a lesson."

"Only it looks like *you're* the one who learned something."

Mo grins and bows. "Touché." He studies me and moves his lips to one side, chewing on the bottom one. "Well, not many people can throw me off guard. I believe you're one of the first."

I wish, I think. Instead, I say, "Guess there's a first time for everything. Don't worry, I won't tell anyone. Might ruin your reputation."

He purses his lips before smiling. "It's all right. Those are overrated anyway. Where'd you learn to move like that?"

I tuck my hands into my pockets so he can't see the lingering tremors from an overflow of adrenaline. "My dad taught me self defense. He was a black belt."

"Hmmm. Smart man."

"Yes, he wa ... I mean ... is." The pit of my stomach boils when I realize I almost used the past tense. My heart sinks, wondering if deep down, I'm secretly giving up. Letting go. I shake off the feeling. No, I will not let that happen. Ever.

Mo eyes my rod. "So let me get this straight. You're a flyfisher, a tracker, and a black belt's protégé?" He flips into a bad American accent. "Grace, you are one whacky chick."

I return to the moment and crack a grin. "Ha ha. What are you doing here anyway? If I was paranoid, I'd think you were following me."

He pushes his longish bangs to the side, out of his inviting eyes. "I was out collecting samples and wondered if you'd be here."

"Thought this wasn't a 'good idea.'"

He laughs aloud. A deep throaty laugh that divides the tension between us in half. "And telling by your reaction, I was right. You out here fishing alone sure isn't the best idea."

"So then why'd you come?"

He claps the dirt off his hands and smears the rest on his pants. "I wanted to be sure you were safe."

I grin and wrinkle my nose. "Only it was *you* who needed protection."

"Who knew?" Mo moves next to me and stares out at the river. His elbow jabs me lightly between the ribs. "Oi. Fancy showing me some of your fishing moves?"

I inch to the right. "I changed my mind. I don't fish with strangers."

He throws his head back and laughs. "Oh! Pardon me, but if I recall, this bloody *stranger* saved your life. That should count for something."

I tap my finger to my lips and contemplate. "Why? You could be a mass murderer, casing riverbanks for your next victim."

Mo shakes his head in disagreement. "That's poppycock. If I were a mass murderer, I'd pick a more populated spot. Nothing 'mass' about it if it's just one poor ole' sod. Anyway, I don't think a killer would take time out to fish. Do you?"

"Maybe it's your cover." I shrug. "Never know these days. The world's a dangerous place."

He smacks his forehead dramatically. "You're not going to make this easy, are you?"

"Did you think I would?"

"I guess not. Oh well, if you're not going to fish with me," Mo tosses his bag over one shoulder and shifts into an odd drawl, "then I'll just *mosey along.*" He begins slowly walking away, every few feet looking back over his shoulder with a sad puppy face.

I giggle at his horrific attempt at a Southern accent and pitiful expression. Almost as bad as my English one, though my puppy eyes could take on his any day. "To where?"

"My *secret* fishing spot."

My smile drops, and I call out to him as he leaves, hopping from rock to rock. "That's ridiculous! I've lived here all my life and know every spot here."

He shakes his head without looking back. "Not this one."

I grow slightly irritated, shifting from foot to foot in a swaying motion. "Impossible. I've hiked out here almost every day since I was three."

"Then you have nothing to fear, my dear. Fancy coming along? Or are you scared you might actually enjoy hanging out with a foreign stranger."

"Hardly." I pause for a few seconds. Part of me needs to stay. Yet a larger piece of me wants to go check this guy out. If he knows of a place I don't, then maybe it's a new place to search. Or maybe I should just go along because I deserve a break. "Fine, I'll bite. What's the catch? No pun intended."

He grins mischievously. "If I show you a spot you've never seen, you have to teach me how to fish."

"Thought you knew how to fish."

He scoops up some water and runs his wet hands through his hair. Little drops land on his lips. "Bloody hell, woman, you know what I mean. Flyfish."

My stomach flip-flops at the thought of spending more time with him. "What if I've been there before? What are *you* going to do for *me*?"

He scratches his scruffy cheeks for a few seconds until his face lights up. "I'll cook you a fabulous dinner."

"Can you cook?"

"Abso-bloody-lutely." I pretend to think for a moment, letting the suspense accumulate. Mo urges me on. "Come off it. What are you afraid of?"

Everything, I think. "Nothing," I say.

"So, you in?"

C３

Yellow star grass borders the overgrown trail. Beams of sun pour through the scattered canopy. Mo walks a few yards ahead of me. I'm preoccupied by his gait as he saunters along the path. He moves with a slight rhythm and confidence.

He sneaks a peek over his shoulder to check on me. I pretend to be studying my footsteps so he doesn't catch me gawking. We traipse along the wooded track in silence, an unspoken agreement not to ruin the peace with mindless chatter.

After tracking our coordinates, I've come to the dreaded conclusion that I probably haven't seen Mo's secret hideaway. I scrunch my face. Crap. I know these woods are vast, but how can some dude all the way from England find a place I don't know about when I've lived here my whole life?

"We there yet?" As soon as I say it, Dad's silly response plays in my head. *What do you mean by 'there'? Because wherever you go, there you are.* I smile to myself thinking about how he never answers a question directly.

Mo obviously doesn't get the joke, because he responds, "Nearly. Does anything look familiar?"

"Keep walking, English boy." I'm not about to admit anything yet. Might as well stretch out my inevitable defeat. I'm not looking forward to confessing the truth.

That I'm wrong. Something I hate almost as much as losing.

After winding around a few more bends, Mo stops in front of a huge rotted tree trunk that stretches across a wide creek. The wood appears to be scarred, battered by Mother Nature. We inch across the log to the other side. He jumps down and holds out his hand to help me.

"I got it." I leap over the gap on my own. Why do guys always assume girls need help?

He points ahead. "We're almost there. Nervous?"

"You wish," I say.

We hike downhill, deeper into the green canvas splattered with brown hues. The broken path disappears as we trudge along a lane decorated with splotches of different-colored flowers. He stops and looks both ways before continuing down a patchy trail.

I tease him. "I'm starting to think you might be lost?"

"Don't you trust me?"

"I'm traipsing through a dark forest with a stranger after only knowing you a day. What do you think?"

He smiles at me over his shoulder. "Sounds exciting!"

A few minutes later, he stops in front of a small opening, surrounded by thick foliage, and motions me through a leafy doorway. "Welcome to paradise, blossom."

Survival Skill #18

If you are unfamiliar with an area,
avoid getting boxed in or isolated.

I blush at the nickname and duck into the tunnel. As soon as I pop out the other side, I gasp.

Walls of glittering rock surround us covered in patches of painted trillium and purple phacelia. The creek we passed earlier has relaxed some, allowing tiny waterfalls to trickle over clusters of smooth boulders.

I lower my guard and squeal in delight. "I've died and gone to flyfishing heaven."

Mo arches his left eyebrow in surprise. "Does that mean you *haven't* been here before?"

I love how he pronounces been as "bean." Ignoring his question, I circle the area, staring up at the rocky towers encasing us.

"Well?" he presses.

I throw my hands up in the air. "Okay, fine! You win."

A beam of triumph sparks across his face as he cups his hand behind his ear. "Sorry, but could you say that a tad louder?"

Playing along, I yell. "I said ... you WIN!"

Mo's smile brightens up even more. "A day to note in history, I'm sure."

I gawk in amazement at the pure beauty surrounding me. "I've lived here a long time and have never seen anything like this before."

"The Smokies are huge. Did you really think you knew every place out here?" He trails his fingers along the moist wall encasing us and pats it. "Look at these limestone formations."

My eyebrows rise. "Interesting."

Mo laughs. "Fine. I won't talk about rocks, but it's time for you to pay up."

I hand him one of my flyfishing rods. "Only if we do it *my* way!"

He bats his black spidery eyelashes at me. "I'd expect nothing less."

"Let's start with the basics. You right handed or left handed?"

He wiggles his fingers on one hand. "A lefty."

My stomach sinks. My dad was also a lefty. I shake my head and fight through the rising sadness. "Haven't even started and already you're high maintenance."

"You're calling *me* high maintenance? I had to save you on our first date."

My heart drops into my belly. "Uh. What … what did you say?"

Mo protects his face with both hands and peers through his fingers. "You're going to smack me, aren't you?"

I giggle nervously, which sounds more like a witch on helium. So much for sexy. "Very funny. Of course not."

He smiles an amazing toothy grin. "Good. My ego can only take one thrashing a day."

I decide it's safer to skip the awkward moment and move straight into the fishing lesson. "I need to change out your rod first." I quickly flip the reel and re-thread the line. "There. Now let's get down to business."

"You're the boss."

I walk Mo through step-by-step instructions. "Grip the rod with your left hand and extend your thumb against the handle, directly opposite the reel." He tries to mimic my hold and I correct his hand placement. "No, no, like this." I move his hand down the rod. Once I realized we've touched, for fear of blushing, I keep my head tipped forward. "There." My eyes meet his. "How does that feel?"

Mo speaks softly. "Brilliant."

I break away and point to the river, pretending to be unfazed by his flirtiness. Reaching into my vest pocket, I pull out a bag of red chenille and pinch off a wad. I tie the fluff onto the end of his line.

Mo tugs his hair and groans. "What? No hook?"

"I'm fond of both my eyes, thank you very much."

"Yes, they are smashing."

This cannot be happening to me. I try not to stutter. "All right, stay close."

Mo lines up behind me, and his breath singes my neck.

I have trouble ignoring how close he's standing. "Uh, where was I? Oh yeah. I'll show you how to false cast until you get the hang of it." Concentrating on the water, I talk him through each step. "See that large boulder in the middle? That's your fish. Pretend you're surrounded by a clock. The twelve is directly above you. Pull the line back, aiming the rod at two o'clock." I demonstrate the technique as I'm explaining it to him. "Then, as the line straightens out behind you, load your rod, and pull into your front cast, aiming the rod at ten o'clock." Gripping the rod, I flick the end forward so the line loops around me like a cowboy's lasso. "Now, you try."

Even after I step aside, his heat remains boiling at each spot on my back where his body brushed mine. Mo begins casting. I correct his stance a couple times and reposition his grip. After a few casts, he picks it up, quite naturally. There's hope for him yet.

The whole time I'm with Mo, Tommy's words go through my head. About living and letting myself put aside my Dad's case for a brief time. Something I couldn't do with Wyn. For the next couple of hours, I try to do just that. Mo practices his casting while I fish a few yards away. We both remain close lipped, except for the occasional comment or joke. Every now and then—that is, about every minute—I sneak a peek at him, trying to decide who he looks more like, Hugh Jackman or Brody Jenner. Not that it matters much. It's nice to fish with someone again. Especially someone hot.

Until today, I hadn't realized how much I missed the companionship.

Eventually, Mo and I take a break just as the sun breaks through the ceiling of cloud cover. We snack next to the river, toasted by the heat. The water continues to stroke the tops of the damp, water-polished rocks, spilling over into small pools. Along the edge, flowers lean their blooms toward each other, exchanging secrets only nature can hear. I eat my double-decker MoonPie and can't resist breaking the silence. "You like MoonPies?"

He shrugs. "Can't say I've heard of them."

"Wow, you are missing out. Guess it's a Southern thing. What is your favorite food?"

Mo straddles the log we're sitting on, facing me. "I'll share, if you share."

I look at him out of the corner of my eye. "Okay, but I get to ask the questions first."

"Fine by me. I'm not afraid to reveal myself."

My body shifts uneasily, and I clear my throat. "Uh, me neither."

"Right. Well? Go on then."

I square my body off to him. "Favorite food?"

Mo doesn't even pause before answering. "Anything cooked over an open fire."

"Heeeey, you have to be specific. Favorite color?"

"Black."

I shake my head. "Cheater. Everyone knows black is not a color. Favorite book?"

He rubs both cheeks with the back of his fingers. "Hm, that's a tough one. It's not really a book, but Wordsworth's poem, 'The World Is Too Much With Us,' would be high on my list."

I try not to appear too amused. "Wow. You must be really smart."

He shrugs and rolls his neck in a circle as if his muscles are aching. I resist the urge to rub his shoulders. "Depends on who you talk to. Now I'll have a go."

"Shoot."

"Favorite color?"

I think for a second. "Sky blue."

"Very specific. Favorite food?"

I pick at a piece of dead bark on the log, exposing a family of slugs. "Hm. Either MoonPies or Spicy Cheetos."

Mo stops and appears a bit shocked. He pulls his t-shirt away from his chest as if he's hot. "Seriously?"

"Sad but true."

"Favorite book?"

Grimacing, I cover my face. "I'm embarrassed to admit I don't read much."

He tilts his head to one side and chews on a pine needle. "Pick something."

"Fine." I tap my forehead to bring forth a random book buried deep in my school curriculum. "I got it. *Stranger Danger.*"

Mo smirks. "You probably wrote it."

I giggle at his joke, sounding a bit like a child who's just heard the word "poop." Attempting to sound more mature, I answer a few more questions with total composure and class. At some point, the Q&A session tapers off, and we sit in silence once again.

Seconds turn to minutes, which feel more like hours. Questions continue to skim through my mind, but I don't dare ask them.

Do you think I'm cute? Do you date geeks? Do these pants make my butt look big?

I distract my crowding thoughts by braiding a few vines of wintercreeper into a flower bracelet and weaving in some orange trumpet flowers. Once I'm done, I hold up the finished bracelet. "Voila."

"Let me see that." He lays nature's jewelry in his palm and studies the details. "Nice little masterpiece. Is it for me?"

I snatch it back. "Nope. These are very, very rare. Priceless, you might say. Only special *blokes* get these."

"Hopefully, I can qualify." He stares at me. For a second, it feels as if the world holds its breath before exhaling.

The comment throws me off guard. My mouth gapes a little. How can he just blurt out stuff like that so easily? My nerves take over my body. "Um, I gotta go!"

I scramble to my feet and grab my things, trotting along the stream. Unfortunately, I move too fast and slip on a slimy rock. My right ankle twists, and I flap my arms, trying to stay on both feet. Definitely not graceful. I fall to one side and grab onto a rock, scraping my arms. Mo reaches out and steadies me so I don't tumble into the water.

"Thanks." A dry klutz is better than a sopping one.

Mo laughs. "Steady on."

I bite the inside of my cheek to keep from snapping at him for finding humor in my clumsiness. I'm also afraid I'll cry from absolute and total humiliation if I open my mouth. Tears swim in my eyes as my arm throbs. I check the damage to my elbow. Deep red lines of blood form a nasty scrape.

Mo bites his bottom lip when he sees it and immediately looks concerned. He holds my arm. "Crumbs, are you all right?"

I try to play it off by reciting Dad's favorite Monty Python line in my mock English accent. "It's just a flesh wound."

Mo laughs as he checks out my arm. "Interesting movie reference." He inspects my cut. "You need a plaster." He walks over to his bag and pulls out a Band-Aid.

"I got one, thanks." I pull out my own first aid kit, hoping I don't look as frazzled as my hair. The only Band-Aid I have left is one with Smoky the Bear on it. Great. My ears heat up as I patch the wound and wince.

Nothing sexier than a big nasty scab covered by a pervy bear that wears nothing but a hat.

To avoid Mo's gaze, I gather my stuff and walk carefully across the pebbled lane, refusing to hint at the throbbing pain in my ankle.

He speaks behind me. "Why are you so nervous around me?"

I don't turn around so he can't see the words 'guilty as charged' written across my forehead. "What? Excuse me, but you do not make me nervous."

"Then why are you leaving?"

I continue focusing on where I step. Stumbling once, a fluke, but stumbling twice, a fool. "Maybe I just need to go. Shouldn't be here anyway. I've got stuff to do. *Very important* stuff."

"Like what?"

For a split second, I think of telling him about my dad but decide against it. "Don't worry about it."

Out of the corner of my eye, I see Mo snatch his bag and hop over the rocks after me. "At least, let me walk you back. Just to be sure you're safe."

I stop and face him with my arms crossed and eyebrows furrowed. "I don't need a babysitter."

He bites his lip and raises his eyebrows. "How about a bodyguard?"

"Considering I took you out, that's a joke, right?" I tighten my lips to keep from revealing the smile that's reluctantly forming inside. "Like I said, I don't need help."

Mo saunters forward, as if he's stalking prey. A sexy smile, with one corner turned up, breaks free. "Maybe I'm not trying hard enough."

I shift onto another mossy boulder. "Stop it. You can't just *say* things like that."

He takes a step forward. "I'm seventeen. If I can graduate early and start a semester of college. Isn't that old enough to flirt?

I back up again and stutter. "Yeah, but ... it's just not *cool*."

He inches closer. "Maybe I'm not trying to be cool. Maybe I'm just being honest."

I retreat a step. "Doesn't matter. You should play hard to get or something."

His eyes are intent on keeping my attention, and his voice sounds raspy. "Why? What's the point?"

My voice gets trapped in my throat, and I swallow hard, still retreating until my back bumps into the stone wall.

I'm trapped.

Mo crowds me, and I try hard not to stare into his eyes. My fear mixes with excitement and anticipation, concocting an explosive reaction. The sweats. Probably not listed in Cosmo's "Top Ten Ways To Attract A Hot Guy." He places his hand on the wall just inches above my head. With his other hand, he moves a damp strand of hair that's clinging to my cheek. My breath quickens.

His silky lips graze my cheek and move to my ear where he whispers, "I like you, Grace."

My nerves trip over my words so all that comes out is a, "Um, okay. Yeah, sure." Oh, great comeback, Grace. Since I don't hear anything else he says, I fixate on his mouth as it moves. His lips have no cracks or creases. Just smooth. Nice and soft. He could be reciting Shakespeare or informing me of another geological miracle and I wouldn't hear a word.

He lifts my chin, forcing me to find his eyes. I stare at the dark pupils and watch them dilate, in and out. He hones in on my mouth and leans down until his lips barely brush over mine, gently like a leaf floating out of a tree and skimming lightly along the water.

Just then, a popping sound echoes in the distance.

Survival Skill #19

A tracker must know when to trust a hunch.

"What the hell was that?" I break out of his mysterious hold and rush forward to scan the woods.

He stands with his hands on his hips, listening. "Maybe an engine backfired."

"Out here? No way!" Shaking my head, I point in the direction of the noises. I brush past him and stand by the trickling river, straining to hear more. "That was gunfire."

Little popcorn sounds drift by again.

Mo touches my arm, igniting a small fire deep in my belly, warming me from the inside out. "Maybe it's those wankers from the other day. Drunk and shooting off firecrackers or something. Whatever it is, it's none of our business."

I stumble around in a circle with my hands cupped on the back of my neck. "You're wrong. It *is* my business."

He draws back and seems slightly irritated. "Really? Why?"

I'm not ready to tell him about Dad, so I focus on the trees surrounding us and avoid his prodding eyes. "Never mind. But I plan to find out." Before he can stop me, I charge off in the direction of the noises.

Mo runs up behind me and clutches onto my wrist with a vice grip. "Bloody hell, woman. In case you forgot, we're in the middle of nowhere and definitely don't want to meet up with those blokes again."

I think about Al and Billy, wondering if Les found them. "Okay, fine. Maybe you're right."

He tugs my shirt. "Come on. Let's get you out of here."

I can't help but appreciate how protective he's being. Kinda sweet. Though I would never admit it.

Reluctantly, I follow him down the path as we pass by jungles of wild rhododendron and a long parade of wildflowers. The setting sun casts shadows along the ground, breaking up the natural light. I've never been afraid of much, except maybe boys, dresses, and poison ivy.

Until now.

My jaws clench as my eyes shift back and forth on the lookout for anything tied to those shots. My lungs retreat into a dark corner of my body. Al's face pops up in my mind. Suddenly, I break into a full-fledged run.

Mo calls after me, his tone a mixture of frustration and concern. "Oi! What's the rush?"

Storming down the path, I trip on a tangled web of exposed roots and bang my knee on a log.

He rushes up and touches my arm, but I jerk away and march up the hill. "I need to get out of here. Now."

This time, he paces himself at my heels. "Away from me?"

I speed walk and answer with a scattered breath. "Yes. I mean … no. Away from *here*. From these guys. From—"

"From me?"

"No."

Mo grabs my arm and spins me around to face him. "What are you hiding?"

My arms fly out to the side. "Nothing! I'm fine." Tears threaten to drown my eyeballs, but I pinch them back.

He searches my face for clues. "I can tell. You're holding something back."

My hands clench into fists as I squeeze everything back. I refuse to make eye contact for fear he'll see right through me. "Please, I don't want to talk to about it."

He cups my jaw and draws my chin upward to face him. "Maybe you need to."

"I barely know you."

"Maybe I want to change that," he says.

Without thinking, I blurt out. "My dad's missing." His shoulders slump, and his arms hang down. I back away from him, awaiting his reaction.

Mo doesn't say anything for a few seconds, as if he's waiting for a translator to decipher what I said so he can fully understand. He speaks softly as if his volume's been turned way down. "When?"

I study my watch. "Three months, eleven days, twelve hours, and forty-three minutes ago."

He laces his fingers on top of his head, knuckles white, and tilts his head. "How?"

A sigh of frustration streams out. "I don't know."

Mo stiffens and shakes his head as if what I'm saying is wrong. "What do the police say?"

I scrutinize the army of trees, still feeling watched. "That he drowned. Fell into the river." I wring my hands together. "They found some of his stuff, but his body never showed up. Everyone says he's dead, but I refuse to believe it."

Mo's eyes remain fixated on mine. Shock mixed with horror distorts his angular face. He allows silence to expand the air between us, waiting for me to continue. I notice how he drums his fingers on his thigh, the thumping noise creating a galloping rhythm.

I prevent my voice from shaking. "I think those guys from the other day and these popping noises are related."

He massages his temples with his fingers then gives me a strange look. The same one I've gotten from Carl, Mom, and everyone else. The look of disbelief, pity, and doubt.

The comfortable vibe once connecting us morphs into sheer awkwardness. "Look, let's just drop it. I shouldn't have said anything." I pivot on one heel and march off.

Mo doesn't say anything as he trails me several strides back.

As soon as I reach my motorcycle, I hop on and nudge the kickstand with my toe, ready to bolt. When I stomp down on the pedal, Luci coughs a few times before going back to sleep. I swear under my breath. Can't even depend on my stupid bike. I step on the foot starter again until Luci catches her second wind. I hug my helmet like it's a football. "Goodbye, Mo."

He straddles my front tire and grips the bike's handlebars so I can't roll forward. "Why are you leaving?"

"You don't believe me."

He hesitates for a millisecond too long. "I didn't say that."

"You didn't have to."

"I believe you." He stops to swallow before forcing out more words. "I do."

"You trying to convince me or yourself?"

He leans in and pecks my cheek. My body relaxes slightly. "Grace, I'm not doing *anything* to anybody."

My voice comes out flat, unemotional. "I have to go."

"Can I see you again?"

Truth is, I want nothing more than to hang out with him. But my heart can't get a grip on that right now, not to mention I can't afford any more distractions. Focusing on questioning these guys once they are in custody and finding Dad are my main priorities right now. I've wasted enough time. "I'm not ready for this."

Mo scratches his head and wrinkles his face. "You lost me. Ready for what?"

I point between us. "This."

Mo sighs and shifts to one side, allowing me to pass. "Meet me at Bear Creek again tomorrow. We can talk more."

I slip on my helmet. "I don't think I can." As I roll away, I glance in the rearview mirror. Mo stands on the trail, watching me leave, reminding me of Humphery Bogart when he watches Ingrid Bergman walk away in Casablanca. My fleeting moment of romance.

I head home to meet my mom for our "dinner date," yet Mo still lingers in my thoughts. I analyze every moment of the day. Remember every smile in my mind. Popping noises reverberate in my head. No way those were firecrackers.

It was gunfire.

And I'm pretty sure it came from the same gun as Al's.

Survival Skill #20

*The reactions of animals provide warnings
of any danger in the area.*

Mom's high-pitched voice sucks me out of a delicious dream. Think Mo plus kiss plus MoonPies. "Why are you in bed? It's almost noon!"

I moan from under a mound of covers as my mind straddles between waking up and going back to sleep. "I'm tired."

She yanks the pillow off my head, letting the bright light find my face. "Why? What were you doing all night?"

I squint, as dots blink in my vision. My hand shields my eyes until my pupils adjust. "Me? Where were you? You didn't show up for our *family* dinner last night. *Again.*"

Mom acts nonchalant about standing me up … again. "I was offered another shift. I called but you didn't answer. You must have gotten home late."

I lean up on my elbows and stare at her. My muddled brain finally flickers on and starts to recall reality. "Really? Because I called the diner. They said you'd already left. Where were you?"

"Out." Mom balls her fists and places them on her hips. "Anyway, I don't have to answer to you."

I cross my arms. "Well, you don't have to *lie* to me either."

She yanks off the bedspread, exposing my naked feet. "Get up. Jim's only chargin' me fifty bucks a session, the least you can do is be on *time.*"

I salute her and rise to a soldier's stance. She ignores my military impression and leaves without saying another word. I sigh as soon as the door closes. Deep down, it sucks fighting with her. Wish I knew how to stop. Surely there's a class or something. *Troubled teens and their messed up moms 101.*

Rubbing my eyes, I stuff my feet into bear slippers and shuffle to the closet. After squeezing into a pair of tan cargo pants, I flip through my collection of vintage t-shirts and choose a Cookie Monster one that says, "One Tough Cookie." Don't feel very tough today. Actually, the opposite. Beaten down. Weak. Spent. I wonder if Cookie Monster ever gets tired of obsessing over sugar. Who knows, maybe this shirt can give me some kind of super power. Like the big S on Superman's chest.

As soon as I make it downstairs, Mom appears from the kitchen, wearing her diner uniform. "Gotta go, I'm late. I made you some breakfast." She pushes through the screen door.

A couple seconds later, I hear the struggling clutch beg for mercy as Mom attempts to murder it once again. I smile. Weird, how the small, dumb things never change. Yet the big, important things you want to stay the same never do.

In the kitchen, I spot my most-important-meal-of-the-day on the table: two pieces of burnt toast, an expired yogurt cup (Hello, lactose intolerant!), and an open can of flat Coke. What ever happened to Wheaties, fruit, and a good ole' glass of OJ? I scrape the black crust off the bread and cram it into my mouth.

It's official. Mom's trying to kill me.

Just as I'm leaving the house for Dr. Head's office, a photo perched up on the mantle catches my eye. The one of Dad and me holding up a huge fish we caught together. I'm wearing a big smile, unaware of the bunny ears he's displaying behind my head. In pretty much every picture of us, he did something silly.

As I stare at his smile, guilt pumps through me. I wasted so much time yesterday messing around when I should have been searching another grid. I need to regroup. Focus. Get back to my investigation. The gunfire replays in my head.

I need to see Les. Check and see if he found those guys. Tell him about the shooting noises. Find out why he never called like he promised.

There's not much time before my appointment, but this can't wait.

Dr. Head is not going to appreciate my "no show." I know how it feels to be stood up when you are expecting someone. Like mother, like daughter. Gives Dr. Head and I something to analyze later.

When Luci and I turn down Station 11's dusty road, Les's truck is in the station's driveway. I park and walk up the porch's rotting stairs, creaking with every step. The ranger office is empty except for a walkie-talkie and ranger gear lying on his desk.

I knock lightly on the wooden frame encasing a torn screen. "Les?"

Muffled noises drift from behind the house. Sounds like whispering voices. I mill around the side to an empty yard. A sudden gust blows by, making a *haaaa* sound as if the trees are laughing at me.

A chill skitters down my spine. "Les? You here? It's Grace." Something scuffles through the underbrush. The hair on my arms tingle, and my heart drums in my chest. "Les? Is that you?"

Suddenly, a midnight-black dog bolts out of the woods. I yelp as Dad's service dog jumps on me and muddies my shirt with his paws. "Bear! Geez, you scared me." Since Dad went missing, Bear has lived at the station with Les. Mom thought it was the best thing for the dog, no matter how much I protested.

Bear leans all sixty pounds of himself against my leg and stares into the trees, waiting for someone to return. I scratch his pointy ears, still convinced he's part wolf. After looking around a little, I leave him there, still staring off into the woods, and trot back up the rickety steps to wait.

As I enter Les's office, a strange smell of tobacco mixed with rotten sandwich meat and bad coffee makes me gag. Two huge rotating fans thump on the ceiling, circling musty air. Papers stack up on every guest chair. I step over random trash and sink into Les's captain chair.

Bored, I flip through his park ranger manual outlining procedures on hunting permits, animal relocation, and wilderness laws. Then I shuffle through the loose papers scattered across the top. A weather report, an email about a new bear sanctuary, and a few old, coffee-stained invoices. Underneath the scattered junk mail, I spot Les's patrol log.

First, I open the book and run my finger down the pages, scanning the most recent notes. There's nothing recorded for the last couple of days. Slacker. Then I get an idea. I flip back to the week Dad disappeared and read a few entries, starting a few days before and after. One in particular grabs my attention.

Wed April 8th: Checked Station 19. Patrolled areas 11 and 12. Poacher citation #1248960.

It's as if the wind has been sucked out of my sail. I fall back in the chair and think for a second. Does this mean Les or Dad issued a poacher citation the day before Dad went missing? And if so, to whom?

I yank the desk drawer where the documents are filed. Locked. I slip the pink Swiss Army knife out of my bag and choose a tool. I jimmy the lock, careful not to leave any scratches on the laminated wood.

After a few tries, it pops open. Scary the things you can learn on TV and the Internet these days. B&E is getting to be a bad, yet fun, habit. I glance outside to be sure Les isn't coming before rifling through his files. As soon as I find the label marked "citations," I slide the manila folder out and thumb through its contents until I find the reference number I'm looking for.

Bingo!

My jaw clenches as I slide out a paper with trembling hands. It's dirty and crumpled, obviously trampled on. The ink is smeared, but I can still read it.

> **Poacher citation #1248960.**
> **Location:** 1 mile East of Station 19, on park border.
> **Offenders:** Alfred Smith and William Barrett. Expired gun license. Suspected of bear hunting off season. No carcasses found.
> **Action:** Issue citation with fine of $500.
> **Notes:** Remington .44 Magnum and a Winchester. Second offense.
> **signed:**

I cover my mouth as I make the connection. Alfred and William.

Al and Billy.

No one signed the bottom. I double check a few other citations and confirm this is the only one without a signature.

Did Les issue this? Is that why he asked me about names? Did he tell Carl about this when Dad went missing?

I jot down the information in my notebook just as the front steps creak, warning me that someone's coming.

Survival Skill #21

Proper rest stops, nutrition, hydration, and your physical condition are key to mountain hiking.

Without hesitation, I shove everything back into the drawer and slide it shut just as Les waddles up to the door.

He stops abruptly when he sees me. "Mornin', Gracie. What are you doin' here?"

I come out from behind the desk and try to act natural, hoping he doesn't notice the big GUILTY sign stamped on my forehead. "Just waiting on you. How are you?"

Les slurs through his tobacco-packed lip. "Oh, can't complain."

I squeeze through the small space between him and the desk before sinking into a musty chair. My knees rise above my waist, but I pretend not to notice. "Were you out back?"

He eyes me. "Yeah, why?"

I shrug. "I heard voices. Was someone with you?"

"Nope. Probably just me yappin' at the dog. Damn dog needs to learn that fetching means he has to bring something back."

Eyeing him, I check to see if he's showing any signs of deception. "Weird. I didn't see you with Bear when I went back there."

"I'm easy to miss." Les snorts at his own fat joke and collapses into the seat. The chair groans from the extra weight. He interlaces his fingers and rests his hands on his belly shelf. "So Gracie, what can I do you for?"

I relax in the seat. "Wanted to see if you got the men I told you about."

Les nods and spits into a cup. "Yup. They're down with Carl at the station."

My body stops moving. "Really? Why didn't you call me?"

When he shrugs, his belly jiggles. "Forgot I guess."

My fingers pick at the foam hanging out of the seat cushion. "Did you find *any* evidence of Dad?"

Les picks his nose. "We didn't find hide nor hair of Joe. But I did find an expired gun license and some illegal equipment. Carl's booked them yesterday so I'm sure he'll question them more."

I sit up as straight as I can. "Yesterday?"

"That's what I said."

A timeline reels through my head. "Do you know exactly what time?"

Les studies a stain on the ceiling. "Don't know. About noonish I'd say."

I groan and drop my face into my hands. "But that can't be. Are you sure it wasn't a few hours later?"

He shifts in his chair; I can tell he's getting irritated. "Of course, I'm sure."

A beetle crawls across the short-haired carpet in front of me, climbing every obstacle in its path.

Les stands and moves around the desk, accidentally stepping on the insect. Poor bug didn't stand a chance. "What's goin' on here, Gracie?"

"When I was fishing last night—"

He frowns. "Fishing? I thought you were going to stay at home until I called?"

I pretend I didn't hear his question. "I heard popping noises out by Dragon Ridge."

He dribbles a tar-like goop into a can, but a few black drops of saliva hang on his lips. "Popping noises?"

"Yeah, like from a gun. At the time, I assumed you hadn't found Al and Billy yet. But if you got them earlier yesterday, then who made those noises I heard last night?"

Les frowns. "Come on, Gracie, are you sure? First these two bozos, and now mysterious noises. This is getting a little farfetched, don't you think?"

"I swear."

He scoops the inside of his mouth, removing a dark glob of gunk and tosses it into the trash. "I'm up there all the time. If something strange was going on, I'd know it."

I think about the unsigned citation in the drawer. "Did you know about Al and Billy? I mean beforehand. Had you ever seen them before."

Les growls a little at first but then forces a smile. "No." His answer makes me wince. Does that mean he really didn't know about the citation, that Dad wrote it, or that he's lying now?

He itches the inside of his ear with his pinky. "Look, I can see you're upset. I know what you think you heard up there. But as you know, sometimes the woods make sounds we don't recognize. Can play with our heads." He taps his temple with his finger. "Make us crazy."

I twist a strand of my hair. "Maybe."

Les chews on one of his nails. "Listen, no matter what you think you heard out there, those two guys aren't going to bother you anymore. You're safe."

A lump sticks to my esophagus as I obsess over his answer to my Al and Billy question. I push past it so he doesn't become suspicious. "How long will they be in jail?"

"Depends on Carl. We didn't catch them with any hides or nothing so if they're hunting off season, I didn't see any sign of it. Even if they get out, Carl'll make sure they leave this town for good."

I perk up after hearing his statement. "What do you mean, *if they get out?*"

Les ambles over to a small fridge and sounds a bit out of breath from exerting himself. "Carl needs some pretty heavy evidence to keep them more than a few days."

"How can that be?"

He pulls out a can and holds it out to me. "Cola?"

"No thanks." My thoughts churn. I can't let Al and Billy roam these woods again. I've got to find something to connect them to Dad. Anything illegal to pin on them. Maybe come clean about how they attacked me. Then again, Carl would probably be more furious at me for getting involved.

As my mind reels, Les pops the top and slurps down the carbonated sugar. I can almost imagine his insulin sky-rocking, reminding his body to store more fat. If that's even possible. He slams the can down on the desk and belches. "Just let me worry about them, okay? I don't want you snooping around anymore."

He tosses the empty can into a recycling box by the front door. Only the can misses and bounces off the wall, landing on the floor. He crushes the can under his boots, putting it out of its misery before throwing it away.

As I watch this, my brain sifts through files of random information until something clicks. I launch myself out of the sagging chair. "You know what? You're right, Les. You can handle this now. I trust you." I glance at my watch and then bug out my eyes. "Whooooa! Look at the time. I gotta go. I'm late for an appointment."

Les blocks the door and gives me a hug, compressing all the oxygen out of my lungs.

I reluctantly return the gesture to escape his hold quicker. The rolls on his belly jiggle under the pressure. Finally, I manage to squirm free. "Thanks, Les."

"You okay?"

"Sure. Never better." I bolt through the door and leap over all four steps to the ground.

Les shouts after me. "Thanks for stopping by. Don't be a stranger."

After flipping him a wave, I jump on my bike and tear off down the dirt road, almost veering out of control and into a tree once or twice.

The image of Les's soda can is etched into my brain. Dad used to buy them at a local government commissary to keep the station stocked with drinks. Al hit Billy in the head with one just like it.

There's only two places nearby where Al could have gotten those cans.

Here at Station 11.

And up at Station 19.

If I can link Al to something up there, he might just rot in jail for good.

◌ঽ

The hike into the Smoky Mountains toward Station 19 is longer than I remember. It's been years since I've ventured up here. Dad covered such a huge district; it took him months to patrol all of it. Took Les even longer.

As I gain altitude, the trail seems to disappear. I pass over a few small creeks, under the canopy of large hemlocks and yellow poplars. Intermittent breaks in the treetops provide views of the surrounding mountain range. The trail is a steady climb and by the time I'm close, my calves are cramping and my thighs burning. It takes me a couple hours to reach the station.

Digging my toes into the soft slope, I push up the hill until I finally reach the top. After winding through trees, I emerge from the dense forest and walk into a small clearing.

The old, dilapidated station leans at a weird angle. A redneck version of the Leaning Tower of Pisa. Just as I'm about to step into the opening, a warning sound clangs in my brain. Something seems off, but I can't tell exactly what.

I hide for several minutes and watch the area. Maybe my paranoia is finally taking over. Eventually, I slink towards the fire pit. When I reach the stony circle, I hold my palm over the small mound of charred sticks and twigs. Still feels warm. I spot the white outline of a boot print, telling me someone's shoe got a little too close to the fire and the sole melted from the intense heat.

As I approach the building, I slide out my knife and remain low to the ground. The door is slightly ajar. I creep up the steps—avoiding the third beam that's always been extra squeaky—and squat under the window. After a few breaths, I rise slowly until my eyes clear the sill. The station isn't how I expected it to be. There's upturned furniture. Open cupboards. Trash scattered everywhere. Including a few of the same soda cans I spotted at Al's camp. On the ground, I find another partial print, same tread pattern. Just as I'm about to take out my camera for a picture, I hear a noise close by. The birds stop tweeting.

What if Al's been released without Les knowing? And worse, what if he's here now? Watching me.

My nerves respond to the thought, and my flight instinct kicks in. Instead of entering the shack, I slink back along the side, like a dog with its tail between its legs, and slip into the safety of the trees. I already learned my lesson with Al. This time, I need to be smarter.

As soon as I'm a safe distance away from the station, I hike off the trail and cut through a different way, constantly looking over my shoulder. Stopping every few yards to listen. The forest seems unusually quiet, making me uneasy. I wade through the underbrush quietly until my foot squishes into a small pool of goopy stuff.

Pausing, I squat down and touch my finger to the dark, tarry liquid and hold it up to the sunlight. It isn't tar.

It's blood.

As soon as the reality hits me, I cover my mouth. Part of me wants to wail. Not because it's blood, but because I don't know whose blood it is. I frantically wipe my hand on my pants and scan the area. I shift into tracker mode and follow the blood trail deeper into the forest until a foul stench slams into my nose. Something rotting. A cross between iron, feces, and old garbage.

My stomach lurches at the familiar smell of death.

Up ahead, a dark mound lies in the shadows. I freeze, not sure what to do. I rise up on tippy toes for a better look but can't make out anything. Wish I had my binoculars. My hands shake and my stomach lurches as I inch forward. No matter how many times I've come across a dead carcass, the smell gets to me every time.

Gagging, I cover my nose with my shirt and breathe through my mouth. I'm relieved to see it's a dead animal. From it's massive size and dark fur, it appears to be a bear. A dead animal I can take. Just not a human.

I circle the carcass wide, maintaining a good distance. The bear's mouth is wide open with its tongue hanging out to one side, as if surprised. Flies buzz in and out of its mouth, searching for a place to land. A frozen snarl on his lips.

That's when I recognize the scar and white tuft of fur.

My heart sinks.

Simon.

"Damn it!" I hiss, pressing the heels of my hands against my forehead and shaking my head. I kick a log. Why Simon? Of all the bears, why did it have to be him? Without warning, a tear slides free, and I drop to my knees and stare into Simon's deep brown eyes, once full of life. I knew I should have kept better tabs on him.

To me, he was a friend. To them, meat. A trophy. Another notch on their sick hunting belts.

I think of the Native American prayer Tommy taught me. The one Dad and I always recited for any dead animals we came across. "May the warm winds of heaven blow softly upon your house. May the Great Spirit bless all who enter there. May your moccasins make happy tracks in many snows, and may the rainbow always touch your shoulder."

I sit still for a minute and let the breeze whisper a goodbye. The only thing I can do for Simon now is find out who did this horrid thing. Before checking him for clues, I tie a bandana over my nose and mouth to block out the stench. Batting at flies, I scan Simon's body for evidence. A gaping wound marks his neck. A single gunshot.

I quickly scan the area. No shells or other signs of anything odd. Someone smart collected and removed any evidence. Tilting my head back, I scan the treetops and spot the remains of an elevated camouflage stand. I shimmy up the tree like a monkey and inspect the small platform. A few pieces of donut and corn kernels scatter along the top.

Someone lured and hunted the bear from here.

I climb back down and approach Simon. I can't help but wonder what kind of person kills a bear, not for meat or its hide, but as a trophy. Then leaves it to rot. I'm not against hunting as long as it's legal, respectful to nature, and not wasted. Dad says sometimes the populations have to be managed in order to be sustained. But that's why we have hunting laws and specific limits.

This kill is what forest rangers call a "want and waste."

I cover Simon with branches and leaves. Other than that, there's nothing else to do.

It's not until I'm about a mile away that my emotions boil over. I try to grab hold of a branch as my legs crumble underneath me. Sitting on an old stump, I bury my face in my hands and let my body tremble. Scenes of my time with Simon run through my head. Part of me wants to punch something, but the other piece just wants to melt down and give up on all this.

I wrap my arms around my stomach and soothe myself by rocking.

If Al and Billy killed this bear for fun, what else would they do? I try not to let my mind consider what they might have done with Dad and refocus.

The only positive thing to come of poor Simon is that now I have proof these guys are poaching. Carl can't set these guys free now.

Survival Skill #22

*When traveling in densely wooded areas, hiking with
a partner is much safer than being alone.*

𝐼 speed down the highway and enter the town limits, passing
derelict billboards, abandoned gas stations, and fading street
signs. Once I reach the main strip, Luci practically slides into a
parking space. Without ripping off my helmet, I bolt towards the
Carl's office.

Before I reach the police station, I spot Mr. Fields standing
outside his store under a grand reopening banner and a revamped
front with new windows, sparkly paint job, and a shiny, red sign.
He smiles at me and waves. "Grace, want to come in for some
tea? It's my reopening!"

I stop in front of the open doors and catch my breath, taking
note of his renovations: new hardwood floors, new shelving
stocked with merchandise, and even an old-fashioned popcorn
machine. The smell of fresh paints teases my nose. Looks like he
finally got the money to stay open. Guess some things can turn
around when you least expect them to. "Can't today, Mr. Fields,
but congrats on the new look."

He wipes his hands on his apron. "Thanks. It's about time us
small town folks caught us a break. No matter what your daddy
said, our town needed a change." The hair on my neck stands on
end at his random comment. He catches himself and turns red
with embarrassment. "Sorry, Grace. That was out of line." He
spins around and leaves before I can respond.

I try to let his comment roll off my back as I sprint the rest of
the way to Carl's. But for some reason, it bothers me even
though I know it probably shouldn't. I mean, who says that kind

of crap to the daughter of a missing person. Especially about someone who loved this town the way Dad did. He wanted the town to thrive, he just didn't think strip malls and chain restaurants was the right answer.

I guess it's true: dumb people say the darndest things.

The inappropriate comment slips out of my head as soon as I round the corner. I yank open the dinging door, yelling. "Captain!"

Bernice jumps to her feet and presses her hand against her chest. "Good heavens, Grace! You scared me!" She checks me out and hands me a tissue to wipe my face. "Sit down, child. I'll get you something to drink."

I flop down in a new leather chair in the linoleum-lined waiting area. "New furniture?"

Bernice rushes over with a paper cone full of cool water. "Don't you just love it? Finally adding a woman's touch to this place."

"Looks good." After taking a swig, I wipe my mouth on my sleeve before speaking more clearly. "Bea, I need to see the captain. Is he in?"

She points out the window. "Here he comes now."

I peek through the mini-blinds and spot Carl and Wyn walking along the sidewalk. Carl's the dad Wyn never had, and Wyn's the son Carl always wanted. Guess having Skyler worked out for both of them.

Wyn opens the door for Carl and trails close behind him. They both look surprised to see me. Wyn mutters, "Hey, G."

I smile back. Thank God Wyn's here. If anyone will back me up on this case, it's him.

"What happened to you?" Wyn raises his eyebrows when he spots me, all dirty and haggard.

I realize how haggard I look. My pants are wet, and my boots are muddy. "Nothing. Why?"

"So dressing to impress then."

I force out a chuckle. "I think you get funnier everyday, Wyn."

He looks proud of himself. "I try."

"Obviously not hard enough." I turn to Carl. "Captain, I need to talk to you. It's important."

Carl removes his baseball hat and hangs it on the rack. "Grace, I don't have time to play P.I. with you today. Believe it or not, I have a slew of other cases that need my immediate attention. Cases that are still open."

I barrel on as if I didn't hear him. "You have two men in custody, and I have evidence that will help you lock them up for good. Proof they're poaching illegally."

Wyn moves directly behind me in the doorway. I find it hard to concentrate with him standing so close to me. Puffs of his breath stroke my neck, and every now and then, his arm brushes against me. Part of me just wants to spin around and hug him. To tell him I'm sorry. That I should have let him help me all along. That I want his help now. Maybe even that I kinda want him back. I block out the thoughts.

Carl passes by us and plops down behind his desk as if I'm exhausting him. "Go ahead then. Tell me."

Wyn touches my back. "Go ahead, Grace."

I clear my thoughts and start to tell Captain everything that has happened in chronological order. At least the rated G version. The gunshots, talking to Les, and the cola can connection.

After all that, I stop to take a breath and Wyn speaks up. "So you have proof they littered? That'll get at least two days and a hundred-dollar fine."

I turn around and glare at him. "Thanks *Watson*. But I'm not finished." I take in a deep breath to steady my heartbeat and describe the state of the shack along with the hunting platform built so close to the station.

Carl frowns. "Station 19? You went all the way up there. Today?"

Wyn interrupts again. "G, that's a hike. You shouldn't be traipsing all over the forest by yourself."

I widen my eyes and purse my lips, hoping he can take a hint to shut the hell up. "I wasn't *traipsing*. I was *hiking*."

He frowns. "Same thing."

"No, Wyn!" My voice is louder than I mean it to be. "It's *not* the same thing!"

Wyn's eyes widen as Carl holds his hand up. "Back off, Wyn. I'll handle this." Carl pats my shoulder. "Take it easy, Grace. Now tell me what you were doing hiking that far up in the mountains. Alone."

"I was following a hunch."

Carl frowns but tries to stay calm. He dismisses me with his hand. "Shoot, teens don't have hunches, cops do. I told you, this is my business."

My fists perch on my hips. "This is not about my hiking patterns or my age bracket, Captain. Is anyone going to let me finish? Because I'm not done yet."

"Sorry. You're right. Go on then. Tell me what evidence you have." Carl leans back in his chair as Wyn pretends to lock his lips with an imaginary key. "*Real* evidence."

"I found something. Something bad. Something awful." I pause trying to figure out how to phrase what I'm going to say next so it has the biggest impact. "I found a dead bear. Shot for fun."

Carl appears a bit shocked but before he can say anything, Wyn comes close to me with a sincere look on his face. He touches my hand. "Are you sure?"

My anger rises again. He knows how much I need Carl to believe me. Why is Wyn interrupting so much? All he's doing is causing Carl to doubt me. He's supposed to be on my side. I yank my hand away. "Yes, Wyn, I'm sure. I think I can tell if a bear is dead or not. Believe it or not, I'm not as dumb as you are about the woods."

Wyn's face turns red. "Chill out. Geez, what's wrong with you?"

I snap back, growing angrier by the minute. "You are! I don't have time to answer two people. Now do you mind if I talk to the *real* detective around here?"

Carl stands up and moves between us. "Grace, he's only trying to help. Now tell me more. Did you get any pictures of the carcass?"

I silently curse myself. "Well ... no, I ... I guess I was so freaked out by it all ... I forgot."

Wyn paces the room. "You forgot? Great. How are we supposed to help you then?"

Carl gives Wyn his "stay out of it" police look and puts his attention back on me. "Okay, let's think through this. Did you get samples or other evidence from the scene that will help me hold them?"

My hands tremble as I shake my head. How could I forget something that important?

Carl wipes his face with a green handkerchief. "Then there's not much I can do. These guys have been in custody since yesterday so without concrete evidence, we can't prove they did anything anyway."

"Wait, you can't release them! They threatened me, and I want to press charges. That should keep them locked up. Right?"

Wyn frowns at me. I notice how the vein in his neck throbs. "What? You didn't tell me this."

Carl puts his fists on the table. "That's quite an accusation, young lady."

I nod emphatically and press on, ignoring his expressions. "The big one came into the store. Wyn saw him. I heard them talking at the diner about hunting and followed them to see if they had anything to do with my dad and—."

Carl cuts me off before I can finish. His face turns beet red. "You what?"

I cower. "I'm sorry. I was trying to help. But they saw me out in the woods and threatened me."

"What?" Wyn rubs both hands over his face, seemingly stressed. "When was this? What happened?"

Pulling down the collar of my t-shirt, I point to the scratches on my neck. "They had a knife to my throat."

"Those are some serious allegations, young lady." Carl narrows his eyes at me as if I'm lying. "When you came and saw me last week after trekking around the woods, you had scratches all over your face and body."

I can see where this is going. "I'm telling the truth."

Wyn studies me for a moment, looking directly in my eyes. I nod slightly to let him know I'm being honest. Finally, he faces Carl. "Maybe you and Les can hike out to the station and get some evidence to nail these guys. I don't think Grace would lie about something this serious."

Carl eyes me for a couple more seconds. Then he takes a deep breath and exhales as he pats Wyn's shoulder and addresses me. "Fine. I'll take your statement to hold these guys for another day. I'm heading out of town tonight, but I'll call and see if Les can get up there first thing in the morning."

My body is shaking like I've had too much coffee. This time, I roar at both of them. "No! We have to go now!" Carl glares at me, and Wyn's mouth hangs open. Tears burn the back of my eyes again, and I lower my voice back down to a whisper. "What I mean is, you have to go *tonight*. The evidence could be gone by tomorrow. This could be a link to my dad."

Carl raises his voice slightly and deepens it to reflect his authority. "I can't just drop my commitments because you tell me too. I said I would get Les on it. It's the best I can do on short notice."

I look out the window and spot a couple of raindrops trickling down the glass. "I won't let you blow this off."

He flexes his jaws. "Grace Wells, you are pushing where you don't want to push. You will stay out of this and let Les handle it or I will throw your butt in the slammer for a night. Just for interfering. You and me, we made a deal."

I chew my nails, knowing I've stepped way over the line—so far over for the line, I can't even see where that line is any more. Even though my head warns me to stop, I can't hold back. There's no one else willing to fight for Dad, so I'll take Carl on if

I have too. "What about your end of the deal? Have you tested the bag yet?"

Wyn looks back and forth between us, contemplating whose side to jump on.

Carl squints his eyes. "It's at the lab now."

"What's taking so long?"

He huffs in frustration, kinda like a bull warning me he's about to charge. "Oh, so you're a forensic scientist now too? As much as you want to take this out on me, I'm not in control of the goddamn lab!"

"Fine. Then I'll meet *my* end of the deal when you meet *your*s." As soon as the words escape my lips, I know I'm toast. I cower, wishing I could blend into that wall.

Carl screams. "I've had enough of this nonsense!" He slams both fists down on top of his desk.

I bite back tears. This time, my mouth falls open and my eyes widen. I've never seen Carl get this mad. Never heard him yell. Not like this. Not at me Not at anyone.

Wyn steps forward. "Captain—"

Carl puts his hand up in Wyn's face. "No! You need to stop defending her. She's gone too far this time, and I've been patient long enough." He faces me. Beads of sweat break out on his forehead, and his cheeks turn scarlet. "This case is over! I'm telling you to let it go, or there will be major consequences. Do you understand me, young lady?"

I bite my quivering lip and nod. The room blurs a little as tears pool in my eyes.

His voice bellows in the small room. "For some stupid reason, I'm still making silly deals with you. A damn kid. You're sticking your nose where it doesn't belong, and I won't have it anymore. Now you better get out of here before you tick me off even more."

Without another word, I storm out of the office, purposely pounding the floor, leaving a track of mud as I bolt out the front door. When I clear the corner, tears tumble down my cheeks. I quickly wipe my fists across my face. Carl thinks I'm being dramatic. Irrational. Maybe even making all this up because I'm "grieving." What do I have to do to get him to believe me? Why has he given up on my dad, his friend, so easily?

Just as I'm mounting my bike, Wyn jogs up. "G, wait up!"

I scowl at him. "Go away … *traitor.*"

He looks confused. "Traitor? If I recall correctly, *you're* the one holding out on me. Why didn't you tell me about those guys?"

I shrug and push away from him. "I just didn't. Why were you questioning me back there? Now Carl thinks I'm crazy."

Wyn rubs his temples. "Uh, news flash, I know your crazy. But to be honest, I'm thinking your grade A attitude and that big chip on your shoulder didn't do you any favors." He pauses and swallows as he stares at me. "And I'm starting to wonder if you have any marbles left."

I hear myself gasp a little. "You don't believe me?" I close my eyes and let my shoulders fall forward, suddenly feeling more alone than ever. My voice barely breaks the surface of my lips. "So you're turning your back on me now too? Figures."

His close-shaven face softens, and his eyebrows turn down in concern. "That's not fair. I'm trying to help you, but if you don't let me, what else can I do? You're fighting me every step of the way. Lashing out at the police. You can't tell Carl how to do his job."

"Why not? Maybe then he'll do it better."

He crosses his arms and gives me an icy stare. "Wait a minute. That's not fair. Carl's a good cop. Just because he needs a small thing called *evidence* doesn't mean he isn't doing everything he can to help you. And that goes for me too. I've seen him going over and over that case file. Have you ever thought he might be as frustrated as you?"

"No." I lean into him and wait for him to hug me.

"At least you are honest." When he says that I feel sick, knowing I haven't been truthful with him. He kisses the top of my head and rubs my arms. "Why are you shaking?"

"I'm cold."

"So you *are* frigid?" He smiles at the joke I totally saw coming.

I shake my head. "This isn't the time to kid around."

"Something is upsetting you more than just some old dead bear. You've seen a ton of them and in some horrific ways. So, what is it really?"

Wyn knows me so well. I don't have the strength to hold out on him anymore. Someone has to know what's going on. "The dead bear I found at Station 19—" I pause to swallow and wait until the threat of tears recedes to a safer level. My voice comes out much softer than I plan. "The bear was Simon."

Instantly, Wyn pulls me into him. My face presses against his chest. "Ah, man, G." He strokes my hair. "I'm so sorry. No wonder you're so upset. Poor Simon."

I'm engulfed by the scent of his musky cologne, making him smell like some kind of businessman. Maybe I should just let him help me. "Wyn, I think this is all related. That guy in the store did this. I'm sure of it."

He holds me at arm's length so he can see my face. "Did they … you know … *touch* you in any way?"

"It's not what you think, but they did threaten me." I stare up at him, our faces only inches apart. "Will you help me? I can't do this without you."

He pulls my hair back in a ponytail at the base of my neck. "Man, those big green eyes of yours should be classified as deadly weapons." He pulls me back into him.

Even though he's erased the space between us, I try to keep a thin invisible wall between us. I don't want to lead Wyn on. Now when I'm still confused myself, it might lead him on and that wouldn't be fair.

He rests his chin on my head. "Tell me the truth. Have you told me *everything?*"

My confession about Mo rises to the surface, threatening to come out. Instead, I pinch my lips together and hold back. This is not the time to upset Wyn. I force out my answer. "Yes."

He cups my chin with his hand. "Then I'll help you." A long sighs fills the only space left between us. He rubs his thumb along my jawbone as he stares at me. His breath is warm and his touch, soothing. He breaks our gaze and looks off to the right. "So then, let's go."

I look around for a second. "Did I miss something? Go where?"

He points to the mountain rimmed in a halo of fog. "Station 19. Show me what's going on up there. We still have enough time before it gets dark."

My laugh comes out as a cough. "You? Hiking? It's almost five miles. You don't even walk that in a month. Come on, be serious."

He presses the heel of his palm against my forehead. "Excuse me, but I was the Rooster Run champion two years in a row."

This time, I laugh in his face. "Hello! That was in second grade!"

"Hey, it's more than you can say. You didn't even place."

"'Cause it was for *boys*."

He scoffs. "Since when does that stop you?"

I pinch back a smile. "True."

Wyn lightly touches the dimple in my chin then the tip of my nose. "Seriously, I'll go up there with you. I don't want to lose any evidence if it's all we got. Beside, you and I both know you're not gonna wait until morning anyway, and I don't want you to go alone. You need protection."

"From who?"

"Yourself mostly. So let's get a move on then. We'll hike up together and take some pictures for Carl. Maybe it'll light a fire under him and Les."

I chew on my cuticle, feeling guilty for not coming clean about Mo. "You'd do that for me?"

He smiles and ruffles my hair. "That's the kind of great guy I am."

"But you hate to hike. You hate the woods."

Wyn shrugs. "Whatever, I *own* these woods. Besides, how can I refuse to hike when I live in the mountains?"

"My point exactly."

"Unless you can think of something better for us to do." He plasters on a silly sexy face, resembling a soap opera star with one eyebrow arched and lips puckered.

Rolling my eyes, I cover his mouth so he doesn't speak. "Not now, please." I laugh and scoot forward on the seat. "Hop on, *sucker.*"

He straddles the space behind me and grabs hold of my waist. "You know if I wasn't a total *gentleman*, I'd take advantage of this position."

"If you weren't such a *sissy*, I'd let you drive."

He laughs as we take off down the road. His warm breath strokes my ear. Heading up into the mountain, I'm very aware of Wyn's arms cradling me. How at every turn, they tighten a little. How he leans against me. How his legs rub against the back of mine. Only a thin layer of cotton clothing is preventing us from touching skin, yet a little heat still manages to simmer between us.

Survival Skill #23

Signs of passage include signature footprints, broken limbs, or flattened vegetation.

"Are we there yet?" Wyn calls out from a few yards back as he crashes through the leaves.

I continue sliding through the underbrush without any issue. Daylight is fighting for extra time as darkness invades. The sky has blackened and the rain has already started. Every fifteen feet or so, I stop and wait for Wyn to catch up. "You hike like a girl."

"How would *you* know?" Wyn's breath comes out in spurts. I'm pretty sure he hasn't had this much exercise since we were five.

I can't help but stifle a snicker when he gets tangled in a web of branches and begins battling against the menacing vines. My little woodland warrior. "You sure you're okay?"

He pushes a branch that slaps him back in the face. "No." A few steps later, he breaks free and trots to catch up. "At the risk of sounding like a total sissy, I should have changed my shoes. These Converses are toast." He lifts up khaki-colored shoes soaked in mud. How Wyn ended up so neat while living in a small mountain town is one of North Carolina's greatest mysteries.

"I'm not even going to respond to that." I break off a crooked stick and hand it to him. "This might help."

Wyn grabs the thick branch and chuckles. "Three legs are better than one."

I flick his ear. "Do you kiss your mother with that mouth?"

His face scrunches up as if he's sucked on a lemon. "If I *kissed* my mother, you'd have more to worry about than my *sick* sense of humor and sexual innuendos."

"Hm. Good point."

Wyn and I walk for a few more miles, chatting about nothing, ribbing each other, and getting digs in whenever we can. When we reach the top of the trail, it splits into two. We veer right and head up. The deeper we travel into the woods, the darker it gets.

As soon as we reach another mile marker, I check my GPS. "We're almost there."

He rests on a boulder and wipes his forehead with his sleeve. "Why does it have to be so hot?"

I take a swig of water and hand him my canteen. "Don't get too tired, we still gotta hike back."

He groans as he guzzles my water.

A scratching noise catches my attention. I press my finger against my lips as my heart flips around in my chest like a fish on land. "Did you hear that?" Wyn stops in mid-gulp and shakes his head. Then I hear a noise, like a door is being slammed. Without explaining, I dash off toward the station. Wyn crashes after me. Once I reach the site, I hide in a bush at the edge of the clearing. Watching.

Panting, Wyn squats next to me and hits my arm. "Thanks for the warning."

With one finger to my lips, I poke him. "Sshhh. I heard someone."

"Well, it can't be those guys you were talking about. They're still locked up."

We both peer over the bushes at the crooked station. Something's different, but I can't tell what. I signal Wyn to follow, but he shakes his head in disagreement. He points to the space next to him, telling me to stay put.

Ignoring his protest, I emerge from the bushes and slowly approach the building. Scanning the dusty earth, my eyes hone in on some faint parallel lines, resembling rake marks. I point them out to Wyn, but he only shrugs. Clueless.

Something draws my attention to the fire pit. It's empty. No old ashes. No charred sticks. Nothing but a circle of small boulders. I motion to Wyn again, trying to hint that something is wrong. Again, he appears clueless. Continuing up the steps, I stop in front of the rickety door.

Wyn bumps into me from behind.

I glare at him and point to a window without saying anything.

He peeks in and blurts out. "There's no one in there."

Hissing, I struggle to keep my own voice low. "Sshhhhh! You'd be an awful Indian. Tommy would be very disappointed."

He waves me off. "Whatever. Why are we sneaking around acting as if we're behind enemy lines? We're alone."

"You can never be too safe. Wait until you see how messed up this place is." I push open the door with both hands and step inside. Particles of dust bounce around in the streams of sunlight. My breath catches in my throat. The inside is perfectly clean, untouched.

The same parallel lines from outside mark the floors.

No mess. No cans. Nothing. The place is spotless.

Wyn stretches his lower back. "Boy, if this is a mess, what do you call your room? A disaster area?"

I ignore him. "I can't believe it. Everything's clean."

He strolls around the inside, inspecting drawers and cupboards. "Maybe Les did it."

Shaking my head, I inspect the room for tracks. For a sign telling me who was here. "No. Les told me he hasn't been up here. Besides, how would he get out here before us? And why would he clean up? His office is a pig sty." Then Simon pops into my mind. "Oh no!"

Before Wyn can stop me, I bolt out of the station and run in the direction of the dead carcass. Searching the weeds. Please let him be there. It's the only evidence I have against these guys.

Wyn thunders after me, pounding down the steps like an elephant. "G! Wait!"

Hopefully, whoever was here is long gone because Wyn's lack of silence is astounding. If we were in a war, he'd have to be sacrificed first or we'd both be dead. I approach the area where I first found Simon. I stomp my foot and yell at the world. "Damn it!" There's no carcass. Only a slightly mashed area of grass. I hunt around for tufts of hair, blood anything, but the brief rain shower from earlier must have erased anything left behind.

Wyn huffs up next to me and bends over with his hands on his knees, out of breath. "What's wrong?"

All my stealthness goes out the window. I speak loudly so anyone hiding around me can hear. "Everything that might have gotten Carl to take me seriously is gone." I sweep the area looking for any signs of heel digs or that something was dragged out of here.

He glances around. "You're sure it was here?"

I shove him away with both hands. "Do you think I'm mental?"

He pushes my shoulder with one arm. "First of all, I *know* you're mental. Second of all, chill out, ya woodland freak. I only meant, are you sure this is the *area*? What's gotten into you lately?"

My hands automatically wipe across my cheeks as if erasing any tears before they even fall. I want to scream, wishing I could curl up in the weeds and let them grow over me. "I can't seem to catch a break, and time is ticking by. Now we don't have any evidence so Carl's going to let those guys out."

He cups my neck and lifts my chin with both of his thumbs. "I don't know what to say, G. There's nothing here."

"You don't believe me."

Studying his eyes, it dawns on me how much they resemble stormy skies with a high chance of rain. "I believe you saw something horrible and I'll try to help you figure this out. No matter what it is. I promise."

I nod as helplessness fills my body. I can tell Wyn is losing faith in me. I see it in his face. Hear it in his voice. He strokes my face and stares at my lips. For a brief second, I want him to kiss me. To replace the pain in my gut with something sweet and nice. Tell me everything's going to be all right. That Dad's going to be okay. That I can go back to being the carefree girl I was before this mess happened.

But the fleeting moment—whatever it was—drifts away. I collapse into Wyn and hide my face in his neck, now sweaty and dirty.

He pecks the top of my head. "It's getting dark. We need to head back. There's a long hike ahead of us. One I'm not too thrilled about."

"Okay." I hand him my flashlight and trail several steps behind him. A rising half moon provides little light. Without uttering a word, we hike back through the columns of spruce, fir, and beech trees.

There's nothing to say.

After all the extensive hiking I've done today, my feet and legs grow angrier with every step. My exhausted body's heavy, making it feel as if I'm sleep walking. With each step, I feel heavier and heavier, anchored to the earth by fatique, sadness, and confusion. I think about the ransacked station. Am I really making something out of nothing? *Am I just seeing what I want to see?*

A rotting oak tree on the side of the path catches my eye. I touch my finger to the long chipped sections of the bark. Something hit it hard. Marked it for life.

Something like a bullet.

I scan the area for shells or human tracks, but only find a few broken limbs and flattened grass. When I part the branches with my hands, a faint signature print reveals itself. The edges of the track cave in when I brush them lightly. Definitely fresh.

A smile touches my lips.

I'm not a total nut job nor a dramatic teen. Someone was here. I take out my camera and take pictures of the boot print. Wyn calls my name from a distance. I quickly smear away the print with my hand, erasing a page in the story of this track. He doesn't believe me anyway. Why waste my breath? He'll probably question it like he does everything else.

I stand up just as he walks comes around the bend. "Did you find something?"

Sweat weaves down my back as I wipe my hands on my pants. "Nothing important."

"Let's go then. I'm over this place. It's too spooky." He stumbles off into the dim light until his shadow blends into the outline of the trees.

Trailing behind, I can't help but wonder who would clean up so fast and how.

03

On the way home, the wind whips across my face, stinging my eyes. When I pull into Wyn's driveway, his mom waves at us through the kitchen window.

Wyn dismounts. "You want to come in for dinner? We can call Carl together."

To avoid mumbling through the shield, I remove my helmet. "Can you just tell him? He won't yell at you."

"Sure."

I gaze over his head at the mountains spiking in the distance. "Thanks." Wyn nods and unexpectedly leans down. His face is only a few inches from mine. I panic and turn away. If I go down this road, there's no turning back, and this time I could just lose the only friend I have. "I better get home."

He pecks my cheek and steps up onto the curb. "See yah later, Little Miss Independent."

I rebuckle my helmet. "I owe you one."

"Shoot, you owe me more than that." He shoves his hands into his pockets and winks. "I'm sure I can think of something."

"Don't hurt yourself." I drive away, smiling. As I round the corner, the spot on my cheek where Wyn's lips briefly visited still tingles. I can almost still feel him sitting behind me.

By the time I get home, it's pitch dark outside and Mom's still MIA. Shocking. I grab a snack and run upstairs, anxious to Google the names listed on Dad's citation. Seems like forever since I found them, yet it was only this morning. I wait for my computer, aka Munster, to boot up. Nine minutes and fourteen seconds later, the Google search bar appears. I type in Billy's name, *William Barrett*. Chewing my thumbnail, I beg the screen for results. Nothing pops up. Poor Billy. If you can't be Googled these days, you aren't anybody important.

My fingers peck the keys for *Alfred Smith* and wait another two minutes and fourteen seconds for results. This time, a few hits pop up. Skimming through the links and images, I click on a picture taken at a Tennessee hunting club party.

It's Al.

I stare at the picture, almost seems as if he's staring right back at me. I quickly close the file and page through the other articles. One in patricular catches my eye.

Tennessee man fined. Hunting privileges suspended.

Townsend, Tenn. A local judge has suspended the hunting privileges of a man who pleaded innocent to a felony charge of bear poaching.

Federal wildlife agents arrested Alfred Smith in December after receiving a tip that he was hunting and killing game out of season while using illegal weapons and forbidden trapping equipment.

He was charged by Game Warden Will Cameron for six counts of poaching and multiple counts of commercialization of wildlife.

Sitting back, I put my feet up. Just as I suspected, Al's been in trouble before. After he did some time, he must've moved to North Carolina and started hunting again. Once an illegal hunter, always one. Dad probably busted him and issued a citation for killing off season. Maybe he ran into Al on that last day. Al knew he'd have serious jail time with a third offense.

Makes me wonder why Carl can't keep him in custody longer. Surely he's seen this article. One felony should be enough to book him.

In my notebook, I log a few unanswered questions: *Who was at Station 19? What is Sidehill? Why are Billy and Al killing bears for no reason? And, most importantly, what did they do with Dad?*

I sit back and cup my head with my hands. What now? More waiting. I glance around the room, trying to figure out my next step.

Then I spot my camera on the table and jolt to life.

The pictures! How could I have forgotten those. Maybe I can find a match.

My heart races with anticipation as I upload all the photos I've taken over the last couple of weeks to my computer. Scanning through them, I print off the picture of the print by Al's truck and the other photo I snapped up at Station 19. I study each one by zooming in on the tread, comparing them.

They don't appear to be the same.

I flop onto my bed and sigh. Thought for sure the one at Station 19 would match one the ones by Al's truck. Another dead end. There's got to be another way.

Something Wyn said pops in my head. About the place in Cherokee that sells custom boots.

After Googling it, I find out Mama Sue's place isn't open tomorrow so I make a plan to visit first thing Monday morning.

Maybe she can help.

Survival Skill #24

A fire is essential to wilderness survival, but it can also be the key to keeping positive and calm.

After a sleepless night, Wyn texts me first thing the next morning to inform me Al and Billy are still in custody and that Carl isn't returning from his trip until later. Good news for me. But then if Al and Billy are still locked up, who was sneaking around Station 19? My head reels with twisted information, not knowing what is true or real anymore. Maybe Les was right about the woods messing with my brain. But being stuck indoors isn't helping my mental state either.

No matter where I go, the walls seem to be closing in on me.

All day, I hide in my room until Mom finally heads into work. I try to piddle around the house for a while but eventually I just can't take the boredom anymore. The woods are safe now that Al and Billy are behind bars, and it's obvious nothing's going to happen in Dad's case until Carl gets back.

I need to escape the shrinking walls of my house and meet Mo at Bear Creek. Even if I'm a little early, I can just fish until Mo gets there.

If he even shows. I wouldn't blame him for not coming, considering how I acted the other night.

I spend the whole afternoon fishing alone. The woods are alive and singing while the sun is warm and comforting. Once I'm done, I sit cross-legged on the embankment and wait for Mo as I watch the water roll by. The sun starts to droop behind the trees, spraying a yellowish glow across the water. A barred owl announces the day's retreat, and the river babbles back. In the forest, night comes quicker than anywhere else.

My mind wanders. The popping noises, Al and Billy, the dead bear, the citation, and now, the station. It's all connected. But how? I pluck a purple hepatica and weave a bracelet along with a matching head wreath. Braiding makes me realize how three equally separate things can easily be interwoven. It's a matter of putting them together in the right way.

When it's finished, I place the flower wreath on my head. "I now crown you, Grace, Idiot of the Forest."

A voice behind me replies, "Every queen needs a king, no?"

I spin around and jerk the flowery crown off my head. No matter my effort, being cool isn't coming so naturally to me lately.

Mo sits on top of a boulder, chewing a piece of grass. His eyes smile without requiring his face to follow. "Didn't think you were coming."

He was thinking about me? I shrug it off. "Why? Were you worried?"

"More disappointed. Figured I scared you off."

I relish in his smooth accent as it washes over me. "I don't get frightened off that easily."

"So you *say.*" He tilts his head toward the river. "Fancy fishing?"

I pretend my nerves aren't bouncing around inside like a spaz on a pogo stick. "Actually, I want to show you something. If that's okay."

Mo raises his eyebrows. "Sounds mysterious."

"You're not the only one who knows cool places around here."

He throws his bag over one shoulder. "Didn't know it was a contest."

I nip at my cuticle. "Do you want to see it or not?"

He beams, causing my stomach to do a pirouette. I gnaw on my bottom lip as he glides toward me. He motions me to walk in front of him. "After you, blossom."

The nickname makes me beam like a little girl. I walk past him, fighting the magnet threatening to pull us closer together.

As I lead him through the vivid green forest along a rocky path, I can't help but wonder if he's looking at it right now. When I walk over a log, Mo presses his hand on the small of my back to steady me. The gesture sends my heart skating. The whole time, I pretend to be cool as an ice cube.

Eventually, I stop in front of a steep rocky wall and point up. "Think you can climb this?"

Mo shields his eyes and looks up at the ridge. "Does an Englishman drink tea?"

I motion to him. "Age before beauty."

He doesn't hesitate and quickly scales the face of the wall with ease. I crawl up behind him, gripping the tiny ledges with my fingertips. Right when I reach the edge, Mo holds out his hand.

I shake my head. "No, thanks. I can do it."

He smiles at me. "You know, it's okay to accept help sometimes. Doesn't mean you're weak or anything."

Man, this guy nails my psyche better than Dr. Head. "Fine. I'll let you this one time, but only because you *begged* me." I clasp his hand and allow myself to be swept up by him.

The flat ridge overlooks a deep canyon unobstructed by trees. The sky stretches out before us, creating a ceiling painted with the grey of a pending rain mixed with the pink of a long-setting sun. The stars peek through the blazing sky and a teasing wind flicks the back of my hair.

Mo's voice is breathy. "Brilliant."

I smile. "Told yah."

I suddenly realize we are still holding hands. The moisture between our palms keeps my hand cool. It seems embarrassingly personal to share sweat. We stand close together. Wait, am I dreaming? I subtly pinch my thigh with my other hand and wince.

Nope, this is real all right.

As we clutch hands, the crimson sun dips slowly behind the green curtain of treetops. Bands of orange, red, and pink transform into a blueish gray as the fading light casts an odd-shaped shadow over the mountain narrows. Silhouettes of bats flutter and zing across the sky, feeding on unsuspecting insects.

The air turns a bit cooler. I don't want to break our connection, but I do want to show him I can take care of myself.

I let my hand slip out of his. "I'll start a fire." I gather sticks together and tuck clumps of dry moss under the miniature twig teepee. Using my flint, I set off a few sparks until a small fire takes hold of the mound. Then I blow lightly until the flames dance out from under the twigs.

Mo moves closer. "Wow, a cute girl and a warm fire? Who could ask for more."

My face heats up, and I'm not sure if it's from the flames or the compliment. I poke at the fire with a branch. Sparks twitter in the air and flit off into the darkening night.

He leans back against a tree with his hands behind his head. "See, I'm fine letting a girl take care of me."

"I bet you are."

He exhales and relaxes his whole body. A silly smirk on his face. "How'd you find this place?"

I snap a few twigs in half and toss them onto the fire. "I come up here sometimes to clear my head."

Mo pats the seat next to him. "To think about your dad?"

I twirl the bracelet on my wrist. "Among other things."

"You want to talk about him?"

I sit next to him, not too close, and check him out in the orange light. Slivers of shadows flicker across his face. "Not really."

He draws back the drape of hair hiding my face and tucks it behind my ear. "We haven't really talked about him since you told me about everything. You still worried about those noises?"

"Yes. And I found a dead bear."

Mo stares at the fire. "That's bad? Don't people hunt up here?"

"It's not bear season. That makes it illegal." My mind flashes to the last time I saw Simon ambling away from me. Never thought it would be the last time. "It was Simon. The bear I told you about the other day when we were fishing."

His mouth arches downward. "Crumbs. Poor sod. I know he was special to you."

"Yeah, well. I'm used to losing things."

He leans in and squeezes my hand. "Don't say that, blossom. I'm here."

I stare out at the night sky. "I thought those guys from the other day did it, but evidently they're in custody."

He tilts his head a bit, the light highlighting the crinkling lines curving around his eyes. "So they got arrested?"

I fill him in on my conversation with Les and how he brought the two guys in for questioning. "But don't worry, I didn't mention you."

He rests his chin in his palm. "Did you tell your mum about everything?"

My body tenses at the question. Jabbing the logs with a stick, I focus my eyes on the fire. "No. She's pretty much a total basket case right now anyway."

"Can't blame her really. But I'm sure she'd want to know what's going on with you."

"I'm fine on my own." I steal another glance at him.

"Of course you are." He smiles, sending a light feather drifting along the insides of my belly. His eyes dig into my soul, searching for the real story.

"What is *your* mom like?"

Mo shifts to the side a tad until our legs aren't touching anymore and his shoulders slump so slightly that most people might not notice. But I do. "You mean, what *was* she like?"

I don't know what to say. He hasn't talked much about his family until now.

He closes his eyes then clears his throat. "My mum passed away a few years ago." His voice sounds a bit detached. Flat. A little rehearsed.

"I'm sorry. I had no idea." Suddenly, I want to crawl into his arms and make him feel better. Instead, I lightly touch his elbow. Little zings of electricity buzz through my fingers. "I shouldn't have brought it up," I whisper.

He shakes his head and pats my hand. "Don't be daft. You asked a simple question." Sadness engulfs his dark eyes as he inhales a deep breath. "My mum died of cancer—" He abruptly stops, making me think the story's gotten all tangled up in his throat. Eventually, he breathes in deep as if he's just plunged into freezing water. "She was an American. My parents met when she went to school in England. Several years ago, after she was diagnosed with cancer, she wanted to come back and be with her family. So my dad got a job and moved my sister and I over here. Mum died less than a year later."

"I'm sorry."

He drops his head. "Me too."

At the risk of appearing totally cheesy, I reach into my pocket and pull out the flower bracelet I made by the river. "Here, this is for you."

Mo smirks. "I think I fancy the crown more."

I laugh. "No way! You gotta work up to that one."

He pats his pants. "I want to give you something too."

"You don't have to do that."

"I want to." He reaches into his pocket and pulls out a small velvet pouch. He opens the drawstrings and pours a jagged light-green rock into his hand. "Here." He places the stone in my palm and curls my fingers over it.

I study the jade stone, admiring its sparkle and smoothness. "What is it?"

"Alexandrite. Named after Alexander II. Stands for grace and purity. Supposedly, when a person carries this stone, they remember things aren't always what they seem and are encouraged to seek the truth. I want you to have it. My mum gave it to me."

I try to return it. "I can't take this from you. It's too special."

He places two fingers over my lips and stops me from saying anything. "So are you."

I can taste the salt on his fingertips. Part of me wants to melt into him. Like the chocolate in a freshly made s'more. The other part wants to hide deep into the mountains, away from the emotions he's stirring up. I don't know how or why, but this guy makes me want to lose control.

"Grace?" Mo lifts my chin and runs a finger down my neck. His eyes dart back and forth between mine. I can't move because my body has become part of the rock I'm sitting on. He cups my face with his strong hands and stops an inch away from my lips. "May I kiss you?"

My first thought is, *It's about time!* I search Mo's eyes for a sign this might be a joke. They reveal nothing but kindness. I nod because I can't really say anything for fear of ruining the moment. He loops his arms around my waist and pulls me closer.

Anticipation floods my senses and, suddenly, all I hear is the erratic rhythm of my own breath.

His lips attack mine with such force, mine forget to fight back.

Survival Skill #25

*No matter the hemisphere,
the positions of stars can provide directions.*

A surge of warmth zips through my veins as if someone has shocked my body back to life after my heart has ceased beating. My hands shake and my knees wobble a little. Mo kisses my lips, one at a time. It's the kiss I've always wondered if I'd ever receive. The kind where everything fits together perfectly like a little puzzle. No awkward moments or fumbling. And only once do I think of Wyn. How different this kiss is. Then the memory slips away into the abyss of my brain. Like Mo's kiss erased everything going on in my head. Especially anything about Wyn.

I interwine my hands behind his neck as his mouth cradles my top lip. My heart cracks open and I feel a small part of myself let go. I'm not sure how much time passes but, eventually, he pulls away. I hover for a minute with my lips slightly puckered and eyes still closed. Hoping he'll kiss me again.

Mo clears his throat. "You see that cluster of stars?"

Wait a minute! Is my brain on kissing while his is on star gazing? I can still feel the sensation of his lips on mine but pretend to be uber-interested in astronomy. "Which ones?"

"Over there. Northwest from the moon."

"Says the cute compass."

He points up. "Seriously, do you see it?"

I squint at the small polka dots decorating the black canvas stretched above us. "Yeah, I think so. What is it?"

"Scorpius. Some say Orion fled from the scorpion by swimming across the ocean to see his lover, Athena. Apollo, the son of Zeus, didn't much care for Orion. So he tricked Athena.

In a challenge, he dared her to shoot an arrow at a black shape in the water. Athena loved competition so she hit the target and unknowingly killed her one true love, Orion. Poor sod."

"Poor Athena."

Mo stares up at the sky. "Can you imagine? Being responsible for the death of someone you love?"

I think about Dad. "Sometimes I feel that way."

Mo hugs me but doesn't push me to reveal anymore. I assume he knows how hard that was for me to admit. I make a conscious effort not to pull away. "How do you know about stars?"

He clears his throat. "My dad was in the United Kingdom Special Forces. Spent a lot of time in the woods with him. The stars were his compass."

"Does he love rocks too?"

Mo laughs unexpectedly. A puff of air tickles my forehead. "No, but he would listen to me go on about them for hours. When I was little, we spent a lot of time hiking in England's Lake District. I'd collect rocks, and my dad always helped me cart them home so I could identify them."

"Are you guys close?"

"Very."

"How does he feel about you being out here? He must miss you."

Mo doesn't answer for a very long time. Once he finally speaks, his voice is scratchy. "If you don't mind, I'd rather not discuss him right now."

"Sure, no problem." I rake my fingers through his hair.

He sweeps my bangs to one side and kisses my forehead. "We better get you back, blossom. It's getting late."

I don't protest even though I'm disappointed the night is ending. The whole hike back, I clutch onto Mo. Even though his hand is strong and callused, his touch is soft and reassuring. In the humid weather, my face has frozen into a permanent, goofy grin.

"You look happy."

I try to pull my face down and look less giddy. "Why do you say that?"

"The cheeky grin gives you away. Don't worry, I won't tell anyone," he says, his voice low and his accent mesmerizing. "Let's meet again tomorrow."

Even though I want to, I've already decided to head into Cherokee to find out more about the boot treads in those pictures. "I can't. I have stuff to do."

Mo tilts his head. "Anything I can help with?"

I shake my head. "I wish."

"Well, if you change your mind, I'll be at the same place. Late afternoon." Mo leans in and grazes my mouth with his lips. He sees me grin again and points at my mouth. "There it is again. You're smiling. What are you so chuffed about?"

My cheeks ache a little and I try to be serious. "Nothing."

Everything.

Later, as Luci and I zigzag along the windy road, I replay the night in my head and lick my lips where Mo kissed me. *I can't believe this is happening to me. Now.*

But as usual, questions begin chipping away at my happy thoughts.

What if this guy breaks my heart? What if he moves back to England?

I notice my speedometer and slow down a bit.

Maybe I'm going too fast. Then again, what if I'm holding back too much?

My toe of my shoe presses down the gas pedal and I fly home all the way home.

Survival Skill #26

Tracks, especially human prints, lose their sharp edges over time due to weather conditions.

First thing Monday morning, I get up and head out before Mom even wakes up. Mama Sue's place is the only store within a hundred miles that makes custom hiking boots. So maybe she can help me figure out where these prints came from.

After cutting through the town of Cherokee, I turn off the main road and onto Hwy 1410. The crowds are already lining up outside Cherokee's Bear Park, waiting to "experience nature up close and personal."

When I realize the store is only a few doors down from the bear pit attraction, a sick feeling ignites in my belly. I hate this place. People hitting animals with rotten apples. Bears living in cement corners without so much as a blade of grass in sight. Obese cubs begging for crappy food.

Stretching along the beautiful Oconaluftee River, the bear park is massive, offering a variety of bear species, a gem mine, a tubing center, a shooting range, and an indoor mall. For reasons I still don't understand, the park isn't subject to any national bear laws. Keeping animals in an unnatural habitat with these awful conditions is not only disrespectful to nature, but it goes against everything Native Americans represent.

I park and notice Wyn has already called twice and texted once. I turn my phone off to avoid him. The more I hang out with Mo, the more I find myself hiding from Wyn. I'm stuck between wanting to tell him what's going on and not hurting him. A part of me is afraid I'll lose him again too.

I head toward the shop, keeping my face down. I'm not supposed to be here. Chief Reed banned Dad and me from the reservation last year because of our persistent protesting. Hopefully, the chief isn't around today.

As I walk by the reinforced walls of the complex, I hear snippets of the things going on behind the scenes. Bears groaning, kids screeching, and people shouting, "Bear! Bear!" Don't those people see how unhappy the bears are? Maybe if they understood the animal's natural behavior, they'd be more appalled. What's worse is that the chief doesn't see it either. Or doesn't care.

At last, I reach Mama' Sue's. The scent of leather wafts through the store, its walls lined with shoes: cowboy boots, hiking boots, and wellies. A few clothing rounds break up the large, open space, displaying outdoor wear for fishing, hiking, and camping.

Mama Sue is helping a customer in the back. Dad always liked Sue, called her "Mama Grizzly." From what he said, the woman is hardcore and tough as a rhino's horn. Once, after being attacked by a bear, she crawled back to her cabin and sewed up her own head before calling for help.

Everyone knows Mama Sue doesn't fool around.

As I wait for her to finish, I browse the store. A few articles about her attack hang on the wall next to a large bear hide. I'm guessing Mama Sue got her revenge after all. I lean in to read one about how she used to live so remotely that she could only provide her address by giving the latitude and longitude.

"Well, hello, young lady. How can I help you?"

The scruff voice startles me. I spin around and face Mama Grizzly. She's wearing a leather river hat, chambray shirt, and black jeans. Her kinky brownish-gray hair is braided and hanging down to her waist. She crosses her arms. "Well? Speak up, child. I don't have all day. Come to think of it, at my age, I probably don't have much longer *at all*." She coughs then smiles. "That means, you had better ask me something now. Before it's too late."

I make a point not to stare too long at the three deep scars running down her left cheek. "You're Mama Sue?" Dumb question, I must be nervous.

She grips the blue spectacles hanging from a chain and balances them on the end of her pointy nose. "Maybe. Who wants to know?"

If she can take down a four-hundred-pound bear, I can only imagine what she could do to the average sixteen year old. My voice cracks. "I'm Grace Wells, and I wanted —"

She cuts me off. "Grace Wells! Good Lordy. As in Joe's daughter?"

"The one and only."

"My. My. Look how much you've grown!" Her face brightens. She yanks me into a bear hug with a vice grip that shows exactly how strong she really is. "Why, you look just like your daddy." She wraps one arm around my shoulders and leads me in front of a photo hanging on the wall. She points to the picture of her and Dad. "He was a fine man."

All I hear is the past tense. The room tilts a little bit, and for a second, I feel like I'm going to pass out. I center myself and can't help but tug on the top of my t-shirt, hoping to stretch the collar to keep it from squeezing my throat. "Yes … he *is*."

Her eyes soften as she nods slowly. "Is. Was. All the same to the big man upstairs." We look in each other's eyes for a second.

I prickle. "Well, it's not the same to me."

She pats my shoulder and smirks. "I see that. You know, you're spunky. Like Joe. I like that. Now, why are you here? You must have come for something other than nothing."

I slide the pictures out of my back pocket. "I want to know if you can tell what kind of boots made these prints."

"Honey, do you know how many boots are out there? What makes you think I would know one from the other?"

I point outside. "Sign says, *We know boots*. I assume 'we' is *you*. Unless it's false advertising. Which I doubt. Plus Dad always says you're the best."

Mama Sue busts out laughing. "You got guts and a sense of humor. Good for you." She takes the pictures from me and studies the one I found by Al's truck. She walks over to the wall and inspects the treads of a few shoes. "Hm. This one here is probably a High Tec. Size 10. I can tell by the tread. Pretty common around here." She points to a larger print. "However, this bigger one looks custom made. Probably a size 11."

I study the prints over her shoulder. The smaller one must be Billy's and the custom one has to be Al's. I summarize what's she's said to be sure I understand. "So these are definitely from two different boots?"

Mama Sue nods once. "That's what I said."

I stare at the custom one. "Has anyone been in here recently for custom-made boots?"

She scoffs. "A few. But none of these are mine."

The knots in my stomach form a noose around my gut and cinch tighter. "How do you know?"

"Most boot makers I know mark their work with a signature tread." She holds up a shoe. "This is mine. I try to do an S in the pattern. This one looks to have a couple notches in the heel."

I hold up the picture from Station 19 and pray her assessment is different than mine. "What about this one? Do these prints match either one of those?"

She studies the photo for barely a second. "Nope. This one's different."

I sigh in defeat. Just as I feared. Why can't anything be easy? If these are all different, who was the person at Station 19 that day?

Mama Sue takes off her glasses and studies me for a minute. "I know most of the people who do custom boots around these parts. Why don't you let me keep these photos, and I'll do some digging for you?"

I only hesitate a second. If Dad trusts her, so can I. After making copies of the pictures for Mama Sue and leaving her my cell number, I leave the air-conditioned store, but not before sneaking a peak at the photo of my dad.

Outside, the heat attacks my skin and fills my lungs with hot air. This time, I cross the street and walk in the shade on the opposite side of the bear pits.

I shuffle along the sidewalk, staring at my feet. I'm so close to figuring this thing out, but something is sitting just beyond my mind's grasp. Think, think.

Just as I round the corner, I smack right into a man.

A deep voice chastises me. "What the hell are you doing on my reservation?"

I shield my eyes and look up to find Chief Reed staring down at me. Something tells me to note specific details about him in my head. Dressed in faded jeans and a white button-down shirt, he plays with a Native American bolo tie made of braided leather, silver, and turquoise beads dangling from his neck.

I stutter at first, trying to come up with a good explanation. "Visiting Mama Sue." I back up a few steps to put some distance between us and collect my wavering confidence. "Besides, just because you ask me not to come here, doesn't mean you scare me away from trying to close these bear pits."

His face remains stoic, his eyes black and menacing. "I didn't *ask*, I forbade it. Do you want to get arrested?"

I scoff. "You can't arrest me."

He plays with his braid. "The rules are different here on my reservation. You may not know that, but your dad sure did."

My lip quivers. "What's that supposed to mean?"

Chief Reed shrugs. "He knew the consequences of hanging out around here. You should too."

I grit my teeth. "What are you saying? Did you have something to do with my dad going missing?"

"Me? Why would you say that?"

I cross my arms to hide my shaking hands. "My dad was all over you about those bears. Was close to shutting you down, which would cost you millions of dollars in profits."

"Those bears are well taken care of."

I wrinkle my nose. "Wow, you're either really dumb, lying to yourself, or just plain evil. Last year, you wrote in your book 'respect of nature, the animals, the winged ones, and every living creature is honored as demonstrating sacredness.' By the way, I didn't buy it. Just saw it at the bookstore. Wouldn't give you a dime; I know where it all goes." I point to the bear pit.

Chief Reed acts all innocent, but I see a smile hiding behind his eyes. His amusement frustrates me but I try to hold back from saying anything. "On the reservation, accusing a Tribal Council official could be considered a crime."

"You can't do that. Free speech."

He grabs my arm and leans in with a fake smile on his face as to not attract attention. "On my reservation, I can do what I please." He taps his finger on my forehead. "The sooner you get that into your sweet little head, the safer you'll be. Now get out of here," he sneers and winks, "before you disappear too."

Chief Reed walks off and shakes some hands of a few tourists. I'm left standing alone, steaming, with my mouth hanging open. Wishing more than anything I could throw his butt in a cement pit and toss tomatoes at his head.

He looks back over his shoulder and waves goodbye.

Here I am, stuck on Al. But maybe there's a suspect I haven't considered yet.

Chief Reed.

Survival Skill #27

Proper navigation consists of three distinct stages: orientation, navigation, and route finding.

𝕢 spend the rest of the morning and early afternoon, searching for more evidence. As usual, no finds. I pick up my rod and wade into the water to wait for Mo. As I cast, I allow some of my frustrations to drift away in the water's ebb. Eventually, my body relaxes and Mo's smile creeps in.

Goosebumps prickle my arms as I picture our first kiss. Again. I'm so caught up in my daydreaming that my line gets caught in a tree.

"Hello, blossom," a low voice says.

I jump. "Why do you always do that?" I spin around to find him perched on top of a large boulder.

He's lying on his back with both hands behind his head and one knee propped up. Perfect and poised. Like some kind of lazy nature God.

My cheeks blaze in embarrassment, wondering if he can hear my thoughts. "How long have you been watching me?" I can't see his eyes through the dark sunglasses.

"Long enough."

"Why didn't you say anything?"

"I was afraid to."

"Very funny."

"Actually, I just fancy watching a pretty girl fish. Is that a crime?" He smiles and motions to my line, still dangling from a limb above. "You trapped?"

I want to say, *You have no idea.* Instead, I smile. "Not quite." I jerk my rod and the line slumps out of the tree, snaking around me. I wade through the rippling current toward the embankment. "Wanna join me?"

Mo pushes his sunglasses up on his forehead. "What happened to *stranger danger*?"

"I think we've made progress."

"Well, how can I refuse then?"

I skip across a few slimy rocks until my foot slides out from under me. I attempt to recover, but this time, I lose the battle and timber into the shallow stream. A bit shocked, I roll into a sitting position and wipe my face with my shirt, hoping the redness washes off with it.

I'm an idiot.

Mo bends over me with a big grin strung across his face. "Bloody hell, are you all right?" He stretches out his hand to help and, this time, I accept it.

Only instead of pulling up, I yank on his arm, catching him totally off guard.

A look of shock replaces his blazing smile as he tumbles into the river. He catches himself with his hands, but not before his face smacks the water. I immediately crack up. It feels good to laugh again. Like really laugh.

Mo springs to his feet in a nanosecond and plasters on an I'm-going-to-get-you expression. He cups his hands together and splashes me, soaking the small part of me that's still dry. I fight back with a fury, kicking water in his face. At this point, we're both hysterical. When I see my chance, I slop off through the water, lifting my legs high for speed.

Mo chases after me.

Screaming, I try to escape, but he tackles me. As I scramble to get away, he clutches onto my ankle and pulls me backwards. Rolling over, I fight him by squirting water in his face.

Instead of splashing back, he holds down my hands and kisses me. I feel as if I'm gliding on top of the river like a canoe. The water sloshes in my ears. We kiss for several long minutes before parting.

I frown. "I think that was cheating."

"All's fair in love and water war. Couldn't let myself be brought down by a girl again." Deep crinkles spray the corners of his eyes. Water droplets fall off his dark hair and land on my lips. "Your eyes are the same color as the Alexandrite I gave you."

I tilt my head back and laugh. "Are you serious? That's your line! Wait, are they twinkling like the stars too?"

He smirks. "How come every time I give you a compliment, you make a joke?"

Because I'm scared to death? "Because I'm naturally funny?"

He doesn't bite. "Maybe you're afraid of something."

I shift uncomfortably at his insight. "Of what? You? Hardly."

Mo pecks my forehead. "No, not me. Of *us*."

Us? Are Mo and I an "us"? A "we"? My face singes. For once, I can't come up with a clever retort.

He opens his mouth as if he's going to speak but stops short. "What is it?"

He props his butt on his heels. "Nothing."

"You were going to say something." Mo doesn't respond. Instead, he slicks back his wet hair and pulls his soaked shirt away from his toned chest, making a sucking sound. I click my lips. "Now who's pushing who away?"

Mo holds out both hands and lifts me to my feet. Our wet bodies press against each other. He wraps his strong arms around me. "Is this close enough?"

I shrug. "Not quite."

He pecks me on the lips. "Come on, then."

"Where to?"

Mo tosses his backpack over one shoulder. "To my place."

"Out here? Isn't that a little strange?"

He shrugs like he's never thought about it before. "I don't think so. I like it. It'd be harder to hike in everyday and find samples. Why not just enjoy it before my semester starts up again?"

"Good point." I try not to appear too excited at the thought of heading off into the woods with him. "But I'm all wet."

"Don't worry, there's no dress code. I'll get us warm. Plus I owe you some home cooking."

I bite back another protest and follow him up the embankment. After gathering our things, we trek deep into the woods scattered with shadows dancing in the dimming light. The further we go, the thinner the path and the thicker the foliage. The sun is still setting in the sky, but down on the forest floor, it's already night time, making it hard to follow his outline.

"Mo? Where are you?" I whisper.

A beam of light breaks through the trees a few yards ahead. "I'm over here."

I steer in his direction, with my hands out in front, protecting my face from protruding branches and creepy spider webs. I wince as a wiry branch snatches onto a clump of my hair and rips several strands at the root.

Up ahead, an arching line of light sweeps across the ground and reflects off something shiny to my right. "Hey. Shine the light over here a second. I want to see something."

Mo doesn't answer.

Squatting down, I press the faint LED light on my watch. Something glimmers from under a pile of wet leaves. I brush my hand along the ground until my fingers touch something hard and cold. I hold up the shiny object, trying to make it out in the glow of my watch. Too dim. I try to note the coordinates too even thought it's hard to see.

"Mo, I need your flashlight." He doesn't answer so I stuff the object into my pocket. "Mo?"

I try to focus on anything in front of me, hoping my eyes will adjust. The woods grow quiet. My heart flutters.

Then out of nowhere, someone grabs my shoulder.

Survival Skill #28

The type of shelter needed depends on the equipment, terrain, and climate.

Directly in front of me, Mo flips on his light with it glowing under his chin. "Boo!"

I clutch my chest, checking to see if my heart has stopped or fallen out. I hit him with both hands in the chest. "Geez! You're lucky I didn't flip you over my shoulder."

"Come on. You knew it was me."

"Doesn't matter! Any time someone jumps out in the dark, it freaks you out."

"Sorry." He squeezes my hand. "Come on, my place is over here."

I stumble behind him as his boots crunch through the dead leaves.

He stops me with both hands and holds me still. "Stay here." I stand solo for a few seconds, watching the shadows move around me until a lantern offers a reassuring light. "Time to relax." Mo motions for me to sit down as he pokes a long stick into a heap of charred twigs.

Minutes later, twirling flames illuminate the area. It takes a few moments for my eyes to adjust before I notice his man-made, lean-to shelter. A roof, made of leaves, nestled between two tall trees. Under the shelter, a piece of black tarp stretches along the ground. A rolled-up, army green sleeping bag and a wool blanket rest on the artificial floor.

He catches me staring. "Fancy what I've done with the place?"

"You have great taste. I'd say a little country mixed with a dash of rustic."

He nods. "Spot on. That's exactly what I was going for."

I check out his sleeping quarters. "So no tent? This is where you stay—every night? Still seems a bit odd."

"That coming from a girl who talks to a cranky bike named Luci."

"Touché." I can't help but laugh, knowing he's so right.

"Besides, I told you. I'm on field study for school." Mo pours some water from his canteen into an iron pot and hangs it over the fire. "Cuppa tea?"

"Sure, but isn't that a little formal for a fire pit?"

"Nothing but the best for you, blossom."

A few minutes later, he pours the steaming liquid and hands me a stainless steel cup. I welcome the warmth between my hands. Even though it's the end of summer, the nights are growing cooler and being damp doesn't help. I shiver while sipping the hot liquid, the strong black tea trailing warmth through my body. Even though I'm more of hot cocoa kinda gal, the tea is surprisingly good.

Mo reaches into his duffle bag and pulls out a dry t-shirt.

I whine. "Hey, no fair! How come you get to be dry?"

"Bloody hell. Have some patience, woman." Mo strips off his wet shirt without any notice. A thin layer of moisture glistens on his ripped body. I ignore my urge to jump him and force my jaw to stay shut. Don't care who you are, gaping mouths are never sexy. I keep my eyes on him. If I look away now, it'll be obvious I'm uncomfortable. He slips both arms in the holes, before popping his head through the middle.

Then he tosses me a different shirt.

I don't move quickly enough to catch it so the shirt lands over my face. I frown under the cotton. After today, "graceless" will be my new middle name. I pluck the draping shirt off my head. "You could've warned me."

"Sorry." Mo pinches his lips together, stifling a laugh.

I smile, wondering if my face is as red as it feels. "Okay, maybe I'm not the most coordinated person." For some reason, around this guy, my brain won't send the right messages to the right place in time.

"Always? Or just with me."

Is this guy a mind reader or what? "Don't flatter yourself, mister." I smell his woodsy scent and fight the urge to bury my nose in the shirt like a bloodhound. Just as I go to change, I stop, realizing he's watching me. "Privacy, please."

Mo snaps his fingers in jest and spins around. "Can't blame a bloke for trying."

I peel off my damp t-shirt and slip into his dry, comfy one. A scent of smoked wood lingers in the cotton. I steal a quick sniff and hug myself, feeling protected by the thin layer of fabric. I tie a knot at the waist and rip the hairband out of my matted ponytail. I tousle my damp, stringy hair. "It's safe."

When Mo sees me, his mouth drops open. My heart sinks. Nothing sexy about wearing dirty pants, an oversized shirt with a bulging knot, and wet, moppy hair. He exhales. "You look smashing."

I wave him off. "Please, good thing it's dark. Must be the shirt."

He inches closer. "You look fabulous to me, shirt ..." He raises his eyebrows. "Or no shirt." He grins at his remark and cups my face. I drop my head back, inviting him in for another kiss. I want so much to be close and connected to him again, even if it's only for a few seconds.

Mo tilts his head to one side and kisses me. As his lips encircle mine, I hold the back of his neck tightly, forbidding even an inch of space to come between us. Don't want to give him enough room to pull away. His warm tongue sweeps across mine, teasing me to play. Mo's breathing quickens, and he wraps his fingers through my hair, tugging me closer. His heart pounds against my chest as our kiss intensifies.

A few seconds later, he steps back and composes himself.

I move closer. "What?"

"You hungry?"

Since he's stolen my breath away, I can only nod.

Mo begins cooking. He seems so comfortable in the woods. Not many people can be.

Something dawns on me. Maybe I've finally found someone just like me.

After enjoying a juicy dinner of fish cooked in foil and more tea, he shows me some of the rock samples he's collected. The night air makes me tired, and I yawn as he explains that granite is North Carolina's state rock.

Mo chuckles. "There's my clue to stop talking about rocks."

I shake my head. "I think it's North Carolina's cue to pick a more exciting rock. I mean, granite? Honestly. What about rubies or diamonds?"

"If it makes you feel better, emerald is quite abundant here as well." He massages my shoulders for a few seconds, causing me to yawn again. "Tired?"

"Relaxed."

"Come here then." He wraps a blanket around us. We cuddle as we stare up at the canopy of branches above us. Lightening bugs twinkle around us, like strands of blinking Christmas lights.

I nudge him with my elbow. "Thanks for the dinner. It was delish. You sure know your way around a fire."

A crimson glow from the campfire illuminates the side of his face. "Anything for you." Mo rolls onto his side, pulling me down with him, and gently plants little kisses all over my cheeks, throat, and nose, Little ripples swim along my arms. He teases my lips until I surrender. His tongue twirls through my mouth, searching for a dance partner.

Somewhere inside my head, I want to be consumed. To crawl inside Mo's body and hide from my life. Like a yolk tucked safely inside an eggshell. Surrounded, protected.

Without warning, he moves back a fraction of an inch, hovering over my lips, tickling them with his breath. He searches my face for something. "I know this sounds strange, but I'm falling for you, Grace."

How does he just throw that out there? No holding back. My heart pounds with excitement, fear, and disbelief all mixed in one. "It doesn't sound crazy at all. I feel the same way."

He traces one finger down my ribs, making me squirm. Then he puts a few inches of distance between us. "We should stop. Maybe it's time to get you back."

Before I can think of a response, I blurt out, "No!"

Mo's eyes widen. "Let me know how you really feel. No to stopping or no to going back?"

Could I be more obvious? Maybe I should back off too. "No. We probably should stop. But I don't want to leave." For the first time in a long time, I'm happy and don't want it to end.

Mo frowns, revealing deep creases in his forehead. "Is it a good idea for you to stay?"

"Best one I've had in a long time."

He kisses my forehead as I nuzzle my face into his neck. "What about your mum? Won't she worry about you being out all night without her permission?"

I pull aside the edge of his t-shirt collar and trace the contour of his shoulder with my lips as I talk. "I'm sixteen and, in case you've forgotten, you're only a year older than me. Besides, she's working a double so she won't be home until tomorrow morning. I'll get back before she does." Before he can talk me out of it, I roll him on top of me and entwine my legs through his.

A sharp pain shoots through my butt cheek.

I struggle to ignore it as he pecks my face with kisses, refusing to ruin the sweet moment. His moist lips brush back and forth across mine. The pain digs deeper into my tailbone, causing me to wiggle and groan in discomfort.

Mo lifts up into a push-up position. "Are you all right?"

I open my eyes. "Yeah. Why?"

"You appear to be in pain?"

"Don't worry about it." I pull him down closer. When he presses on top of me, I yelp. "Ouch."

This time he rolls off to one side. "I'd rather you be thinking of pleasurable thoughts than painful ones. What's wrong?"

Huffing, I blow my bangs in frustration. Only I could ruin a special moment. I feel on the ground underneath me, expecting to find a stone or stick.

Then I remember the shiny thing from the woods jammed down in my pocker. Totally slipped my mind. Mo does that to me.

Slipping my hand into the tight pocket of my pants, I grip the cylindrical object and hold it in front of the firelight.

I immediately jolt upright. "Holy crap!"

Mo peeks over my shoulder. "What is it?"

Survival Skill #29

*The silence and isolation of the wilderness
can play tricks on the mind.*

Ꟗ vault to my feet and hold my discovery up to the lantern for a better look. "It's a bullet."

"What do you mean?" Mo appears next to me and grabs the tiny brass cylinder. "Where'd you find this?"

I snatch it back and twirl the casing between my fingers. "In the woods on the way here. Whoever it belongs to must be close by."

Mo shakes his head. "Must be old. If some blokes were shooting around out here, I would have heard it."

"Do you know what kind it is?"

Mo studies the find. "Not a clue." He throws a rock into the fire.

"What's wrong? Did I say something to upset you?"

He stares at the sky as if he's collecting words from the heavens. "Blossom, I don't want you getting involved in whatever it is you're getting involved in." He faces me with his face stern. "This sounds dangerous, and I think you should stay out of it."

I turn away from him and cross my arms in front of me. "No way. If this has something to do with my dad's death…" My arms drop to my side, hanging like broken limbs. My breath jams in my throat, reminding me of the time when I was little and ate a whole jar of creamy peanut butter with nothing to wash it down.

Mo comes behind me and rubs my shoulders. He whispers in my ear. "What is it?"

His hand's rhythmic motion relaxes my stiff muscles. The moon plays hide and seek behind the dark trees. Suddenly, I want nothing more than to hide too. My eyelids flicker open and shut.

I clear my throat, trying to make room for words and air. My voice pours out in spurts. "That was ... the first time ... I said my dad was ... is ... dead."

Mo hugs me, erasing any space between us. "Grace, it's all right to let go. You can't be strong forever."

For the first time, I feel like someone actually understands me. An army of tears presses against the back of my eyes, determined to break the long-standing barrier. I spin around and lean into him. "I have to find out what happened to him. No matter what, I can't—no, I won't—stop until I do."

Mo twists my hair into little curls around his fingers. "That's what I'm afraid of."

My lower lip quivers as I fiddle with my bracelet, wishing it would do as it says and help me fly out of here. "I don't know what to do anymore. I've tried everything and nothing seems to be working. What would you do?"

He hugs me close. "Listen, blossom, it's late. Why don't you get some sleep? You're not going to figure it out tonight."

Pressing into him, I stare at the forest's green awning. An owl hoots above me. Oddly close. In the fire's dying light, I scan the limbs fanning out above us, the bird's eyes glow in the dimming light. Soon, he spreads his huge wings and glides away for his nightly mission. I think about Tommy's owl carving.

The owl gives us the power to extract secrets and know the truth.

Haven't I uncovered enough? How many more secrets can there be? I fight back a barrage of mixed emotions, curl into the crook of Mo's arm, and blanket myself with the smoky aroma of his jacket. For a short period, we share the same small space of air.

His face relaxes and his lips part slightly with every breath. Soon, our rhythms are the same. His exhale becomes my inhale and vice versa.

Just as I am about to drift off, a crack echoes in the trees.

I sit up.

Someone hisses my name. "Grace. Help me."

I stand and walk the edge of the small campsite, tracking the sound. "Dad?" Further ahead, a figure moves through the fog. I take off after it. But the crowded underbrush roots my feet to the earth. I cry out after the shadow. "Dad? Joe? It's me. Grace!"

Behind me, footsteps pound the ground. They're closing in fast, growing louder and louder. A deep voice calls out again, sounding desperate yet sad. "Grace!"

"Dad!" I force my way through a drape of vines, but the sticky strands hold me back, pinning me like a fly in a web. Flailing around, I rip one hand from a leafy shackle and grip the knife Tommy gave me, slashing at the vines surrounding my wrists.

A man walks out of the shadows as I try to break free. I can tell by the way the silouette walks, it's not Dad. The figure grabs me just I thrust the knife into his chest. A deep scream travels through the forest. Everything goes quiet and then, suddenly, my hands drop free. I scramble to get up and trip over a body crumbled in the center of the path. Blood flows out of a deep wound and pools along the dusty ground. The man doesn't move.

My adrenaline surges as I inch around to see who it is.

It's Mo.

Survival Skill #30

If you are hiking or camping alone, be sure someone knows the plan in case you do not return.

₵ jerk upright, still shrieking.

Mo crouches next to me, knife in hand. "Cor Blimey! What happened?"

For a minute, I remain completely still, too stunned to move. Then I squeeze his face and turn his head toward me. He has no choice, but to look me in the eyes. "I killed you."

He speaks through squished-up cheeks. "It was a dream."

"A dream?" I rub my forehead. "But it seemed so real."

He returns his weapon to its sheath and sits next to me as I hug my knees close. "They always do." He strokes my head. "By the way. Who's Joe?"

I sift through the details of my dream, trying to remember if I said his name. "My dad." Mo doesn't move. As if my words have paralyzed him. I lay my head on his chest and listen to his heart thumping. "I thought he was here. That's all." He strokes my hair. The steady rhythm calms me. "Mo?"

He buzzes in my hear. "Hm mm?"

I pause before asking the question I've been wanting to ask since we met. "How long are you staying here?"

He stops combing my hair with his fingers. "As long as I need to. Why do you ask?"

My voice blurts out in a squeaky whisper. "I don't want you to leave."

Mo kisses my forehead. "I don't want to hurt you."

"Then don't."

He spoons me from behind. "Go to sleep. We'll head out at first light so you can get home."

A few minutes later, Mo's breath finds a consistent rhythm. I focus on his soft breaths, in and out, wondering how he sleeps so soundly when I can never seem to catch a wink.

In my dream, his breath was nonexistent, and his death was my fault. What would I do if I was responsible for Mo's death? Or Dad's for that matter? I promise myself I won't let that happen.

Eventually, my mind settles in for the night, and my eyelids close from the weight of the day.

I drift off to sleep with Mo's arms encircling me in a ring of safety.

ೞ

Early the next morning, after making plans to meet up again, I reluctantly leave Mo. As Luci and I approach the house, I see Dad's truck parked in the driveway. Great. The one time I stay out all night, Mom decides to come home early.

I creep inside, praying she's asleep. Maybe she doesn't even know I'm gone. It wouldn't be the first time she didn't notice me. After leaning my backpack against the wall, I tiptoe into the kitchen and listen at the doorway.

The house is quiet. No movement.

As soon as I round the corner, the light flips on. I jump out of my skin. "Geez! You scared me."

Mom stands in the middle of the room with her fists planted on her hips. "Where the *hell* have you been?" Her voice quivers. "Do you know how worried I've been?"

I mumble. "Sorry. I went camping."

Her face pinches into a scowl as worry lines travel in parallel lines across her forehead. Dark black patches hide under red, puffy eyes, informing me she's been crying. "Camping? Then, why—in God's name—didn't you tell someone?"

"Sorry."

Mom goes from being quiet to sounding as if she's in TMX stereo and screams at the top of her lungs. "Is that all you can say? It's 6 a.m.! I've been calling you on your cell all night!"

"You know I don't get reception on the river."

She rubs her temples and lowers her voice about half a decibel. "I called Tommy and Les. Even Wyn. No one has seen you since yesterday!"

I raise my voice a bit. "I said I was sorry. You don't need to lecture me about it."

She yells again. "Don't talk to me that way. I'm your mother!"

"Could have fooled me ... *Mary*." I bound up the stairs and into my bedroom.

Mom storms after me. "Don't walk away from me when I'm talking to you. What's gotten into you lately? Skipping appointments, staying out all night. You are not yourself."

I spin around and face her, steaming mad. "Hi *Pot*, my name is Kettle."

She gives me a stern look. "Damn it, Grace, I'm your mother, and you *will* respect me. This is my house you're living in, and my hard-earned money you wasted when you didn't show up for your session the other day."

This time, I yell back. "I'll pay for the stupid session! I make my own money, in case you forgot."

She shakes her head. "That's not the point. You need to tell me where you're going and what you're doing. You're only sixteen."

My mouth gapes open. My mother's MIA for months and now, the one time I'm happy, the one time I don't check in, she wants to be my mother again? I don't think so. "So, what ... you can stay out all night, but I can't go camping without sending home a freakin' status report every hour?"

She screeches. "I don't have to answer to you, I'm an *adult!*"

I squawk back. "Then act like one! Because you haven't since Dad went missing."

Mom screams in my face. "You mean, the day your dad *died!*"

I yell even louder. "Uh, news flash ... he's not dead!"

Before I know what's coming, Mom's hand comes out of nowhere and makes contact with my face. Shocked, I touch a hand to my stinging cheek and stare her down. She's never slapped me before.

Mom takes in a deep breath, and her shoulders hunch forward. "I'm sorry. I shouldn't have done that … I didn't mean to hurt you."

I shield my face and turn my back so she doesn't see me tear up. "You never do."

She speaks in a monotone voice as if she's a computerized robot. "That's it, Grace. I've tried to reason with you. But you seem determined to fight me every step of the way. I can feel you slipping away. It's like you're a different person. Out of control."

I cross my arms with my back still facing her. "Oh! Now you care. You sure you're not mad because you can't control me anymore? Or is it because you can't control yourself?"

She sighs, and her voice becomes monotone. "That's it. You're grounded."

Spinning around, I scream in a high-pitched voice. "What?!" Balling my hands into a fist, I dig my nails into my palms. Squinching my face, I challenge her. "You can't *ground* me."

Mom cranks up her volume again. "The hell I can't!"

I shrug as if I don't care. "Whatever. It's not like you'll be here to enforce it anyway." The second the words spill out of my mouth, I wish I could reel them back in.

She frowns and raises her eyebrows in a question. "Oh, really? If that's what you think, I'll just take your bike with me."

I grit my teeth, holding back what I really want to say for fear I'll be slapped again. "You wouldn't dare."

She leans in close to my face. "Watch me."

We stand there in a stare down, waiting for the other to cave. I crack first and break eye contact, like a dog submitting to his Alpha.

Mom switches her voice into a softer tone. "Listen, Grace. I'm sorry about everything. I never meant to let you down. I know I've made mistakes. Your dad's death has been hard on both of us. Maybe we can find a way to put all this behind us and start over."

"He's not dead," I mumble.

She continues pretending I didn't utter a word. "So when you're ready to apologize, come talk to me."

I throw out my last dagger. "You mean, *if* you're available."

Mom tightens her lips into a thin line and stomps out of the room, slamming the door behind her. I smash my face against the glass and make foggy clouds on the window as I watch her dragging Luci into the back of her truck. After fifteen minutes of wrestling with my bike, Mom tears out of the driveway, leaving a cloud of dirt behind her.

I throw myself onto my bed and punch a pillow. It isn't fair. I'm more responsible than she is, and I'm grounded? She has no business touching my bike. I can't wait to leave this crappy house, crappy town, and crappy life.

As tears blur my vision, I flop down on my bed and stare at a line of glowy stars pasted along the white-pocked ceiling. Mo's constellation pops into my head. The thought of him relaxes everything stirring around inside. Then I realize being grounded means I can't be with him. Mom's already messed up my life. I'm not about to let her screw that up too. My night wth Mo was the best thing that's happened to me since all this happened.

As soon as I think of Mo, the bullet pops into my head. I run to get my bag. In all the drama, I'd completely forgotten about it. I dig through the front pocket of my backpack until my fingers touch the cold metal. After pulling out the cylinder, I twirl it in the light. The bullet is long and thin with a steel point on one end and a welded seam running down one side. A long scar.

Maybe I can find it online. I race downstairs to the kitchen where I left my laptop and sit at the table. For the next several hours, I skim through pictures of bullets from rifles, pistols, and shotguns. Some look familiar, but I can't tell from the blurry photos. Dad used to have a book about guns in his office. Maybe that would be better.

I walk down the hall and stop in front of the office door. My breathing quickens. I haven't been inside this room since before Dad disappeared. I cup the knob to stop my hand from shaking and slowly turn. The door clicks and swings open. The room is dark and chilly. Even musty.

Like a tomb.

Reaching in, I flip on the light. As the room lights up, my heart darkens. Everything is in its normal place except for one thing. Dad. I move in front of his mahogany desk and wipe my hand across the silky surface, streaking through a thin layer of dust that's collected while waiting for his return. When I sit down in his old tweed chair, Dad's scent overwhelms me. I vault out of the chair and back away before noticing the old sweatshirt hanging on the back. My body trembles as I clutch the garment and raise it to my nose.

The faint scent of pine needles mixed with wood teases my nose. Tears fill my eyes. I miss his smell. Something I never thought about before he left. Emotions clog my chest, creating shallow breaths. I flop back down in Dad's chair and lay my head on his shirt. Touching his pens, I can almost picture him writing, taking notes. Next to his antique phone sits a brass frame holding a picture of our family, hugging and laughing. I clean the glass with the edge of my t-shirt.

If it wasn't for these grainy pictures collecting dust around the house, I don't know if I'd remember as much as I should. Somehow, even though I fight it, the details are peeling away. The little things are fading, no matter how hard I try to hold onto them. The day Dad disappeared changed everything I believed about families, about the woods, about my life. Like dynamite exploded under the foundation of my world. The ashes of my memories are all that remains.

Charred, disintegrating, and floating away.

I focus away from the photo and skim the bookshelf. For some time, I flip through books on hunting rifles and ammo and find some facts to note. Eventually, I make my way back to Dad's desk and comb through the drawers for paper to write on. When I pull out a few sheets, a manila folder lies hidden underneath.

Curious, I take out the file full of articles and pictures.

One news clipping discusses how bear parts are a hot commodity in Asia used to make food and medicine. Anything from bear claws, gall bladders, and bile. A few pictures slide out and drift to the floor. I drop on my hands and knees to collect them from under the desk. My stomach churns at the graphic images of mutilated bears, all missing four paws. Bears locked in cages with tubes running from their bodies, collecting bile. Photos showing a row of bear hides and boxes of bear parts confiscated by customs. Then I come across a stack of stapled memos from the U.S. Fish & Wildlife Service and skim through the headings:

Bile and body parts, taken from bears using horrifically inhumane means, feed an illegal trade in bear products, which extend worldwide.

Poachers will hunt and remove bears from their natural habitat and deliver them into a life of pain and suffering in the bear farms.

Wild bear gall bladders are of higher quality than those of farmed bears.

It is the black bear in North America that has become the victim of poachers looking to turn a quick profit in the Asian medicine market.

Bear Poachers Busted as Congress Considers Federal Bear Bill.

I never heard Dad talk about this level of bear poaching before. Not to such an extreme. At the bottom of the paper stack is a letter. When I read the name, my breath catches in my throat.

Chief Reed.

Basically, he politely threatens Dad if he "continues creating a stink about the bear pits." Evidently, Dad's constant chatter is "real bad for business."

Unable to absorb any more, I return the file to the desk and scan the empty room, imagining Dad sitting in the squeaky chair with his feet propped up on the edge. That's when I notice the fireplace. I walk over and kneel in front of the soot and half-burned logs. Little pieces of paper with charred edges hide in the soot. My breath catches in my throat as I pick up a small piece. It's the remains of Mom and Dad's wedding picture. On second glance, there are several more, all burnt. My dad would never do that. I frown. Only one person could've done this. Mom.

In that one moment, I hate her. Why would she do this? She's Miss Scrapbook.

Mom's betrayal and Chief Reed's letter fill my mind. Followed closely by the disgusting images of mutilated bears.

I take out the bullet and twist the cylinder between my fingers.

What does it all mean? There seem to be several pieces from different puzzles scattered around me. But none of them match to make a complete picture. Or at least one that makes sense.

Just then, someone bangs on the front door. My heart bounces around in my chest, clambering for steady rhythm. I sneak out of my dad's office and tiptoe over to the door.

Just as I peer out, a face pops up in the window.

Survival Skill #31

As a survivor, you must get a rescuer's attention by sending a message they can easily understand.

I scream as Wyn presses a piggy nose against the glass.

Sliding off the chain lock, I swing the door open. "Dude, you gave me a heart attack."

"Why?"

I stand there, holding the door wide open. "Your face scared me."

Wyn strolls by me without being invited. "Gee, thanks."

"Anytime." I slam the door shut and follow him into the living room.

"Man, it's been ages since I've crashed your pad." He walks around the house looking at things before he jumps into another subject. "So, where yah been? I've been calling you the last two days." He doesn't face me.

I try not to stutter. "Oh, my phone isn't charged. I keep forgetting to plug it in."

He points at the bag of Spicy Cheetos on the counter. "I see you're eating a nutritiously balanced meal."

"Yup! Carbs, fat, and protein."

He wrinkles his face. "I don't get the protein part."

"Cheese!" I shove a fistful of cheesy nuggets into my mouth.

"That's disgusting."

I flash him an annoyed look. "Surely, you didn't come over to discuss my eating habits. Why are you here?"

"Well. Your mom called my house last night looking for you. She was kinda wigged out."

I roll my eyes. "Yeah, sorry about that. She's a little drama these days."

He studies me in an odd way. "Seems to run in the family. Saw your bike in her truck at the diner. Is it broken or something?"

I scoff. "Believe it or not, she *grounded* me."

"Seriously? What are you, ten?"

"My point exactly."

Wyn sits down with one foot up on his leg and bounces his knee. "So where were you?"

I twist my hair into a bun. "Uh … no place special. Just out and about."

He probes further like he knows something is up. "Not really your style to stay out that late by yourself, is it?"

I suddenly feel like I'm under a spotlight, and everything I'm hiding inside is glaring. Leaning back, I put my feet up on the coffee table, trying to appear casual. "Didn't know I had to check in with everyone. The rules around here change as much as Joan River's face."

"That was bad." He moves next to me on the couch. "So you're not going to tell me either?"

I rub my hands across my pants. "Nothing to tell. I was out searching for more clues and decided to camp out."

Wyn scoots down to get more comfortable, but his face is still tense. "And? Find anything?"

"Actually, a lot. Nothing makes much sense, but I have a theory forming."

He sits back with his hands behind his head and stares at the ceiling. "Okay, let's hear it."

"You sure?"

"I'm all yours."

I stand and pace, playing with my hair as I talk. "I found an article about Al. Evidently, he got nabbed for hunting in Tennessee. Got off on a technicality though. He probably came down here and started killing bears. I'm guessing Dad caught him and tried to bust him. Obviously, Al didn't want to go to jail so he must have kidnapped my dad and hid him somewhere." I slump back down next to him. "What do you think?"

He thinks for a moment. "I guess it sounds plausible."

"Nothing else makes sense. I just need to find enough evidence to keep them behind bars so we can get them to crack and tell me where they're keeping Dad."

Wyn shakes his head. "Crack them? Wow, you are watching too much TV."

Ignoring his comment, I think out loud. "Wonder if Carl tested the bag yet. Maybe it has new evidence to hold them."

Wyn rolls his hands together and watches the clock. "You know Captain. If he did, he wouldn't tell me."

I prop my feet up on the table and lean back, mimicking Wyn's posture. "I went over to Mama Sue's yesterday. She's trying to help me nail down the boot treads. Still hasn't called though." I crumple up the Cheetos bag and chuck it into the trash can. "Two points!" When I face Wyn, he's staring at me with a funny look on his face. "What's wrong? Why are you looking at me like that? You think I'm missing something?"

Wyn shifts in his seat and inches closer. Then, without warning, he leans in and parks his lips on mine.

It happens so fast, I melt into him before I realize I'm kissing him back. Hard. His breath echoes in my ears, and he tastes minty and fresh. His kiss isn't electric like Mo's but it's gentle and familiar. Comparing the two kisses brings me back to my senses. I place my hands on Wyn's chest and gently push him away. "Wyn, wait."

He looks half surprised and half hurt, but keeps staring at my lips when he talks. "What's wrong?"

"I'm so sorry." I whisper back, hoping a lower volume will lighten the blow. "But I can't do this. To you. I mean, us. It's not fair." I drop my head down. How could I do this. Kiss two guys in the same day. I'm disgusting.

"Why don't you let me think for both of us?" He cups both hands around my neck and pushes my chin up with his thumbs, drawing me in again. His lips find mine, and I briefly surrender.

185

Again. It feels so nice to be wanted, to be with Wyn like this, but I can't help but wonder if it's because of how it used to make me feel. That is, it takes me back to when everything was okay and Dad was safe. When I didn't have anything to worry about.

I'm not that girl anymore.

Wyn weaves his fingers into my hair and holds my hand with the other. For a minute, I feel like I'm suspended under water, floating. Not resisting but not giving in. As I rise to the surface, I realize that maybe something is missing between us. Something small I never knew was there; yet somehow, it has become significant enough for me to finally notice.

With Mo, everything is different. Like a huge firecracker exploded in my heart. With Wyn, it's more of a sparkler fizzing inside before extinguishing too quickly, leaving darkness until the next sparkler is fired up. Thinking of Mo makes me feel awful. I'm a total cheater.

My eyes spring open, and I jerk back. Further this time, to a safe distance. That way, the burning embers still smoking between us can't touch me. "Wyn, I'm serious."

In defeat, he slouches back. "Too serious, if you ask me."

"Well, I didn't."

He studies me as if probing my thoughts before attempting to speak. "Grace ... I ... came ... here ..."

I hold up my hand, stopping him before he finishes. "Wyn, wait. Don't say anything. The last time we were together, it almost cost us our friendship."

He slides a bit closer. "Maybe I don't want *just* a friendship anymore."

"Don't say that." I shift a little, trying to get comfortable. Not knowing what to say. I don't want to hurt Wyn, but I can't lead him on either. My life is complicated enough without this on top of it. "Come on. What about Skyler?"

Wyn rubs his chin. "What about her?" He bends forward again, teasing me. "She knows I'm still into you."

I scoot back on the couch in a full retreat. "Please, don't do this. You're my best friend. I don't want to mess this up. We broke up, and we both moved on. Let's not go back and try to replay this differently."

He sighs and gets up. "I wish you would've told me this sooner before I made an ass out of myself. I thought maybe you wanted me back. To try again. You said you needed me."

I'm stunned. Almost unable to talk. Not sure what to say to make this all better. "I did, I mean, I do need you. As a friend."

Wyn points to where we were kissing on the couch. "That did not feel like friends. There is still something there."

I drop my face into my hands. "I'm just confused. I don't want to hurt you again."

Wyn strokes my hair. "We'll be fine as long as you're honest with me."

I take in a deep breath, wondering if I should drop my love bomb. Wyn still doesn't know about Mo, and there never seems to be a good time to tell him. Then again, maybe I'm afraid it'll change everything between us. Am I ready for that? I've lost Dad, and what if I lose Wyn again? The last few weeks have been better because we're talking again. What if I can't find Dad without Wyn? I stare at my annihilated fingernails and notice there's nothing left to gnaw.

He clears his throat. "Why are you so quiet? Is there something you want to tell me?"

I nibble on a frayed cuticle and shake my head. My legs pump up and down. A confession hangs off the edge of my tongue. To tell or not to tell, that is the question. "Maybe there is something."

Ready to come clean, I look up, but notice Wyn isn't listening to me anymore. He's too busy studying something on my computer screen. A confused look washes over his face and he points to the laptop. "What's this?"

It takes me a moment to realize what he's reading. "Hey! That's private!" I leap forward and try to snatch the computer off the table.

He shoots to his feet and holds the laptop high in the air, out of my reach. "You studying to be a marksman or something?"

I bounce up and down like a basketball player blocking a three-pointer. "It's research."

"Hunting rifles and huge bullets? Is there a rabid elephant loose in the area I don't know about?"

I stop hopping. "Why do you care about my Internet surfing habits? I mean it's none of your business what I do anyway. Not that I'm *doing* anything."

He hands me the computer. "Ah ha! Defensiveness equals guilt."

I shut the lid and set it on the kitchen counter. "Nosiness equals rude."

He narrows his eyes and rubs his chin. "You're acting suspicious. And don't deny it because I've known you and your antics all your life. What's going on with you?"

"Nothing." I stop. "Fine. I found a bullet."

He remains silent for a few minutes, as his brains works to process everything. "Where?"

"In the woods." No need to mention Mo. I'm not going to lie, just can't tell him the whole truth.

Wyn cocks his head. "So what? You think the bullet belongs to that guy from the store?"

"Al? Yup."

Wyn shrugs. "Well, then let's take the bullet to Carl. He can check for prints."

I wrinkle my face. "Um, we can't. I didn't know what it was when I grabbed it so my prints are all over it."

He slaps his forehead. "G, what were you thinking? You don't seem to be all here these days. It's like you're a different person. You've lost your edge. Forgotten everything you know."

I dip my head to one side and purse my lips together. "Come on, Wyn, cut me a break."

His face softens. "All right. All right. Let me see it."

I rub my eyes. "See what?"

"What else? The bullet, ding dong."

I retrieve the casing from my jean pocket and place it in his hands. "Here. It's not gonna help though. I already looked online and combed through Dad's books. They all look the same. Probably from a standard hunting gun."

Wyn holds it up to the lamp and inspects it before blurting out, "Holy shit."

Survivor Skill #32

When hiking, be aware of hunters and know when hunting season is for certain animals.

ꟼ glance over his shoulder. "What is it?"

Wyn points to a ridge that runs down both sides of the cylinder. "Dum dum."

I flick the back of his head. "Dude, stop with the ding dong and dum dum crap."

Wyn thumps my forehead back. "Not *you*, silly. That's what this is called. A dum dum."

"What do you mean?"

He faces me, still pinching the bullet between his pointer fingers. "It means this isn't really a standard .308. These dudes are making their own bullets in the woods. They're serious about this, and they don't want to get caught."

"How do you know?"

"Captain's talked about these types of bullets before. I think he caught someone using them a while back. One-Stoppers. At least, that's what he calls them. Here, I'll show you. Give me your knife." I hand him my pink Swiss Army knife, and he jams it into the seam. After jiggling the end, the bullet pops open. A couple small steel balls roll across the table. "See. These guys are loading bullets with ball bearings. The bears don't have a shot in hell."

I pick up one of the little balls and roll it around in my palm. "What does it do?"

"The bullet expands on impact, making the hole much bigger. Guarantees a kill, and the bullet is completely untraceable. Wonder why they're using these? Not really standard for your average jerk hunting off season."

My eyes widen as another puzzle piece falls into place. "When I was in Dad's office earlier, there were some articles about bear poaching. Talked about hunters selling bear parts—gall bladders and paws—for a ton of money overseas."

"What about the bear at the Station 19? Was he cut up?"

I picture Simon lying on the ground. "No, he was intact. Nothing seemed to be missing. From what I saw, it was a thrill kill."

Wyn whistles. "Well, if anyone is poaching and selling bear parts, it's more serious than we thought. It's a federal offense. We gotta tell Captain."

I plead with him. "Wait. Not yet. I need your help first."

He shakes his head and frowns. "Noooo way. I know that look. Your idea of help is either a felony or a hike up Mount Kilimanjaro." I stare at him, pleading with my eyes. His face softens, and he pokes the dimple in my chin. "Damn it! I hate that I can't say no to you."

I grin. "No, you don't."

"You don't deserve me." He releases an exasperated growl before answering. "What do you want me to do this time?"

"I need to get on Carl's computer."

"You're nuts!" His voice has a pinch of panic mixed with dash of anger. He pushes me aside and hops to his feet, pacing the room like a caged animal.

I grab his arm and get him to look at me. "Hear me out first. I saw a note in my dad's case file that Carl found a bullet shell. If I can see a picture of it, maybe it'll match this one."

"Captain would have noticed a dum dum."

"Maybe he missed it."

His body tenses, and his lips purse. "I doubt it."

"Then maybe he knows about it and isn't saying anything," I blurt out.

Wyn glares at me and his voice rumbles. "So what, Captain's *crooked* now? You've gone too far this time. I'm outta here." He storms toward the door.

191

I block him from leaving. "Wait, I'm sorry. I didn't mean that."

He crosses his arms. "How dare you accuse him? First of all, he's the closest thing I've known to a father, and you know how I feel about him. Secondly, Captain's known you your whole life. Not to mention he busts his butt for this town. In more ways than one. Take it back, or I'm leaving and you can do this on your own."

I hang my head. He's right. I'm so desperate for answers, I'm accusing friends and family of crazy stuff. "I'm sorry. I'm tired. This is starting to get to me."

He takes in a deep breath. "Starting to? Look, I know you're having a hard time, but you gotta be careful what you say. Blaming innocent people because your world is messed up is not going to change anything."

Clutching his hand, I nod. "I know. I'm sorry. Will you help me? I need to get that evidence file. Find out about that bullet." I grab my notebook and start rifling through the pages. "On *CSI*, they catalog everything in some kind of evidence software."

"Only this isn't *CSI*. This is real life and, if you get in trouble, it doesn't end in an hour."

I hold up my notebook and point to the file name, smiling. "See. Here it is. If I can match this bullet to the ones in the file, we'll have proof there's a connection. But I need your help."

Wyn sighs. "Fine. But this time … you better get in and out."

I pounce on him and hug his neck. "I'll be as quick as a cricket."

"Let's hope you don't get squashed." I realize we're embracing so I peel my arms off his neck and we separate. Even though we are now standing a few inches apart, I can feel the heat drawing me in.

He clears his throat and steps back. "Captain's still out of town until tomorrow night. It's the only day we can go."

I follow where he's going. "Yeeeaaaaahh. Only Bernice will be there."

He waves me off and struts toward the door. "No problem there. I can get her outta the office, but it won't be for long. She's real picky about leaving the place unattended in case Captain calls."

Then I snap my fingers. "Shoot, I have an appointment with Dr. Head. Mom'll kill me if I don't go."

Wyn strolls over to the door and flings it open to leave. "With the current condition of your psyche, I would recommend you never miss it. So I'll meet you there when you're done."

Survivor Skill #33

In the wilderness, denial can be dangerous when facing real fears and challenges.

The next morning, I hide in bed until Mom screams up the stairs. "Grace, we're leaving in five minutes!"

I throw back the covers and linger in front of my closet. What does one wear to a B&E? In addition to attending my second felony, I plan to meet Mo later. With or without my bike, I'll find a way. This time, I want to look extra good. Not like I-tried-too-hard good or that would be totally obvious, considering my idea of formal is a clean shirt. I'm going for sporty boho.

After sifting through raggedy clothes, I choose a pair of tan pants from the back of my closet that I've never worn, my good hiking boots, and a black fitted t-shirt with a cool butterfly design on the front.

Before getting dressed, I glance at the covered mirror and stand in front of the old sheet for a moment, mustering up the nerve to peek. Reaching over, I grip the corner of the cloth and yank. The cover slides down the glass and curls into a heap on the rug. I gaze at my reflection.

My long dark hair fans out over my shoulders. I barely recognize my own body. My legs reach up higher than I remember. My boobs are still small but slightly fuller. I smile. And my reflection smiles back.

I have to say, I look pretty good.

With Mo, I feel beautiful. Like a woman, for the first time.

℃ξ

The whole way into town, neither Mom nor I say a word. Eleven point seven miles of awkward silence. Makes a twenty-minute trip seem like an eternity. I cough a few times to add noise on top of the truck's choppy melody. Every time my mouth opens to talk first, Luci jostles around in the back, making me steam all over again.

Finally, we reach Dr. Head's office. I'm so relieved to escape the quiet ride from hell, I practically fall out the door.

Only then does Mom speak. "I'll pick you up at work."

Without answering, I shut the door ultra hard to be extra obnoxious. The window rattles, threatening to shatter right alongside our relationship. I charge straight into the brick building with purpose and slam the door behind me, never looking back.

Once inside, I peek through the thin, cheap drapes and watch her sitting in the truck with her head hanging. She opens the door slightly as if she's coming in and then slams it shut again. She sits there until her shoulders start to shake. I stand frozen, watching Mom cry, not knowing what to do, but wanting so much to run out and comfort her. Just talk. Like we did before Dad went missing.

Like we haven't done since.

A few minutes later, Mom wipes her face and rolls out of the parking lot, taking her frustration out on Dad's clutch. Tears clutter my vision as I watch the distance between us grow until the truck becomes only a dot on the highway.

Once she's gone, I drag myself upstairs to Dr. Head's office. This is the first time I've ever been punctual. It'll probably give him a heart attack. Or worse, he'll think, "we're making progress."

When I push through the door, Dr. Head jerks his head up, startled as expected. He checks his crazy-eyed clock. "Grace, you're on time."

I study my watch. "Actually, I'm a minute and forty-three seconds early."

He comes out from behind the desk and sits in his therapist's chair with a notepad on his lap. "Didn't think you would show after you missed our appointment the other day. You know I'll still have to charge your mom."

"Trust me, I've heard *all* about it. And if you don't mind, I'll just pay for it myself."

Dr. Head looks a bit surprised. "That's nice of you."

"It was my fault. Besides, it will make life a little easier at home."

He doesn't miss a beat or a chance to dig into my psychological state. "So your life at home is hard?"

I plop down in my assigned chair. No use fighting it anymore. "That's an understatement."

Dr. Head lights a pipe and props his feet on a small fabric stool that reminds me of my granny's old Sunday hat. I cough, emphasizing my annoyance at the smoky intrusion on my lungs. Doesn't bother him any. No matter what the situation, he always seems unfazed. He blows out a smoke ring before asking anything. "Because of your dad?"

"What else is there? Though I'm pretty sure Mom would say it's because of me." I huff at my bangs, realizing we're already talking about my problems, and I've haven't even been in the chair for a full minute. Obviously, I've lost my touch.

"I wouldn't be so sure of that." He takes his glasses off and cleans them with the corner of his button-down shirt. "She's going through a tough time too, ya know."

"Yeah? Well, maybe I'm tired of worrying about her. Maybe *she* should worry about *me* for a change. She is the mother. I mean, she drove me here and didn't talk the whole way. What parent does that for no reason?"

Dr. Head gets up and pulls his chair next to mine. He breathes through his teeth, sounding like a balloon with a small leak. "I need to tell you something."

I sit up straight and prepare myself for some psychobabble. "About me or my mom?"

He sits up straighter and exhales before speaking. "Actually, it's about your dad."

My mouth clamps shut. It takes a lot of energy to toss out a word. "Okay."

He scratches his chin, but keeps a straight face. "I talked to your mom last night."

I groan. "She called you too? Geez, does the whole town have to know I was out late? It's not exactly front page news ."

He butts in. "Actually, she came here to see *me*."

My chest rises and falls much quicker than before. Otherwise, I don't move. Can barely swallow. "To talk about me?"

He exhales before answering. "You could say that."

"And?"

"She wanted me to discuss something with you."

I shift in my seat as sweat dribbles down my back. "Dr. Head, can you just tell me what you're trying to say?" I grab the armrests and brace myself for something to crash into me.

He reaches over and grabs the tissue box.

"Thanks." I grip the box in my lap, crushing the cardboard sides. Is he expecting major waterworks or something? Whatever he's about to say isn't going to be good. I relish in the moment of ignorance, waiting for him to spill the beans.

He speaks very slowly. "Grace, your mom got a call from Carl yesterday."

My mouth dries out like the Sahara in summer. Great, now my mom knows about the evidence I found. This will cost me at least six more months in therapy. "Is this about the Cheetos bag? Did Carl find something?"

Dr. Head looks confused. "The Cheetos bag? No. I'm afraid it's something else." He pauses to pack his pipe. "They found a shirt floating in the river." Everything seems to stop as I wait for his next sentence. "It's your dad's."

It takes a second for my brain to play back what he said. Both hands slide up and cover my mouth, allowing only a whisper to escape through my fingers. "Oh God. Is there more?"

He frowns and nods at the same time. His eyes even look a little moist. "It was shredded to bits and had ... blood on it."

I stare at him as if I didn't quite hear exactly what he said. Then I close my eyes and picture Dad walking away that final morning. How he stopped and saluted me as I stood watching out my window, barely awake. I can't imagine not ever seeing him again. My throat tightens, and I cough a few times to clear any blockage.

Dr. Head is still talking while my eyes are shut. "They are officially closing the case and declaring your dad—"

"Dead." I choke out the word. It tastes bitter in my mouth, making me gag.

"Carl think the shirt confirms the drowning theory."

I release the breath I've been holding for God knows how long. I study the bracelet Dad gave me, not able to quite comprehend that this may be the last gift I'll ever get from him. "Why didn't Mom tell me?"

"I think she tried to find you. Then I guess she thought it was best for me to tell you in here. In case you need to talk about anything."

"Maybe I just *need* her."

Dr. Head nods as he lights the tobacco. "She was barely able to tell me without crying. She didn't want you to see her like that. But I agree the communication between you two needs a lot of work."

I sit there unable to process anything. As if there's a wall surrounding my brain, preventing some information from passing through. I can't imagine what happened to Dad, but even I know this isn't a good sign. The blood is proof he's hurt in some way. And being in the river doesn't look good either.

Dr. Head pinches the bridge of his nose. "I'm so sorry. It's normal to be sad."

Normal? Nothing about my life is normal. My heart pounds out a Morse code emergency signal. The well-constructed dam holding back my emotions cracks as a single tear breaks loose and rolls down my cheek. I wipe it away immediately. "I'm fine. This doesn't mean anything. The blood only proves he was hurt."

Dr. Head closes my really, really thick file and rocks in his chair. "I'm sure it was quite a fall. None of us want to believe he drowned. But we can't change it. He's gone, and your mom is worried about you holding on so tight. Maybe this will help you move on."

My heart is knocking against my ribs, begging to be free. "No." The raspy tone doesn't come close to resembling my real voice.

Dr. Head replaces his glasses on his nose and peers over them like an old librarian. He keeps his voice steady. "The longer you wait, the harder the grieving process will be. The sooner you accept where we are, the faster you can heal."

"Maybe I don't want to heal."

I sit there, shaking my head until he places a hand on my shoulder. "Don't punish yourself. It's time to let go."

I push his hand away and speak through my teeth in a growl. "*Don't* say that." I need to get this quack out of my head.

"When a kid loses a parent, it's common to want to blame it on someone. Deny the facts. It's hard for a kid, especially your age, to understand that accidents happen and sometimes they are unexplainable. That sometimes people, parents, die and that doesn't make it anyone's fault."

"He's not *dead!*" Without warning, I jump out of the chair, sending a lamp crashing to the floor. Without another word, I storm out of the room, stumble down the stairs, and burst through the double doors. In the sunlight, my mouth gapes open, like a fish gasping for air.

How could Mom have done this to me? Why didn't she tell me herself?

Anger I've never known surges out into a piercing scream that rides the wind before disappearing. I spin around and search for a way out in every direction.

Where do I go from here? What do I do next? Where can I hide?

A door slams behind me.

Glancing back through rage and watering eyes, I find Dr. Head standing on the sidewalk. Slowly, I retreat with my fists up, ready to defend myself. "Leave me alone." He advances toward me. My words burst out, this time even louder. "I mean it, Doc. Don't touch me!"

He ignores my threat and embraces me in a bear hug. "I'm so sorry, Grace."

I writhe, trying to get loose, but he holds me tight.

My body tires easily and slumps into him. I bury my face into his cheap, polyester shirt. My legs buckle. It's as if the ground's been yanked away and now, I'm hanging over a huge crevice, ready to fall. Dr. Head supports me, refusing to let me drop away into a cave of nothingness. A wail climbs through me and escapes my locked jaws. Tears pour out. The wall of denial surrounding me crumbles, and the dam floods over, drowning my hope.

My heart collapses from months of tireless beatings, and a sob escapes my lips. "I miss him."

Dr. Head keeps his grip on me. "I know, Grace. But you're going to be okay. I promise."

I cry for a few minutes, my whole body shaking uncontrollably. Spasms tear through every crevice that still wants to believe Dad's alive.

He clears his throat and speaks in a near-whisper, assuming that if he says something softly, it might make this all hurt less. "I know it's seems impossible to accept. But you will in time."

Behind him, Mom pulls up and gets out of the truck. She freezes on the sidewalk when I catch her eye.

I support myself and shove Dr. Head away. "No! You're wrong. I won't accept anything any of you say. Not until I have proof."

My mom starts to walk toward me.

I put up my hand and scream, "No! It's too late."

Her lip quivers and she manages to speak. "I'm sorry, Grace. It's going to be okay."

I point between her and me. "We will never be okay.' I swallow and force out something I've never said to either of my parents. "I hate you."

Survival Skill #34

When tracking, it's the combination of evidence that provides the whole picture.

After running away from both of them, I hide in the alley for over an hour and sob until I'm drained of tears. Empty. Even though I don't want to, I force myself to keep my meeting with Wyn. My legs feel weighted, as if they're filled with quicksand from the ankles up. I can't—won't—let this setback prevent me from pushing forward. A little blood means Dad was hurt, and the wet shirt just tells me he's not wearing one anymore.

It doesn't prove he's dead.

Does it?

I shake the thought from my head. Even if he is, I have to uncover the truth, the whole truth, for myself. Panic sets in. I have to find him and bring him home.

Dead or alive.

Before I enter the police station, I check my face in the window for any signs of my breakdown. Or a "breakthrough," as Dr. Head would call it. I wipe my face on my t-shirt and push through the door.

Bernice squeals when I walk in, but as soon as she sees my face, Bernice sticks out her bottom lip. Her voice softens. "Grace, sweetie. How yah doin'? You holdin' up okay? I'm sorry about your daddy. May he rest in peace." She bows her head a little and puts her hands in a prayer position.

Anger stirs deep inside, threatening to expose itself. People can say the most inappropriate things sometimes without even realizing it. I ball my hand into a fist behind my back and try not to show any emotion on my face. "Thanks."

She comes over and cradles my shoulders. "Lordy, you're wastin' away before my eyes."

I force my lips to curl upward. "Must be what I'm wearing." On the other hand, it could be that the life is draining out of me each day Dad's not here. Little by little. Drop by drop. I'm shrinking.

Into. Nothing.

"You know darlin', Captain's still out of town. You may want to come back tomorrow." She plops back down at her computer and starts pecking on the keys with her fake nails. The noise reminds me of Bear's doggy toenails clicking on the hardwood floor. When she realizes I'm still there, she stops typing and eyes me, lowering her voice to a whisper. "Unless you came to see Wyn?"

On cue, Wyn emerges from the storage room. Streaks of dirt smudge across his face, giving him the linebacker look. He's wearing old battered jeans with holes ripped at the knees and no shirt. Sweat glistens on his lean body. I don't remember the missing shirt being part of our plan. Surprisingly, I'm kinda digging the improvisation. I avoid staring and feel my cheeks searing like a piece of meat on a grill. What's wrong with me? How can grief and lust fill the same space? I try to focus on an image of Mo's face. He's the one I connect with the most. These feelings for Wyn are just old feelings that have been stirred up. Like when you kick up dust. It floats around for a while, but eventually it settles again. As if it was never there.

Wyn speaks in a flat tone. A little too rehearsed if you ask me. "Hey, G. How are you? Long time, no see."

Averting my eyes from his, I can't help but wonder if he knew about Dad's shirt last night. And if he did, why didn't he have the guts to tell me.

I push everything aside and focus on what I need to do. Get that file. "Hey, Wyn."

He veers off script and shoots me a concerned look. "You okay, G?"

I shake it off, not meeting his gaze directly. "Sure, I just thought Captain would be back."

He returns to our script with Bernice. "Whew, Bea, you sure are workin' me hard today. What's a guy gotta do to get some water?"

Bernice launches out of the chair. "Gracious me, where are my manners? Let me get you some ice-cold stuff. Captain'll appreciate everything being done when he gets back. I know I do." She bends over to fill the triangle cup and hands him the water.

He throws back his head and gulps down the liquid before letting out a long sigh of relief. "Aahhhhhhhhhhhhhhhhh! Thanks."

I roll my eyes. He's laying it on a bit thick for my taste. The average person might catch on. However, we're lucky. As sweet as Bernice is, she's always been one fry short of a happy meal. Totally unsuspecting and undeniably gullible. Especially when it comes to Wyn.

She blushes and coos. "Thanks, Wynnie. Lucky for me, you were here to fix the A/C, especially in this heat."

I speak up. "Yeah, *Wynnie*! Sure is lucky you were here to save the day. Real knight in shining armor. Only ... without the armor." I point to his bare chest and try not to blush when his pecks flex involuntarily.

Wyn scowls at me then addresses Bernice. "Oh my goodness. I didn't realize it's already lunch. I better get started on fixin' the toilet so I can eat. Boy, I'm starved!"

Bernice hops up out of her seat again like a bunny in spring. "Good Lordy me! Forgot all about lunch. How about I go get us somethin' from Barry's place?"

He flashes his double-dimpled smile. "You sure, Bea? That'd be great. If you don't mind."

"Of course not! I insist." She faces me. "Grace? You want somethin'?"

I stand up and get ready to leave. "No, thanks. I need to get to work. Tommy'll kill me if I'm late again."

She flashes a lipsticky smile and heads for the door with her flowered purse in tow. "Okay, darlin', if you're sure. You tell Tommy I said hello, and I'll tell Captain you came by. Wynnie, I'll be right back with some fuel for your engine."

Wyn winks. "I'll wait at the rest stop."

Oh brother. Bernice giggles and waddles through the door.

He immediately faces me. "You've been crying?"

I act stupid. "Me? Crying? Yeah right. Since when do I cry?"

He looks at my face. "Contrary to what you want me to believe, I know you're not dead inside. What's wrong? Did something happen since last night?"

I mumble. "I don't want to talk about it." Maybe he doesn't know or maybe he's just testing me.

He pulls back my bangs. "G?"

If I'm going to do this, I need to pull myself together. "Look, I promise I'll tell you all about it later. Soap opera and all. But right now, we don't have time." I split the blinds with my fingers and watch Bernice hobble down the sidewalk. "By the way, nice acting. I knew you were full of it."

"Shoot, I have to be full of something if I'm hanging out with you," Wyn bites back. "Seems to be one of your upgraded features. The new and improved Grace on fire. Drama included."

I furrow my brows. "Ha ha." As soon Bernice is a safe distance away, I jump into her chair. "Wanna time me?"

"I'm glad you think this is a game." Wyn peers over my shoulder. "How are you gonna get in?"

I point to a post-it note stuck to her screen. "Use the password."

He snickers. "Man, you are one lucky chick."

"Nah, I saw it here last time."

He breathes on my neck when he talks. "You know, using up all your nine lives and luck before the age of eighteen isn't a great idea. You're bound to run out."

I push him away. "Can the peanut gallery keep it down while I do my *thang*?" I scan the desktop and search through Carl's folders until I find the CrimeStar application. When the sign-in

205

box pops up, I type in Bernice's user name and the password. As I wait for the application to open, I tease him. "Hey, *Wynford!* Did you know your name is her password? Something going on with you two?"

"Gross. You think you're funny, but you're not." His hot breath tickles my ear, and the smell of his musty sweat teases my nose.

"Well, I crack myself up." I squash the old feelings resurfacing deep inside and focus. Finding out about this bullet is the only hope I have left. We both stare at the hourglass on the screen. I bounce my legs, waiting for the computer to quit buzzing.

Wyn pipes up. "Now what?"

I swat his nose. "Look, I can't concentrate with you breathing down my neck. Keep an eye out for Bernice in case she comes back sooner than we expect. She always rushes when you're involved."

"Fine. I don't want to be a part of this anyway." He strolls over to the front window and peeks through the mini-blinds. "You better find something big, and soon, or you're gonna get promoted to numero uno on my shit list."

"Nothing new." Finally, the main screen pops up. "Yes! I'm in!" I buzz through the menus until I find the right folder and scroll down, looking for the document name. The arrow mouse hovers over the file icon. I hesitate a nanosecond before double clicking. Please let there be something here I can use.

After opening the folder, I scan through the evidence catalogue, studying every photo. I finally open one that shows a bullet lying next to a ruler, measuring its length. "Yes! I think I got it! And as far as I can tell, it looks to be the same type."

Wyn calls out. "Well, you better wrap it up because Bea's on her way back."

"Already?"

"It's not like this town is huge or anything."

My heart thumps as I print off the picture of a bullet. "Just a few more seconds. You gotta stall her."

"G, come on!"

At the bottom, I spot a link to some articles and references. "Just do it!"

Wyn faces me. "Fine. But only if you go to dinner with me."

I stop typing and check to see if he's serious before shaking my head. "Come on, Wyn, you know I can't do that."

He gives me a mischievous smile. "Well, you better or you're going to get busted."

I frown at him. "Are you serious? You're blackmailing me? Now?"

He crosses his arms and stands tall. "No better time than the present. You had better decide because she's just passing Larry's Hardware. What's it going to be, food or felony?"

I keep my eyes on the screen. "Fine, but I hate you."

Wyn shrugs. "Noted." Then he bolts out the door. I watch as he points towards the station then back at the diner. She nods, and they walk off together, obviously getting me food too.

I launch the article and read the title. *Tennessee ranger killed in hunting accident.*

This is about the ranger that died last year. I read the article until I see a name, William Cameron. Why does that name sound familiar? Instantly, it comes to me. Will Cameron. From the news articles I read last week. The game warden who busted Al in Tennessee. I cross reference the name in the database, and a photo pops up. The man seems familiar. I stare at his features for a few seconds before something clicks.

I reach into my bag and pull out the tin with Dad's photo. The one of him winning the excellence award. The one I snatched from Carl's file.

William "Will" Cameron is one of the men standing behind Dad in the picture.

My heart races. Is it possible the two cases are connected? Carl said they weren't but maybe he's wrong. I get up and peek through the blinds to check Wyn's status. He's across the street talking with Bernice and Postman Louie. He can surely kill time with them.

Man killed by a hunter, bullets unidentifiable, no hunter comes forward, death ruled an accident by the coroner. Survived by son, Morris, and daughter, Fiona.

A caption under a picture of a body covered in a white sheet reads: *Son finds dad's body and tries to revive him until paramedics show up.* My stomach clenches at the thought of watching a family member die and being completely helpless. Another photo caption reads: *The Cameron family in happier times.* I click on the photo link and wait as it launches in a new window.

The pixels slowly fill the screen and become crystal clear.

I freeze as an invisible stake pierces my heart. My stomach churns. Life stops for a split second as my brain processes what I'm seeing. I squeeze my eyes shut, hoping the picture will be different. I open one eye. No such luck.

Outside, Wyn sounds off a sharp whistle warning me that Bernice is on her way.

I punch Print and exit the application. As she walks through the door, I snatch a stack of papers off the printer and stuff them into my bag. Wyn trails close behind, eyes wide, like he's seen a naked female ghost.

Bernice holds up a brown paper sack. "Wyn says you want lunch?"

"Uh, yeah, that was sweet. I wish I could eat with you guys, but is it okay if I take it with me? Tommy wants me now."

She hands me the bag. "Sure, sweetie."

I bolt out the door before she or Wyn can ask me any questions. Around the corner, I pull the photo out of the bag and stare at Will Cameron's son.

It's definitely Mo.

Survival Skill #35

Asking yourself questions can't lead you home;
your answers matter most.

Tommy stands behind the counter conversing with a customer. He waves as I walk in the door.

As if nothing's wrong, I pin on my nametag and begin straightening the new display of touristy crap. Hats, tomahawks, and moccasins. Since when did Tommy start selling this stuff? He must need money bad.

When Tommy heads to the back, I take out my notepad and scribble a few notes about everything I've learned in the last hour.

Mo's dad was killed, and his dad knew *my* dad. His dad busted Al for hunting, then he was killed.

Why wouldn't Mo tell me about his dad, and how much of this does he really know? After everything I've confided in him, he just kept it from me? I try not to be angry because he didn't really lie or anything. Guess I can relate to keeping secrets. Some things are too painful to say aloud.

Makes them real.

Confusion surfaces and, suddenly, I've accumulated more questions than I've answered. I jot them down, still trying to process all the facts jumbled in my brain.

1) *Where is Sidehill, and who is the anonymous tipper?*
2) *Why are Al and Billy using homemade bullets?*
3) *Is Mo's dad's case related to mine? Is that why Mo is here?*

The nagging questions rattle me. I bite on the end of my pen and stare at the pictures around the store.

Someone taps me on the shoulder.

I flinch.

Tommy smiles. "Little jumpy?"

"Guess I'm in my own world." I shove my notebook into my pocket so he can't see what I'm writing.

"What's up?"

I frown. "Nothing. Why does something always have to be *up*?" I try to act normal, but I can feel myself unraveling after the morning's events. I tidy a clothing rack, dropping a few fishing vests onto the floor. As I bend over to pick them up, my butt knocks over the display behind me, sending it crashing to the ground. I drop to my knees and gather the scattered items.

Tommy squats down to help. "You sure you're okay? You seem on edge."

I grab a fishing tin from him and place it on the rack. "Everything's fine. I always knock stuff over."

"Your mom called here last night."

I restraighten the same rack. "She definitely likes to reach out and touch *everyone*. Called the whole dang town. So what? Am I going to get the Spanish Inquisition from you too?" I shuffle between the displays, adding some distance between us.

Tommy follows me into the fishing tackle section. "Who's doing that? What's wrong with you?" He can usually sense when something's off. He calls it his Indian intuition; I call it guessing.

"Your vibes must be getting a little rusty. I'm fine."

"Come on, Elu. You can talk to me."

Without thinking, I blurt out, as if the lid's been blown off a boiling pot, "They found Dad's shirt. It had blood on it."

Tommy appears horrified and opens his arms to hug me. "Gaest-ost yuh-wa da-nv-ta."

With my hands up, I back away from him. "Don't be sorry. It doesn't mean anything."

He looks confused and answers me slowly. "Okaaaay."

I toss out some more breaking news. "Wyn kissed me last night."

Tommy smiles. "I was wondering when you two would start up again."

210

One more shebang. "But I'm seeing someone else."

He stops walking. A slew of emotions slog over his face. Confusion. Disbelief. Annoyance. "Wait, what? Who?"

"His name's Mo."

Tommy squints. "Where's he from?"

I wave him off. "You don't know him. He's a freshman at Appalachian State. Studies rocks."

"College boy? Isn't that too old for you?"

I realize I'm still backing up when my butt bumps the counter. "He's only 17."

"Then how can he already be in college? That's usually 18, isn't it?"

His questions knock me off balance, and my world seems to tilt as I stammer for a response. "He moved here from overseas, so he's ahead in school."

"How'd you meet him?"

After every answer, I get more and moreout of breath like I'm running from something. "He's been living in the Appalachians, collecting rock samples for a school study."

Tommy frowns. "You met him in the woods?"

I snap back. "Noooo, not in the *woods*. On the river. Fishing."

His face remains furrowed. "So he flyfishes?"

"Well, not exactly. He's a bait fisherman. But he's learning."

Tommy shakes his head as if too much information has jammed inside. "Wait a minute. Let me get this straight. You met a strange foreign boy in the woods who says he's in college, and he doesn't flyfish?" He catches my eyes with his. "You hate bait fisherman."

"I don't *hate* bait fisherman."

Tommy touches his palm against my forehead, checking for a fever. "You must be sick."

I smack his hand away. "I think I'm old enough to look past his fishing preferences. Besides, he's the one who saved me from those men."

He scratches his head. "You've been seeing him since then? This whole time? Why didn't you tell me?"

I reverse down the aisle as anger pumps through my veins. My armor is cracking. I have to get out of here before I crumble into a heap of pieces. "Geez! What's up with the thousand and seven questions from everyone? Why can't anyone be happy for me? I tell you I'm dating someone and am happy for the first time. In a long time. And you grill me?"

His eyes are wide, and he appears shell shocked. "I'm not grilling—"

I snap back before he can finish. "Just because he's not from this crappy town, doesn't make him a bad guy, okay? Just because he doesn't flyfish, doesn't mean he's dangerous."

"Dangerous? Who said anything about—"

I beeline for the door. My only escape hatch to avoid being trapped into a lengthy interrogation. "Besides, I don't know if I *like* Wyn. So why's everyone pushing him on me?" My voice grows louder with every word.

"Who's pushing?"

I stop retreating and steady my voice. "Look, do you need me here today? 'Cause it looks pretty slow."

He checks out the empty store. "Well, no, I guess not but—"

"Good. I gotta go." I race out of the store before he can stop me. But not before tripping twice and knocking over a display of sunglasses.

Tommy calls after me. "Elu? Wait!"

I duck down the alley and slip into a dark doorway, allowing my pity and anxiety to consume me. It's official. I'm alone. I've messed up every relationship important to me. They're all disintegrating before my eyes. And there's not a dang thing I can do about it. Mom, Wyn, Tommy. Evidently, even Mo doesn't trust me.

I bury my face in my hands. But before I can break down, muffled voices float through the alleyway. Easing out of the shadow, I slither my way between all the parked cars. Last thing I need is for someone to catch me cowering behind the trash like a scared rat.

Up ahead, a truck is partially concealed behind a couple stinky dumpsters. Two men appear to be arguing, but I can't hear them over the idling engine. Waddling like a duck behind the car bumpers, I inch as close as I can without being seen. When I peek around a bumper, my heart cartwheels in my chest.

Al and Billy are out of jail.

Survival Skill #36

When night hiking, make a note of any landmarks and use your five senses.

Billy's voice squeaks. "What do we do now? We probably shouldn't hang around here."

Al cracks his knuckles. "I got a plan, don't worry."

"Shouldn't we run everything by the boss first? We could get in some hot water and don't need any more trouble."

Al growls and grabs Billy's collar, lifting him off the ground. "You on my side still? Because you don't want to be on my bad side."

Billy looks terrified. "I'll do whatever you say."

Al drops him to the ground. "Then let's go. I want to find him before it gets too dark."

My hands sweat. When were they released? My legs are cramped and start to tingle as they fall asleep. I shift from one leg to the other, and my toe grazes a tin can. It clinks across the asphalt.

Al snaps his head in my direction. "You hear that?"

I flatten my body against the pavement and slide under an Oldsmobile. My lungs burn but I refuse to take in air for fear they'll hear me. I know things won't go well if these guys catch me snooping again. From my position under the sedan's oily belly, I can see their ankles.

Billy pipes up. "What do you think?"

Al grunts. "Probably just a racoon." He pulls a green bandana out of his pocket and wipes his brow. "Come on! Boss comes back, he'll be more than pissed if we's still hanging around here."

After the men leave, I exhale through my nose and shimmy out from under the car. I try to make sense of everything floating around in my clouded head. I squeeze my eyes shut and replay every second of the scene, trying to pick out any additional clues. Who let them out? And what boss are they referring to? Then something clicks as I replay their short conversation. *I want to find him before it gets too dark.*

They're probably going after Mo.

Energy pumps through me. I need to warn him before Al gets there first. I glance at my watch. He'll probably be at the river. How can I get there without my bike?

I sneak out to the main drag and am about to cross the street when my phone rings. I immediately recognize the number and pick up, stepping back behind the corner. I keep my voice somewhat low. "Hey, Mama Sue. Did you find something?"

As I'm on the phone, Les walks out of the convenience store. He doesn't see me as he heads toward his truck.

Mama Sue's voice crackles through the fuzzy connection. "I sent the photos we copied to a custom boot guy I know in Tennessee. You'll be happy to know he found a customer order and a name that matched that print by the truck."

I slide out the picture I printed off Carl's computer and smile into the phone. "Let me guess, Alfred Smith?"

She pauses. "Well, yes. How'd you know?"

"Lucky guess." I watch as Les chucks some stuff into the bed of his truck. "Did you find out any more on the print at Station 19?"

"No, even if that one was custom made, it'll be impossible to trace."

I prop the phone against my cheek. "Even for you? Why?"

"The tread's too light. Barely visible."

My eyes follow Les as he trips then bends over to tie his frayed laces. When I focus in on his ancient boots, I almost swallow my tongue. "Let me guess. If the tread's too light, the boot is old. Right?"

Mama Sue pauses before she answers. "Ancient." I eye Les's boots as he climbs into his truck. My head starts to spin a few more pieces into place.

It can't be.

Mama Sue pipes up. "Grace, there's more."

I lean against the wall when my legs start to shake. How much more can there be? "What is it?"

"I enlarged the pictures by the truck and found a different print. One you may not have seen." My head clouds over in confusion. "That print has the same faint tread as the one you saw at the station. Do you understand what I'm saying?"

My voice sounds raw. Almost hoarse. "No."

"The person who made the faint print up at Station 19 also left a print by the truck."

As soon as I get off the phone, I spy on Les until he pulls down the street and turns out of town. Then I sink down until I'm sitting on the sidewalk. Stunned.

Both prints belong to Les? That means he was at Station 19 when he said he wasn't, but that he was close to Al's campsite. So what, he knows Al? But Les acted as if he didn't when I mentioned Al and Billy. Did he know I was at that campsite too? My mouth drops open. I suddenly feel as if my head's being held under water, and I'm flailing to catch a breath.

Les must be the boss Al and Billy were talking about. What other explanation could there be for his boot prints to be at Al and Billy's site *before* I gave him the coordinates? He already knew about them because he was working with him.

He's been in on this whole thing!

I gotta find Mo and fast. Maybe he can help me put the last few pieces of this puzzle together once and for all. After all, his dad is obviously a critical piece. But how? My eyes find the diner and suddenly I'm running. Thunder cracks in the distance as clouds roll in. I race around the back to where Mom parks her truck.

Luci sits helpless in the bed, begging me to set her free. Dragging over a piece of thin plywood, I build a ramp and rescue my motorcycle from its unjust imprisonment. Quietly, I roll Luci out of the truck and down the street.

When I'm a safe distance away, I start her up and head off to find Mo.

Before Al can find him first.

♔

Mo is now officially fifty-one minutes late for our meeting. After pacing for nearly an hour, I've worn a faint path in the carpet of pebbles and grass. He wouldn't keep me waiting this long.

Something's wrong.

Without thinking, I sprint in the direction of Mo's campsite. Maybe he didn't think we were meeting today or maybe he's still hanging out at his place. Seems logical since that's the last place we were together. I travel deeper into the woods, moving in the direction we headed the day before, begging the sagging sun for more time. It grows more shadowy as I head into the belly of the forest. Nothing and everything looks familiar. Luckily, I noted the coordinates of where I found the bullet so Mo's campsite can't be far from there.

The underbrush grows dense and a thin trail wiggles through the trees, twisting and turning. I stop to study my watch again. According to my position, I'm close. Moving on, I attempt to track Mo by searching for tramped grass or other signs of disturbance. The forest's ceiling turns from green to grey. Maybe it's smarter to go home and get help.

No, I can't give up. I'm determined to warn Mo. If anything happens to him, it will be my fault.

After a few more yards, I check my position again.

This should be the place.

I take out my flashlight and step into a clearing. The area is bare. No sign of anything. Undisturbed. I stumble around, looking for signs of his fire pit. Could this be the wrong place? Maybe along the way, I went off track? Turned around?

217

An owl hoots above me, perched in the safety of his wooden nook. His eyes glow in the dim light. My mouth falls open and I sink to my knees, remembering his call from the night before.

This is Mo's site.

But he's gone.

The tarp's vanished along with his man-made shelter. The mound of ashes from his fire pit has disappeared. There's no trace of him. At least not any I can see in the dim light.

It's as if he didn't exist. How can it be that two important people in my life are seemingly untraceable?

How could Al possibly get here before me? They didn't even know where to look. Or did they?

No, that's ridiculous.

I must be the reason Mo's gone. Maybe I said something wrong or messed up without knowing. Maybe I scared him off. I reanalyze every second of our last night together, searching for a sign. Dissect every word, every kiss, every moment.

Pacing the campsite, I look for signs, a clue, something. Maybe a trail pointing me in the right direction, showing me which way he went. My light arcs back and forth along the ground. That's when I notice the faint, parallel lines scrape the dirt in perfect rows. As if someone has raked the ground. It takes a few seconds before I make the connection.

Someone's cleared Mo's campsite. Hiding the evidence.

Just like they did at Station 19.

I drop down on all fours and scout around for more clues. Searching under bushes. Around trees. Studying leaves. Checking trunks. I find a few chips in the bark of one. Identical to the ones I found with Wyn. I check the leaves along all the paths leading out of the space and find a shoe print.

I know without even looking.

They match Al's. Perfectly.

I abandon the trail and follow the tracks. They lead away from the camp until they just disappear. Right when I'm about to give up, something gleams from underneath a thick bush.

I plunge my hand in and touch something small and cold. I know what it is before I even see it.

I hold it up in the light to analyze it.

Another dum dum.

My world plays on slow motion for a short period. I collapse onto a log. My mouth arid, my throat clogged, and my legs can no longer support the burden of everything that's been dumped on my shoulders in the last twenty-four hours. It takes a few seconds for logic to override my shock. After being paralyzed for a short time, my gut springs alive.

Al and Billy were here.

They must've found Mo before I did.

I have to tell Carl.

Behind me, I see a beam of light. Sweeping. Searching. My heart does jumping jacks in my chest. I hop to my feet and hide. Hoping it's Mo.

Praying it's not Al or Billy.

Survival Skill #37

If you have a map or a compass, you will most likely be able to move toward help.

From behind a tree, I watch as a shadowy figure hovers under the leafy cover.

Against my better judgment, I call out to the shape. "Mo? Is that you?" *Please let it be you.*

A silouette emerges from the spindly cover.

I immediately recognize the movement and flick on my flashlight to reveal a friendly face. My heart sinks and a sliver of frustration pops out in my voice. "Tommy! What are you doing here?"

He shines his light in my face. "I should be asking you that question."

I shield my eyes. "How'd you find me?"

He shrugs. "I tracked you. Have you forgotten I taught your dad everything?"

"I don't understand. Why would you do that?"

He wraps me in a hug. "After you ran out of the shop, your mom came by. Said you stole Luci after being grounded. She didn't know where you were."

I huff. "I can't *steal* something that belongs to me."

Tommy places a hand on my shoulder and squeezes. "She's worried about you. Wyn is too. He came into the store right after your mom left. When he found out you'd left on your bike, he told me everything that's been going on. Said you found something on Carl's computer that upset you."

I nod as tears stream down my face.

Tommy hugs my shoulders. "Come on. Let's get you inside so we can talk this out."

"Where?"

"Let me be the leader for once." He twitches his eyebrows and offers a strong hand. My mind races as we hike together. All the while, it's as if my brain's rebooting. The events of the last few weeks spew out in random order. I scroll through a list of crazy theories about Mo's disappearance. About Les. About Dad.

Tommy breaks my concentration. "What do you think?"

Slightly disoriented, I squint in the moonlight. As my eyes adjust, I slowly make out some kind of hut made from woven saplings, mud, and poplar bark. "What is this place?"

"My home away from home." He motions me inside. "Ehiyha."

"Thanks." I push the door open first and stand in a pitch black room. Behind me, a bright lamp flickers to life, instantly brightening up the cozy space. The room is scattered with rustic furniture made from pine logs. Lanterns swing from metal rods, and a stone fireplace frames one wall.

Tommy slides out a small wooden chair from under the hand-carved table.

I lower myself into it and relax. "Did you build this?"

He makes his way around to the other side and places his hands on the back of a chair. "This hut's been a part of the Qualla Boundary history and in my family for years. Since the Trail of Tears. Ama and I made some changes to make it more livable. Even built the furniture ourselves. It was our special place to get away." Looking sad, he walks to the fireplace in the corner and hangs an iron kettle in a rod before sitting down next to me.

"How come I never knew about this place?"

Tommy glances around the space and shrugs. "Not many people know about it. If they did, it'd probably end up a tourist site. Small chance of finding it out here in these woods so I just kept it quiet. Your dad knew about it though."

My heart performs a bellyflop when he mentions Dad. Reminding me of my situation. He and Mo are gone. And it's all my fault. If I'd gone with Dad that day, he might be here. If I hadn't followed Al to his campsite, Mo wouldn't be in this mess either.

Tommy pours some steaming water into a cup and drops in a tea bag. "Do you want to tell me what's going on? Maybe I can help."

Everything spills out in a random sequence. I ignore punctuation and don't even breathe between sentences. Some of what I say, Tommy's heard, but some of it's new. The whole time I talk, he doesn't say a word. Not a doubt. Not a question. He only nods. As if everything makes sense. Which, of course, is impossible. None of this makes any sense. I stop when there's nothing else left to say. My shoulders slump forward in exhaustion.

Tommy exhales, telling me he's held his breath this whole time too. He whistles. "Wow. You're in deep, Elu."

"I know. What do I do?" To burn off the adrenaline pressing against my chest, I stroll around the open space, studying the Cherokee artifacts that decorate his walls.

He shakes his head. "Maybe I should've helped more? Then you wouldn't be in this position."

I stop at his desk and eye an old picture frame, hanging on the wall. "It's not your fault Dad's missing."

He mutters behind me. "Maybe."

I call out over my shoulder. "What do you mean? What does any of this have to do with you?"

Leaning in, I inspect the art surrounded by an old gold frame. The paper is so old, it's now sporting a yellowish-brownish hue. As I stare at the details, I realize it's some kind of old map.

Tommy doesn't answer.

Just as I'm about to try and convince him, something catches my eye. My stomach sinks, and the room begins to tilt.

I spin around and face Tommy in disbelief. "Oh, my God. It was you?"

Survival Skill #38

*Having knowledge of proper navigation, the enemy,
and the terrain are key to the planning process.*

Tommy blinks but doesn't say a word. He doesn't have to.
His eyes confirm everything.

I point at him. "You were the anonymous caller?"

He breaks eye contact. "I don't know what you mean."

The reality settles in and releases my pent-up anger. "You're
the one who called in the tip." I tap on the old map with my
finger. The glass trembles in fear. "And it's right here. *Sidehill.*" I
want him to deny everything. To tell me I'm wrong.

Tommy's face doesn't lie.

Before he can say anything, I erupt again. "This whole time,
you've known all about it? You've known where Sidehill is!" My
voice echoes through the small cabin. So loud, I almost want to
cover my own ears.

His voice comes out flat. Cold. "Yes."

I stumble back a few steps as if he kicked me square in the
gut. Suddenly, I want to press rewind. Pretend the last few
minutes never existed, yet the rawness of my throat reminds me
of the truth. Covering my mouth with both hands, I try to trap in
my words. "Oh, my God."

Tommy won't meet my eyes. "Gaest-ost yuh-wa da-nv-ta."

I holler at him, mimicking a screech monkey. "No! You don't
get to apologize and pretend it's all okay. So are you gonna tell *me*
what is really going on?"

He surrenders with his hands. "Calm down, Elu."

I shake my head. "Calm down? *You* don't get to say that to
me. You're part of the reason I'm a total basketcase. You lied to
me. Tell me what's going on ... NOW!"

He jerks back, seemingly surprised at my verbal attack and glass-shattering volume. His voice quakes. "A few days before your dad went missing, I was hiking back to town from an old Indian burial ground, Sidehill, and came across some type of camp."

The butterflies in my stomach are replaced by a deep, twisted feeling. I place my hand on my belly to settle my spinning nerves. "What kind of camp, Tommy?"

He practically whispers, as if saying the truth quieter makes it hurt less. "I'm not sure."

"Why did you report it?"

Tommy thinks for a moment. "It smelled funny. I left before I got a good look. Didn't want them to find the burial or anything."

"You *left?*" My voice bounces into a higher octave. "Let me get this straight. You found some type of stinky campsite, weird enough for you to call the police with an anonymous tip, but you *left* without checking it out? And even after my dad went missing, you kept it from me?"

His sad eyes droop. "I called it in, but I assumed it wasn't connected."

"But you didn't *know* that." I lean against the wall for support. Speaking words this fast and loud is sapping my energy. Making me lightheaded.

Tommy repeats himself. "I'm sorry."

"Stop saying that." I study Tommy's face in the flickering light. Suddenly, I realize this isn't the man I've known my entire life. My stand-in grandpa whom I've loved so much is gone. He even looks different. Like a complete stranger.

Panic gushes through me. Everyone I care about has betrayed me. Carl's shut me out, Mom's abandoned me, Les is a traitor, and now Tommy's lied to me. I reenter my body and will my lungs to breathe.

Tommy answers me. "Elu, I didn't mean to keep anything from you. I assumed the police checked it out already and it wasn't connected."

224

I slam my hands down on the table. "But the police probably couldn't find it, Tommy! It's not on any modern trail maps!"

Tommy looks horrified. "Are you sure?"

"Yes, I'm sure. I wouldn't lie to *you*." In a flash, something clicks. Some pieces move into place. "Al and Billy must be hiding in the woods and killing bears to make a quick buck. Dad must have found out and they had no choice but to take him. Maybe even wanted him to help them track. Sidehill must be where their real camp is. This whole time, you could've made a difference."

"I didn't want to get involved."

I plaster on a disgusted look. "Involved? Don't you care what happens to my dad? Your friend?"

"You know I do. But it was the police's job. I have my own things to protect."

I grab my hair and tug in frustration. "What things? What's so *important* that it's worth turning your back on my dad? Lying to me?"

Tommy sighs in defeat. "Every year, a few of the Eastern Cherokees hike up to Sidehill on the anniversary of Tsali's death."

I'm confused. "Why?"

"To pray. *Sidehill* is Tsali's resting place. One of the only Cherokee burial sites still intact."

I shake my head as facts stream by. "I thought you said Tsali was buried under Lake Fontana?"

"That story was concocted years ago to throw people off. Thousands of sacred places have been destroyed by tourists, even historians. When someone tampers with a burial ground, they disturb the resting spirits. I didn't want to call any attention to where it was. Have people tracking in and out up there."

My mouth gapes open. "I can't believe what I'm hearing. You're the same man who gave up everything to help Ama fight cancer. To keep her alive. Now you're giving up on the living and are more focused on the dead then ever. So my dad ... has to suffer ... for a man who died ... over a hundred years ago?"

225

Tommy looks at me with tears in his eyes. "He wasn't just a man! He is my blood, and he's a hero. He's protecting Ama in the afterlife until I join her."

Tears stream down my face. "He's dead, Tommy! Dad might still be alive. Besides, Tsali gave up his life for the people he loved. What have you done to honor that? Nothing. You've turned your back on me, on Dad, on everything Tsali stood for?"

Tommy stares down at his moccasins. "You wouldn't understand what's important to the reservation. Only our ancestors understand."

I screech. "You mean *ghosts*!"

He shakes his head. "I told the police. What more could I do? They were the ones who decided it wasn't important. Not me."

"No, you just didn't do anything to make sure." I rip the framed picture off the wall and smash it on the ground. When I snatch the map from the shattered pile, a piece of glass slices my hand. I'm so numb, I barely feel the cut across my skin. "You know what? I'm not turning my back on Dad the way you have. I'm going to help the people I love. Like Tsali. Unlike you." I stomp out of the hut and storm off into the darkening woods.

Tommy calls after me. "Elu! *Higinelii!*"

All I can do is scream goodbye. "You're no friend of mine! *Do-na-da-go-v-i!*"

I grab my bag and run from the house without looking back. I can't bear to see the stranger standing there, making excuses. Tears streak my face as I fight my way through the trees. A thick mist hovers over the forest floor. I don't even know where I'm going but I know I'm too angry to stop.

Then, a dog barks in the distance. I'd recognize that bark anywhere.

It's Bear.

Wonder what he's doing so far out here, so far from the station? I head off in the direction of the sound. About a half a mile later, clapping noises echo through the woods followed by more barking.

I freeze. It takes a second for my brain to process what I just heard.

And this time, I know exactly what they are.

Gunshots.

Survival Skill #39

Mental preparation is a vital part
of the rock-climbing experience.

𝕴n an instant, the forest transforms from a peaceful refuge into a danger zone. Without hesitating, I bolt toward the ruckus, running over thickets, jumping rotted logs, and protecting my face. Another shot rings out followed by a yelp. I try to figure out which direction they are coming from and maneuver over uneven ground.

Then I spot a dark mound ahead. I inch closer and see Bear lying in the leaves with red patches of clumped fur along his chest.

"Jesus." I slide in next to him and lay his head on my lap. "It's okay. I got yah."

My hand feels warm and when I pull back, I notice it's covered in blood. I quickly take out my bandana and press it on Bear's wounds. Within a few seconds, the rag soaks with blood.

Bear stares up at me with brown eyes. His eyebrows twitch. Like he's asking me what's going on and I have no answers for him. Then his eyes droop a little and flutter.

I bury his head against the warmth of my body so I can't see his face and listen to the slowing of his breath, my hand covering his creeping heart. For some reason, I start rocking back and forth, humming some song I can't remember.

My tears splash along his muzzle as I stroke Bear's head. I remember all the times he'd curl up and sleep on my bed until Dad got home from work. Memories of Bear come flooding back. Him as a puppy chasing squirrels through our house. Him at Thanksgiving when he stole Mom's turkey. Him laying in the station's driveway for days, waiting for my dad to come home after he went missing.

Eventually, his labored breathing is consumed by complete silence.

My hand trembles as I check for a pulse. Any sign of life.

But Bear is dead. My dad's dog is dead.

Then I feel Bear's body relax fully and lighten.

In that moment, I realize there's a glimmer of beauty found in death. When something bigger sweeps in undetected and cradles the dying. In the last breath, the place where pain finally surrenders to complete peace.

After covering his body with leaves, I sit facing the mound and cradle my head with both hands. Tears and sweat dribble down my face.

Soon, my sorrow and confusion shift into rage.

My body tenses and I clamp my jaws together, gritting my teeth.

Why are these men killing innocent animals for fun?

I stroke Bear's fur at the same time I'm scanning the woods, on full alert. Even though I don't want to leave Bear behind, I know I need to push on and end this thing, once and for all.

Whoever killed Bear is involved in the disappearance of Dad and probably Mo too.

I unfold Tommy's map and plan my route to Sidehill. It's critical I make good time and get as close to the camp as possible before the sun sets.

I will get my dad back, if it's the last thing I do. At this point, that's all that matters. I can't see anything else.

I stand and march away. Leaving behind so much. A friend, a life, a family. But no matter what, I don't look back. Step by step, I move away from safety.

Towards who knows what.

 C3

Hours pass by, but I push on without stopping for food, water, or rest. My feet ache, and my muscles cramp. Over the long hike, my adrenaline and anger have faded, allowing logic and pain to seep in. If I'm going to stay alert, I need to get rehydrated and reenergized. I gulp down some liquid and pour a stream of water over the back of my neck. The coolness shocks my body, causing me to gasp. For the first time, I notice my stomach is grumbling. I can't remember the last time I actually ate. While taking note of my coordinates, I slip the emergency pack out of my backpack and eat a stale granola bar.

I'm halfway there.

As I check my path, Tommy's betrayal resurfaces. I can't understand how or why he turned his back on me. On Dad. What was he thinking? I should have taken this trip months ago. Tommy's lies and secrets have held me back from solving this whole thing.

Because of him, I've failed Dad.

As the minutes tick by, my body surrenders to exhaustion. I feel heavier, as if I'm becoming a part of this place and growing roots that keep me here. Alone. Forever.

The woods have a way of messing with you. Of tearing you down. If you're not careful, it can break you. The isolation. The darkness. It can sweep through you unexpectedly.

I toss aside the weighted feelings and force myself on my feet. Sidehill is still so far away. The thought of Les struggling up this path actually makes me smile. Maybe there was a reason I never favored him, even though Dad loved him like a brother. I wonder if Dad knew about Les's involvement with Al and Billy.

I snatch a walking stick for extra support and move up the steep mountainside. A thin path zigzags up the hill as I push through the snaking weeds and tangled vines. Eventually, I come to a rocky wall. Taking a small stick, I clean out the packed dirt and pebbles stuck in the lugs of my boots.

Hoping to make up some time, I scale up the cragged side. As I slither up the ridge, the edges of sharp rocks dig into my palms. I'm reminded of my climb with Mo—how quickly he scaled the wall. After recovering on a few slips, I finally reach the top and peer over the ledge to confirm it's safe. Then after grabbing hold of a hanging root, I attempt to pull up.

The prickly vine snaps under my weight.

Suddenly, I'm sliding back down the sharp, rocky side. Scraping my hands down the wall, my fingers fumble for a crevice while the tips of my toes search for any foothold. I grab a thin ledge and cling to the wall by my fingertips. My arms burn, and my breath becomes jagged. Panic threatens my sanity as the weight of my bag begins tugging me backwards into the mouth of the mountain. Slowly, I manuever my foot around until it lands on a tiny shelf. My body presses into the uneven rock wall.

When I look down, my breathing speeds up as the sensation of plummeting to my death taunts me. I'm dangling a hundred feet above the ground.

Waiting to be unlodged. Like a pebble on a mountain.

My adrenaline and survival instincts kick in. Slowly, crack by crack, I creep back up the rocky face. This time, when I reach the top, I keep a firm grip and hoist myself over the crag. As soon as my body finds solid ground, I flip onto my back and stare at the dark sky through the treetops. The grass tickles my neck, and the wet ground seeps through my shirt.

I peer over the cliff and smile. I made it. Sometimes, things don't look as hard as they really are until you conquer them. The drop is straight down. I whisper a prayer of thanks to whoever is watching over me on this mountain. The Big Man upstairs deserves a huge bonus for working overtime these last few weeks.

I stand up and turn to leave, tripping over something hard. Seems like I'm on my butt more than my feet these days.

Brushing off my pants, I look back and find two eyes staring right at me.

Billy.

Survival Skill #40

If stuck in the wilderness at night, be sure to set up your camp and start a fire before nightfall.

Death has such a distinct smell, I don't know how I didn't detect it sooner.

A burning sensation slides up the back of my throat. I scramble away from the body and swallow a few times to settle my churning stomach. I've never seen a dead body before. Animals, yes, but not humans. The scent is so powerful, I can almost taste the rotting flesh. My stomach clenches, and all of a sudden I'm wretching. Luckily, there's not much in my gut.

Once I finally stop heaving, I wipe my mouth on my sleeve and cover my nose. Breathing through my mouth, I look at Billy long enough to analyze his mangled body. He has a vacant look on his face and has obviously been dead for a few hours, given the bugs crawling in the cavities of his body. A large bullet hole sits in the center of his forehead. Streams of thick, coagulated blood streak out of his nostrils and ears. His mouth hangs open as if he was singing or yelling when he died. His arm is folded behind his head in an unnatural way.

Immediately, I double over and hurl again. My body convulses and my stomach cramps, but I can't stop staring at the gray, bloated body.

Billy almost looks fake. Like some kind of strange yoga mannequin.

I glance up and study the palisade. A few broken branches cling to another cliff towering above me. Obviously, someone shot Billy and launched his skinny body over the side. Now what? Should I frisk him? Maybe I would find something. Something useful. The guys on *CSI* rifle through the pockets of dead people all the time and usually find something useful to their case.

Maybe Billy has something I need?

I steal another glance at the dead man and shake my head. No way I'm touching a stiff. Don't care what he has on him, I gotta draw the line somewhere.

Wanting to put distance between me and the body, I charge off down the path. Not only away from Billy, but also what he represents. Death, deceit, and everything evil. My sporadic breath buzzes in my ear, and my heart beats against my temples. A wail sneaks out of my lips. My quiet life has become a bad B movie. Murder. Betrayal. Even zombies. If they can kill Billy, that means they can kill my dad without even blinking?

Billy's warped body haunts me. His contorted face. Empty eyes. The cramped posture of his body. I can almost still smell him. The scent of rot. I gag and bend over the weeds. This time, only dry heaving. There's nothing left inside me to purge.

I'm hollow. Empty. A shell.

Crouching down on the path, I crawl into a downed tree trunk to hide. A tree's long roots drape around me, helping me feel safe. Sobbing, I smother the sounds with my arm and curl into a ball like a roly poly, wanting to disappear. Let the weeds grow over me until I'm no longer here.

I close my eyes and wish myself away to a special place.

Home.

ଓଷ

I must have cried myself to sleep because when I wake, the sun's disappeared behind the trees. Squinting, I check my watch. Six p.m. Even though I don't want to stop, I have no choice but to set up camp in the dark.

I force myself to leave the safety of the bushes. About a half mile down the path, I find a carved-out space dug into the mountainside. Good enough to provide some protection, shelter, and concealment. Not to mention, protect me against an ambush from the rear. Sitting against the rock, I do a quick inventory of the few supplies left in my bag. Unfortunately, I didn't plan on camping so I only have a few items left: a small plastic tarp, a flint, a knife, a flashlight, a few pieces of gum, Bea's smashed paper bag lunch, a small rope, and a poncho.

Deciding to make a lean-to shelter, I cut my tarp into two pieces. Half to make a waterproof roof and the other half for bedding. After collecting large, leafy branches, I construct two Y-shaped supports and hammer them into the ground with a rock. Then I suspend a long pole along the top and lean strong branches against the beam. Next step is to weave saplings over and under the sloping branches, creating a thick lattice that will not only hide me, but keep me from being exposed to any rain or wind. I go back and forth about starting a fire, wondering if it's the safest thing to do. But I haven't heard any out of place noises in a long time so I can only assume the guys are long gone and not looking for me.

A fire is one of the most important things to have if you're lost or stuck out in the woods. Somehow it lifts your spirits. I stack up a small nest of tinders and use a flint to catch a spark. As soon as the pile starts to smoke, I blow lightly to massage any flickers of flame. Once a fire begins to dance, I break a few sticks and stack them on top until it's roaring with warmth.

I sit on my rain poncho and rub my hands together. There's something about making a small fire that makes you feel safe. The light cuts the darkness in half, preventing me from being swallowed. I grip the handle of my knife and keep it close.

Just in case.

Mosquitos hum in my ear as the dying embers mesmerize me. I can't help but think about my last night with Mo. How we cuddled in front of a similiar fire. Was that only a day ago? I tuck my legs underneath me. In the distance, thunder warns me of the approaching rain. The ground shakes to get my attention.

A few seconds later, lightning cracks the sky in half, and the clouds begin to cry.

I know how they feel. I try to quiet my spinning thoughts. Mom pops into my head. Even though I know it's out of range, I check my phone for a signal. It's official, I'm on my own. She's going to have a field day with this when I get home.

If I get home.

Even though I don't want to admit it, I miss her.

∽

I barely sleep a wink. As soon as dawn approaches, I put out my fire, careful to stir the ashes, and bury any evidence. I disassemble my shelter and erase any sign of my temporary camp. Soon after packing up my stuff, I plod deeper into the mountains. Nothing stops me, as my body is on autopilot. I trudge on for miles. Hours. Nothing goes in or out of my fogged-over brain, as if I'm on cruise control. The tough terrain saps my energy, but I push forward, munching on the rest of Bea's now-soggy sandwich for energy.

According to the map, Sidehill should only be a couple miles further. My calves cramp from propelling me up the steep slope. My legs have morphed into two stiff boards, aching with every step. My pants are still damp from the night's drizzle, leaving me soggy and uncomfortable. This trip seems to take longer, the farther I go. I'm miles away from anywhere, anyone, or anything. Several times, it crosses my mind to give up and turn back, afraid of what's ahead.

Right when I think I can't take one more step … I smell smoke.

My heart stumbles. This is it.

I stop and kneel, preparing to crawl closer. First, I tie my knife and sheath to my calf and conceal it with my pant leg. After tightening the straps on my backpack, I smear dirt on my face to tone down the flesh color. Slithering into the trees, I follow the scent of the fire, taking in the smallest details of my surroundings with all six senses. It's critical I detect them before they notice me. I move like a shadow, blending in and conforming my shape to the surroundings, every few yards performing listening halts to detect any sound that's out of place.

Eventually, male voices drift through the trees and cut the silence. They remain muffled so the words aren't easy to make out. Up ahead, firelight splits the dark tree line. Cautiously, methodically, I slink toward the skipping light. An overwhelming stench punches me in the nose, and my stomach convulses.

I can't take another corpse encounter.

After gagging a few times, I bury my nose in my sleeve. I strategically place my feet along the path, knees shaking, and keep my arms tucked in tight, minimizing my form. Eventually, I drop onto my belly and crawl commando-style under the thick vegetation.

When I reach the edge of the hill, I peer over.

A horror I never imagined reveals itself.

Survival Skill #41

*To be camouflaged in the woods, cover up in mud,
hide in vegetation, and move in the shadows.*

The remote camp consists of several tents arranged in a U-shape. A huge bonfire roars in the middle of a circle of men wearing faded fatigues. Green bandanas cover their mouths and noses, allowing only their eyes to be seen. There's an added strangeness when you can't see people's faces. It's why I hate Halloween.

On one side of the camp, bear hides hang from the spindly trees. An assortment of ice coolers lie underneath stretched-out skins and alongside heaping buckets of what looks like salt. My dad's articles come to mind. The coolers probably store organs, and the salt must be to preserve the skin.

Several dead bears line up along the ground like sardines in a tin can. A man with a machete marches up to one of the carcasses. Without hestitation, he chops off the paws in four quick blows. Then he reaches inside another bear's stiff body and removes a blobby mass. An organ of some sort. After packing everything in an ice chest, he scribbles a number on the top.

My brain has a hard time reacting to the scene, refusing to process any of this in a way that makes sense. This is much larger than anything I could have imagined. A few grunts and roars echo through the area. What was that? I pull away from the horrific images and sneak along the cliff line toward the sounds.

Once I clear a clump of trees, a few large bears stand cramped in tiny cages. The bars of the cages dig into their hides, leaving open sores. Long, metal tubes protrude from their guts as a milky liquid, which I can only assume is bile, drains into large containers. At the end of the row, a large bear thrashes inside the small cage, banging his head against the prison. Others make horrible snorting sounds, gasping for every last breath.

A man yells over the crowd, and a group of men begin to gather in front of a large tent. A few pat each other on the back as if they're meeting at happy hour for cheap beer. A man steps out of the canopy and whistles.

I instinctively duck when I recognize him. Chief Reed. I stare at his face in disbelief. A hush sweeps over the small crowd as he holds up a fat stack of money. "It's payday, boys! Better to pass it out here than in town where someone can see us." The men break into a cheer until Chief Reed whistles for them to quiet down. "Let's run over our numbers to date."

He glances down at a piece of paper. "So far, we've harvested a hundred and seventy-two bear paws and forty-three gall bladders. As some of you know, the gallbladders go for about thirty-five hundred a pop and around two hundred for each paw. Two pounds of bear bile is now going for up to four-hundred thousand dollars. Do the math, boys. Better than last month." The men high-five each other as Chief Reed passes out rubber-banded bundles of cash.

How could this happen in my own town? With people I know? Usually these kinds of extremists are whackadoos from other places. Florida or California. Not from here. I remain frozen on the hill. Afraid to move. Afraid to breathe. I can't do anything but watch the merciless mutilation and killing of these animals. The same ones Dad and I worked so hard to protect.

Everything I've learned falls into place and begins to make sense.

As if that's even possible.

This is a poaching ring. A big one too. These men are slaughtering bears and shipping them overseas for money. I know from Dad's articles that bear claws, gall bladders, and bile are hot commodities in the Asian market. From what I read, some of these animals live in bear farms their entire life. Their parts are used in bear paw soup, bile medicines, bear bile powder, and claw jewelry.

I happen to know that only one or two percent of all U.S. poachers get caught. That means lots of people get away with the illegal hunting and selling of our wildlife. It was the main reason Dad worked as a game warden.

To help catch the ones that got away.

A few grunting noises catch my attention and yank me out of my daze. I spot a bear cub tied to a tree on the slope below me several yards away. It wails under a muzzle and thrashes around, clawing at the rope strapping it down. The men either ignore it, don't hear it, or don't care. I slither along the trees until I'm directly above the little animal. A large dead female lies beside him. Probably the mother. Her gut is sliced open, and all four paws are missing. The cub yelps and chews on his leash.

At first, I ignore him. I can't sacrifice myself to save an orphaned cub. Who will take care of him? The more I hear his cries, the more my heart tugs inside my chest. Dad would never leave an animal behind, no matter how dangerous things ever got. I think about Simon as a cub. I couldn't save him, but maybe I can help this little guy to make up for Simon's unfair death.

The pants and dark shirt work well in the woods but I need to be sure my skin is concealed. I smear some more mud on my face and arms before sliding down the slope. The cub is tied behind a tent so at least there's a barrier between the men and me. Once I reach the bottom, I shimmy across the ground until I'm only a few feet away. In the background, Chief Reed's voice fills the air. I make my way behind the tent and step into a pile of steel traps. Luckily, they weren't set. Picking up one, I study the large rusted jaws. Illegal and inhumane.

I lay it to the side and approach the cub. He sniffs the air and rises onto his back legs, yelping a series of groans and squeaks. I stop and wait. Even though he's only a baby, cubs can weigh seventy-five pounds and are total powerhouses of muscle. One swipe of his claw would slice me in half. I mimic a few noises, hoping to calm him.

The little cub drops down onto all fours and slinks toward me. He sniffs my hand until I scratch his little head. He snuggles against my leg as I untie the double knot. As soon as I slip the binding off his neck, the cub lumbers over to his dead mother. He groans a bit and nuzzles her, trying to get her to move.

The scene brings tears to my eyes, reminding me so much of the day we found Simon. I gently pet the bear's head. "She's gone, buddy," I whisper.

He stands up and hugs my arm with both his paws, wrestling and grunting.

I jerk my hand away and scold him quietly. "No playing. Now shoo. You gotta get outta here." The ball of black fur cocks his head and rubs against my leg. I push him off. "Go. Before they hear you." After several attempts, I climb back up the hill toward the path, hoping the unsuspecting bear will follow me to safety. As I expected, he lumbers after me. Once we reach the top, I push him down the path. "You don't want to hang out with me. I'll get you killed."

The cub stares at me for a moment as if thinking about what I said. Then he scoots off. As he disappears into the thick, shaded greenery, I notice the peculiar white comma marking his rump and try to think of a name. "You better never try and eat me … Lucky."

Chief Reed's voice pulls me back to my mission. I sneak back around to the front and listen, totally disgusted that I've actually eaten dinner at his house before. At his table! It was along time ago but still. Makes me wonder what I was eating. Now I'm starting to think the bears in his pits got off lucky compared to these.

"Okay, men. Lets stick with the program. We need to keep working at the same pace before we move on. We have free rein until the new bear sanctuary opens. Until they start tagging bears, they won't be able to detect any change in numbers. As long as we stay clean and quiet, we'll be rich. No sloppiness, and no thrill kills. Got it?"

The crowd of men chants. "Yes, sir!"

Chief Reed claps. "We have a small window to get as many bears as possible. If the Bear Protection Act ever passes, it'll be harder to transport these parts out of the country." He paces in front of the cluster of men with his hands clasped behind his back, like he's a drill sergeant. "Listen up. I'm giving you guys a free ride here. If you break any of the boss's rules, don't be fooled. You will be killed. No questions asked. Understand?"

I cower at his statement, but the men sing out in unison as if in a church choir. "Yes, sir."

"Pick up all casings, do not hunt for fun, and if you kill a bear and can't haul it back, record the coordinates so we can go clean up your mess. We don't want nothing left behind that would raise any flags. Got it? Good. Happy hunting."

The men cheer again as Chief Reed disappears into the tent. The crowd slowly disbands as a few of the men remove their face cloths. I watch as the masked men slowly transform into regular-looking humans. A few of them I recognize from town. Postman Louie and Mr. Fields are the two that surprise me the most. I guess now I know the source of Mr. Fields's renovation financing. That means Les has been working his magic in town. I wonder who else is involved. I think through all the other shop owners and can't think of any more likely suspects. Most of them are women.

I step back a few steps. This operation is way too big for me to tackle alone. I've got to get some help before these guys leave the area. Noting the coordinates on my watch, I snap a few pictures with my digital camera. This will be just enough to get Carl up here when he gets back.

As I turn to leave, I focus in on one man rubbing his hands through his hair. He turns in my direction and pulls the bandana off.

I scream when I see his face.

241

Survival Skill #42

To throw pursuers off track, change the course of
action unexpectedly.

℘t's Mo.

I squeeze my eyes shut, hoping the vision will disappear. It's only when I hear my wail reverberate through the forest do I realize how loud I really screamed.

Mo snaps his head in my direction. We stare each other down for what seems like an eternity. In those few seconds, a series of expressions wash over his face.

A few other men point toward me. That's when I notice I'm standing on both feet and out in the wide open. I couldn't be more visible if I'd been wearing a red shirt that said *kill me*. In hearing the commotion, Chief Reed barrels out of the tent and glances in my direction. His eyes narrow, and his teeth gnash.

"Damn it, grab her!"

A small crowd sprints up the hill toward me. Even as they charge in my direction, I remain frozen in place a few seconds longer than I should, taking in Mo's face. The last moment of the old "us." I'll never see him in the same way again. It takes everything I have to rip my eyes away.

A bullet zings through the woods, a small missile searching for a target. Missing my head by mere inches, it splinters a tree next to me, spraying shards of bark onto the deserted path. It's as if someone snapped their fingers next to my head, I wake up from my brief daze and take off, hoping to hide in the shelter of the woods.

Branches slap me in the face as I tear through the trees. My backpack bumps against me with every swerve and hop. I skid to a halt at the fork in the path, not sure which trail to choose.

Adrenaline bursts through my veins as another puff of dust explodes at my feet. Trees slap me in the face, stinging my cheeks, and the trail spits mud at my pants. I veer east and weave through the trees. As my feet beat hard down the broken path, my mind blocks out any thoughts.

I don't stop. I can't stop.

White dots spiral across my eyes as my body begs for air. I slip behind a tree to catch my breath. Behind me, deep voices echo, but only muffled words reach my ears. I can't tell what they're saying or from which direction they're coming.

At the thought of being captured, fear coils around my chest like a boa constrictor. My head pounds with pain as my brain threatens to escape. My eyes dart across the monotonous woods, searching for a way out. The voices float all around me but I can't see them so I still have some time before they close in.

I have to be smart about this. I need a plan or I have no chance.

Think. Think.

I listen for the slightest sound, search for the tiniest movement.

Nothing.

As a wildlife enforcement officer, Dad believed the woods would talk to me if I could be still enough to listen. Closing my eyes, I concentrate on the space around me.

Listening. Waiting. Afraid to breathe.

A light breeze slithers through the ghostly forest. The leaves rustle and the trees hiss as if whispering secrets to each other. The forest appears to exhale then hold its breath. Everything goes as quiet as a graveyard at midnight. Nothing scurries, burrows, or twitters. The trees stop swaying and freeze, as if they're hiding too. And then I hear it: the distant snap of a random twig. The hair on my neck bristles.

They're still after me.

In the silence, Dad's voice reminds me what to do. *Our tracks are the earth's reaction to us and give proof of you. If you don't want to be found, erase any evidence that you exist.*

Suddenly, a strange calmness pumps through me. I lick my finger to test the wind's direction so I can stay upwind. Then I quickly pinpoint my coordinates and map out a different route to Luci. I can do this. I just need to be smart about it and quiet.

Once I'm ready, I tiptoe out of my hiding place and backtrack a few feet down the trail. Sticking to the side, I cover any evidence of my existence. As soon as I reach the cliff edge, I secure my backpack and rub the bottom of my boots off on a dry rock to clean them before scaling the mountainside. The knifelike edges rub the lacerations already on my hands, but I fight through the pain. To achieve smooth climbing, I only move one body part at a time. Foot, hand, body. At the top, I propel myself over the ledge.

For miles, I evade the men and inch toward Luci. Everything aches. My heart and body weigh down as if big blocks of ice have been tied to my shoes. Only one thing keeps me going.

If I want to find Dad, I have to get back to Carl. Alive.

I round a bend in the path and bend over to catch a quick breath.

Out of nowhere, something hard slams against the side of my head.

My vision blurs. I have no idea which way is up, but my body leans to one side. Suddenly, I'm trapped in an invisible hourglass, and someone's flipped me upside down. Eventually, my face and body slam into the dirt. I glance up through the thick fog rolling across my brain and make out the shape of a man.

Chief Reed stands over me with a large gun in his hand.

"Hello, Grace. Can't say I'm happy to see you here."

When I attempt to push myself up, he stomps on my back with a boot, flattening my chest against the rocky dirt. Moaning, I roll onto my side. My whole body throbs as every muscle seems to punch the inside of my body. I touch an oozing gash on my forehead and wince at the sting.

I begin to pray. *God, please help me.*

Fighting against the urge to pass out, I rise up on my hands. Chief Reed kicks me hard in the ribs. I crumble into a heap and spit. Red-speckled saliva sprinkles the dusty ground. A wave of agony travels through my limbs and hammers into my brain. I peer up through the overwhelming pain, billowing dirt, and bright sun.

His blurry shadow looms over me and yells something I can't understand. I focus in on his face, but large, white dots of light keep the picture dull and fuzzy. As a last attempt, I try a defensive ground-kick by driving the bottom of my heel into his kneecap.

I miss.

He reaches down and decks me in the face, sending me spiraling into space. A disgusting growl gurgles in my throat. In that second, I suck up any pride and throw in another prayer, wondering if God gets mad if you ask for the same thing twice.

Dad's face flashes in my mind, and a second wind kicks in. I fumble for Tommy's knife still strapped to my leg. My fingers wrap around the cold, ivory handle and pull out the steel blade. Somehow, I scramble into a seated position and face my attacker.

At the very least, I'll die fighting.

The shadows of the trees hide Chief Reed's tan, angular face as a few strips of light highlight his cold eyes like a white mask. He sneers as he points a gun in my face. I fixate on the barrel and brace myself, half expecting to hear the shot that will end my life. Still clinging to the knife, I drop to my knees with my hands above my head in surrender. Chief Reed walks behind me and presses the cold steel against the back of my head. The feeling of death runs down my spine.

I glance up at the trees for guidance and spot a spiderweb hanging between two limbs. It catches a random sunray and shines. My body relaxes, thankful this is the last thing I'll see before I die.

The click of the safety being released echoes in my ear. I squeeze my eyes shut, anticipating a big boom. A round of shots rings out, sending a slew of birds cackling off into the trees. I wait for the pain to set in. For my heart to slow. When nothing happens, I get frustrated. Why does death have to take so long?

Then I hear a thump behind me and glance over my shoulder to find Chief Reed sprawled out on the ground. A few holes decorate his back. It takes a second for me to realize our roles have been reversed.

I'm alive, and he's dead.

I hear my name called. My eyes finally focus as Mo stomps over to me and grabs my elbow. "Get up!"

A sliver of gratitude and relief mingle with hate and confusion. I jerk my arm away. "Don't you *dare* touch me!" My attempt to stand fails as a surge of pain rips through my torso sending me back down to the ground. Mo lowers his gun and tries to help me up.

I pull away and growl at him. "Leave me alone!"

Mo moves past me and checks the pulse of the guy he shot. He shakes his head and kicks a large rock, sending it running down the path. "Damn it!"

Obviously, Chief Reed's dead. "What? You're surprised? You *shot* him." My voice squeaks. "What did you *think* would happen? He'd skip off into the wildflowers?" I'm shaking as I grab a tall stick and push up, using it to support my weight.

Mo squats and supports his elbows on his knees. He remains in that position for a few minutes. "I never wanted to kill anyone." His voice is low and raw.

I glare at him. So much hate and confusion and darkness course through my veins. Waves of adrenaline dilute my fear. "Oh, really? Well, that's what happens when you run around with *crazy killers*, Mo." I limp away on my makeshift crutch, refusing to succumb to the ribbons of agony weaving through my insides. I squeeze back tears. Wouldn't give him the satisfaction of seeing me cry.

"Come this way." Mo jogs up and grips my arm.

I attempt to elbow him in the ribs. "Get away from me! I don't have to do anything you say."

"You do if you don't want to *die*." Mo tosses the gun strap over his shoulder and scoops me up in his arms. Against my will.

I holler in pain as he explains in a very matter-of-fact voice. "Those men'll be here soon, and I'm not leaving you."

I pound on his chest with my fists. "Those men that YOU ARE WORKING FOR!" Winded, I stop fighting.

Mo flinches as if a gnat has irritated his skin. "The only person you're hurting right now is you."

I stare him in the eye. That's the moment my guard comes crashing down. I can literally feel my heart shatter into a gazillion pieces.

His eyes soften as he walks with me in his arms. "I don't want anyone to hurt you."

Unable to fight anymore, I go limp and look away. "No, you just want to do all the damage yourself."

Before he can answer, voices ride the breeze.

Mo hisses. "They're coming."

As Mo barrels through the forest holding me, the trees move by so fast they lose any definition. Is this really happening to me? Or am I just watching it happen to someone else? I rest my head on Mo's shoulder and watch the world blur by. Everything hurts, yet somehow my body is numb. Soon, it feels as if I've left Mo's arms and am floating up with him.

I hear Mo yell in my face. "Grace! Stay with me!"

The blazing ball of sun that hangs above the leaves summons me.

I focus in on its bright, radiant light.

The only beacon in my night, guiding me home.

Survival Skill #43

When choosing shelter, be sure it is dry, offers concealment, and has an escape route.

Slits of light break through the darkness engulfing me, as if mini-blinds are opening. I'm surrounded by a dingy gray color and total silence. Am I dead? My brain muddles through some random scenes as I piece together events. The fuzzy world fades in and out. A peach with black fuzz moves into my frame of sight.

A hand touches my forehead.

A voice speaks to me. "Try to relax, blossom."

Facial features slowly come into focus. I manage to whisper, "Mo?" Saying his name alerts my brain, and my memory comes flooding back. A streak of anger zips through my body. I ball up my fist and punch him square in the chin.

Mo stumbles back, stunned. "Bloody hell! What was that for?"

"That was for me." I sit up and take stock of my situation. I'm in a cave somewhere with a total traitor. Mo's face is scruffy, and his face filthy. I try to hit him again. This time, he grabs my wrists and holds them tightly in front of me.

The anger boiling inside me gives way to my broken heart. I feel like a broken china dish someone has tried to glue back together. Appearing fixed, whole, but with a hairline crack, a weakness, preventing me from being truly whole again.

I lower my head and whisper, "I hate you."

Mo releases my hands and rubs his jaw. "That makes two of us."

"Leave me alone." As I scoot across the sandy floor to get away from him, pain pulses through me, as if a burning knife is slicing open my gut. I lean my head against the stone wall and breathe.

Mo inches closer but doesn't touch me. "You have to relax."

"Fuck ... you." Then for some strange reason, I smile. For years, Wyn's tried to trick me into blurting out those two little words, but I could only muster a *fudge you* or an *F you*. Now I realize Wyn was right. Two words *can* make me feel better.

Mo ignores my verbal breakthrough and holds out his hand. "Take these."

I smack his arm away, sending two white pills sailing through the cramped space. My voice comes out sharp. "No."

He picks them up and offers them again. "They'll make you feel better."

I turn my head away and purse my lips in defiance. "I don't *feel* anything anyway. Besides, it's probably poison."

He smirks a little. "No. I couldn't find any of that out here."

"Why should I do *anything* you ask?"

His eyes try to bear into my soul, but I turn my face toward the wall. It's like he's Medusa and can only have power over me if I look him straight in the eye.

"You've got to trust me." The cute English accent that once made him sexy, now makes me sick. I can't even hear his voice anymore without thinking of him in his psycho mask with those crazy men.

"HA! That's the line of the year. Look, I don't need your stupid aspirin or whatever it is you're trying to shove down my throat. And I certainly don't need you." I push back even further. Bolts of fire shoot through my stomach, and I double over in pain. "Ow."

Mo points to the pills in his open palm. "You sure?"

I snatch them from his hand, knowing I want the pain to die down more than I need to make a point. He holds up a canteen of water, but I slap it away and chew the acidic medicine raw. Even when some of the powdery stuff glues to my throat, I still refuse his water. After several minutes, the pain lessons a tad.

"Where are we?" I croak.

"Don't worry about it."

I frown. "Is that why you didn't tell me who you were? Because you didn't want me to *worry about it*. Gee, you're so thoughtful, Mo. What a great guy. What a *bloody good* catch you are."

This time, Mo doesn't smile. He remains serious. More serious than I've ever seen him. His muscles are tense. "I'm sorry. I didn't want you to find out this way."

"Was there a better way for me to find out?" He opens his mouth to say something, but I cut him off. "You're a liar and a murderer."

Mo doesn't flinch. "You wouldn't understand."

I cross my arms in front of me. "You never gave me a chance to. You just lied. About everything."

"I'm sorry."

"Stop saying that!" I yell. "It doesn't mean anything! You owe me more than that. You owe me some kind of rational explanation. You owe me the truth."

"I didn't choose this path. I want to be a geologist, for God's sake."

I push him hard, and he falls back on his butt. "*You* don't believe in God. What you believe in is something crazy and absurd. You believe in killing animals, threatening people, and blood money." I stop talking and catch my breath.

"That's not true," Mo says quietly.

Something shifts inside. Any feeling I have drains. I'm using logic with someone who's completely illogical and irrational. Probably crazy too. My words come out flat and unemotional. "Then tell me. What is true … *Mo*? Or should I say, *Morris*."

He gets up and paces. "How do you…?"

"I found an article online about you and your father. It was in my dad's case file." I stop suddenly, tired of talking, and stare at the guy in front of me. The guy I started to love. The guy who's not the same person I kissed a couple days ago. Mo stares out the entrance. His confident posture refuels my rage and I egg him on,

250

wanting so much to hurt him the way he's wounded me. "Your dad would be *disgusted* with you right now."

Mo glares at me. His piercing brown eyes reveal a hint of hurt. "You don't know anything about me or my dad. Just because you read some article, you think you know everything now?" His eyes flip from anger into sadness before I can even blink.

I soften my tone, hoping to extract some information. "Then tell me ... what's going on?"

He sighs. "Last year, I was in the woods with my dad when he was shot."

"Did you kill him?"

Mo spins around and slams his head on the low-rocky ceiling. "Ow! No!" He touches the small cut above his brow and winces. "How could you even say that?"

I keep my eyes on him, refusing to let him off the hook until he tells me more. "I don't know what to think anymore, Mo."

His body loses its posture and his shoulders curl forward in defeat. "My father was murdered. By these guys. In cold blood."

"The article said it was an accident."

Mo kneels down. "Grace, the article was wrong."

Survival Skill #44

*When in a survival situation,
sometimes it's better to listen.*

Mo sits down across from me on a rotted log. "My dad was a special agent with the U.S. Fish & Wildlife Service. He was investigating a major poaching ring that was sweeping across Tennessee. He was tracking these guys. They found out and killed him."

I eye him suspiciously. "How do you know this?"

Mo's eyes flash something I can't decipher. "My dad told me everything before he died. Told me where his files were. All his notes on the case."

I think about what he's saying, trying to make some sense out of it. The image of him trying to revive his father sticks in my brain. He looks sincere, but how do I know he's not snowing me all over again? "This sounds crazy. Why would he tell you that?"

"My dad said some of the locals were corrupt. Before he died, he told me to take all the information we'd gathered to the head of his squad. His leader would know what to do."

"Who was that?"

He pauses for a minute and sucks in enough air to state his answer. "I didn't know at the time, but now I know it was your dad."

His answer slices through me. I shake his words out of my head. "No, that's impossible. My dad wasn't a special agent. He was a game warden." Actually, this crazy scheme is probably something Dad would get involved in, especially if it meant protecting or saving bears.

Mo remains still, no movement, and answers very simply. "Obviously not."

"What did you do with the files?" I rub my temples, desperate to relieve the pressure that's built up inside.

Mo fiddles with his shirt. "I took my dad's case file and started hanging out at the local gun show in my town, chatting it up with a few guys in the group. By the time I'd gotten in with them and we relocated here, your dad had already been taken. So I hid them."

"How do I know you are not lying to me again?"

He strokes my fingers with his warm hands. "Because you know me."

I glare at him. "Why didn't you tell me this sooner?"

Mo shrugs. "I didn't want you involved."

"Is that why you packed up and left?"

He nods as he talks. "I didn't really think about you being connected to all this until you mentioned your dad missing. But by then, I was already smitten. I thought I could keep it all separate until you mentioned his name that night at my camp. That's when I knew I needed to stay away from you. It was the only way to keep you safe."

I poke him in the chest. "Yeah? Well, you were wrong. I saw footprints and gun shells at your site so I got more worried. Found out Al was involved and assumed he found you and did who knows what."

"Al's involved, but he's not in charge. Fields is the leader of this one group, but he's in contact with someone on the outside."

I skim through more questions backing up in my brain. "I think it's my dad's old partner, Les."

Mo shakes his head. "I don't know a Les. But I don't know a lot of the guys' names here. Most of them use an alias for obvious reasons."

"Are there more camps like this?"

"Yes. There are a more in different parts of the States. It's part of a larger operation. All mostly run by locals to avoid suspicion."

"All for money?"

"Yes." He leans in and cups my face in his hands. Even though I divert my eyes, he finds them and grabs their attention.

"But this isn't about money for me. It's about getting justice for my dad. You know that, right?"

I swallow, afraid to ask my question. "Okay, but how *involved* are you? Are you killing bears?"

Mo wrings his hands. "No, how can you even ask me that? I'd never be able to do that."

"No. You just let them die. Without doing anything about it."

His eyes water. "I was just trying to get close enough to find out who was the top guy. I swear."

I cradle my head in my hands. It's heavy with the information bogging it down. Too many free weights have been stacked on my shoulders. "I don't know anything anymore, Mo. Especially not about you. You've lied to me this whole time."

Mo refuses to believe me. "Crumbs, you're the only person who knows me, Grace. The real me. Everything that's happened between us is real. Not telling you about my dad and this group was my way of keeping you safe."

I point to the cave we're sitting in, then to my swollen face. "How's it working for you?"

He shakes his head. "I know. But I tried to warn you."

I jerk my head up as the main question pushes forward in a long line of inquiries crowding in my head. "So these guys kidnapped my dad?

He refuses to look at me when he answers. "Yes."

A wave of energy jolts to life and pumps throughout my body in tandem with my blood. My breath escapes in short bursts of air. "Is he alive?" It takes him too long to answer so I stand and push him with both hands. "Tell me!"

Mo remains stiff. "I don't know. They had him at the camp for a while. He escaped a couple times but they caught him."

I almost smile thinking of Dad getting away. Must have been irritating for them. "Did they kill him? Just tell me."

"I really don't know. I haven't seen him since then. But I promise, I'll help you find out what happened, either way. These people took both of our dads from us. I'm going to make sure they pay for it. Okay?"

I shackle down any escaping emotions. This is not the time to crumble. I have to keep it together until I find out what happened for sure. "So now what?"

Mo rubs his hand over his mouth. "I don't know. I can't go back. As soon as they find out I killed Chief Reed, they'll know I helped you. And if they find me now, they'll kill me, especially if they think I told you anything. I need to keep you hidden for a few days until they leave. Then we can go to the authorities."

"You can't keep me prisoner here."

He tugs on his hair in frustration and grits his teeth to keep from raising his voice. "Bloody hell. Is that what you think I'm doing? I'm saving your life."

"Or are you saving yours?" I let the words hang in the air before saying more. "Besides, I'm not going to hide from these creeps. Lets go see Carl. He's the police captain, and we can tell him everything."

Mo raises his voice. "No, we can't trust anyone but us. The whole town's dirty."

I almost laugh. "Believe me, you can trust Carl." I think about how much by the book Carl has always been. "The guy doesn't even know what it means to break a rule. Trust me, I've tried."

"Fine, but telling Carl only stops this group, and we may not find out where all the others are." Mo thinks for a second. "I saw some maps back at the camp."

I clutch onto his hand and squeeze. "If we can help Carl find these guys, we can shut this operation down."

He massages his scalp as if he's shifting thoughts around.

A glimmer of hope warms my heart when I realize he's thinking about helping me. Maybe he isn't bad after all. "Let's go to Carl. Before someone else gets hurt. Please, do this for me. For us."

He finally softens to my touch and leans his forehead against mine. His voice is almost too quiet to hear. "For what it's worth, I've never killed any bears or anyone. Until that bloke was going to kill you first."

This time, I don't pull away. "I know."

He clasps my face and kisses my cheeks. His eyes gleam with moisture. "In that moment, when I thought he would kill you, you were all I cared about. Grace, I don't want to be without you."

The armor around my heart unhinges. "Thank you for saving me."

He strokes my hair as if he can't believe I'm in front of him. "Can you ever forgive me?"

I rub his chin. "I know what it's like to do what it takes for someone you love. Promise me you're being honest now and that you'll help me fix this."

He smiles and holds up two fingers. "Scout's honor." Not even a second later, Mo's face jerks toward the entrance. He places a finger to his lips and points.

My heart slams into my rib cage as I watch terror sweep over his face.

Something scuffles outside.

I grab onto Mo just as men swarm the cave.

Survival Skill #45

The best way to handle any attack is to try and get away. Never be taken to another location.

"Leave her alone!" Mo screams.

I look over to see Mo struggling with a couple of men from my town.

He jerks an arm free and punches my dad's barber, Ned, in the face. Then he kicks our real estate agent in the gut and moves in my direction. Before Mo can reach me, a third man pistol-whips him across the temple. His eyes roll back in his head. Then he doubles over on the ground and curls into a ball, like a little boy, vunerable and scared. A trickle of blood dots the corner of his mouth.

We lock eyes and he mouths the words, *I'm sorry.*

A bunch of hands grip my armpits and drag me out of the shelter, my legs scraping the ground behind me. I try to scream, but only a moan escapes. Rocks and sticks tear at my knees. The pain returns and sprays through all my limbs.

As soon as it registers what's happened, I fight back, kicking and screaming. Little stars flicker across my vision, but I manage to muster up one last dose of energy to flail. This time, I break free and kick Tony in the kneecap. Then I sweep my foot across the ground in a wide circle, taking out another pair of legs. Ned flops backwards and lands on his butt. A third man from my church jumps on top of me, pinning me down with his knees. I buck like a wild horse until someone presses a damp cloth over my nose and mouth.

My vision is affected first. The leaves outside the cave morph into butterflies that flit off into a blurry backdrop. I gag at the pungent smell as a bitter taste fills my mouth.

Soon, my world dissolves into blackness.

CB

The only point of light I see is high above me. It's either the moon or a distant star. When I sit up, my stomach churns as every place on me throbs. My fingers graze over a bump on my cheek. I groan and push through the sharp pain in my torso, feeling my way along the moist wall. Jagged rocks formed into some sort of underground tomb.

Where am I? In a cave? Maybe deep underground.

Buried alive.

Panic wells in my chest as claustrophobia kicks in. I cry out to the dark space. "Help! Is anyone here?"

Then a familiar noise floats through the cramped space.

Whistling.

My body trembles. I know that sound. How could I forget it?

A door opens and a shaft of light illuminates the black space. A huge figure crouches through a man-made door and holds up a lantern. I shield my eyes until they adjust.

The first thing I focus on is Al's evil grin.

"I'm baaaaaaack." He bursts into laughter as he glides closer to me, dragging a large blob behind him. "And I bear gifts. Who says I'm not a nice guy?" He tosses the mound on the floor.

I stare at it, expecting a dead body until a cough pierces through the darkness.

"Mo?" I crouch down and pull back the sheet. His face is battered and swollen. Duct tape is spread out over his mouth, and one eye is swollen shut. Dried blood dots his chin, and a small gash across his eyebrow drips down his face. He moans through the cloth stuck into his mouth and struggles against the ropes hog-tying him.

I mask my fear and glare at Al. "Let him go."

Al pretends to think for a second. "No." He sneers and gives Mo a kick in the gut.

I shield Mo's body and scream. "Stop it!"

Al chuckles and glides toward me. He clutches onto my arm as if his fingers are huge talons. He smells my hair. His voice sizzles like drops of water splashing into a hot pan. "But don't worry, I'll give you another chance." He presses me against the wall and twirls a piece of my hair. "Wouldn't want you to be lonely down here."

Mo moans under the material and flips around on the sandy floor. His eyes flash dark, and he wraps his legs around Al's ankle, pulling him down.

Caught off guard, Al stumbles backwards but catches himself against the wall. He pulls a gun from his holster and presses the muzzle against Mo's cheek. "Check, mate."

I yell. "Wait!" Al sneers at me, so I try softening my voice. "Please don't."

Al seems amused. "You know what, Mo? She's right. Why don't you watch our little party first? Then, I'll kill yah."

Behind him, someone bellows. "You'll do no such thing!" Les appears through the door, holding a gun. His face and shirt are drenched in sweat. "Didn't you learn from Billy's mistakes? Drop the gun, Al." Al lets his gun clunk on the ground as Les hobbles over to me and shines a light in my face. "You okay, Gracie?"

I shove against his blubbery body. "Get away from me, traitor!"

Les appears shocked. "I came here to help you. I warned you to stay out of this."

Tears well in my eyes. He's right, but what other choice did I have. "How could you be involved in all this? Dad loved you!"

Les keeps his gun on Al who's eyeing him like a lion does a lamb. "I don't have time to argue with you now. Come with me."

Mo watches me but remains still on the floor.

I lift my head and speak emphatically. "No."

Les frowns and grabs my arm, pulling me toward the door. "Gracie, you don't know what you're talking about. Now you have no choice but to come with me, or you will die."

Just then, someone hits Les over the head, and he drops to the floor with a grunt.

Survival Skill #46

When in a survival situation, always trust your instinct. Usually, it's right.

Another man enters the shrinking space. "Damn it, what the hell is going on in here?"

My mouth drops open, and I smile. "Carl!"

Al bends over and snatches his gun off the floor. "Man, I thought you'd never get here."

Carl ignores me and frowns at Al. "You're making things messy. First Joe, then thrill kills, and then you toss Billy over the canyon. Now, you've got two teens down here? How long do you think it'll be before people start snooping around, looking for them?"

I watch as they talk, my head swinging back and forth, not understanding what they're talking about.

Al shrugs as he speaks. "Didn't hurt us with Joe, did it?"

I interrupt and address Carl with tears in my eyes. "Wait. You're in on this?"

Carl ignores me and lifts his hat off his head to smooth his hair. "Damn it, Al. You're risking everything. Getting careless. I'm not letting you take me down on this one."

Al pushes Carl who backs up a few steps. "Look, don't be getting in my face. You had your chance to lock me up a while back. Instead, you wanted in on this. So don't be threatening me, you're in this just as thick as I am. If not more."

Carl grits his teeth. "Look. I started this operation months ago, and I can do it without you."

Al puffs up his chest. "You wouldn't. I don't care if you're the boss or not. It was my idea."

"These are my people out here, and they'll back me up if they need to. Without me, you got no operation. So shut up if you want to get paid. Get Les outta here, and try not to kill anyone else. We got enough blood on our hands."

Al salutes. "My pleasure, *boss*." He grabs Les by both arms and drags him through the door. "Damn, it's like hauling a hippo." I can hear Al cackling at his stupid joke all the way down the tunnel as he grunts and groans from dragging the extra weight.

Once Al's gone, Carl faces me and clicks his tongue. "Now what am I going to do with you?" Suddenly, skinny Carl appears large and in control.

Shaking my head, I move in front of Mo, protecting him. "No, you can't be involved with them. Not you. Not this."

Carl smiles an impish grin. "Sorry to let you down, Grace. But things are more complicated than you realize. A man's got to take care of his family and life the best way he knows how."

Tears fill my eyes. Memories of Carl plague my mind. How he helped Wyn and me hang up a tire swing or how he taught us how to shoot a can from fifty feet away. "I don't understand. How could you?"

Carl glares at me. "What choice did I have? It was either this or watching a town I love, the town I grew up in, slowly crumble to dust." I stare at him blankly, but he goes on without my response. "Surely you've seen what's been going on. Shops closing. People leaving. Who do you think is breathing life back into it?"

I speak slowly. "You're not doing this for the town. You're doing it for yourself."

"You should thank me," he snaps back. "Our town would have dried up and washed away if it wasn't for the money I've been putting into rebuilding it. Then where would we be? Poor, jobless, no future!"

"But this isn't the way to do it!"

Carl shakes his head. "What do you know? You're a teenager. You don't have bills to pay. You don't have to worry about anything. This town is all most of these people have. Without it, who would they be? What would they do?"

"So the whole town is in on this?"

He plays with the guns on his hips. "Not everyone, but I got a few others on board."

A tornado of thoughts twist through my head, destroying everything in its path. "So Les isn't working with you?"

Carl laughs. "That buffoon? Are you serious? He's been riding my ass for weeks. If you hadn't warned me about Al leavin' that bear, Les probably would've have caught us. Lucky we got it cleaned up just in time."

"Les was protecting me?"

"Ever since your dad fell into … unfortunate circumstances … Les has been tailing you, making sure you were safe. Nabbed Al when he was stalking you and that boy by the river." He motions to Mo who's still bound and gagged on the floor.

My head swirls. Les was protecting me? I swallow hard. Feels as if my saliva's hardened and can barely fit down my throat. "What about my dad?"

Carl sighs and takes off his hat. "That was all Al. Joe was an unfortunate liability. One I tried to prevent, but he was about to blow our operation wide open. He and his English friend. For a while, his tracking skills came in real helpful in locating bears. Until he got … difficult."

The thought of Dad helping these guys makes my stomach churn. I can't imagine how he felt doing that. "Give him to me. Now."

Carl shakes his head. "Hm, you are persistent. I'm afraid I can't do that. He's dead."

"Dead?" My body sags, and my back slides down the wall until I'm slumped in a seated position. Burying my face in my hands, I run through what he said but remain in denial. "No, no, it can't be." I blink back tears and lock my jaw to keep from screaming. "You're lying."

Carl kneels down beside me and strokes my hair. "Wish I was. But you know Al. He's a little uncontrollable. I tried to protect

Joe, but he wasn't cooperating." If looks could kill, I would have already put Carl six feet under. "At least I got here before Al could hurt you. Right?"

"Yeah, you're a real *hero.*"

Carl smiles. "I've always admired you, Grace. You got spunk. A lot of guts. That's why I'm going to help you. So don't go anywhere, I gotta go do some damage control."

"I don't want your help."

"You better. I'm all that stands between you and Al. Trust me, you don't want him unleashed. It's not a pretty sight." Carl nudges Mo with the toe of his boot before ducking out the doorway. "Don't worry, boy. We haven't forgotten about you. Al will have fun with you later."

After Carl leaves, a large boulder rolls over the hole, blocking us in.

As soon as we're alone, I yank the tape off Mo's mouth and choke out, "I thought he was going to kill you." I fiddle with the knot for some time because my hands won't stop trembling. Finally, the rope surrenders and releases Mo's hands.

He rubs the red-inflamed markings on his wrists. "I'm abso-bloody-lutely positive it's won't be too long before he does." Mo checks me over before touching my cheek. "Look what they've done to you."

I lick the dried blood coming from a cut in the corner of my mouth. "I'm in better shape than you." I lightly touch his swollen eye. "Are you okay?"

"Shoot, you should see the other bloke." Mo begins checking out the place. "We gotta get out of here. Now that I know Carl's the top guy of this whole operation. I gotta get some help."

"This is insane. I cannot *believe* Carl is caught up in this." I sit back and prop my elbows up on my knees, wondering where Wyn is right now. If he has any idea what his idol, Carl, has done. Though maybe I should have known. The Dixie song in his office. The green bandana. Not to mention, he's been holding me back from solving this case since day one. If it hadn't been for

Wyn defending him all the time, I may have caught onto Carl weeks ago.

Mo kneels next to me. "I'm sorry about all this."

All my unasked questions resurface. "So, does this mean you've known Al and Billy this whole time? Were you there when they attacked me?"

"I was out collecting a sample, because believe it or not, I do want to be a geologist. I saw you snooping around their truck and head off into the woods. I remembered you from the river and followed because I knew what those guys were like. When they attacked you, I had no choice but to intervene. At the risk of ruining my cover." He stops, probably expecting me to ask a question.

"Why'd you pretend not to know them?"

Mo wipes his bloody brow with the hem of his t-shirt. "We worked out a deal later to keep it all quiet so none of us would get in trouble. That's why I've been here so long. Waiting to find out who's running this whole thing. Now I know."

"Then why'd you show up at the river that day? Seems like it would've been safer for you to just stay away."

He looks up at the faint light source, as if thinking of a response. "Pretty daft of me. I knew I shouldn't, but after our time in the cave, I was worried someone would see you. Hurt you like your dad." He rubs my shoulder with one hand. "I'm sorry."

I crouch over and suck in gulps of air. "I can't believe all this is about money."

Mo agrees with me. "Carl has the perfect set-up. He can have his men kill bears without anyone knowing. He's been in charge out here and only one person could stop him—"

I finish his statement. "My dad." Then I mutter under my breath. "Well, don't underestimate *me*."

He grins. "I wouldn't. I've seen your moves. Up close and personal."

I try to smile back, but my lips seem cemented in place. "I wish I knew what happened that day at the river."

Mo sighs. "Your dad found out what was going on. He walked right into a trap." He averts his eyes, refusing to meet mine.

The look on his face scares me. "Is he really dead?"

Mo hugs me and whispers in my ear. "I honestly don't know, blossom. These guys are unpredictable. Who knows what they've done. The thing we need to do right now is get the hell out of here. Alive. Get help. We can come back for answers later. And we need to move fast because I have a feeling we don't have much time left."

"But how? This is some underground tomb. Only one way out." I point at the door Carl exited through.

He motions toward the natural skylight. "Not the only way."

I look up. "Yeah, but how in the world do we get up there? It's too smooth to free climb."

He runs his hands though his hair. "I have no idea."

For some time, I remain curled up in a fetal position. My body's crashed, like an old computer. Unable to perform any of the basic functions. Standing, talking, even breathing. I've seen it happen to the people Dad's rescued on the mountain. Shock is a powerful weapon for the enemy. My body is unresponsive to any activity swirling in my brain. As if the hope's drained out, leaving behind an empty shell.

As if I'm already dead.

Mom's face pops into my mind. I wonder what she's thinking right now. Is she worried? Is she fed up? Does she think something's wrong or wonder if I've run away for good this time? It's hard for me to calculate how much time has passed since I saw her last. Hours? Days?

Mo paces the cave, searching for a way out. I track him with my eyes, noting every detail. How he thinks with his tongue sticking out of his mouth. How he fiddles with his hair when he's frustrated. Every few minutes, he musters up the energy to try something new. Attempting to move the boulder in front of the tunnel with a large stick. Trying to scale the slick wall using shoelaces as temporary footholds. But of course, nothing works.

The more he fails, the more I realize that this could really be the end.

I stay curled on the ground, unable to gather any energy to help. I focus in on the night sounds. Crickets and frogs compete to see who can make the loudest noise. An owl hoots from far away, and the cicadas chirp in rounds.

Mo squats down next to me and strokes my hair. The dead flower bracelet I gave him scratches my hand.

I smile and kiss his forehead.

As he resumes his obsessive pacing, I stare up at the moon's face, peering down on us from high in the sky. I can't help but think of Wyn and all the times we argued back and forth about whether there really was a man in the moon. Even when I pointed out facial features, he still said he couldn't see it.

Now I miss him annoying me. I wonder if he's thinking about me too.

The owl calls out again. This time, it sounds much closer than before.

An idea crosses my mind. It's a long shot, but it's possible.

I stand up and hoot toward the punched-out hole in the ceiling.

Mo moves next to me. "What is it?"

"What do you think? It's an owl." I focus on the patch of light. Watching. Wondering. Hoping. The owl hoots again. I answer back one more time, just in case. My hunch might be crazy, but if I'm right, I just might get us out of this hell hole.

Mo squints at me in the dim light, looking confused. "Are you expecting an owl to rescue us?"

I shush him as the shadow of a head appears over the side.

Survival Skill #47

Before moving away from safety, always plan a course of action and a contingency plan.

q squeeze Mo's arm. "It's Tommy!"

Mo and I stare up at the entrance. Seconds later, a climbing rope uncurls in front of us.

He motions us up at the same time I hear voices yelling in the distance. Tommy changes his mind and climbs down the rope, never once making a sound. When he reaches the bottom, he puts his finger to his lips and stares up at the entrance until he thinks it's clear. Then he whispers. "Sorry, I was going to just pull you up until I thought they saw me. There's a swarm of people up there."

I barely even hear what he says because I pounce on him. "Tommy!"

He clutches my arms. "Elu, *(t)do-`hi-tsu!*"

I nod. "I'm fine. How did you know where we were?"

He squeezes me hard. "I had a hunch you'd come here so I came prepared. Just in case."

I pull away and search his face. "Wait. I thought you didn't want to get involved."

He winks. "I changed my mind."

I smile and pat his hand. "Well, then, it's true. You *can* teach an old dog new tricks."

His face softens. "Can you ever forgive me?"

I peck his cheek. "Already have."

Tommy smiles, and I hug him again. As he holds me, he sticks out his other hand to introduce himself. "You must be Mo."

Mo looks at me as if to ask for my permission in answering him. I nod. This isn't the time to bombard Tommy with all the details I've uncovered about Mo today. I'll fill him in on everything later, once we're safe. I owe him that much.

"Yes, sir." Mo shakes Tommy's tan hand. "How did you know we were down here?"

Tommy frowns at me while answering. "By the time I got here, I saw them dragging you guys into camp. Unfortunately, there were too many of them around you so I had to wait. You both okay?"

"Yes. Did you see Les?"

Tommy shakes his head. "Saw the big dude dragging him out of here. He didn't look so good. What's going on?"

I mutter. "Les's been protecting me this whole time. Carl and some other people in our town are involved in this. Did you know what was going on?"

Tommy drops his head and makes a clucking noise. "No. But Carl came into my store a few days ago saying he had someone who wanted to finance the store. Maybe help me expand. Acted kinda strange when I asked him where the money was coming from. I turned him down. Kinda like my store the way it is."

"I thought you wanted to make it bigger?"

"Changed my mind. Lucky I did." Tommy takes off his fishing hat. "Man, how money can change a person."

I clutch his forearm. "Have you seen any sign of Dad?"

Tommy shakes his head. "Not so much as a clue or a track. I looked. Is he here?"

Mo remains silent so I just shrug. "No one knows."

Tommy points up. "Well, I'm thinking we should get out of here. Probably don't have much time before they come back for you two." He addresses me. "You strong enough to climb this rope?"

I tug on the frayed end. "Thought you'd never ask."

Mo stops us. "Wait. First, we need a plan. I can tell you what I know about the layout of this place." He squats and draws a diagram in the dirt with his finger.

Tommy and I lean over him, studying the squiggly lines as he moves his finger along the picture. "Once we get up there, we'll have a chance if we head out this way." He points to a triangle shape. "The back side of the camp is less covered. It's night, so they'll be taking shifts. One person will be over here…" He points to a spot and then draws an X in another area. "Over here, there are usually two men patrolling the border."

Tommy looks a bit perplexed. "Wait? How do you know all this? Didn't you both come here together?"

I interject to cover up Mo's involvement. For now. "Mo was watching the camp before we were caught."

Tommy searches my eyes for the truth. I simply smile, acting as normal as I can. He pushes the swinging rope toward me. "Let's get you out first, Elu."

Mo catches the rope. "Sir, if you don't mind. I'll go first. Then, Grace. And, then you. That way, I can keep an eye on things while you two climb out."

Tommy pats Mo's shoulder as if he's an old friend. "Makes sense to me, son."

I place my hands on my hips. "Does anyone want my opinion?"

Mo and Tommy answer in unison. "No."

Tommy smirks and points at Mo. "I think I'm gonna like this guy."

I smile. Tommy's always had a good sense about people and can peg a bad seed in a field of clover. Maybe there's hope for Mo yet.

As planned, Mo curls the rope around his legs and shimmies up through the hole. When he reaches the top, he motions for me to go next.

My shoulders throb and my arms shake with each grip, but giving up is not in my vocabulary today. I pour every ounce of strength and wrap my legs around the rope. As I climb the rope, sharp stabs of pain shoot off in all directions. I'm pretty sure I've broken some ribs and who knows what else. I block it all out, focusing on moving one hand over the other. I'm getting out of this dismal place.

Alive.

At the top, Mo clasps the back of my shirt and hauls me over the side.

I crouch next to him and wait for Tommy to appear from the darkness. Even though he's in his sixties, Tommy reaches the top much faster than me.

The three of us squat, and no one says a word. We have darkness on our side as long as we stay out of the light given off by the hanging lanterns.

Mo points ahead and Tommy nods in approval. As they communicate with hand signals, Mo squeezes my hand and smiles.

In this one moment, I'm only sure of one thing. Mo really does care about me. My pulse quickens, and I feel a twinge of guilt for ever doubting him. No matter what he's done, he's obviously had one important reason. His dad. I know how love and fear can drive someone to do crazy things.

At Mo's signal, the three of us hunch over and creep along the ring of tents. Several times, he holds up his hand, warning us to stop. As we slink through the camp, men's voices float around us, coming from different directions.

A gunshot slices though the silence. The three of us flop onto the ground. Pebbles digs into my skin, but I don't dare move. We wait, expecting to be attacked, but no one comes.

A few minutes later, a few more cracking sounds are followed by a thunder of drunken laughter. Just what we need. Crazy drunk guys with guns. Mo motions us to continue, and the three of us crawl toward the border of the camp in single file line.

Mo stops at the corner of the last tent and sits back on his heels. He points to a man's head bobbing above the bushes. He's the only thing standing between us and freedom. If we get past him, we might have a chance at getting help before anyone realizes we're gone.

Mo gives us a signal to stay in place and points, informing us he's going after the lone gunman.

I shake my head violently, begging him not to leave, and point in a different direction, suggesting we leave another way.

He winks at me and eyes Tommy who grips both of my shoulders, holding me back. Mo crawls into the thick shrubs on his belly.

I shift back and forth from leg to leg as anxiety pumps through me.

Tommy clutches on to me tighter, knowing how impulsive I can be.

Time slows down. I scan the area, wringing my hands. Where is he?

A few seconds later, Mo pounces out of the bush like a wild cat and lands on top of the hunter, knocking him to the ground. The man fights back. Mo cups his hand over the guy's mouth and tries to drag him into the leafy cover. Unfortunately, a gun discharges and sprays the treetops with bullets.

Tommy and I stop breathing. Praying no one heard the disturbance.

Suddenly, voices ring out all around us.

The next few minutes of my world seem to play out over an entire lifetime. In an instant, everything reverts to a snail's speed, as if someone's pressed the slow motion button on my life. A fog rolls over me, leaving everything sounding muffled. Eventually, the sound shuts off too, like an old silent film.

Mo tosses the man's gun to Tommy. He catches it and presses the middle of my back, pushing me.

I slug forward a few steps, but don't move far because my legs seem to be lodged in a vat of jello.

Mo clutches my hand and drags me behind him. My legs seem to be circling underneath me, but I can't tell if they're actually touching the ground.

I glance over my shoulder to find Tommy, but a guy tackles me. My hand rips out of Mo's. I try to scream, but no sound comes out. Before I can think, the heel of my hand shoots out and clips the guy's nose. Blood splatters on my arm as he falls to his knees, clutching an injured face. I quickly kick him hard in the chest, and he flies backwards into a tent, which collapses on top of him.

Tommy shoots me a thumb's up, and Mo tugs on my sleeve to remind me to keep moving. A man clambers out of the trees. I must have screamed because Tommy spins around just in time to duck a punch.

I notice how fast he moves for his age, how confident and strong he seems all of a sudden. I run backwards after Mo and hold out my hand to Tommy as he runs to catch up.

The man scrambles to his feet and jumps on Tommy's back, dragging him down to the ground.

Tommy rolls around with the guy on top, trying to scoot out from under his weight.

Horrified, I yank against Mo's hand, trying to break free from his vice grip, to go back and help. Mo locks his hand on harder and jerks my arm in the opposite direction. He's stronger than me so I stumble behind him watching Tommy fight off a guy half his age and twice his size.

I trip over something and lay in the dust, paralyzed in fear. Mo yanks me to my feet by my t-shirt.

Out of nowhere, a man grabs my leg.

Mo slams the butt of his gun into the guys's temple.

Still on the ground, I look back, searching for Tommy amidst smoke and gunfire. He's still wrestling the same man. And this time, it doesn't look like Tommy's winning because he's moving slower.

In that second, Tommy glances up and our eyes meet. The light from the lanterns highlights the strong angles of his face. Something passes between us. I'm not sure what. Acknowledgment. Regret. Fear. Maybe all three. His face softens and he mouths one word, "Go."

Just as I get to my feet, faint popping noises break through my bubble of silence.

Tommy jerks around as if he's doing some strange dance before tumbling forward in slow motion. He slams against the ground, and his body jolts for a few seconds until all movement stops.

I push through the terror muting me until total sound reenters my world.

This time, I hear myself scream his name. A sound so primal and comes from somewhere deep.

"Tommy!"

Survival Skill #48

Use body movements or positions to convey a message in a dangerous situation.

Mo's arms clutch onto my waist as he tugs my stiff body forward. But I can't seem to move. As if someone's has nailed my feet to the ground. I stand there, gawking at Tommy's body, speckled in red. Mo blocks my view and yells in my face. "Grace! Grace! We've got to go! Now!"

"Tommy!" My voice sounds raw and broken, as if I've been yelling for days. I jerk my arm away from Mo's grip and sprint back to Tommy who's not moving. I drop onto my knees next to his body. A couple of red holes dot his chest, and blood drips out of his nose and mouth.

I shake him. "Oh, God! Tommy, Tommy. Please! Please don't leave me. Oh, God. Please!"

Tommy doesn't answer me.

Panic roars through my chest, making me frantic. Unleashed. Wild. I sob and try to drag his limp body behind me. My feet slip and slide in the loose dirt. Tommy's body is pure dead weight, and it pulls me down.

Mo slides in next to me, spraying dust into the air, and hollers in my face again. "Grace! He's gone. We have to go!"

All I hear is that he's gone ... because of me.

I notice the tear stains on Tommy's face. "I'm so sorry." I kiss his cheek. *"Gv-ge-yu-hi."*

I don't want to leave, wishing I could stay with him, but Mo grabs my hand and pulls. "Come on!"

Gunfire echoes around me. I jolt to life as full sensation returns to my body. The world around me springs back to life, and my survival instinct kicks in. I peel myself away from Tommy and sprint alongside Mo down the dusty path. He clutches my sleeve and yanks me left and right, practically jerking my arm out of its socket. As I run, Tommy's sweet face clouds my vision. For a split second, I want to go back.

I need to go back.

I can't just leave him behind. But I don't want to die either.

Mo pushes me up the hill. Behind us, a couple of men from town stomp along the path. We both duck down beind a bush and press our bodies into the murky leaves to hide. I fight to suck in air while still remaining quiet. It's as if a huge boulder has rolled onto my chest. Pools of tears threaten to wash away the vivid image of Tommy's last few moments replaying in my head. A quiet moan slips from my lips as I try so hard to hold everything inside because I have to be quiet.

I shake my head over and over. This isn't happening. It's all a bad dream. Tommy isn't dead. Dad is still alive. I just need to wake up. From where we hide, I can still see his body still lying in the clearing and I will him to stand.

Get up. Get up.

Mo drapes his arm over me and pulls me close. I bury my head into his shoulder, smelling the familiar and once-comforting vanilla scent. He strokes my hair a few minutes before whispering in my ear. "Listen to me. You hide here. I need to go back down there for something."

I cling to his arm. "Wait, why? What for?"

He runs his thumbs down my jawline. "It's a hunch I have. It's important. Trust me. I want you to stay here."

My fingers dig into the fabric of his shirt. "Please. Don't."

He brushes his lips along my forehead. "I'll be right back. I promise."

Even though I don't want him to leave, grovelling for him is worse. I take in a deep breath. "You promise?"

He kisses my knuckles. "Abso-bloody-lutely." Then he places his gun in my hand. "You know how to use this?" I study the pistol and give him a 'what do you think?' look. He pats my shoulders. "Okay, I was just checking."

Before I can answer or argue one last time, he charges back down the hill. I watch as he sneaks across the campsite. My body shudders in fear. *Where's he going?*

I scan the area, hoping to catch a glimpse of him. The swinging lanterns give off a faint light, barely enough to see.

Off to one side, I spot a shadow creeping out of a tent with a rope in one hand and a bag draped over his shoulder. I sigh in relief as Mo steps into the dim light, checking both ways before crossing the path. Squatting, he pulls back a tarp blanketing the ground to reveal another large hole similar to the one we were in earlier. His mouth is moving as if he's arguing with someone. *Who's he talking to?* He drops the rope down the hole and leans in.

Off to my right, a few men make their way through the trees, heading straight for Mo. They move methodically in a V-formation, randomly poking bushes and kicking leaves.

I whisper to myself. "Come on. Hurry up. Get out of there."

The men inch closer.

How can I warn Mo they're coming?

I replicate Tommy's owl call, hoping to jog his memory. He doesn't seem to notice. Before I can get out another warning, a man charges out of the woods and tackles him from behind. Mo tosses the man onto the ground. All in one smooth movement. Not missing a beat.

Mo falls on his belly and stretches his arm down the hole.

Al pops out of a tent and charges Mo with his gun drawn.

What can I do?

A memory of me and Dad shooting at the gun range resurfaces. Dad's words unravel in my head. *You're good with a gun, Gracie, you could be a marksman.* Not something I thought was handy.

Until now.

Without hestitating, I hold up Mo's gun and zero in on Al's thigh, pausing for a second.

Al points his gun at the back of Mo's head.

I close my eyes and fire.

Al drops to the dirt and writhes in pain.

At the sound of the shot, Mo spots me on the hill me and gives me a thumb's up.

I signal back but am relieved. Whether Al deserves to live or not, I'm glad I didn't actually kill him.

Mo reaches in the ground one more time and pulls. A head breaks the surface, and a skeletal figure rolls onto his back. Mo helps the man to his feet and wraps one arm around his waist. They both head in my direction. The frail man stumbles to his knees a few times, but each time, Mo is right there to hold him up.

I squint through the tree limbs, waiting for them to get close so I can see the man's face. My heart pounds in my chest.

Mo sprints to the hill and pushes the filthy man up the slick grass.

The man claws at the dirt, but obviously isn't strong enough to make it.

Men swarm in from all directions, heading for the slope.

I yell down to them. "Mo! Hurry!"

The scrawny, filthy man looks up and smiles when he sees me.

I gasp. I'd know that smile anywhere.

Survival Skill #49

Knowing how to tie good camping knots is an invaluable skill in wilderness.

I scream and slide down the hill. "Dad! Dad!" As soon as I reach him, I throw my arms around his filthy neck. He smells of urine mixed with mud and blood but I don't care. "I knew you were alive." I push him back and check him over quickly. Mud covers his bloody body from head to toe. His face is swollen from obvious beatings, and his lips are cracked from dehydration. I touch his bearded face. "Are you okay?"

Dad doesn't say anything. Or can't. He just nods and smiles. That wonderful smile.

Mo hollers up the hill. "Grace! Go! Go!"

I grab Dad's hand and tug him after me, but I can't seem to get good traction. His tattered boots slip along the grass, almost dragging me with him. Clutching both of his wrists, I try to hang on but his hands are too slimy. He rolls halfway down the hill.

Carl charges down the path and points a gun at us.

I scream at him. "Carl, no!"

He grins and aims straight for Dad. We all sink into the underbrush. A few bullets peck the hillside around us, kicking up plants and dust. Carl tries to shoot again, but his gun jams.

Without any warning, Al limps up behind Carl and shoots him in the back. As Carl crumbles to the ground, Al sneers at me and points his gun.

Mo claws his way up the hill and throws himself over my dad as more shots ring out.

I cover my head until they stop. Then I hear grunting below me. "Mo, are you okay?"

He shifts a little and looks up, gritting his teeth. "I'm fine. Get your dad out of here. I'll be right behind you!" Mo struggles to get my backpack off his shoulder.

"Don't worry about my bag! Let it go!"

He coughs, and a splotch of blood paints his lip.

"Oh, my God. You've been shot!"

Mo gives me a sad face, like a puppy begging for food.

I cover my mouth with one hand and stretch down as my mind floods with worry. "Take my hand!"

He shakes his head. "No! You have to go!" He tosses my backpack up and holds his side. "Get out of here! Your dad won't make it without you." I stare at him as if I don't understand any words coming out of his mouth. He pleads with me. "Grace, don't let this all be for nothing. Save him. It's what you came to do."

I look back at my dad lying in the weeds. "Fine. But, if you die, Morris Cameron, I'll never forgive you!"

Even his smile is too weak to move. "I'll be right behind you, blossom."

"You promise?"

He nods once. "Abso-bloody-lutely."

I half drag, half walk Dad down the path as gunfire erupts behind me, trying to ignore any creeping thoughts about Mo's fate. Dad leans his full weight on me as we stumble along the path. Every few feet, he collapses from exhaustion. It takes everything I have to keep him moving.

As we round a bend, a whistling noise drowns out the hissing trees.

I stop in my tracks and slowly turn around.

Al is following us, slightly hobbling from my shot to his thigh. He spits to one side. "What? No hello? How rude."

"I'm not afraid of you anymore."

"You should be." Al points his pistol and fires.

Dad jerks his arm out of my hand and before I can stop him, he steps in front of me acting like a human shield. The bullet must connect, because he yells and slumps to the ground.

I scream. "No!" Before I can help him, another bullet grazes my shoulder. Pain shoots through my arm, and I tumble to the ground. Dad tries to get up but collapses against a tree. I can't do anything except writhe in pain as Al converges on us.

He stands over me. "Damn. Kinda wanted a good challenge. Thought you'd be tougher than that. Your old man was too easy. I told Carl we should've killed him months ago, but Carl didn't have the balls."

The comment pisses me off. I didn't come this far to give up now. Holding my arm to keep from bleeding out, I stagger to my feet and take a defensive stance between Al and Dad. "Get away from him."

Al faces me and sneers, revealing bloody teeth. "Didn't think I'd let you get away, did yah?" Then he points the gun at my head.

Wyn always teases me about having nine lives. Last I counted, I didn't have any left.

My brain recalls every survival move I've ever learned with ease. I decide to distract him. "Too bad I hit your leg. I was aiming for your heart."

Al laughs. "What are you talking about? You didn't shoot me."

"If you say so." I smile, even though my legs quiver. The whole time I'm only focusing on one thing. Knocking that gun out of his hand.

He steps forward and extends his arm, the gun's only a few inches from my head. Just a few more steps. "You're lying."

I shift on my feet and slide on forward. "What? You got something against being shot by a girl? Doesn't make you much of a man, does it?"

Al leans in and hollers right in my face. "Shut up!"

The fact he's so close proves how much he underestimates me. I take the opportunity to head butt him right in the nose. His nasal cavity crushes and starts to bleed. But he doesn't seem to notice because he wraps his large hands around my throat like a steel vice.

My vision blurs as oxygen is depleted from my lungs. I sag to the ground under his force and try hard to remain conscious by breathing shallow, but my refusing to pass out only encourages him to squeeze harder. A black veil slowly wipes over the image of Al's face.

Before my vision totally disappears, Dad's face pops up over Al's shoulder. He barks an order. "Get the hell off her!" Before Al can react, Dad slams a log down across his back.

Al tumbles over and lies on the ground, whining. When he pushes up to on fours, Dad hammers on him again. This time in the back of the head. Al flops over on his side.

My shoulder's on fire, but I manage to crawl over to Dad who's slumped against a log. "Nice shot."

His breath seems labored. "Those stupid golf lessons your mom got me finally came in handy."

That's when I spot the blood. At first I think it's mine or Al's, then I notice Dad's side. "Dad, you're bleeding."

He closes his eyes and mumbles a little Monty Python, "Nonsense. It's just a flesh wound."

"I gotta get you outta here."

Jumping up, I stand at a safe distance and nudge Al with my shoe. He doesn't move, but I can see he's still breathing. Out cold. I uncurl some twine from my backpack and bind his ankles and wrists, using a double reef knot so it holds. My hands work feverishly as I expect him to sit up and grab me like in a horror movie.

When he's finally secure, I remove the green bandana hanging out of his pocket and shove it into his mouth. I mumble under my breath, "Jerk," and give him one extra kick in the butt. I look at Dad. "Sorry. I couldn't help myself."

"Don't apologize to me. I don't blame you." Dad coughs as I run over and help him to his feet.

We head off the path and crash through the underbrush. With each step, Dad grows weaker and weaker.

Behind us, voices grow louder, reminding me they are still after us. I search for a quick place to hide as my vision goes in and out. I almost pass out but somehow hold it together. Every time Dad collapses from exhaustion, I push through fogged vision and pain to support him.

Up ahead, I spot a small chance at safety.

I drag Dad into a small opening in the rocky hillside. Working quickly, I lay him down and pull a few logs in front of the entrance, hoping to conceal us from the path. Panting, I crawl in and collapse next to him. My heart is pumping so hard, I can almost see the outline of it pushing against my chestbone. The crunching of the men's boots along the pebbled path outside makes me hold my breath. They sound so close. Any minute, I expect them to bust through the flimsy barrier like they did before.

I grip my knife and stare at the opening, waiting.

Survival Skill #50

Hope, belief, and the willpower to survive can be the difference between life and death.

As the noises grow faint, Dad moans softly from the corner. I slide over next to him and position his head in my lap. "Ssshhhh. We have to be quiet." His shirt is bloodsoaked, so I take out Tommy's knife and cut it lose in the front to assess the damage. Once I see the wound, my throat clenches. It's a stomach wound and much worse than I thought. My SAR skills flood back as I tear his shirt into strips and press them on the wound, hoping to slow the beeding.

I quickly assess the rest of his body for signs of major injuries. A few gashes line his forehead and stretch down around one ear. His pants are torn, revealing a huge gash on one leg. Blood lines the border of the wound. Doesn't look fresh, but I tighten a few strips around his leg, just to be safe.

By the time I finish, the bandages on his stomach are soaked.

I stop and stare at the blood on my hands before wiping them on my pants. I hear myself talking, "What else can I do?" Tears stream down my face and splash on his cheek. But he doesn't answer me. There's nothing else to do now but pray.

Stroking his matted hair, I focus on Dad's gaunt face. It's the first moment I've had a chance to see who he's become. I stare at the person who raised me in these woods.

His sallow face is as white as the moon and as thin as a skeleton. He's no longer the strong man I once knew. Now he's scary thin with a scattered, gray beard, and he stinks.

I grip his bony hand. He gives me a weak squeeze. This is not the dad I lost three months ago. This is a man who's struggled. A man who's been betrayed by almost everyone he trusted. This man is no longer just my dad; he's a survivor.

I bite my lip as I cry quietly, not wanting him to hear or see me break down. Suddenly, I'm scared. He's been held captive for over three months, tortured, and starved. But this bullet wound is much more serious and needs urgent medical care.

Panic rips through me. I'm out here miles away from anything or anyone that can help him. I kiss his forehead and whisper, "I knew you were alive."

He smiles up at me without opening his eyes. "Felt like I was dead, sometimes." His voice is raspier than usual, as if a thousand pine needles have scraped along his vocal chords. He reaches up and touches my face, but not without wincing.

Emotions rise like a high ocean tide, but I force them to recede. Dad doesn't need any more stress, especially from me. I stroke his clammy forehead and can tell he's burning up. I pour some of my water onto my cloth and press it against his head.

He lifts his fingers and touches my face. "Thank you, Gracie."

I shrug. "For what?"

He eyes me. "Gee, I wonder. For finding me. For not giving up after all this time. For putting yourself in danger."

"Yeah. You owe me, big time."

"How's Mom?"

"Not good. She'll be so happy to see you. But you should see your 'to do' list."

His brief laugh becomes a fit of coughs. A drop of blood speckles the corner of his mouth.

I rub his forehead. "You sure do pour it on thick, huh?"

He closes his eyes for a moment before answering. "It's okay, you know."

"What is?"

"I may be hurt, but my brain still works. I know you."

"Dad, what are you—"

He interrupts me. "I know you cared about Morris." Hearing Mo's name gets me right in the gut.

My eyes flood. "Don't be silly. All I care about is you."

He lifts his head up and forces out words. "He did what he did for his father. Will was a good man and a good friend. I don't blame Morris—or Mo—and I don't think you should either." Dad lays his head back on my lap and stares at the ceiling. "It's such a shame he got dragged into all this. He's such a smart young man."

I chomp down on the inside of my cheek to keep from choking up.

Dad studies my face. "I want you to know that when I was down in that pit, Mo was there for me. Even though it compromised his cover, he helped me whenever he could."

"Then why didn't he rescue you?" I press my lips together, creating a barrier to remaining sobs.

Dad stares at the ceiling, a distant look wipes over his face. "He wanted to, but I wouldn't let him. What he was doing was more important than me. It was everything Will and I worked on for a year. Until they killed him. I wouldn't be alive if it wasn't for Mo. He convinced Fields to keep me alive in case they needed leverage. Mo even took that bullet for me."

"I guess."

"His heart was in the right place. I'm sure he cared about you. Knowing him, I'm pretty damn positive that was real."

I press another strip of cloth to his stomach, hoping to stop the flow. "Shhhhh. Get some rest. We can talk later. We're not out of the woods yet, in case you haven't noticed."

"No pun intended." Dad touches my face. Tears appear in the corners of his eyes as he studies my face. "All I wanted was to see your sweet face again. To tell you how much I love you. I didn't get to do that when I left."

I sob into Dad's shoulder. "I love you too, Dad. But you gotta stop talking like this. You're going to make it. I promise."

He shakes his head slightly. "We both know that's not true."

My heart aches as I sit helpless in the fading light, awaiting our fate, the adrenaline that once pumped through my veins now replaced by pure exhaustion.

Dad mumbles in the darkness. "Take care of your mother. Tell her how much I love her."

I shake my head no and act strong no matter how I feel inside. "No! You tell her yourself. I'm not doing your dirty work for you."

His face drops to one side, and his breathing quickens. Tears trickle out of his eyes, puddling in the dirt. "Tell her ... I'm sorry for leaving her."

I shake him. "Don't you dare start saying goodbye. You're going to be fine." Horrible thoughts invade my mind. What if he dies right here in my arms? After all this time? After I just found him? That would mean everything I did, everyone that's died, would all be for nothing.

I watch his chest rise and fall like an accordian, willing it to continue. Soon, his breath becomes short and erratic.

"Dad?" I pat his face a little to wake him up. Sobs take over my body. His head flops to one side, and his body goes limp.

Tears spring to my eyes as I cradle his face with my hands and shake him a little. "Dad, stay with me." I press my ear to his chest. "No, please no."

I lean over him and perform CPR. "Dad, don't leave me!" While pumping his chest with my hands, I scream out the opening, not caring who hears me. As long as it gives Dad a chance. "Help me! Please!" I perform a few more rounds and check for his pulse again. This is not happening.

I clasp my hands together and slam down his chest several times. "Don't you dare leave me! Do you hear me! I'll never forgive you!"

Silence fills the cavernous space as I abruptly stop fighting. I hold my breath waiting for him to take another breath. Waiting to see his chest rise and feel his heart beat. Waiting for him to live.

But it's too late, he's gone.

Survival Skill #51

*When hiking, always mark your trail
so you can easily find your way back.*

𝕴 have no idea how long or why I sat there holding Dad. Maybe because I was hoping he was asleep and would wake up. That I'd made some bizarre mistake, and he was still alive. That everything I did had amounted to something. That Tommy's death had a purpose and was not just a big fat waste.

My sobs reverberate throughout the small space. I clutch onto my dad's shirt and moan, shaking him slightly. "I'm so sorry. Please, please don't leave me." His face is peaceful and relaxed. I take out a cloth and wipe the dirt from his cheeks.

Suddenly, I'm overwhelmed by all the things I'll never know about my dad. Things I never thought to ask. What was he like when he was young? How did he feel when he met Mom? And what did he think about the day I was born? What did he want me to be when I grew up? What made him the most happy?

Now, I'll never get the chance.

I bring my head down to touch his forehead for my last goodbye. My mind explodes with total grief for everything I'm going to miss about him. All the moments we'll never share. All the time I wasted taking things for granted. But mostly, that I couldn't save him.

No matter how hard I tried, I failed.

Sadness is replaced by anger. Why did he have to die, now, right after I found him? How could he leave me after everything we've been through? I wish I could rewind the last few months. Go back to that spring morning when Dad left and pause life for just a second. Run after him and beg him not to go. To change the events by changing time. Keep him home. But I can't. The only thing I can do now is get him back so he can have a proper burial.

So Mom gets her chance to finally say goodbye.

"Bye, Dad. I love you." I start to cry again as I cross his arms over his chest, promising to come back for him.

Then trying to collect myself, I wipe my face and force myself to stand. I peek out the makeshift door, listening for gunfire.

All is quiet, as if the woods have completely forgotten the invasion. Oddly, everything out here has already gone back to normal.

Yet from now on, my normal will never be the same.

I push the vines back and climb out over the dead logs blocking the entrance. An owl hoots above me. The noise sends my heart into spasms. I strain to spot the large bird soaring through the trees before being swallowed by the leafy forest.

Native Americans believe owls guide spirits from this world to the next. I wipe my eyes and recall the poem Tommy said at Ama's funeral.

I whisper one of the lines to the wind. "There is no death. Just a change of worlds."

Cautiously, I walk back towards the camp, hoping I can spot Mo. My shoulder is now throbbing with pain, my arm coated with blood. As I stumble along the path, I feel like a big heavy wet blanket has been draped over me. My body is anchored to the earth, my feet feel sluggish, and my mind is foggy. Like it will take everything I have to make it back. At one point, I just want to collapse to the ground, cry, and let the woods swallow me so I don't have to face what has happened.

But I push on. For my mom. She can't lose two people. It will kill her.

As I backtrack along the trail, I do my best to tear small strips of material off my t-shirt and tie the small pieces of cloth to various branches, marking the path so we can locate Dad. I have no choice but to head back to camp. It's the closest place that might have some food or supplies. Seems totally stupid but it's all

I can think of right now. I can't help but wonder what I'll find when I get there. Maybe I'll find Mo.

I trip and stumble forward through the pain in my heart and arm, wishing Mom was here to tend my wounds and reassure me everything's going to be okay. I wipe a tear from my face, wondering if I'll see her again. Hoping we can repair what's been broken for so long.

In the distance, pitch black smoke hovers along the forest floor, creating an eerie mist for me to follow. When I finally come to the top of the hill, I squat down and peer over the side. Everything in the camp is either on fire or already charred. A few red splatters blemish the dusty earth, marking the end of life.

I sigh a breath of relief when I spot some men from the U.S. Fish and Wildlife Service swarming the space, dressed in green jackets. A couple of agents tend to the bears trapped in cages while another man drags a body down a side path. One agent sits in front of a tent with bloody bandages on his legs, arms, and torsos.

I make my way down to the center of the camp and come up behind one of the agents.

He spins around and points a gun directly in my face. "Don't move!"

I freeze to the spot. My hands shoot up in the air as I stammer to explain myself. "I'm Grace ... Grace Wells. Joe and Mary's daughter."

The man smiles and lowers his weapon. He comes closer and pats my shoulder. "Miss Wells. Thank goodness you're okay. Where have you been?"

I swallow not sure if I can find the right words. "My dad, Joe Wells, is in a cave about a mile up the path along that ridge. Can you please go get him? He ... he's ... he's dead." Hearing the words come out of my mouth, in my own voice, makes my stomach churn. Something I've avoided saying out loud since dad went missing. And now, it simply rolls off my lips. I give the agent the coordinates of the location and explain how the trail is marked.

He takes off his baseball camp and looks distraught. "We'll take good care of Joe. He was one of us. You wait here." The man unclips the radio off his belt and walks away so I can't hear what he's saying. He mumbles and waits until a jumbled voice answers through the static.

Moments later, a group of men sprint up the hill with a stretcher.

Just as they disappear into the woods, someone shouts my name. The voices sends a surge of emotion into every nook and cranny. I spin around and search the trees.

Mom is runnning across the camp with her arms stretched out. "Grace! Grace!"

I sprint toward her. "Mom!"

As soon as we reach each other, she wraps her arms around me like a shawl and starts to cry. "Oh, thank God, you're okay." I finally allow my body to collapse, and she holds me until I can steady myself. She pushes me away and scans my body for wounds. That's when I notice her face. Puffy and swollen with black streaks down her cheeks. She's been crying. About me. "Oh God, you're hurt."

I look at my shoulder. Blood is still dripping along my arm. "I'm fine. Dad saved me."

She wipes my tears with her thumbs and steps back a small step. "Dad? What do you mean?"

I clutch both of her hands and look her in the eyes. "Mom, I found him." Before her eyes can reveal any hope, I break her heart once again. "He took a bullet for me and … then … then he died."

Mom turns white as a ghost. A dazed look washes over her face as I summarize what happened as much as I can. She appears stunned. Then she tips her head to one side as if trying to hear what I'm saying. "You found him, but now he's dead?"

Tears stream down my face. "I'm so sorry, Mom. I tried, but I couldn't save him. He was hurt too bad." I clutch onto her hands. "This is all my fault. He was alive, and I got him killed."

Mom squeezes me hard. Her voice cracks when she talks like a bad radio connection. "No, it's not. Grace, if you hadn't found Sidehill, we may never have found your father at all." She tucks my hair behind my ears. "This is not your fault. You did everything you could. You believed, when no one else did. Now we can at least bring him home."

She's talking through her own tears now as her arms tighten around me. "We're going to be okay, Grace. I promise. You and me." I nod and sob with her. Already missing Dad more than I can bear. She whispers hoarsely. "Let's get you taken care of." Before I can say anything, Mom waves both hands in the air. "Les! Over here!"

Les waddles out from behind a van. His arm is hanging in a bloody sling, and his face bruised with one eye swollen shut. My mouth drops open, and my body freezes for a second as I watch him lumber down the path. I assumed Al had killed him.

Les smiles at me. "Gracie, I'm so glad you are okay."

When he walks up, I hug him as hard as I can. This time, I don't let go. "I thought you were dead."

His round cheeks turn a bit pink, and he squeezes me back. "Not yet."

Before I can say anything, Mom whispers, "Grace found Joe. He's dead."

Les squeezes my good shoulder and fills his lip with tobacco. He plays with his hat. "I'm so sorry. How?"

"Dad tried to protect me so Al shot him. Al's tied up along the path too."

Les frowns. "Son of a bitch." I watch him as he radios a couple men instructing them to find Al if it's the last thing they do. He studies me. "You're hurt. Let's get you fixed up."

I clear my throat. "Les? I'm so sorry I doubted you. I didn't realize you were trying to help me in that cave. I thought you were one of them."

He bends over and cups my shoulder. "Water under the bridge, Gracie. No need to speak of it again."

I nod. "How'd you find me?"

Les spits on the ground. "Tommy called. He told me everything. About the bullets you found, about Sidehill. Mentioned you bolted off to find Sidehill. I called a friend of Joe's at the USFWS."

One word sticks out in my mind. I barely manage to choke out. "Tommy?"

Les lowers his head and fiddles with his cinched belt. "I'm sorry. I told him to let me handle it, but he was so worried about you. Said something about it bein' his fault."

I can't blink, as if my eyes are super-glued open. My throat feels like sandpaper. "I can't believe he's ... dead too."

Mom butts in and clutches both of my shoulders to get my undivided attention. "No. Grace." She smiles and strokes my hair. "He's alive."

Les nods. "He's in pretty bad shape. But alive."

My heart explodes with relief. My shoulders straighten and a small weight falls off my shoulder. "What? Where is he?"

Les points up the hill. "He's there. We're getting ready to wheel him up to the North Ridge so a helicopter can take him to the hospital."

I rub my hands through my hair. "Unbelievable. Can I see him?"

Les nods. "Make it quick. He's stable but needs medical attention."

I take off up the hill, yelling at a man in a suit pushing a stretcher. "Wait!"

Survival Skill #52

Escaping a survival situation can be life altering.

The paramedic stops as I run up. Tommy is lying down with tubes in his nose and eyes closed. A sheet soaked with blood is draped over him.

I swallow and whisper in his ear, not wanting to disturb him. "Tommy? Are you okay?"

He opens one eye. "Never better." His voice is hoarse.

I rest my head on his chest and cry. "Tommy, *gaest-ost yuh-wa da-nv-ta.*"

He shakes his head. "You don't have to apologize, Elu."

"This is all my fault. Please forgive me."

His eyes look wet, tears stuck in the corners as he winces from pain. "How about we make a deal? I'll forgive you if you forgive yourself."

A lump rises in my throat thinking about Dad, not having the heart to tell him.

Tommy whispers. I lean down to hear him. His breath tickles the little hairs on my ear. "Don't worry. I already know about Joe."

I kiss his forehead and watch a tear roll down his face. "I tried."

He sniffs and winces. "I know, Elu. I know." He grips my hand and stares at his watch. "Think it's time I got this fixed?"

I smile. "I thought time was nothing but an illusion."

He takes in a raspy breath. "It was until I got more of it."

I remove the watch from his wrist. "I'll take care of it. It's the least I can do."

The paramedic interrupts us. "Miss Wells. We need to go ahead and transport him to the hospital. He's in pretty bad shape but should recover just fine. Do you need a ride there?"

Mom walks up and answers for me. "Yes, thank you." She twists my hair back into a ponytail like she did when I was a little girl.

I cross my fingers behind my back before asking him a question. "Sir? Do you know if anyone else survived?"

He nods. "A couple were detained and charged."

"So some lived?"

"I think so." He motions toward a few gurneys. "Those are the unlucky ones."

My heart lifts. "So if someone's not here, it means they could be alive?"

The man nods once. "That's right." The wheels squeak as he pushes Tommy up the path.

Mom speaks gently into my ear. "Try not to look, honey."

I grip her arm as we head up the pathway. A couple of stretchers line up side by side, carrying bodies covered in black tarps. I spot a hand hanging out from underneath one of the covers.

Something's dangling from the wrist.

My bracelet. The one Dad gave me. The one I gave him.

My breath sticks in my throat as I move closer. I feel my Mom clutch my arm to hold me back but I pull away.

If it's Mo, I have to know for myself.

I stare at the facial features outlined under the cloth and reach out to clasp the edge of the sheet.

Just then, the man in a black suit blocks me with both arms straight out. "Trust me. You don't want to see this." He spins around and pushes Mo up the hill without another word.

I slump to my knees in a prayer position and watch the man load the body in a van. I bury my face in my hands and weep. Not just for Mo, but for everyone and everything that's been murdered today. And I can't help but feel I'm responsible for the deaths of all these men. I cry for Mo and Dad. I also shed some tears for me.

For the ray of hope in my heart that was so easily snuffed out.

For the broken vision of my future.

And for everything I've lost.

Visions of my time with Mo zoom past. I picture his beautiful smile. The way he called me blossom. Our kisses. Our laughs. Like a movie trailer, a bad montage of our short but very real relationship rolls on until the end.

I cry and spit and choke and cough. Afraid I'll never care about anyone in that way again. How can I go back to being without him when he brought out so much in me?

Mom kneels down and is crying too. "Oh honey, I'm so sorry, sweetie. About everything." I'm not sure if she even knows what or who Mo was to me. But nevertheless, somehow she understands and is finally here for me.

And this time, I let her be.

"I really cared about him."

She whispers in my ear. "I know."

As I wipe my face and nose on my t-shirt, Mom helps me to my feet. She clasps my hand and pulls me down the path.

Slowly, step by step, I walk away, leaving behind a piece of myself.

A piece that, someday, will be untraceable.

Three days later...

Epilogue

Life is short. Be sure to make your mark.

𝓘 stand out in the hallway of the U.S Fish and Wildlife Service building just outside town.

Les steps out of an office. "Sorry for calling you in here, Grace. I guess it's standard procedure."

My nerves jitter and twitter. "It's okay, I understand."

"They'll call you in a couple of minutes."

Before he turns away, I grab his arm. "Les, did you find out about Carl?"

Les bows his head. "Yeah. He didn't make it. The wounds were too severe."

My hand clasps over my mouth. "Oh no. Does Wyn know?"

"He and Skyler were with him at the end."

Just then, we see Wyn exit the room next to us into the hallway, his hands stuffed in his pockets. His frazzled hair juts out in all directions and puffy, dark circles under his eyes make him look as though he's been awake for weeks. He doesn't even look like the same person. I'm used to seeing him smile, but now, he's frowning. I've never seen him so broken.

I race up to him. "Wyn, are you okay? I heard about Carl. I'm so sorry."

He stops for a second and mumbles, "And I'm sorry about your dad. He didn't deserve all this." Then he pushes me aside and walks past me in silence without another word.

I pace myself next to him. "Thanks. It was awful. I tried to call you a few times but you never picked up."

Wyn keeps his eyes down and continues moving. Like a robot, every step is the same distance and the same pace.

296

I squeeze his arm and try to tease him a little to crack through the barrier he's forced up. "You know, you can't ignore me forever."

He suddenly spins around and glares at me. "The hell I can't. You've ruined my life."

I stop in place, shocked at his strong reaction. "Wyn, I didn't know Carl was involved, I swear. I tried to talk to him. But he was ... crazy."

He stares at me blankly with dark gray eyes. "Well, *you* would know." His voice is cutting and cold. He takes in a breath and stares forward at the door.

My lip quivers. "Wyn, I had no idea who was behind all this. I thought it was Les." I stop. Really, I just want to hold him and tell him I care about him and that we're going to get back to where we were before all this happened. That everything will be okay. "Carl is the one who betrayed us all."

He faces me and looks sad. "I know how he feels."

"Wyn, you're my best friend, and I know you cared about Carl. But he made his own choices."

He shakes his head, and his eyes swell with tears. He gets a little choked up and forces out some words. "You think this is about Carl?"

I glance up at him. My heart is aching for how much pain I can see he is in. He loved Carl. "Isn't it?"

Wyn looks at me as if he doesn't know me. Like he can't figure me out. "I know what Carl did. This has nothing to do with him."

I stare at him and shrug. "Then what is it?"

He throws his head back in frustration and yells. Everyone turns to look at us. "God, you're still lying to me. You just can't help yourself, can you?"

My stomach churns as I search for something to say. "I don't understand."

He barks back at me. "Why didn't you tell me about your little boyfriend? Mo, is it?

My mouth gapes open. "I—"

He crosses his arms and cuts me off. "What? You didn't think I would find out? Or did you think I was so into you, I wouldn't care?" I go to open my mouth, but he holds his hand up in my face, and his eyes flash something I've never seen before. A spark of hate. "Don't even bother lying or coming clean now. It's too late. Tommy mentioned it. Guess he didn't know it was such a *secret.*"

My brain fights for something to say. A way to ease his anger. "Wyn, I can explain."

"Explain what? How you led me on? How you lied to me? How you took away the only man who's ever cared about me? Or how you don't care about anyone but yourself. Especially me."

I shake my head and grab his face. "That's not true. I do care about you."

He clutches both my wrists and pulls my arms down. His eyes narrow, and his mouth fixes into a straight line. "I have nothing to say to you. Ever. Just leave me alone. I'm done with you. I'm done with this." He spins around and storms out the front door.

My heart drops as I yell out. "Wyn, please!"

Just as I'm about to go after him, Les calls out to me. "They're ready for you, Gracie."

"I'll be there in a second." I race to the window and watch Wyn climb into his Jeep. Skyler is in the passenger seat with her head hanging forward. I watch Wyn pound the steering wheel with his hands. She falls into him and hugs his neck. It looks like they're both crying. Together.

It's the first time I've seen Wyn cry since the time he fell out of our tree and broke his arm. Suddenly, it's like I don't know him anymore. Like we're strangers all over again. And Skyler has taken my place. I lied to Wyn because I didn't want to push him away. Instead, I shoved him straight into Skyler's arms.

He starts the car and peels away, leaving only a cloud dust behind for me.

The minute his car leaves my sight, I miss him. His smile. The way he makes me laugh. As far as I'm concerned, Dad is not the only one in my life that died this week. Wyn died a little too.

And maybe, so did a piece of me.

I shuffle after Les, feeling awful about hurting my best friend. Wanting nothing more than to jump on my bike and race after him and beg him to forgive me. But this time, I've done too much damage. Damage that's unrepairable.

Les's crappy old boots squeak against the linoleum. The noise irritates me. After all this, my world is turned upside down and will never be the same, yet some things never change.

Once we enter the room, two men sit behind a long table. One is wearing jeans and a button-down shirt with a blue blazer; the other is the same tall stoic agent that drove Mom and me to the hospital.

Les ushers me through the door and drags out a metal chair. It scrapes against the floor, sending a chill down my spine. I flop down next to him. "Now, Grace. These men have some questions for you. Let me say up front, you're not in any trouble. They just need to clear up a few things. Then I'll take you back to the hospital to be with Tommy and your mom."

I swallow. "Sure, okay."

Les plays with his ranger hat and points to the man in the blue blazer. "This is Agent Sweeney. He's a special agent from the U.S. Fish and Wildlife Service." The man nods at me. For some strange reason, he looks familiar. Then again, my brain is mush from the last few months. Les motions to the other guy. "I believe you've already met Agent Todd."

Agent Todd leans forward. "Have some water, Miss Wells."

Hanging on the wall behind the men is the same picture of my dad winning his award. My chest clogs with sadness. The hole in my heart left open by my dad's death stings. I quickly pour a glass of water and take a sip. The cool liquid washes through my dry mouth and drowns the lump in my throat. "Just call me Grace." The men stare at me with intense eyes, causing me to shift in my chair.

Agent Todd frowns. "Let's talk about one of your friends. How do you know Morris Cameron?"

I glance over at Les. He nods that it's okay to answer. "I met Mo in the woods. We ended up hanging out some."

For the next hour, Agent Todd grills me about every single move Mo made during the few weeks I knew him. If I knew his bathroom schedule, they would have been interested. A pit forms in my stomach as I tell them everything I know. About Mo's family, the poachers, and his role in this whole mess. I even tell them about the other camps Mo mentioned. I end with, "He was trying to help."

Agent Todd sits back and folds his arms. "He didn't give you any more details than that?"

I think for a moment. "Nope, that's pretty much it. Why? Isn't that enough?"

"You never saw any of his dad's papers that he mentioned?"

A bit baffled by his question, I shake my head. "No."

Agent Todd leans forward like they do in fake interrogations on TV. "You sure?"

I'm getting a bit irritated by all the stupid questions. "Positive."

Agent Todd stands up. "I'm done here. Sweeney, you have anything?"

Agent Sweeney speaks for the first time. "I have a few more questions if you don't mind, Miss Wells."

"Sure, why not. I love to play twenty questions. Twice."

Agent Todd leaves the room as Agent Sweeney flips through his notes. After a few moments, he scratches his head. "Les? Would you mind getting us some coffee?"

Les pushes up from his seat. "No problem. Black?"

Agent Sweeney plasters on a smile. "As the night. Thanks."

Les squeezes my shoulder. "I'll be right back, Grace. You're doin' good. We're almost done here."

As soon the door closes, Agent Sweeney leans his chair back against the wall and props his feet up on the table. "You need anything?"

"That's a loaded question."

Agent Sweeney beams. "You're a pretty smart girl, aren't you, Miss Wells?"

I eye him. "It's Grace. And it depends on who you talk to. Not sure my science teacher thinks so. Look, am I in trouble here?"

Agent Sweeney grins. "Should you be?"

I shrug, but my legs shake under the table. "Not in my mind."

"We analyzed your computer and your ID. We know all the web sites you've visited recently. All the information you've collected. What do you have to say about that?"

I gawk at him. "Well, unless Facebook is a crime, nothing. And any articles I researched were probably to help find my dad."

"So you were just researching poaching and bullets on a hunch? You sure Mo wasn't feeding you information or helping you in any way?"

I scoff, thinking about how much Mo *didn't* help me at all, at least not until the very end. "I wish. Mo never told me anything. I didn't even know he was involved at all until I saw him at the camp. I've told you everything I know. Is that why you *stole* my computer?"

Agent Sweeney makes some noises with his lips. "I assure you, Miss Wells, we had a search warrant. We needed to know if you found any information that would help us in this case."

"The only thing I know is that Mo said there were maps at the campsite with codes or something."

Agent Sweeney twiddles his thumbs. "Well, we didn't find any papers."

I think for a second, making sure I remembered everything that Mo told me. "What about the men you arrested? Did they tell you anything?"

He sifts through his paperwork. "Not that I see."

"Well, what information do you have? Maybe then I can help you."

Agent Sweeney licks his fingers and pokes through the loose pages in a folder. "Let me see. We arrested three, and we had a few … casualties. Mr. Robert Fields isn't talking. At a minimum, all the men will be charged with thirty-three counts, including murder, animal cruelty, illegal poaching, and kidnapping. With your testimony, I'm sure they'll be in prison for a while."

I sigh, totally relieved Mr. Fields would be locked up for a long time. Wonder what will happen to his store or his family now. "What about Al?"

Agent Sweeny closes the folder. "Who?"

"Alfred Smith. Where is he?"

He shakes his head. "We never found Alfred Williams."

My stomach lurches, and I lean forward in my seat. "What?"

"He disappeared."

I shake my head. "That's impossible. I tied him up on the path for you. Good too. Practically wrapped him with a nice bow."

Agent Sweeney rubs his head. "He was gone when we got there. The rope had been cut."

I gasp. "Then someone helped him."

Agent Sweeney disagrees. "We've accounted for everyone at that camp except Al. He must have gotten out on his own."

"No way. That was a good, solid knot. Did it myself."

"We asked all the men in custody."

My blood bubbles as anger pumps through me. "So what you're telling me is that he's still out there somewhere?"

"Yes. But don't worry. We have around-the-clock protection on you and your mom. I doubt he's hanging around though. Probably took off. Far away from here."

"Great, thanks," I choke out.

"If it makes you feel any better, we confiscated a lot of stuff from the site and even saved a few bears."

Finally, a bright spot in this mess. "What will happen to them?" Please don't say bear pits.

"They'll be a part of the new sanctuary Les is going to run for us. Once they recover, that is."

"Did you find a small cub?"

He checks his papers. "No, all adults. Mostly male." I smile, thinking Lucky got away safely. Agent Sweeney watches me for a second then his eyes twinkle. "You seem to be a smart young lady to have solved this on your own."

"Watching TV comes in handy."

He winks. "One hell of a computer gal too."

"I can Google, if that's what you mean."

"Dabble in grades much?"

I think about Wyn but don't say anything to incriminate myself. "Excuse me?"

He leans in and teases me. "Don't worry, Miss Wells. I won't tell anyone what you and Wyn did. Think it's pretty clever myself, changing grades. You must be much better than a Googler if you can hack into the school system. You want to come intern with us? With your research ability and nature skills, we could turn you into a fine agent someday."

I laugh. "Oh right. Agent Grace."

He leans back and cups his neck with both hands. "We do some stuff I think you'd find interesting. Your dad loved it."

My heart sinks at the thought of my dad. "I'll be sure to keep that in mind."

Behind me, the door opens, and Les comes in with two steaming Styrofoam cups in his hands. "You guys done in here yet?"

Agent Sweeney takes his coffee. "Abso-bloody-lutely!"

I stand to leave but before I take a step, I freeze. "*What* did you say?"

He shrugs. "What? Oh, it's just a phrase I picked up recently. A guy on my team says it. Why?" Agent Sweeney shakes my hand. "Thank you for your cooperation, Miss Wells. You're free to go. We'll call you if we have any more questions. Here's my contact information. If you think of anything, please call me. If not, I guess I'll see you at trial."

My hands tremble, and it feels as if I've slid into a tunnel. I'm barely able to grab the business card and mumble a response. "Thanks."

The phrase Agent Sweeney said repeats in my head.

My world spins in a fast circle as the last few pieces of this twisted puzzle fall into place. I bolt out of the office and push through the two front doors. As soon as I break into the sun-filled world, my lungs are finally able to refill with fresh air. The bright light burns my eyes.

I sprint around the corner to Luci and take off.

Away from town. Away from Agent Sweeney.

Away from everything that's confusing.

I head up into the Smokies, the sun at my back and a tinge of rain in the air. Leaning into every turn, I pick through the jumbled knot that's formed in the corner of my brain, searching for something.

What am I missing?

My conversation with the agents replays in my head. Agent Todd asked me several times if Mo gave me anything. I said no, but now that I think about it, Mo went back for my bag. I thought it was strange at the time, but the bullets distracted me from questioning him much.

On the next turn, I pull over and unzip my backpack. As I rifle through the crap inside, I pray for something. Anything that might help piece everything together. Once and for all. I fish around until my fingers brush something.

Hidden all the way down at the bottom.

How could I have missed it?

I scan the area to be sure I'm alone before pulling out a small tube. I pop off the lid and tip it over, letting a stack of dirty papers slide out. I take off the rubber band and unroll them. Pages of maps, rows of numbers, and some kind of code.

Why did Mo give these to me? Did he want me to have them? Or did he know he was going to die and needed someone safe to take them?

I sift back through my memory bank, searching for any clue. Then it hits me. The reason I recognized Agent Sweeney is because he's the same man from the woods. The one pushing the stretcher. The one who wouldn't let me look at Mo's body. The one wearing a blue blazer when the man with Tommy was sporting a white lab coat.

You don't want to look at this one.

Was Mo alive under that sheet? If so, why would Agent Sweeney sneak him out of those woods?

I sit down on Luci's cracked leather seat before I can pass out. My limbs tremble as the facts and events from the last few weeks buzz through my mind in chronological order. I reevaluate everything I know about Mo. About the last few weeks. About everything he said.

I reach into my pocket and pull out the Alexandrite stone he gave me that night. I can almost hear his voice whispering it's meaning in my ear.

A person carrying this stone is reminded that things are not always what they seem and must seek out the truth.

What was he trying to tell me? That he wasn't working alone? That he was working undercover too?

I cover my mouth. *Is Mo still alive?*

I smile to myself.

Because I think I already know the answer.

Uncontrollable,

Nature of Grace #2

Coming Summer 2012

Shout Outs!

First, I'd like to thank the children's book publishing industry for loving books as much as I do.

To Harold Underdown, Lexa Hillyer, Emily Lawrence, and Supriya Savkoor for helping me make this book the best it could be.

Alyssa Henkin, for all the time you spent supporting me and helping me grow as a writer.

I'd like to thank all the beautiful bloggers for their support.

The best part about being a writer is all the people I have metespecially The Bookanistas, The Hopefuls, The Calliope Circle, Southern Breeze, Midsouth, and all of SCBWI.

A special shout out to Lindsey Leavitt, Sarah Francis Hardy, Suzanne Young, Lisa and Laura Roecker, and Elana Johnson for their friendship and undying support since the early days.

To Kristin Tubb, Jennifer Jabaley, Beth Revis, Gretchen McNeil, and Megan Miranda for reading my book(s) and offering constructive feedback.

To Vania for her creativity and bringing this book to life.

To Katie Andersen, Jessica Dehart, and Nancy Tuttle, I would not be here without your advice, daily chats, and honesty.

To Beth, Catherine, and Amy for sharing my rants, tears, fears, and happiness throughout the years. No matter what.

To Kendra and Ursula for healing words & positive energy.

A special and heartfelt thanks to Kimberly Derting for believing in me and this book—sometimes more than I did. Her loyalty and friendship is priceless. (And, I'm so so glad she is NOT a big hairy guy who wears white skiffies. ☺)

To my family, who has always been there for me:

- Fiona for her encouragement and Jeff for not being afraid to tell me why my ideas would or would not work.

- Gary and Michelle for always asking me WHEN, not IF, I was going to be published.

- My dad for always pushing me and teaching me I could accomplish anything if I worked hard and never gave up.

- My mom for being my friend and #1 fan. Thank you for reading my book(s) over and over again, yet always being excited as if it were the very first time.

To my sweet dog Bud (and Connor), I still miss having you at me feet; and to Charley, for picking up where Bud left off.

To the two best things I ever did in this world, Madelyn and Gray, thank you for the patience, unlimited giggles, hugs, and smiles. You gave me the inspiration and confidence to know I could create unbelievably special things.

To my wonderful hubby, best friend, and soulmate, Alistair, who has stood beside me every step of the way since I started this crazy rollercoaster ride. You've been the one person in this universe who believed in me more than I ever believed in myself. Thank you always encouraging me to keep writing—no matter how down and defeated I got. *Am byth a thu hwnt!*

And, most importantly, to all my beautiful readers, I am so grateful to you and hope my words touch your heart in some small way.

Last, but certainly not least, to the Big Cheese upstairs, even though it may not always seem so, I thank you for the ironic moments, universal signs, twists and turns, and helping me find the strength and faith to continue - when I needed it most.